**This Large Print Book carries the
Seal of Approval of N.A.V.H.**

THIEF OF GLORY

Sigmund Brouwer

CENTER POINT LARGE PRINT
THORNDIKE, MAINE

This Center Point Large Print edition is published
in the year 2016 by arrangement with WaterBrook Press,
an imprint of the Crown Publishing Group,
a division of Penguin Random House LLC, New York.

The text of this Large Print edition is unabridged.
In other aspects, this book may vary from the original edition.
Printed in the United States of America on permanent paper.
Set in 16-point Times New Roman type.

ISBN: 978-1-62899-929-7

Library of Congress Cataloging-in-Publication Data

Names: Brouwer, Sigmund, 1959– author.
Title: Thief of glory / Sigmund Brouwer.
Description: Center Point Large Print edition. | Thorndike, Maine :
Center Point Large Print, 2016. | ©2014
Identifiers: LCCN 2015051417 | ISBN 9781628999297
    (hardcover : alk. paper)
Subjects: LCSH: Mothers and sons—Fiction. | World War,
1939–1945—Fiction. | Family secrets—Fiction. | Indonesia—History—
Japanese occupation, 1942–1945—Fiction. | Java (Indonesia)—Fiction.
| Washington (D.C.)—Fiction. | Psychological fiction. | Large type
books. | GSAFD: War stories.
Classification: LCC PS3552.R6825 T45 2016 | DDC 813/.54—dc23
LC record available at http://lccn.loc.gov/2015051417

THIEF OF
GLORY

In March of 1957, much in love, with all that they owned in suitcases, a young couple from the Netherlands boarded a ship to cross the Atlantic for an unknown future in Canada, both leaving behind the events of what the Second World War had inflicted on them as children.

As a small girl, she watched German soldiers take away her father for hiding a Jew in their house. Halfway across the world, at about the same time, the boy's father went from teacher to soldier to prisoner of war, and Japanese soldiers forced the boy's older brothers onto the flatbed of a truck that left the boy and the other siblings behind.

In Holland, the girl's father eventually returned, but she endured the remainder of the Nazi occupation without her mother, who had died from pneumonia. In the Dutch East Indies, the boy's father did not return, a victim of the brutal conditions of forced labor during the building of the infamous Burma railway, and the boy spent the war years with his mother and remaining siblings barely surviving a series of concentration camps.

All these years later, at the time of the writing of this novel, they are still together, still much in love. They have six children, fifteen grand-children, and six great-grandchildren. In the truest sense, this novel was inspired by that young couple—by stories of their childhoods and by how they lived and loved since that Atlantic crossing—my parents, Willem and Gerda. Because of their example, it was not difficult to imagine another decades-long journey in *Thief of Glory*, where Jeremiah and Laura share a similar enduring love.

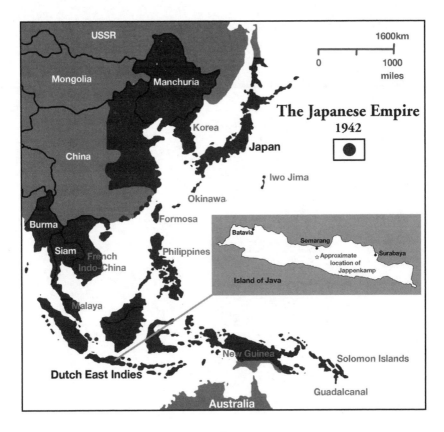

COLONIAL NAME	PRESENT DAY NAME
Batavia	Jakarta
Dutch East Indies	Indonesia
Siam	Thailand
Burma	Myanmar
French Indo-China	Cambodia, Laos, Vietnam
Formosa	Taiwan
Manchuria	China
Malaya	Malaysia

One

Journal 1—Dutch East Indies

A banyan tree begins when its seeds germinate in the crevices of a host tree. It sends to the ground tendrils that become prop roots with enough room for children to crawl beneath, prop roots that grow into thick, woody trunks and make it look like the tree is standing above the ground. The roots, given time, look no different than the tree it has begun to strangle. Eventually, when the original support tree dies and rots, the banyan develops a hollow central core.

In a kampong—village—on the island of Java, in the then-called Dutch East Indies, stood such a banyan tree almost two hundred years old. On foggy evenings, even adults avoided passing by its ghostly silhouette, but on the morning of my tenth birthday, sunlight filtered through a sticky haze after a monsoon, giving everything a glow of tranquil beauty. There, a marble game beneath the branches was an event as seemingly inconsequential as a banyan seed taking root in the bark of an unsuspecting tree, but the tendrils of the consequences became a journey that has taken me some three score and ten years to complete.

It was market day, and as a special privilege to me, Mother had left my younger brother and twin sisters in the care of our servants. In the early morning, before the tropical heat could slow our progress, she and I journeyed on back of the white horse she was so proud of, past the manicured grounds of our handsome home and along the tributary where my siblings and I often played. Farther down, the small river emptied into the busy port of Semarang. While it was not a school day, my father—the headmaster—and my older half brothers were supervising the maintenance of the building where all the blond-haired children experienced the exclusive Dutch education system.

As we passed, Indonesian peasants bowed and smiled at us. Ahead, shimmers of heat rose from the uneven cobblestones that formed the village square. Vibrant hues of Javanese batik fabrics, with their localized patterns of flowers and animals and folklore as familiar to me as my marbles, peeked from market stalls. I breathed in the smell of cinnamon and cardamom and curry powders mixed with the scents of fried foods and ripe mangoes and lychees.

I was a tiny king that morning, continuously shaking off my mother's attempts to grasp my hand. She had already purchased spices from the old man at one of the Chinese stalls. He had risen beyond his status as a *singkeh*, an impoverished immigrant laborer from the southern provinces of China, this elevation signaled by his right thumbnail, which was at least two inches long and fit in a curving, encasing sheath with elaborate painted decorations. He kept it prominently displayed with his hands resting in his lap, a clear message that he held a privileged position and did not need to work with his hands. I'd long stopped being fascinated by this and was impatient to be moving, just as I'd long stopped being fascinated by his plump wife in a colorful long dress as she flicked the beads on her abacus to calculate prices with infallible accuracy.

I pulled away to help an older Dutch woman who was bartering with an Indonesian baker. She had not noticed that bank notes had fallen from her purse. I retrieved them for her but was in no mood for effusive thanks, partly because I thought it ridiculous to thank me for not stealing, but mainly because I knew what the other boys my age were doing at that moment. I needed to be on my way. With a quick *"Dag, mevrouw"*— Good day, madam—I bolted toward the banyan, giving no heed to my mother's command to return.

For there, with potential loot placed in a wide chalked circle, were fresh victims. I might not have been allowed to keep the marbles I won from my younger siblings, but these Dutch boys were fair game. I slowed to an amble of pretended casualness as I neared, whistling and looking properly sharp in white shorts and a white linen shirt that had been hand pressed by Indonesian servants. I put on a show of indifference that I'd perfected and that served me well my whole life. Then I stopped when I saw her, all my apparent apathy instantly vanquished.

Laura.

As an old man, I can attest to the power of love at first sight. I can attest that the memory of a moment can endure—and haunt—for a lifetime. There are so many other moments slipping away from me, but this one remains.

Laura.

What is rarely, if ever, mentioned by poets is that hatred can have the same power, for that was the same moment that I first saw him. The impact of that memory has never waned either. This, too, remains as layers of my life slip away like peeling skin.

Georgie.

I had no foreshadowing, of course, that the last few steps toward the shade beneath those glossy leaves would eventually send me into the holding cell of a Washington, DC police station where, at age eighty-one, I faced the lawyer— also my daughter and only child—who refused to secure my release until I promised to tell her the events of my journey there.

All these years later, across from her in that

holding cell, I knew my daughter demanded this because she craved to make sense of a lifetime in the cold shade of my hollowness, for the span of decades since that marble game had withered me, the tendrils of my vanities and deceptions and self-deceptions long grown into strangling prop roots. Even so, as I agreed to my daughter's terms, I maintained my emotional distance and made no mention that I intended to have this story delivered to her after my death.

Such, too, is the power of shame.

Two

Laura.

Beneath the banyan, a heart-stopping longing overwhelmed me at the glimpse of her face and shy smile. It was romantic love in the purest sense, uncluttered by any notion of physical desire, for I was ten, much too young to know how lust complicates the matters of the human race.

The sensation was utterly new to me. But it was not without context. At night, by oil lamps screened to keep moths from the flame, I had three times read *Ivanhoe* by Sir Walter Scott, the Dutch translation by Gerard Keller. As soon as the last page was finished, I would turn to page one of chapter one. I had just started it for the fourth time. Thus I'd been immersed in chivalry at its finest, and here, finally, was proof that the love I'd read about in the story also existed in real life.

I was lost, first, in her eyes—unlike many of the Dutch, a hazel brown—which regarded me with a calmness that pulled stronger than gravity. She looked away, then back again. I felt like I could only breathe from the top of my lungs in shallow gasps. Her hair, thick and blond and curled, rested upon her shoulders. She wore a light-blue dress, tied at the waist with a wide bow, with a yellow butterfly brooch on her right shoulder. She stole away from me any sense of sound except for a universal harmony that I hadn't known existed. So as the nine-year-old Laura Jansen bequeathed upon me a radiant gaze, I became Ivanhoe, and she the beautiful Lady Rowena. Standing at the edge of the chalked circle, I was instantly and irrevocably determined that nothing would stop me from becoming champion of the day, earning the right to bestow upon her the honor of Queen of the Tournament.

As I was to discover, it was Laura's third day in-country and her first visit to the village. This meant I was as much a stranger to her as any boy could be, but the emotions that overwhelmed her, which she recounted to me years later, were as much a mystery to her young soul as my emotions were to mine.

16

I would shortly discover that Laura had accompanied her *oma*—grandmother—on the voyage from the Netherlands. Her *oom* Gert— uncle Gert—worked for the Dutch Shell Oil Company as a refinery engineer, and his wife had recently died from pneumonia. Laura and her oma had come to help Gert and his large family through the difficult situation.

That morning I surveyed my opponents gathered around her, a motley bunch of boys I'd vanquished one way or another at events where Dutch families gathered to celebrate a holiday or other special occasion. From marble games to subsequent fist-fights that resulted from marble games, the fathers monitored our battles but wisely kept them as hidden from the matriarchs as we did. I knew all of these boys. Except one.

As the other boys took involuntary steps backward in deference to my established reign, I felt goose bumps run up my spine. The parting of this group had revealed a boy at the center whom I'd never seen before. He was kneeling, with a marble held in shooting position on top of the thumbnail of his left hand, edge of the thumb curled beneath index finger, ready to flick. Left hand.

The marble I noticed too. For good reason. It was an onionskin, purple and white, with a transparent core. The swirls were twisted counterclockwise and that made it even more of a rarity.

Inside the chalked circle was an *X* formed by two lines of twelve marbles. At a glance I could tell none were worth the risk of losing the onionskin. Without doubt, stupidity was not part of this boy's nature, so either he was very good or he came from wealth that allowed him to not care about the worth of the onionskin.

When he stood, it was obvious that he had two inches on me, and a lot of extra bulk. His arched eyebrow matched my own. Dark hair to my blond. Khaki pants and tousled shirt to my pressed-linen shorts and shirt. Wealth, most likely, against the limited salary of my father's headmaster position.

I would learn his name was Georgie Smith. He was the son of the American sent to oversee the refinery where Laura's uncle worked as an engineer. He'd arrived by the same ship that had carried Laura and her oma.

I doubt Georgie's conscious brain registered the deferential movements of the other boys, but his animal instinct would not have failed to miss it. Or the reasons for it. Like an electrical current generated by rising tension, hatred crackled between us. I believe that had we each been armed with clubs, we would have charged forward without hesitation at the slightest of provocations.

This unspoken hatred was established in the time it took to lock eyes. With effort, I pretended not to see him as I moved to the edge of the chalked circle and squatted. I could feel the burn of his gaze on my right shoulder, as I imagined the caressing smile of Laura warming my left shoulder. It was no accident I had chosen a position that placed me between them.

"Who is next?" I asked, keeping my eyes on the marbles.

"We've been saving a place for you," Timothy said. He was eight years old, and a snot-nosed, obsequious toad, but his answer established that I was leader.

Still watching and waiting for the onionskin to enter the circle, I fumbled with my belt. I always carried two small pouches of marbles tied to my belt and tucked inside my shorts.

"He's not playing," Georgie said.

This earned a respectful gasp from the other boys.

I turned my head to give him a direct stare.

"He wasn't here when the game started so he can't be part of it," Georgie continued, speaking of me in the third person as if I were not there in front of him. "He should run back to his mother and she can inspect his pretty clothes so she can make sure he hasn't smudged himself or wet his pants."

He smirked and waited for my response.

Three

With Georgie only a few steps away, every nerve of mine tingled; I was intensely aware of the full challenge he had thrown at me and of the significance of how I responded. Not only in Laura's eyes, which was what mattered most, but in how it might change my status among my peers. Over the years, my role in the pack of local boys had been clearly established. I could roam through their territory as I pleased with a well-earned diplomatic pass. Preteen boys do not articulate this, but our genetic imprint demands a pecking order. It unfolds whenever boys who are old enough to walk grasp at toys in the hands of other boys.

I looked away from Georgie.

"What is your name?" I asked Laura, for of course, I didn't know it then. What I believed already, without doubt, was that she was destined to be my lifelong love.

"Laura," she answered. "My name is Laura Jansen."

Laura.

"Her father works for my father," the American boy said. His Dutch had an accent to it, but, I had to admit, he appeared to be able to speak it fluently. "At the refinery."

At this, I saw the slightest flinch on Laura's face.

The power of the human brain to read mere flickers of body language, the tiniest of voice inflections, and the subtlety of eye movement, all to draw instant and subconscious conclusions beyond the reach of studied logic, should never be underestimated. Children learn early to assess a parent's mood and react accordingly. Because I was the only one seeing her face—absorbed in it as I was, despite the threat from Georgie—only I understood I had just won the war against the boy I already hated. What remained, however, were the battles.

"Hello, Laura," I said, as if only she and I shared the shade of the banyan, for in a way, of course, that was true. "My name is Jeremiah Prins. Are you here at the market with your parents?"

"I was told to watch her," my enemy said, giving more evidence that she was someone he wanted to impress. "She came with me."

Laura flinched again, and those hazel brown eyes lost some calm.

"I came with my oma to the market," Laura answered. "Georgie asked to join us because he was bored."

She finally glanced at him. "I don't need *anyone* to watch over me."

He understood how clearly she was making her choice known, and his body went rigid.

"This seems to be an unpleasant situation," I told Laura, echoing how I believed a knight like Ivanhoe would speak. "Would it be all right if I took you to your oma? The market is confusing, and if it's your first time, I can make it easier for you."

I was rewarded with the smile. I reached for her hand, and she took a step toward me. Away from Georgie.

"Coward," Georgie said with full sneer.

"Oh," I said, having fully expected and anticipated that he would not let me walk away without a challenge. I did not want to walk away. "Coward? Afraid of what?"

"A fight," he said.

I was disappointed that my hand had not reached Laura's and that I needed to turn to face him before I could feel the touch of her fingers against mine.

"Who wants to fight me?" I asked. Already I could tell that I would be able to twist and skewer him with words.

He grunted with frustration. "I just called you a momma's boy."

"Actually," I said, "you suggested that she inspect my clothing. I don't need help with that. It's rather silly to suggest that a boy our age needs help to know if he's wet his pants."

I paused. Timing is everything. "Unless it's happened to you."

That earned laughter. Like an arrow, it had the desired effect on Georgie, who clenched his fists.

"I was insulting you," he said. "Are you that stupid? It should make you want to fight me. Unless you are chicken."

"If you want to fight," I said, "why don't you just ask?"

This was entertaining for the other boys. I knew it and enjoyed it.

Georgie spit in my direction. "I'm going to pound you so bad you'll bleed from your ears."

"How can that be if we don't fight?" I asked.

"See. Chicken."

"That doesn't sound like a question to me," I said. I turned to Laura, who had giggled when the other boys laughed. "It will be embarrassing to him if I need to explain what a question is. Let's find your oma."

Georgie began to gurgle. Such is the power of deliberate insouciance.

"Come on," Georgie half shouted. "Let's fight."

"All you need to do is ask," I said. "Is that so difficult to understand?"

Georgie had no idea how easily I had taken control of the situation. But then, I had no idea of the extent of his cruelty and preference for inflicting pain. Yet.

Before Georgie could do what I was essentially commanding him to do, Klaus Akkermans stepped onto our stage. Klaus was one of the older boys, almost thirteen. Slicked-back hair and a gap between his front teeth. Twenty pounds heavier than I. During our fistfight a few months ago, he'd hit me so hard in the belly that I had thrown up on his feet.

"I wouldn't ask," Klaus told Georgie. "Jeremiah doesn't lose fights."

"He's fast," Timmie the Toad said. If Timmie was publicly choosing sides this early, then the invisible opinion of the group had shifted in my favor. "When Jeremiah was four, a cobra crawled into his bed. He grabbed it by the neck and went into the kitchen and cut off its head. Right, Jeremiah?"

I shrugged. Truth was, I couldn't remember it, and family stories, I'm sure, have a way of getting exaggerated with each retell.

"It's not that he's fast," Klaus told Georgie. "Although he is. He just doesn't lose fights."

Georgie looked back and forth between Klaus and Timmie the Toad, trying to evaluate this new information.

"Not even the teenagers fight him," said Alfie Devroome. He had the slightest of a clubfoot on his left side. When we chose teams for races, I always made sure he was my second or third pick. First would look too patronizing.

"He can't win fights against teenagers," Georgie said. "Look at how little he is."

Klaus shook his head. "Nobody said he *wins*

fights. He just doesn't lose them. We've just about all had our turns against Jeremiah." He glanced around, then looked back at Georgie. "When I fought him, I hit him so many times my hands hurt, and he was bleeding everywhere. He even threw up on my shoes. It only ended because I had to tell him I was tired."

Klaus put his hands on his hips. "Like I said, he didn't win. But he didn't lose. Older boys know they would have to kill him to end the fight, so they leave him alone."

"You also lost some teeth," Timmie the Toad reminded Klaus. "He did hit you a couple of good ones."

"I've told you," Klaus answered. "Those were loose anyway."

"And don't forget about how he whacked a sow in the head with a hammer and killed it," added Simon Leeuwenhoek, a chubby kid and the only one in the bunch I had not fought. Simon was too good-natured for that. And his parents were rich so he didn't care much about how many marbles he lost. "Jeremiah was only nine."

This I did remember.

"I didn't kill it," I said. "I just hit it once. Because it was attacking me."

The previous summer, we had been visiting a plantation of a family whose children attended my father's school. I had ignored my mother's warning to stay away from the sow and piglets inside the pen, and the sow had torn a chunk out of my left calf as I was scrambling to climb out.

As happened when I was threatened physically, a switch inside of me had flipped on and numbed my body to anything except cold and calculating rage, accelerated by all the benefits of accompanying adrenaline. It means that when I fight, I still have clarity of thought, and I'm aware that this is a rarity of inheritance in which I can and should take no pride.

I'd returned to the pigpen with a hammer found in a nearby shed. When the sow charged me again, I had brought it down with both hands and solidly struck it between the eyes. Knocked it cold. The fathers had not chosen sides, but an argument escalated between the mothers. Mine made the accusation that dangerous animals should be controlled, and the other mother suggested that I, not the sow, was the dangerous animal and that I was a bad example to the other children. Even though the sow only swayed sideways when it got up and walked, and I needed thirty stitches to pull together the ragged skin and muscle of my calf, the other mother insisted I was to blame and we hadn't been invited back. I'd promised not to do something like that again because it had upset my mother. She spent hours alone in a dark, cool room when things upset her. Her spells frightened all of us children in the family.

"I'm not scared," Georgie told our audience. To his credit, he didn't sound scared. He wanted to fight me as badly as I wanted to fight him.

"Then ask," I said. I could sense the coldness at the edge of my gut, and I wanted to feel his nose crack against my fist. "I'm not allowed to ask for a fight. And I'm not allowed to take the first swing."

Those were my father's rules. He said Jesus had not been one to fight. However, Father allowed that it would be impractical to live without any kind of self-defense. His corollary advice was that if you had to strike back, do it far out of proportion to the attack because that will dis-courage future attacks. This counsel had a certain kind of logic if you were hoping to be able to settle back to living like Jesus, but Georgie, as I would learn in the coming years, was just as determined to escalate his hatred against me as I was against him.

There was silence as Georgie realized that asking me to fight would be his first defeat, but he had no choice.

"Will you fight me?" Georgie finally asked. His tone suggested that he was stunned to find himself in the position of a supplicant, and still trying to figure out how it had happened.

"Yes," I said. "But first I'd like to ask Laura if she will leave and shop with her oma in the market. This will be ugly."

"I'm not afraid of ugly," she said. "I'm not a sissy."

A slight flicker of indignation crossed her face. This girl, it was obvious, did not like being told what to do. That simply made her Dutch. I recovered with an immediate explanation.

"I just don't want you to have to lie about it when the mothers ask later," I said. "If you don't see anything, you won't have to lie. It's a way of protecting me."

Lots of unspoken assumptions in there, all favoring me, like the assumption that she would want to protect me, even enough to lie for me. What was artful was that nothing in my request suggested she should protect Georgie, even though his father was the boss of her father.

"Oh," she said to me. "Since you asked. Yes."

It hadn't occurred to me that she would give any other answer.

I turned to Georgie. "We're going to need to find a place where mothers can't see us. Just past the village there's a stream and a small fenced pasture for goats. The boys will take you there and I'll have both pieces of rope. I know where I can find some in the market."

"Rope?" Georgie would have been inhuman not to ask.

"I don't want you running away," I said. The cold inside me was mushrooming, and horrible as it is to confess, I was savoring the sensation and the chance to inflict punishment on him. I had no concern about the punishment I'd have to endure for that chance. "The pasture is fenced. We tie our own waists to a fence post with enough slack in each rope that we can reach each other. Once we are tied to the fence posts, one won't be able to run away from the other. Then we fight."

I grinned at the taller and broader boy in front of me.

"Unless," I said, "you are chicken."

Four

What I didn't know was that while I was escorting Laura to her oma, Georgie had procured a weapon. Later, any of the best guesses from the other boys was that he'd accomplished this as they passed a construction area. A concrete pad had been freshly poured for the foundation of a small house at the edge of the kampong, and a spare piece of rebar must have been lying handy for him to pick up, then tuck into his pants at the small of his back, hidden by his shirt.

Rebar is made of steel. It's a rod about the thickness of the shaft of a golf club and varies in length. It's used to carry tensile loads in concrete, because concrete is a material strong in compression, which is a pushing force, but weak in the opposite force, tension, which is a pulling force. As I would learn in my first-year engineering course on my way to becoming an architect, rods of steel embedded in concrete compensate for concrete's lack of tensile strength. This near-perfect marriage is of little fascination to anyone, I suppose, except to engineers and architects. When temperature changes, steel and concrete expand at roughly the same rate. This makes steel the best material for reinforcement. If one material expanded with heat or shrunk with cold at a different rate than the other, the steel would eventually shred the concrete around it. But the marriage, like any other, is not immune from external threats; the biggest risk of compromise between steel and concrete happens from rust, which, as I would discover later, is also a relevant threat to marriage between humans. In a perfect symbiotic relationship between the concrete and steel, there is enough of a concrete cover to prevent rust. However, without enough concrete, the rusting of the steel takes up more room than the steel, which causes severe pressure that can eventually lead to internal structural failure. On the other hand, if there is too much concrete around the rebar, it loses tensile strength, and the concrete cracks, also leading to structural failure.

Too often we fail to look deep enough. Our buildings and bridges remain stable because of internal structural details that have taken

centuries for mankind to understand. As for mysteries of the heart, it would have never occurred to me to use a weapon in a fistfight against another boy. Likewise, it would have never occurred to Georgie to manipulate and humiliate someone with words the way that I had done to him in such a casual manner. Had I not been so cruel beneath the banyan, he may not have escalated the fight beyond the regular aggression of boys. Perhaps a mere fistfight would have resulted in grudging mutual respect, each of us remaining wary of the other. Instead, the escalation from that piece of rebar would follow us into the concentration camp, leading to consequences that would take seven more decades for him and me to resolve.

Just inside the market, Laura told me good-bye, insisting she could find her oma by herself. I made her giggle by kissing the top of her hand, as any chivalrous knight would do. Before leaving, I stopped at a nearby stall and used some money given to me for my birthday to obtain two stretches of rope. I carried both the quarter mile or so toward the goat pasture, picking up a rock twice the size of my fist along the way.

When I arrived, the boys were leaning against the outside of a wooden rail fence, without much conversation. I tossed the rock just inside the fence, where it landed with a thud in the thick grass.

"You're going to fight with a rock?" Georgie asked. "Is that what you think you need?"

"Not against you," I said. "It's for the goat."

Fifty yards or so away, a billy goat and a half-dozen nannies were gathered near a salt block, feeding on a particularly tall patch of grass that had grown lush and deep green in the tropical heat and moisture.

I unbuttoned my crisp linen shirt, then began to remove my shorts, taking care to keep my two marble pouches secret.

"What is he doing?" Georgie asked, refusing to address me directly.

Timmie the Toad was quick to answer. "He always fights like that. It keeps his clothes clean. So his *moeder* won't know he was in a fight."

In only my sandals and underwear, I placed my clothing on the fence post, satisfied that I wouldn't spoil any of the material with blood-stains.

"He's crazy," Georgie said.

Such statements have been made about the Dutch for generations. Stubbornness is often confused with craziness. The Dutch will not quit, even when we have begun something that makes little sense in the first place. This obstinacy makes us swell with pride, even as we freely admit the senselessness of it. Yet without such stubbornness, a fifth of our country would not exist, for in battling one of the greatest forces of nature, we have carved out our land in continual defiance of the entire North Sea.

"Roman gladiators fought like this," I said. I had no idea if that was true, but it was a suitable romantic vision for me, even if I lacked a gladiator's glistening skin and rippled muscles. My arms and neck and face and lower part of my legs were darkly tanned, yet the remainder of my body, which had been covered by clothing, was pale and skinny. My hair, near white from exposure to the sun, gave no suggestion of Roman heritage either.

I climbed over the fence, then tied one end of the rope around my waist. I tied the other end to a fence post. I held up the second piece of rope and spoke as I tied it to the same fence post.

"This is called a strangle knot," I told Georgie. "My father taught it to me."

I looped the working end around the post and left a small gap. After that, the important point was to cross the second turn over the first turn, then pull the end under both turns. Much easier to show than to explain.

I tugged on the rope. "You don't need to worry that it will come loose."

I tossed the other end of the rope into the pasture, where it appeared to snake across the grass.

There it was. An invitation in the form of that rope, as dangerous as an actual snake. Once he accepted it by tying the other end of the second rope around his waist, we would be intertwined until one or the other surrendered. We didn't know then how our lives would remain like that, long after that rope rotted.

Georgie climbed over the fence. He kept his clothes on and stayed at a distance, as if he expected me to jump him while he was preoccupied with securing the loose end of the rope around his waist. That's how it goes, isn't it? We believe others will behave the way we would behave.

He stared at me, still a respectful distance away.

"You have to take the first swing," I explained. "My father won't let me fight otherwise."

"A goat," Georgie pointed. "Coming our way."

I glanced over my shoulder. It was the billy goat. Black all through, even the spare beard that held broken blades of grass. Its horns curved back over its skull.

"You think it would learn," I said. "Wait a minute, will you?"

I untied the rope at my waist and took the rock and paced toward the goat. Its shoulders were about waist high to me. Yellow eyes.

"You must be very stupid," I told the goat. I showed him the rock. "You don't remember this?"

It snorted and lowered its head and charged.

I didn't bother trying to hit it between the eyes as I'd done the previous summer with the sow. I'd already learned the hard way that there was a reason billy goats used the top of their skulls as battering rams. Instead, I stepped sideways and grabbed one of the horns with my left hand, then used my right hand to swing the rock as hard as I could across the side of its head. The goat toppled with a strangled bleat.

I watched to see if it needed another clout, but it remained on its side, blinking and panting for breath. I brought my face down to its yellow eyes and spoke to it again. "There's more of that if you don't leave us alone."

The goat squirmed and managed to get its hind feet on the ground, then its front knees. I grabbed its horns and yanked it upward so that it could find its front feet.

It swayed. I watched and waited. Finally, it turned away and staggered back toward the salt block.

I walked back to Georgie and retied myself to the rope. I had hoped my nonchalance would form an impression upon Georgie and was glad to see horror on his face. He now knew what he was up against if he wanted to fight a Dutchman.

"We should be okay now," I said. "So if you don't mind swinging at me, we can get started." I could be casual about this because I'd been in many fights. The first few times, it's all about breathing in gulps of panic as time rushes in a whirlwind about you and you madly swing in all directions. By now, I'd had lots of experience and could remain relaxed.

"Sure," Georgie said. He reached behind his back with his left hand and pulled out the piece of rebar and advanced on me.

"Hey," one of the boys shouted. "Not fair!"

"Fair fights are for losers," Georgie said. He took another step.

I have often wondered if his initial intent was to scare me into an immediate surrender. Had I been prudent and done as he'd hoped, the fight would have been over. I could have even claimed the moral high ground. But I had the confidence of a ten-year-old who had yet to meet an opponent he couldn't quell.

My own blood lust—cold and calculating yet white hot—prevented a peaceful solution. The sight of that rod of steel in his hand snapped the switch inside my brain, and I wanted nothing more than a chance to get my teeth into his ears or nose and rip flesh away from his head. I grabbed the rope that attached Georgie to the fence post and jerked on it as hard as I could, hoping to cause him to stumble. Technically, he hadn't yet attempted the first swing, but I was confident that if I had to justify my actions to my father, he would deem them reasonable.

Georgie lurched toward me. Instinct kept me from diving for his legs, for that would have exposed my head to a blow with the piece of deadly rebar. Instead, I rushed at him and stayed as vertical as possible, hoping to bring him into a clinch that would make it impossible for him to swing with any force.

But he was fast. Faster than I expected. He swung the rebar toward me, and I felt, rather than heard, the crack of steel across the bone of my right arm as my momentum carried me into his body. My chest crashed against his, and he fell backward. I slid forward and pinned his arms to the ground with my knees. With no hesitation I pounded my left fist into the right side of his face. Once, twice, three times. So hard that my knuckles would remain swollen for days afterward. I leaned in and chomped my teeth on his ear.

I expected him to scream, but he did not. It was eerily silent, and into this silence broke a commanding female voice.

"Stop immediately!"

Adult authority was simply not something to be questioned, and the voice rang so clearly that both Georgie and I froze. As I released his ear from my teeth and looked down on Georgie's face, he smiled, then spit upward, covering my eyes with phlegm. Of all the things Georgie has done, this single act is the one that conjures up instant hatred in my soul. His act of spitting had been hidden from the female voice, and if I responded by smashing his face, he would look totally without blame.

I did not move off his body until a hand yanked my left arm, near the shoulder. I stood and wiped the spit off my face with the biceps of my left arm.

Georgie stood, leaving the steel rebar in the grass at his feet, where it was invisible. "He started it," Georgie told the woman. "If his friends say differently, they are lying and they are lying because they are his friends."

"Georgie," the woman answered in a flat voice, "it's time to go home. Laura is waiting for us at the market."

This was Laura's oma then.

Children have no sense of the age of adults, except within a decade or so, just as adults can usually only guess a child's age within a couple of years of accuracy. Couples back then married young and had children young, so on that morning, Laura's grandmother, Sophie, was yet years away from her sixtieth birthday. That wasn't something I knew then, nor cared about on that morning, but even at age ten, it didn't escape me that Sophie was amazingly beautiful, set apart from Dutch omas who tended to wide hips and heavy busts as life wore them down. Sophie was wearing a yellow dress from her neck nearly down to her ankles, and her blond hair was pinned back.

There I stood, in my underwear, tied to a rope that was tied to a post. Sophie glanced at me, and then her gaze moved back to Georgie, who had begun to untie himself while keeping his eyes on me.

I became conscious of how badly my right forearm hurt just above the wrist. I lifted my arm slightly and fought back a scream at the bolt of agony I felt when bone grated against bone. I let my arm drop again. It wasn't an injury that would appear immediately obvious, but Georgie's right eye was already turning purple. Blood dripped from the obvious tooth marks in his ear.

I expected to be immediately harangued and decided I would not make an excuse or try to justify my actions. But when Laura's oma spoke, her Dutch was elegant and enunciated with the assured clarity that comes with inherited wealth.

"We're going to need to do something about your ear," she told Georgie. "In this climate, infections can be very dangerous."

She looked at me. "I trust you'll stop this imitation of a savage and dress yourself at your earliest convenience?"

I nodded, too surprised at her calmness to speak.

She addressed the rest of the boys. "All of you, back to your mothers."

They scampered off, probably as shocked as I was at the lack of reprisal. She led Georgie away through a nearby gate, leaving me alone in the pasture.

I fainted twice as I struggled to untie myself and woke the second time with the billy goat's nose only inches from my eyes. It bleated something that sounded like triumph, but it spared me further battle, as all decent opponents will do when victory is assured. I might have fainted again, except by then the stinging ants had found me and I had good motivation to get back on my feet.

When I finally found my mother in the market, I was looking as good as I always did, in my freshly pressed linens. Enough time had passed that my right forearm, however, had swollen to grotesque proportions in the rising temperatures. I told her I had fallen from a tree. She was accustomed to my injuries and responded to them as I had learned to respond to a fight. Panic the first few times, but after that, as long as she was not entrenched in one of her dark moods, she responded calmly and efficiently. In this case, it was a trip to the doctor—after she completed her shopping list.

A boy falling from a tree hard enough to break both the radius and the ulna should be wearing dirty clothes and should not bear the scraped mark of a steel bar where the skin had almost split. My lie should have been obvious. But my lie was safe since before presenting myself to my mother, I'd first tracked down the other boys and forced them to agree on a story that would be presented in common to any inquiring mothers.

The doctor did not speculate about how my arm got broken, and I didn't see him again until weeks later, when he gave permission for the cast to be removed. That was the day before three Japanese soldiers pushed open the front door to our home and, armed with authority and a machine gun, they began the invasion of our lives.

Five

In early 1942, during the six weeks it took for the bones in my right forearm to fully knit, I struggled to write and mail a sonnet to Laura Jansen, continuously irritated that I was forced to use my left hand to put ink on paper. This was the worst of my concerns, for I was innocent of the impact the Japanese Imperial military forces were having on the world in the midst of a war I knew very little about.

Not until many years later would I understand that from the day my arm was broken in late January, to when the cast was removed in early March, how much their forces accomplished in such a short time. The Japanese began and completed the siege of Singapore by forcing British troops to surrender, completed an air raid against Australia, invaded Sumatra and Java of our own Dutch East Indies, forced American President Roosevelt to withdraw American forces from the

Philippines, and invaded Burma and New Guinea and Bali and North Borneo. En route to completing the takeover of the Dutch East Indies and forcing the surrender of the Dutch Governor-General on March 9, they inflicted a series of major defeats against the combined Pacific naval forces of the United States, Britain, the Netherlands, and Australia.

Not to be overlooked is that in the same six weeks, they also attacked the American mainland by sneaking a submarine in close enough to the California coast to shell an oil refinery in Santa Barbara, and also make a return to Pearl Harbor for another bombing attack.

This impressive display of military prowess may seem like more than what I accomplished in laboring over every word of my eighteen-line sonnet and going back and forth a dozen times to the kampong post office to mail it. I would change my mind and, with stamp still in hand, return home to work up enough bravery to go back again another day. It wasn't until the thirtieth copy of the sonnet that I was satisfied it was good enough for Laura, both in content and appearance. The Japanese Imperial forces may have been motivated by oil, but my quest was one of pure love.

Yet, strictly speaking, the Japanese were motivated by a devotion to the Emperor Hirohito, whom they considered to be a god, a god who had been facing an oil embargo imposed on him by the Dutch and British and Americans since July of the previous year. The only way for more oil to reach Japan was if Hirohito relinquished decades of hard-won territory in Asia—including significant control over China—and gave up on the cherished ideal of a "New Order" where the Japanese, as the supreme nation, were entitled to rule all of their part of the world.

It was a profound dilemma for a proud warrior nation. There was no honor in bowing to the West, and Japan was nothing without honor. But it would also be nothing without the oil it desperately needed to import. There was oil for the taking in the Dutch East Indies—refined and stored in quantities sufficient for any war machine—but it was protected by ninety-three thousand Dutch troops and another five thousand American and British soldiers. Furthermore, it was protected by a ring of destroyers and other naval ships that formed the Malay Barrier.

If the notion of a nation of racially superior people seeking dominance by war sounds familiar, that's because Hitler, as an ally to the Japanese, was an inspiration in ideology, practicality, and treachery to Hirohito and his military. Shortly after signing a nonaggression treaty with the Soviet Union, Hitler surprised his relaxed Soviet allies in June of 1941 by launching a gigantic blitzkrieg assault against them that seemed certain of the success he'd had in crushing and dominating mainland Europe. This would give him the resources he needed and help maintain Aryan purity.

The Japanese, then, resolved to move forward with the same audacity. They planned for the bombing of Pearl Harbor even as negotiations with the Americans continued. With the naval resources of Pearl Harbor destroyed, Japan intended to be free to move across the Pacific into the Dutch East Indies, islands that held the richest oil reserves in all of Asia. And thus, the first military action of Japanese aggression that would lead to my entry into a concentration camp some four months later began on the infamous morning of December 7—December 8 in Japan—as the Imperial Japanese Army Air Service attacked a harbor in Hawaii.

Let it not be said that the Dutch easily gave up control of a colony that had been theirs for nearly 350 years and had become a second home-land. In mid-February of 1942, as the Japanese invasion looked inevitable, the Dutch began destroying storage tanks and oil fields and refineries at the river port city of Palembang on the island of Sumatra. Even when hundreds of Japanese paratroopers floated down onto the city, the destruction was delayed only long enough to engage in battle. When the Japanese tried sending a full infantry division up the Musi River from the delta city of Sungsang, we Dutch refused to be cowed and poured a flood of oil onto the river and, with the touch of a lit match, turned the surface of the water into an inferno that destroyed hundreds more soldiers. But, as we were to learn, the numbers of the Japanese seemed limitless, and Palembang fell within a day. We were also to learn that the Japanese were vicious in reprisals—those involved in the demolitions were executed by bullets or sword, and the wives and daughters violated.

As a boy, living what would later become the largely ignored war history of our islands, my concerns were not on the planes marked with large red circles on the fuselage that circled our valley or on the emotional distress in our home caused by those unfolding events. I didn't give much thought to the air-raid sirens that had proved to be false alarms again and again. Since I was accustomed to my mother's mood swings and her fights with my father, I mistakenly believed this tension was just another swing of the pendulum. Most of the Dutch elite were blinded further to the looming threat because they believed the Japanese would need them to maintain the colony.

Not surprisingly, in the weeks before invasion, my mind stayed focused on the lack of reply to my impassioned sonnet. In mailing it to Laura, I'd even included a second envelope addressed to our home, making it simple for Laura to mail back to me any swooning response she might feel appropriate to my marvelous poetry.

My wait finally ended the day before my cast was to be removed. When the family gathered for lunch, one of our *djongos* bowed and set our mail in the center of the table. At the top of the stack, I saw an envelope with our address written in my own handwriting.

I dared not reach for it without permission. My father was a strict disciplinarian and needed to be, given that ours was a family that blended my three older half brothers with me, my two younger sisters, and my younger brother. I existed under a trifecta of teenage dictators—Niels, Martijn, and Simon—who formed a harmonious gang when it came to the young interlopers in their family. They had little affection for me and my lack of respect for their positions of authority.

When not at home or school, they learned street smarts and the art of inflicting physical punishment as they roamed with native Indonesians of their own ages, going to places that few Dutch boys explored.

My half brothers were the reason that I became an expert at reading moods and intentions through the slightest changes of body language. Indirectly, I would end up owing them gratitude for the training they had dispensed. It served me well during my time in the concentration camp, where I also began to realize my perception of them had been colored by my self-centered view of life and eventually came to understand I must have seemed as obnoxious to them as they were to me.

In our sprawling eight-bedroom house, I could avoid being in the same room with them most of the time and overlooked the luxuries of high ceilings, hardwood floors, and constantly turning ceiling fans. Outside, our property had finely trimmed lawns, towering palm trees, and flower beds that suggested Eden. All this would have been extravagant in the Netherlands, and far beyond the salary of a school headmaster.

Here, though, we were able to afford male and female servants for any domestic need. This was a blessing for more than me, as Mother, while movie-star beautiful, was too often frail and brittle. She was my father's second wife. The first had dutifully delivered my half brothers, then succumbed to a bout of influenza. After my father married my mother, he moved from the Netherlands to take the job here in the Dutch East Indies. I was born soon after, followed by my two sisters—the seven-year-old twins Nikki and Aniek—and the baby in our family, four-year-old Pietje.

As we waited for our *kokki*—the cook—to finish the meal at the stove, I stared at the envelope at the center of the table, and the obvious interest was a mistake.

Simon, the fifteen-year-old, casually worked the envelope loose from the pile and examined the writing on it.

"What is this?" he asked. "A letter for Jeremiah. By the return address, it's from someone named Laura Jansen. Who lives in Sampangan."

The village was a few miles downstream from our village of Sukorejo, near the port city of Semarang, where the refinery was located.

Simon waved the envelope. He was big already, like our father.

"Is this your handwriting?" Simon asked as he examined the envelope. "Are you pretending to send yourself mail from a girl?"

"Jansen," my mother said absently, as usual, oblivious to the undercurrents of strife among the children. Another reason I was inured to pain. "Isn't he the one whose wife died last year?"

"Engineer at the refinery," my father contributed. I knew his tone of voice. Cold, almost bitter. That told me that he and Mother were at odds again, although I never understood the reasons, just as I never understood, until later, her mood changes. "Just before Pearl Harbor, his mother had arrived from the Netherlands to help. He and his family left by boat a few weeks ago to escape the Japanese. Along with the Americans."

Laura was gone? Left by boat? My lifelong love was no longer in the Dutch East Indies?

My daydreams of seeing her at the market again collapsed. Perhaps, then, her return letter would have some answers as to how I could reach her again. This made it even more crucial to read the contents. In private.

"Did you perfume it too, *kleine snotneus?*" Simon sniffed the envelope. "No, apparently not."

His continuous use of the phrase "little snotnose" was not meant to be endearing. Despite his admonitions that we should try to be like Jesus, Father never corrected this type of insult. He also wanted his children to be tough and had no qualms about the apparent contradiction. Piety and unemotional severity. A typical Dutch combi-nation.

"If that letter is addressed to me," I said, "it belongs to me." I knew better than to appeal to either of my parents. My mother would wave it away as too minor to be of her concern, and Father especially detested whining or excuses in any form. The emotional bonding in our family— typical of the Dutch then—did not consist of open affection. Neither, at least in our family, it seemed, did a marriage.

"Let's see what this girl sent you," Niels said. "And then I'll be happy to hand it across the table."

He started to open the envelope.

I knew that my father preferred not to inter-fere. He liked to say that his job was not to prepare the path for us, but to prepare us for the path. But he was also fair. Surely Niels had stepped well beyond the normal teasing an older brother was allowed. But just then the classical music on the radio stopped playing. The *Nederlands Indische Radio Omroep Maatschappi*—Netherlands Indish Radio Broadcast, or NIROM—broke in with a special news bulletin.

Halfway across the dining room, our *djongo* froze and remained motionless, tray of prepared food in his hands. The broadcaster reported that our Governor-General, the Lord Tjarda van Starkenborg—Jonk Heer van Starkenborg, in Dutch—had met the day before with the Japanese Lt. General Hitoshi Imamura and agreed to unconditional surrender and a cease-fire. What remained of the ninety-three thousand Dutch troops and five thousand American and British soldiers were to surrender at 1:00 p.m., only an hour away. This was March 9, 1942.

A brief silence followed. Then the NIROM broadcaster said, "We are shutting down now. Good-bye until better times. Long live the queen!"

The notes of the Dutch national anthem began to sound, echoing through our room.

Perhaps I was the only one to see a smile briefly flash white across the dark-skinned face of the *djongo* holding our food. He would be among those in the next few days to meet Japanese soldiers in a crowd, waving flags and crying out "*banzai Dai Nippon*" to the forces that they considered to be liberators. For me, it was my first realization that the native Indonesians were not as happy with life in the Dutch East Indies as were the Dutch. My parents had withheld the news that as the Japanese army had advanced through the archipelago, rebellious natives had also killed Dutch rulers and become reliable informers for the Japanese.

When the Dutch national anthem ended and the radio went silent, my father signaled for the food to be placed on the table.

"*Even bidden*," he said. *All pray.*

It was a perfect time, I would argue, to have asked for divine help in the face of what certainly promised to be a catastrophic time for the Dutch on these islands, but my father merely spoke a blessing over the food and, in so doing, pretended life was normal.

When I opened my eyes, I discovered that in a way, the normalcy of life had not changed. Across the table, Simon grinned at me as he finished opening the envelope sent to me from Laura. He then held it up and turned it over to shake out its contents. When nothing came out, his expression turned to bewilderment.

Six

Early sunlight cast horizontal shadows across my blankets where the blinds could not seal my room against the new day. I had slept on the box spring, and the mattress was on the floor. Still in pajamas, I ignored movement from inside my mattress and sat on the edge of the bed frame. I examined my right hand to gauge whether it had changed for the better during the night. The meat of my palm seemed to have disappeared. My forearm was weak and shriveled; no one had warned me that weeks in a cast would atrophy the muscles. In contrast to the tanned skin of my upper arm, the portion where the plaster had covered from my elbow almost to my knuckles was as white as spots of leprosy. Curious about pain, I curled and uncurled my fingers as I flexed into a fist. I bent my wrist forward and backward, all in efforts to gauge how far I could stretch with any degree of strength. The day before, the doctor had promised this stiffness would gradually disappear, and that soon it would be as if my arm had never been broken.

This was a ridiculous promise. Suggesting that I would forget the day I met Laura was like suggesting I would forget to breathe. Or that I would forget the day that an older American boy had broken my arm. I'd been scheming since then to arrange another fight, and now he was gone, on a ship. With Laura. Who had mailed me an empty envelope. No matter how well the bone healed, it would never be as if my arm had never been broken.

As I was squeezing my right forefinger to my thumb to test how much pressure I could exert, I heard loud thumping at the main door of the house. It was early for visitors. Still, if we had visitors, I needed to look presentable. From my wardrobe closet, I selected my best trousers and a freshly ironed shirt and set them on the blankets covering my box spring. In my underwear, I washed my face with water from a basin on the dresser and ran my wet fingers through my hair. Then I inspected myself in the mirror.

I hid my right arm behind my back and grinned at the handsome image of myself. Because of my older brothers, I knew what body changes were ahead of me, and naturally, I was impatient. I'd seen them naked many times at the river when we swam. Still, in our contests to see who could urinate the farthest, I rarely lost. The secret is in how hard you can squeeze your buttocks and the correct arch in the back.

I moved the clothing and wrestled the mattress back onto the box spring to hide how I had slept. I dressed myself with care to avoid wrinkles in my trousers and shirt. I didn't want to detour to the bathroom until I saw who had knocked on the door. Before leaving, though, I performed a customary check of my hiding hole behind my wardrobe. The two pouches I usually wore during the day were still safe.

In the dining room, I found my mother and father facing three Japanese soldiers, and immediately regretted my decision not to visit the bathroom first.

They were stocky and short. One carried a machine gun mounted with a bayonet and wore a dirty single-breasted khaki tunic with five buttons down the front, matching the color of his flat-topped cap with a single yellow star and neck flaps that hung down to his shoulders. The other two men wore no caps, and their pressed uniforms were darker, almost green, and double-breasted, with narrow red patches on the left shoulder. I hoped my half brothers would come down. They constantly teased me about my fashion standards, but these uniforms were more proof that the way a person dressed indicated status. It was very apparent who were the two officers.

My father, still in his bathrobe, stood stiffly. When he looked at me, I saw that his lips were tight with suppressed fury. My mother stood behind him, eyes looking at the floor, clutching the front of her robe closed.

"Return to your room," my father told me.

"*Kashira naka!*" one officer screamed, and

the soldier waved his machine gun at my father.

Impossible to know the words, but the intent was easy to translate.

I decided the best response would be silence. I held my breath. The same soldier then pointed his machine gun at me. As I stared into the black hole of the barrel, I thought of the eye of a cobra.

He gestured for me to join my parents, and I could feel a cold rage begin to build. I wanted to reach across and grab the finned barrel, then turn the bayonet on him. My father's body language vibrated with the same tension, and the Japanese soldier seemed to sense it, for he backed up a little. My mother sobbed in little hiccups, which seemed to irritate my father more.

The two officers walked over to our dining room table and inspected it. They had a short conversation, then the one that I guessed was the senior officer pulled a tag from his pocket, wrote on it, and slapped it on the table. He wrote pencil markings in a small notepad.

They moved to the cabinet at the far wall. One opened the door, and both began to chatter at the sight of bottles of whiskey, gin, and vodka. The second one closed the door, and the senior officer wrote on a second tag and placed it on the cabinet, then once again wrote in his notepad.

As the two officers left the room, our guard made threatening motions with his machine gun to keep us in place. We stood before him, still listening to the casual conversation between the officers while they roamed the house. Then came unintelligible shouts punctuated by the voices of my brothers and sisters. When they reached the end of the house and Pietje's room, we heard a wail of fear, followed by the thumping of feet as Pietje dashed around the house. When he found us in the dining room, he ran to me and clutched my waist and cried, ignoring the Japanese soldier completely.

"Pietje," I said, drawing out his name, *Peeet-cheh*, to soothe him. I placed my hand on his tousled blond hair. "How many times have I told you not to mess my trousers and shirt? I don't want snot on my clothes."

It was my pitiful effort to make him giggle at my oft-repeated and oft-ignored complaint, but Pietje continued to tremble.

My talking earned another shout from the soldier with the machine gun. "*Kashira naka!*"

I lifted Pietje and held him to my chest. He was warm against me, and I felt more urgently the need to relieve my bladder. I wasn't worried about Pietje speaking, for he rarely put more than a half-dozen words together. We remained like this until the officers returned.

The senior officer pointed at the first tag on the dining room table and said, "*Juu yong.*"

He held up his hands and made them into fists. He put up his left forefinger. "*Ichi.*"

With his next finger, he said, "*Ni.*"

Third finger. "*San.*"

He counted this way until he reached his tenth finger. "*Juu.*"

Then he counted eleven, twelve, thirteen, and fourteen. "*Juu ichi. Juu ni. Juu san. Juu yong.*"

I had no idea then that in the camps, our lives would depend on how well we could count for the Japanese during roll call. I was able to understand his emphasis on *juu yong*, which he repeated as he pointed at the tag, and we confirmed it after their departure. *Fourteen.* He had marked four-teen pieces of furniture with tags. With more gesturing, he made it clear that we were not to touch the tags. He waved his notepad, making it equally clear that he knew where every tag had been placed.

He made my father nod with agreement, and after that, he turned abruptly and marched out. The other officer and soldier followed.

"Children," my father shouted, "come out now!"

My mother moved to the cabinet and poured herself some Bols gin into a teacup. She drank it straight, without a trace of grimace, then added more to the teacup. Normally I would have been impressed. I had once tasted gin from my father's glass, and the sharp burning taste had sent me running for a banana to eat and remove the sting.

As I set Pietje down and he clung to my leg, I

noticed a strange quietness to the house. Our servants had not arrived from where they lived in different parts of the town.

All of the family assembled in the dining room, where my mother sat at the table, staring at the tag.

"It appears that our home has become a shop for the Japanese army," Father said. On my return from the doctor yesterday, streets had buzzed with trucks and Jeeps carrying Japanese soldiers. "Whatever has been marked will be taken by the Japanese. We must leave them marked. Later, I assume, someone will return to take all of it away."

"Not fair," Nikki said. "It's ours."

She and her twin sister were like dolls, and my mother dressed them that way as often as possible. It was a constant battle for my father to try to toughen them up for the real world. I sensed he didn't want them to become as frail and brittle as my mother.

"I've told you many times that life is not fair," Father said. In another household, perhaps, an invasion and subsequent departure by soldiers might have led to one or the other of parents offering comfort to their children. This, obviously, was not one of those households. "I don't like to hear complaints."

The usual silence followed his admonishment.

"And," my father continued, "I don't expect our

58

servants to arrive. So we will make do as best as we can. Each of you go back to your room and straighten up, then we will have our breakfast."

My cold rage had not abated. Despite my aching bladder, I ensured that Pietje and I were the last ones in the dining room, and then I moved to the cabinet. Among the bottles of gin and vodka were three bottles of whiskey. I took them in my arms.

"Pietje, go out and see if the hallway is clear."

He was accustomed to these instructions. My half brothers did not mistreat him, so he could wander the house with impunity that I could not afford. He scampered away, then returned to the threshold and nodded.

Quick as I could without dropping the bottles of whiskey, I retreated to my bedroom. Pietje followed and hopped onto my bed and watched in his typical silence. He ignored the occasional bumping of the mattress.

I moved to the window, lifted the shades, opened the window, and one by one, I poured a few ounces of whiskey out of each bottle. I was nearly dancing by then, so badly did I need to pee. But it was that very need that had given me my idea.

Pietje was my constant companion, so I felt no shyness about undressing in front of him. I care-fully folded my clothes, noting for later cleaning that there actually was a spot on the side of my trousers where he'd wiped his nose against it.

With equal care, I urinated into the first of the whiskey bottles. When it was full again, I replaced the cap and shook it to mix the contents. I wanted just enough in the bottle to satisfy my desire for revenge, but not enough that it would stop the officers from drinking. I did the same to the second bottle, and to the third.

This episode may seem far-fetched, and once, when I wondered whether my memory of this morning was correct, I searched for information and found that a human bladder can hold as much as eighteen ounces of fluid, although the urge to urinate starts at about five ounces, and involuntary urination—micturition—is triggered at about ten ounces of volume.

My bladder had been so full that afterward, I noted with some satisfaction that from the open bedroom window I still was able to splatter the leaves of a tree some fifteen feet away from the house. I'd tried to hit it once before but hadn't looked down first, which earned angry shouts from our gardener and a spanking from my father.

Pietje giggled at my prowess, as I'd hoped. Sure, this was a bad habit to teach him, and I knew he'd try it soon because he always did his best to imitate me. But given that my family had just been threatened in our own home by soldiers with a machine gun, I didn't think there would be much consequence if my mother found Pietje aiming out of his own bedroom window in the next few days.

I had more instructions for Pietje. I said, "Check again to see if the hallway is clear. It's time to return these whiskey bottles."

Seven

A few mornings later, my father and half brothers returned home early after Japanese soldiers had arrived at school and told everyone to leave. Father further explained that our family was not to leave the house. Since Pietje and I were accustomed to entertaining ourselves, this had little effect on us. We were absorbed in our latest venture, sitting in chairs on the lawn near the foundation of the house.

Our house was built off the ground, supported by crossbeams on pilings. It was skirted by lattice meant to keep out larger animals. Beneath my chair was a machete. I held a fishing rod, and the line from the tip fed through a gap in the lattice into the darkness beneath the house. The tip of the rod was continuously quivering at the slight tugs that came at the end of the line.

Occasionally, Pietje would give me an inquiring glance and I would shake my head to indicate it was not yet time to reel in the fishing line. Matters like this required patience, and I wanted to be a good teacher.

Although he and I were not engaged in conversation, we didn't sit in silence. As usual, geckos —*chichaks*—scrabbled up and down the walls, making little clicking sounds. I could not have guessed that within a year, I would be desperate to find them because we had resorted to eating them. The small lizards weren't limited to the exterior of the house. At night, you'd see them near our lamps, waiting for insects attracted to the light. The bigger ones—the *tokeks*—rarely showed themselves.

Around us, the birds, too, twittered and squawked and added to the din. Tawny-breasted honey eaters, friarbirds, mouse warblers, scrub wrens, butcher-birds, orioles—all oblivious to the signs of a country under siege.

The Japanese had taken our radio, so we no longer heard news about the war. Jeeps and trucks continued along the streets, but now more and more of the soldiers were returning after weeks of battle and enjoying their respite. Troops of them ran around in white loincloths like overgrown toddlers in diapers, and it seemed to our ears that their screaming and chattering was no different than a monkey's. They would enter houses at will to find food. Many had already been in our own home, inspecting the flushing toilets and opening and closing drawers to search for any objects of value.

That morning, it was less surprising than it should have been to see our father approaching us and carrying a folding chair to match the ones that Pietje and I were using. He set the chair down and sat beside us in companionable silence for a few minutes, watching the movement at the tip of the fishing rod.

"Is there water under the house that I'm not aware of?" he finally asked.

"No." I was cautious in my answer. Usually my father was direct and impatient. Usually he spoke but didn't listen.

"Aaah," he said, as if that explained everything. But he didn't spend much time around me and Pietje, so I doubted he understood why I had a fishing rod in hand, with the line running beneath the house.

He waited a few more minutes to see if I would explain. I out waited him. He must have had a purpose for joining us, and I had my fears in this regard. Earlier in the morning, I'd heard Simon yell in pain. More than once.

"Niels and Martijn have not slept well the previous nights," he said. "Apparently they have had rats in their mattresses. Has this happened to you?"

"Yes," I said. Each of the last three nights since the Governor-General had announced surrender,

I'd moved the mattress onto the floor and slept on the mattress frame and bedsprings so that the rats could have their privacy and I could have mine.

"Rats in your mattress wasn't something you needed to tell me?" he asked.

"It's best not to complain," I said. "I know you don't like involvement in what happens among us, as long as the furniture doesn't get broken."

I was quoting his own words back to him and wondered how he would take this.

He remained calm. Very unusual, which made me more nervous. "So this means you suspect one of your brothers was responsible for the presence of the rats?"

"You don't like tattletales," I said.

"Niels had a hole in his mattress," he said. "Someone had pushed a few handfuls of peanut butter into the hole. Same with Martijn. Naturally the rats began to explore when it was dark. Is this what happened to you?"

"I can't say whether there was peanut butter in the hole of my own mattress. It seemed best not to put my hands in that deep. I wasn't interested in letting a rat bite my fingers."

Pietje's head swiveled back and forth as he followed our discussion.

"Simon's mattress was untouched," my father said. "Do you find that significant?"

"If that is true, it would be best if Niels and Martijn didn't know that," I said. I was running a bluff. Niels and Martijn had been in my room first thing this morning to see if my own mattress had been tampered with as well. Certainly they would have checked Simon's too.

"I suspect they already know. I found the three of them fighting a half hour ago. Furniture *was* broken, which is why I had to get involved. That's when I learned about the peanut butter in the mattresses."

"And Simon?"

"He swears he didn't do anything."

That answer disappointed me. I had actually been hoping for a medical report. Simon would have put up a good fight, but Niels and Martijn would have been furious at Simon, and I knew the effects of that fury.

"In this case," my father said, "I'm tempted to believe Simon. You would think he'd know that if there were peanut butter in every mattress but his, naturally his brothers would suspect him and punish him for it."

"You would think," I said as neutrally as possible.

"A suspicious person might actually believe that someone else wanted revenge for the other day when Simon opened a certain envelope that had been addressed to a certain other boy in the family." My father examined my face, but in this family, you learned early how to remain expressionless. "Tell me, Jeremiah, does peanut butter wash easily off the hands?"

I handed the fishing rod to Pietje and stood. I now knew the direction this was going. I unbuckled my shorts and lowered them to my knees, making sure my two pouches of hidden marbles were safe. I turned away from my father and took a deep lungful of air and held it. It's best not to breathe during the initial few blows of a flat hand across the buttocks. It internalizes the cries of pain.

"Please sit," my father said, not unkindly. "Our family has far greater things to worry about."

I pulled up my shorts and buckled. Pietje gave me his inquiring look. I glanced at the tip of the rod. It was still quivering. "Not yet," I told Pietje.

I resumed my seat in my chair, and Pietje returned me the rod. "I haven't once told you that I am proud of how you can draw," my father said.

Often, at the end of a school day, while he sat at his desk and graded papers, I would sit at a student's desk nearby and practice those drawings. It wasn't art, but symmetry. I sketched buildings. His indulgence of allowing me time at something that wasn't practical or school oriented told me of his pride. I was startled to hear him state it openly.

"Neither," he said, "have I told you that I know you are a remarkable boy."

My chest swelled with this praise, then deflated when my father said, "I'm going to miss you."

"Are you sending me away?" I asked. Pietje

must have come to the same conclusion. He clutched at my free hand in fear.

What I'd done by planting peanut butter in all the mattresses but Simon's did deserve a spanking, but I hadn't expected to be banished from the household. Of course, I would then be out of reach of Simon, so there was some benefit in it. Eventually, he'd figure out what my father had figured out.

"You've seen what is happening," my father said. "The Japanese are taking over. Dutch currency is being replaced by Japanese currency. I've heard rumors that it will be illegal to speak Dutch on the streets. The Japanese know that to rule this island, they have to control the Dutch."

I listened.

"Accordingly, sooner or later," my father continued, "a truck will arrive to take me and your older brothers. All the Dutch men are going into work camps, and Dutch women and children will go together into different camps. Boys over the age of sixteen are considered men, so Simon will be with us."

I pondered this and had no reason to disbelieve it. It was strange how quickly I had accepted what was happening around us.

"Simon is only fifteen," I said.

"The Japanese count ages differently than we do. On a day that a baby is born, it is his first year, and the baby is considered to be one. The

Japanese will consider you to be eleven years old, not ten. I've changed your birth certificate so that it looks like you were born a year later. You are not tall, and they will believe you are younger."

"You want me to be a nine-year-old?"

"A ten-year-old to them," my father answered. "We don't know how long this war will last. I need you to stay with your mother and Nikki and Aniek and Pietje as long as possible."

Pietje let go of my hand.

"I know how you are," my father said. "I don't need to ask you to keep taking care of your younger sisters and brother. But I ask anyway, because it makes me feel better. I am already helpless in protecting my family."

Now I was afraid. My father, admitting weakness?

"What I've heard," he said, "is that when the soldiers order you from the house, you are given one hour to pack and you are only allowed to take what you can carry. I've already packed a suitcase that you must make sure to take. It's the big brown suitcase with a red ribbon tied around the handle, and I've put it in your room. Don't open it until you get to where they are taking you. Don't let your mother open it either."

I knew exactly the reason for this. My mother was not a practical woman and wouldn't know what to pack. My father, on the other hand, was practical to the point of denying the existence of emotion. I was still reeling from his earlier admissions.

"I'm also asking you to have patience with your mother," he said. "The way she is, is not her fault."

"What do you mean?"

"That you must do everything possible to help her in everything. And when she is cruel or seems uncaring, don't blame her for it. Her illness is no more her fault than catching a fever."

"Illness?" If it was true in some way that my mother was not to blame for the way she was, perhaps it wasn't my fault that she often ignored me.

My father reached into his shirt pocket. He pulled something out that I could not see and left it curled in the center of his closed hand.

"You may think that I don't know you that well," he said. "But that's not true. It's just that . . ." He took a breath. "Sometimes a man has to put so much energy into one area of his family that it appears he doesn't care for other areas. When I'm gone, it will be your turn to watch over your mother."

That seemed to satisfy him, for he left it at that.

"Your fishing rod," he said. "It's stopped moving."

"Eventually it does," I answered. "But a mouse can live for a lot longer time than you would expect."

It was his turn to wait for more explanation, but two can play that game. Besides, I wanted to know what was in his hand.

"When the soldiers come for me and your brothers," he said and looked back and forth between Pietje and me, "I will not give them the satisfaction of knowing how much it hurts to be taken away from you and how afraid I am for what will happen to you when I am not there to protect you. I don't want you to cry, for we will not show them any weakness. Nor will I say good-bye then or how much I love you, and I won't even look back. So I'm saying it now."

"It's all right," I said. "You don't need to—"

Father moved to Pietje and pulled him in close, and to the astonishment of both Pietje and me, Father said, "*Dag, lieve jongen.*"

Good-bye, my loved little boy.

He released Pietje, then put a hand on my shoulder. "I love you. I will miss you."

He leaned back. "More importantly, I respect you for who you are and what you've become. And I dread getting on the truck and leaving you behind."

He opened his other hand and what I saw made me gasp far louder than the hardest of his spankings ever had.

It was a sulphide marble. Transparent green glass. With a miniature statue of a rearing horse in the center.

"I played marbles when I was a boy too," he said. "This was given to my father by his father, and not once did I ever risk it in a game. It is yours now."

He didn't add that it would be something I would have to always remember him, but I could hear it unspoken in the tone of his voice. This was as difficult for him as it was for me.

"I expect," he said, "that you will add it to the pouches you hide in your shorts."

I was astounded. How did he know about my other marbles?

He stood.

"Good fishing," he said. He was making a point that I understood. By not asking about why I had a fishing rod with a dead mouse at the end, he could be as stubborn as I was.

"Yes," I said.

As he walked away, Pietje tugged on my hand, giving me no time to absorb what had just happened. That would come later, when I realized I'd just had my last real conversation with my father.

"Now?" Pietje asked.

"Now," I said, turning my attention to my little brother. I gave him the fishing rod, and he began to reel in the line. I wasn't worried he would get hurt. A poisonous snake would have killed the mouse within seconds before swallowing it, and a bigger one would simply regurgitate the mouse as the line pulled. The fight between our bait and the snake that had taken it had lasted five minutes, so whatever we had on the line hadn't been able to kill the mouse immediately and was so small that the mouse couldn't make it back out past the inward facing bones of its throat.

To the satisfaction of both of us, we had landed a small python.

I gave the machete to Pietje and let him do the honors of chopping off the snake's head, unaware of how that species would later take revenge for this act.

Eight

Days later, the Japanese arrived as my father had predicted. On the street between our house and the muddy river, soldiers jumped out of a large truck. Holding machine guns, they marched to the door and pointed bayonets at my father, screaming in Japanese.

Again, we didn't need a translator. Their orders were obvious, for the open back deck of the large truck was already near filled with men and teen-age boys, each clutching a suitcase and staring at the road.

In less than fifteen minutes, my father, Niels, Martijn, and Simon were on the lawn in front of our house with their own suitcases. The rest of us stood on the steps. Pietje held my hand, and Nikki and Aniek crowded my other side, finding shelter beneath my other arm. I can only guess at the farewell that my mother had given the other males in our family. She remained inside the house.

It was clear that my father had given my half brothers firm orders to remain stoic in front of the conquerors. None of them looked back as they walked away, even with Pietje biting his lip to keep from crying and Nikki and Aniek begging for them to stay.

The four of them joined the other silent men and boys in the truck, and with the crunching of gears and a belch of diesel exhaust, the driver took my father and half brothers out of our lives.

It wasn't until the truck rounded the corner that I remembered I had forgotten to thank my father for the sulphide marble. I turned to Pietje and told him I would be back as soon as I could. Then I ran after the truck, hoping to catch it so I could shout to my father.

But it was too late. When I reached the corner, I saw nothing except cracked pavement and silent houses where all our Dutch neighbors had retreated into their shells in the face of the Japanese invasion.

I refused to weep in public, and I didn't want Pietje to see me cry, for that would have made him afraid. I managed to hold back my tears until I was on the other side of the house in the shade. Then I began to sob in gasping spasms that drove me to my knees.

• • •

For the Japanese, it had been urgent to eliminate any threat posed by Dutch males. A scattered guerrilla resistance managed to form over the next weeks, but to no real effect. Dutch over-lords like my father had been a minority to begin with, and where possible, the Japanese appointed non-Dutch replacements for the newly vacated positions. That meant the rest of the country continued in its usual economic fashion, subsisting on plantations and oil—except that the Japanese were not paying for the oil they used. They merely paid wages to those who kept the wells pumping crude and the refineries converting it.

Without the male income-earner, Dutch households began to struggle financially, and since the Netherlands was under siege by Nazi Germany, distant relatives were of no help. Many of the matriarchs sought ways to make money by sewing or baking or other odd jobs. Then when textiles became scarce, the women sold clothes, bedding, and other fabrics to Indonesians who would pay good money for them. My mother, who did not sew or bake, dug into our trunks and linen closet. Piece by piece she also sold our remaining household furniture, paintings, kitchen items, and other knickknacks. Eventually, our house was bare except for the basics we needed to live and sleep each night.

As it turned out, selling our possessions was

not unwise because young Indonesian extremists had begun looting Dutch homes. One evening, a gang of them pushed open our door but then burst out laughing at the bare interior already scavenged by our mother. They thought it not worthwhile to search the house and never found the suitcases that were packed and ready for the anticipated *Jappenkamp.*

In no time, our household money had run dry, and we were depending on church charity for food. To complicate matters, there came a day when I realized that the swelling of my mother's belly meant that she was pregnant. I began working for an Indonesian launderer. Pietje did what he could to help too, but that was not why he came with me every day. After our father was taken away, he refused to leave my side. The sound or sight of Japanese vehicles—which, unfortunately, were far too frequent—would cause him to freeze, for as much as he wanted to hide and bury his face in my side, he never stopped looking to see if our father might be in one of them.

The Indonesian who hired us—a greasy-faced man with a drooping, thin moustache—paid us half of what he would have had to pay locals, partly because he could but partly because he'd always hated the Dutch. It gave him satisfaction to calculate down to the penny the dividing line between what was enough to make us servile to him and what kept us from seeking employment elsewhere.

Except for Sundays, Pietje and I began at 6 a.m., washing clothes by hand in large barrels with soapy water, then rinsing and hanging them to dry on lines that stretched beneath the tin roofs of an open shelter meant to keep the clothes from rain. One day in early August, with our fingers wrinkled from hours in wet laundry, Pietje and I were walking through the village on our way home after a full day's work. It had been an afternoon punctuated by brief thunderstorms. Our destination was the baker's stall where the elderly baker's equally elderly wife had made a habit of setting aside two-day-old bread for our daily purchase. Unlike the launderer, this was not a petty act of revenge against the Dutch. The selling of our household goods was well known in the village, so the husband and wife understood our family was desperate for anything to supplement what the church could give us. Theirs was the cheapest bread available.

Any older than two days, the bread would grow mold in the humidity. During a particularly rainy time, it could emerge in one day. What the baker might not have known was that our family was at the point where I'd scrape away the first traces of mold that had appeared and not tell my siblings as I gave them their meals.

Just before the baker's stall, Pietje and I

happened upon a native teenage boy kicking at a skinny black puppy that he was dragging by a rope around the puppy's neck. The puppy had braced its feet in the dirt and was gagging with each kick, the rope tightening around its throat.

"Hey!" Pietje yelled. He let go of my hand and burst forward as the older boy lifted his foot to deliver another kick. "No!"

I was surprised by Pietje's reaction, for it was difficult for him to overcome his shyness. The puppy's owner looked as surprised as I was.

"Go away." The boy was barefoot, in shorts so old that dirt had become their color. Bare chested with protruding ribs that looked as if they were drawn by an anatomy student. Nut-brown skin. Head shaved, a sure sign that his family had been infested with lice.

Pietje knelt and placed his hand on the shivering puppy. One of its ears stood up, and the other was folded into a lop ear. It wasn't the cold that caused the puppy to tremble; it probably had a sixth sense about the native boy's intentions. Or maybe we were close enough to the restaurant that it detected the copper smell of blood from previous dogs who had been butchered in the alley and became the dishes of the day. While the Muslims feared and hated dogs, partially because of religious beliefs and partially because of the danger of rabies, the non-Muslims enjoyed *rintek wuuk, sengsu, sate jamu,* and *kambing balap,* all rice and spice dishes with chunks of cooked dog.

"Go away," the boy repeated.

"Jemmy?" Pietje said to me. Pietje's name for me had begun when he was too little to properly pronounce Jeremiah, and he was the only one allowed to call me that.

I moved forward and took a stance between the native boy and Pietje, who was kneeling at the puppy's side. No matter how close I stayed to him all through the night, Pietje had trouble sleeping, and I wondered if this puppy would give him some comfort.

"How much does the restaurant pay?" I asked. Dog meat was a delicacy.

This was a mistake on my part. Pietje wailed, for he immediately understood the implication.

"Restaurant!" He clutched the puppy, then lifted it. The native boy tugged at the rope, and the puppy made the strangling noise again. Pietje did not let go.

I watched the native boy's black eyes flicker as he made calculations, and the figure that he gave me was at least triple what he might get, far more than the amount I had in my pocket from our day's work at the launderer.

"Thank you for that information," I said. "I had no idea dogs were worth that much. Pietje and I will begin looking for our own dogs to sell."

Pietje wailed again, and I made a note to have

a discussion with him about the ways of the world and the value of maintaining indifference.

The native boy shrugged. He also smiled in such a way that showed he knew I was on the hook and would not be able to wiggle loose. I sighed. Then I dug beneath the waistband of my shorts and pulled out my pouch of warrior marbles. I emptied them into my right hand and held my palm open so he could see that it was a good collection. While some were of little worth except as shooters, others, like the swirlies and cat's-eyes, were suitable bait. I didn't say a word because I knew my actions would speak. I put the marbles in two lines on the dirt of the road, forming an *X*. I used my forefinger to draw a circle around the *X,* with the line of the circle a couple of feet from the *X* in the center.

"You first," I told the older boy. "Win the game and the marbles are yours. Lose, and I keep only my marbles and the puppy."

He shook his head and jerked the rope. Obviously, he believed I had more to offer than the marbles, and he was going to enjoy seeing how far I would go.

"I understand," I said. By then, I was well aware of how the majority of Indonesians had welcomed the invasion and how badly the natives wanted independence. "Afraid of a Dutchman. No wonder you needed all those Japanese to fight us for you." The streets weren't empty, of course.

A few other native boys had stopped at the sight of marbles in a circle. I was insulting them too.

I watched the puppy's owner square his shoulders. He handed the end of the rope to another boy. He dug in his pocket for his own marbles—a boy who wasn't carrying marbles was a boy who wasn't a boy—and added them to the *X,* extending both lines. There were twelve marbles in each line. It was winner take all; whoever was the first to take out all twelve of his opponent's marbles would end the game and get to keep all those marbles, plus have his own lost marbles returned.

He squatted at the edge of the circle and dropped a shooter into the hollow of his right thumb where it tucked beneath his right forefinger. He flicked it into the center, where it clicked against one of my swirlies. That made the swirly his, which he pocketed and looked at me with a sneer on his face. He was up one and, by the rules, could continue to shoot until he missed, when it would become my turn to shoot. It had been a long time since I'd lost a game of this format.

He hit three in a row. It didn't worry me. Early in a game, with the *X* in place, any smoothly rolling shooter marble had an excellent chance of making contact. Another flick, another click. Methodically and unerringly, he picked off every single one of my collection without missing once, giving me no chance to become the shooter. He'd taken all twelve of mine with twelve consecutive shots, and all twelve of his remained in the circle. I had never seen this before and was impressed. But I was Dutch. I wasn't giving up.

"You lost the same way to the Japanese," he said, "without much of a fight."

That earned hoots from the other boys. He stood and the natives around him patted his back. By making this a racial challenge instead of an age-old contest between boys, my calculated insult to force him into a game had made him even more of a hero among his friends.

He gave me a mock bow. "My marbles. My dog. Go home, Dutch boy."

"Jemmy!" Pietje said.

I had inadvertently tripled the stakes. I needed my warrior marbles returned, and I needed to get the puppy for Pietje. I also needed to redeem Dutch pride, so the only choice at this point was to risk my secret prize.

I reached beneath my belt for the second pouch. Until my father had given me the sulphide marble with the miniature horse statue, that second pouch had held only one marble. I pulled it out, leaving the sulphide hidden.

The marble I presented was sufficient to draw gasps of wonder. It was a china marble, not named because it came from that country but because it had been made of china. It had been hand painted with the tiniest of delicate brush strokes by a master craftsman, its deep, rich colors heated at kiln temperatures so that the portrait of a fighting dragon made even the roughest-hewn boy respect the artist's accomplishment.

I put the china marble in the center of the circle and pushed it into the dirt so that only the top half was exposed, reducing its exposure to a shooter by half. I also dimpled a mini-circle around it, pushing the tip of my finger into the dirt so that a series of depressions gave a fifty percent chance that any roll of the shooter marble would bounce in a haphazard direction.

"One shot," I said. "You miss, I get my marbles back and the puppy. One shot. You hit it, you own it."

Good as he was, it was a one-in-ten, one-in-twenty, or even one-in-fifty chance that he'd be able to hit the china marble with his shooter. Such was the obvious value of the china marble that he not only agreed to my terms but thanked me for the chance. And such was the obvious value of the marble that despite the low odds of losing it, my palms began to sweat and my gut clenched as he knelt to take his shot.

First, he blew on his own palms to dry them. He sorted through his marbles to find the most balanced shooter. He blew on his palms again, then placed his shooter into position. At the flick of his thumb, he sent it rolling in a fast, straight line.

A dog with rabies or a rogue elephant could

have been coming down the street and we would not have noticed. All eyes followed the shooter as it hit one of the dimpled impressions and careened upward without any misdirection. I felt horror rise in my throat as the line of trajectory took it directly toward the china marble. But the deflection had bounced the shooter marble just high enough, and it landed in the dirt on the other side of my marble, then rolled a few inches beyond. My opponent dropped his head to his chest, and his friends let out a collective groan.

I simply stared at my untouched china marble and blinked a few times. While I had earned back my warrior marbles, it didn't feel like a victory. I had not used any marble-shooting skills of my own. Instead, I'd banked on human nature, no differently than any gambler.

I scooped up my marble and tucked it back into its pouch. If there was going to be a fight, I needed to protect both of those marbles.

"You come by tomorrow," the boy said. "We play again for china marble. I will have another dog for your dinner table."

"If I am able," I said.

I had no intention of risking the marble again but no desire to start a fight either, so evasion seemed the most suitable response. Especially with his friends still clucking and shaking their heads at the magnificent missed opportunity for the glory of that prized marble.

"Pietje," I said, "time to get our bread."

"Coacoa," Pietje said. "That's his name. Coacoa."

I found it reassuring that he wasn't asking me but telling me. Perhaps already some of Pietje's fear had dissipated. And for the first time in a long while, Pietje walked down the street with me without holding my hand. He kept a firm grip on the rope, and his new little puppy, Coacoa, followed without resistance.

When we arrived home, I was prepared to respond to my mother's protests for allowing Pietje to bring home a puppy with fleas that visibly hopped on its scrawny back. I was the family breadwinner—in a literal sense—and I had a right to add one more mouth to the family if I decided. As for the fleas, those would be taken care of with a long soak in warm water with the puppy's nose barely above the surface. The trick was to tie a small piece of wool to the dog's neck so it would float and the fleas could take refuge on it as if it were a life raft.

At home, Mother stood before us wearing a brown cotton dress that bulged at her rounded belly. Her hair was glossy, for she spent hours brushing it, and her eyes seemed large in the little-girl beauty of a face growing thin from hunger. There came no admonishment after I explained that Pietje had wanted to rescue the dog from a soup dish or casserole. Mother just looked first at me, then at Pietje with the dog.

With tragic prescience of what was ahead in the Jappenkamp where we would spend the next three years, she simply looked again at Pietje's glazed smile of joy as he held the lop-eared puppy and said one sentence: "If you really cared about Pietje and cared about the dog, you would have walked away and let that dog die a merciful death."

A little more than a month later, in September of 1942, soldiers returned to our home along the river to put my mother, me, Pietje, and Nikki and Aniek into one of the Jappenkamps.

Nine

At highest count, the Dutch East Indies held one hundred seventy-four such camps for Dutch women and children. Aided by native Indonesians, the Japanese transported us to these tiny, cramped ghettos, surrounded by the natives who then lived for the most part as if we had never existed.

As before, the upheaval began with a military truck stopped in front of our house. This time, however, the open back deck did not hold men and teenage boys.

The Japanese had been in-country long enough to scream in the native Indonesian language.

"*Lekas!*" the soldiers yelled as we dragged our suitcases along the lawn. "*Lekas! Lekas!*"

Hurry! Hurry! Hurry!

But my mother did not. Or could not. I wanted to take her suitcase for her so she could walk faster, but I could only carry one at a time, and the screaming of the Japanese soldiers indicated that I did not have the luxury of making two trips as I struggled to carry the one that my father had left for me. Nikki and Aniek held sacks filled with clothes and the remaining food from our home. Pietje, too, had a sack, so heavy that it almost bent him in half, and Coacoa at the end of a rope. The little pup was just as scrawny and lop-eared as the day we had rescued him, but noticeably taller and, like Pietje, silent most of the time.

Mother's pregnancy was quite visible at this point. The heat had a sauna-like intensity to it, and her dress was stained with sweat at her armpits and where her swollen belly pressed against the material. This did not earn her any sympathy from the soldiers.

I was grateful that this was one of the weeks where she was in cheerful spirits and seemed strong. At other times in the summer, she would have collapsed on the floor in our bare house if the soldiers had arrived, weeping in total unconcern to the threat they represented.

At the truck, I saw that many of the other families had taken mattresses on board. I decided we needed one too. With effort, I pushed my suitcase above my head onto the deck, where a couple of other mothers helped pull it into place. Nikki and Aniek were halfway to the truck, and Mother was still barely past the steps of the house. I ran past the startled soldiers and through the empty dining room to my parents' bed-room. It was a place that children in our household did not visit, and I was expecting to find, like in our own bedrooms, only a mattress on the floor, for we'd stripped our blankets to take to the Jappenkamp. In the threshold, however, I froze as I tried to make sense of what I saw. Most of the walls were covered with pencil sketches on paper. Some of the papers were curling at the edges but some were still flat and new.

I tried to soak it in. The detail on the drawings was astonishing. Delicate pencil strokes, thickened pencil lines, swooping pencil arcs. One wall was filled with sketches of our family, the resemblances uncanny enough to be photo-graphs. Pietje holding Coacoa, the lop ear plain to see. Nikki and Aniek sitting on the broad front porch of our house. Another wall held sketches of village life—street vendors, children kicking a soccer ball, a priest stepping into a church. A third wall showed scenes devoid of people, the volcanic mountains rising up from valley flats, the port and ships of Semarang, a locomotive pulling away from our local station, plume of smoke rising and then flattening and widening to a horizontal arch. The ubiquitous shell-shaped sign at a service station where flags seemed in motion, not the Dutch red and white and blue that had flown for centuries but the red ball of Japan's rising sun. If I stepped into the drawing, I would be around the corner from our house, on the highway that led south to Magalang and intersected another one of the village's main streets. The gas pump had the same cracked glass as the pump I passed every day on the way to the launderer.

Then there was the wall that felt like a kick in the stomach. Dark storms and clouds that swirled into the shapes of monsters, the pencil lines so angry and deep that in places the paper had been punched through. All those times when my mother had succumbed to her dark moods and disappeared into this room for days at a time, I thought she had been sleeping. But she had been pouring her soul into this.

"Lekas! Lekas!" The screams made me jump.

I looked at the mattress and suspected that if I managed to drag it outside, I'd be permitted to struggle with it long enough to get it into the truck. If other families had taken theirs, then they knew something that we did not know about our destination.

Then another sketch caught my eye. It was me, with my mother. We were holding hands, and her dress swirled at her ankles as if the wind were flirting with her. She and I never held hands. In this sketch she also had a smile on her face that I'd never seen before, and nothing about my eyes in that sketch looked as intense and cold as the eyes I sometimes saw in a mirror. Instead, happiness shone from my face.

It was the first sketch I took down, ripping it loose from each corner, which left an empty square where the tacks had held it to the plaster.

"Lekas! Lekas!" The voice was louder, angrier, and it came from inside the house. As fast as I could without ruining the sketches, I pulled down paper after paper and tossed them onto the mattress where I intended to stack them before taking them with me.

"Lekas!" I froze as the voice came from inside the bedroom. I looked over my shoulder at a bayonet on a machine gun held by a Japanese soldier whose eyelids were slitted in anger.

I risked pulling down the last of our family sketches. When I heard nothing from the soldier, I turned and saw that he was at the far wall, staring at the sketches of life in the village.

"Lekas!" Another soldier now stood in the doorway.

As I scooped up the sketches from the mattress, I saw the edge of a pad of paper sticking out from beneath it. I pulled it out and used it to cover the sketches, then slid it inside the front of my shirt.

The second soldier did not have the same reaction to the drawings. He yelled at his companion, who responded in an angry tone of his own, gesticulating at the drawings on the walls.

The second soldier screamed again, then lifted his machine gun and fired at the wall that held still-life images of the village. I was deafened as plaster sprayed everywhere and bullets shredded the drawings that remained. In the silence that followed the aftermath of the blast, the first soldier spat out one word in Japanese that later I would learn to understand.

"Jackass," the first soldier had said.

The second soldier laughed. Then he pointed his machine gun at me and gestured that I should exit the room. I made my way down the hall with him shouting "Lekas!" at my back.

When I stepped out of the house, I discovered that every woman and child on the truck was staring with horror in my direction. My mother was already halfway to the house, her suitcase abandoned back at the truck.

"Jeremiah!" she said, but stopped from running forward and hugging me.

It hadn't occurred to me that they would think I'd been shot, but when I realized their perspective, hearing machine gun fire from the street, I understood why. With all those eyes upon me, I resorted to my normal swagger as I walked toward my mother, wishing that I'd had a chance to shake off the plaster dust from my shirt and shorts and sandals.

"Everything is all right, Moeder," I said in a voice loud enough to reach the other women and children in the truck. "I decided to let them live."

Timing is everything. Just as I finished saying this, the soldiers stepped out of the house. Giggles burst forth from the truck.

"Lekas! Lekas!" the second soldier shouted again.

I was already tired of that word.

Ten

We were the last family to be loaded onto the truck before it joined a convoy parked a few miles down the road. A half-dozen or so trucks were loaded with more women and children and were heading south. Volcanic mountains, draped in thick jungle growth, framed the valleys. The lushness was deceptive, though, since the valley we drove through had no shade. The tires kicked up dust that loomed over us like the monsters in my mother's sketches, and the heat bore down on us. The dust clogged our breathing and formed into clumps on our sweaty bodies as we stood cramped together with no space to stretch.

Our family seemed to be the only one on our truck who had not brought containers of water, and I was furious at myself for not anticipating the need for it. While many of the younger children cried as the day grew hotter, Nikki and Aniek and Pietje did not complain. Their thirst was so obvious, however, that a couple of families took turns sharing water with ours, even as some women glared at my mother for her obvious incompetence in her care for us.

Early in the trip, when I felt the sweat begin to drip down my chest and onto my belly, I surreptitiously removed the sketch pad from under my shirt and slid it into Pietje's cloth sack. I would have loved to have placed it in my own suitcase for safekeeping—I was burning with curiosity about its contents—but I'd promised my father it would not be opened until we were in a Jappenkamp. After keeping my word this long, I would not break it now.

We passed through tiny villages strung along the road like horse droppings, the huts squalid and tiny and primitive. The natives would come out and stare at us as the trucks churned almost at a walking pace down the rough roads, the disrepair of these roads evidence that the Dutch had not been in administration in this region. Some natives jeered as mothers on the trucks begged for water. Others rushed up with buckets of water only to be waved away by the Japanese soldiers. If I hadn't already begun to hate the soldiers, this would have been reason enough to start. What danger was there in letting a container of water reach little boys and girls who were passing out in the heat?

Finally, just as dusk descended, lessening the unrelenting heat, we reached Ambarawa. It was a market town, about halfway between the port city of Semarang and the town of Magalang, and an important rail link of the Semarang-Ambarawa-Magalang line.

One by one, the trucks in the convoy stopped at the open gates of a newly constructed barbed wire fence. In the gloaming, the fence appeared a harmless dividing point between houses on one side of the street and those on the other. As we looked into the neighborhood behind the fence, some of the women began to chatter with optimism. Other camps, I had learned through overheard conversations, were formed in institutes for the insane, or in barracks surrounding parade grounds. Here, we would have houses!

Ours was the second truck of the convoy to stop at the gates. The translator, a heavyset Dutch woman in a gray formless dress, with features difficult to distinguish in the growing darkness, gave orders through a megaphone. We were told to take all of our belongings out of the truck when we dispersed and find a room in a house, one room per family. We could see people from the first truck still streaming down the streets in the neighborhood.

Our family was fortunate to have been on the second truck in the convoy; families in the final four trucks would have fewer choices of houses. We also had been the last to load onto the second truck, which meant we were the first family to get off, and that put us ahead of all the rest in the race for lodgings. And my choice to take the sketches instead of a mattress meant that we had less to carry.

Because my father had given me the responsibility of taking care of our family, I determined what to do next. On the ground, I whispered to Mother, "I need you to carry Pietje's sack while I take him. I'm going to go ahead and when I find a room that's good, I'll send Pietje back to you so you will know where to find me."

I hoped I didn't have to explain anything else. Most families, I guessed, would be so tired that they would want to travel the minimum distance. There would be crowds in the nearer houses, but in the farther houses, the choices would be better.

My legs were cramping from dehydration, but nothing in the last few months had shown that my sisters and brother and I could depend on Mother to look out for us. Her sagging shoulders and indifference to my instructions proved that, so I pushed forward with the suitcase that father had packed for us months earlier. Later, I told myself, I could rest.

Without taking any detours to consider houses

close to the main gate, Pietje and I and Coacoa made a line straight to the end of one street where a two-story house backed up against the barbed wire fence. By my count, we were four residential blocks from the main gate.

The Japanese had obviously confiscated all of the houses and sent the residents of this previously Dutch enclave elsewhere. Before exploring the inside of the house I had chosen, I sent Pietje and Coacoa to tell my mother and sisters where we were.

I roamed the empty rooms and saw that all the interior doors in the house had been removed. A large bedroom on the upper floor looked to be a good choice for us, but it occurred to me that it could be too large. What if we had to share it with another family? Other rooms seemed to be too central; if the house were crowded, people would walk past us constantly, making it a noisy location. I settled on a room on the main floor at the back of the house where foot traffic would be minimal and where we would have the most privacy. It had been a storage room, lined with permanent shelving, and I considered the disadvantage of such a small room against the advantage of having shelves when all the other rooms were empty of furniture. I decided to go with the shelves.

The room did not have a mattress, but a neighboring room did. I was still alone in the house, so I had no hesitation in dragging the treasure to our room. The large mattress almost covered the entire floor, but that didn't matter. At least we had a secure and private place. With my suitcase in the room to establish ownership, I roamed around in the dark. In the kitchen, a battered pan had been left behind in a cupboard. I took it to the cistern and pumped water into it, then splashed the water on my face. I drank so deeply that it felt like my belly would burst. I refilled the pan for the rest of my family when they arrived a few minutes later.

These houses of the Dutch—confiscated by the Japanese as ours had been—had the bathroom and shower area set outdoors, with water fed to the faucets from cisterns that collected rain. The water was always warm and fresh and clean, and in better days, the brightness of the sun combined with the shelter of the privacy walls gave the bathroom area the feeling of a resort spa, complete with friendly geckos that patrolled the area and kept the floors clean of insects.

Our first few moments here alone would be the last of any pleasantness, however, for as the house filled with one family per room, the bathroom area would too soon become a dank area of backed-up sewage.

Pietje insisted on letting the puppy drink before he did, and none of us complained about Coacoa's slurping tongue. It was a good forty-five minutes before other families began to enter the house, long enough that Pietje and Nikki and Aniek had fallen asleep on the mattress, and Coacoa slept on the floor nearest to Pietje.

One woman after another stopped and peeked inside our room, then turned away after seeing it already occupied. One woman returned a few minutes after she'd left and, holding a lighted candle, stepped inside our room.

"*Allemaal opstaan!*" she said. *Everybody up!*

Coacoa growled at the tone of the woman's voice, but my sisters and brothers were too exhausted to be roused.

She was an inch taller than my mother and perhaps a few years older. Her hair was dark with streaks of gray, and its short style matched the expensiveness of her clothing, which I couldn't help but admire. This lady, I thought, had not been depending on church charity when the Japanese arrived at her house.

My mother seemed to shrink.

"It is not fair that some families had first choice," this interloper said. "All of the rest of us latecomers had a lottery in the kitchen, and my number was drawn to give me this room. Take your children and go to the kitchen to find out where your family belongs."

This could be nothing but a bluff, and it clearly came from a person accustomed to having her way with shopkeepers and servants. I searched for the words to protest, but children did not disagree with adults.

"So," this woman told my mother, "off you go." She reached down to shake Pietje awake, but Coacoa's growl deepened, which caused her to hesitate. In the next instant, Elsbeth, my mother, exploded with unexpected fury. As if the shell of despondency that had built up around her suddenly fragmented, she took a single step forward and slapped the taller woman hard and flush across the face.

"Do not," my mother said, "touch my child."

She spoke as if she was barely restraining herself. Coacoa, too, was on his feet and rumbling with a deepness I could hardly believe came from the chest of a puppy that young.

Still holding a candle in one hand, the interloper raised her other to strike back.

"I hope you hit me," my mother said, in a voice barely above a whisper. "Because that will give me the justification to kill you."

The woman froze.

"I have not agreed to any lottery," my mother said. "I doubt any of the others here have either. I don't hear them leaving their rooms. So your lies will not work with me."

"You must clear the room," the interloper said, sounding unafraid and matching my mother's anger. "This room now belongs to my family, as does the mattress."

My old friend, the cold rage, began to build. I debated with myself the ethics of fighting a fully grown woman. It would be unthinkable to attack a girl, but perhaps this woman's size and age would offset her gender and allow me to fight with honor.

"What is your name?" my mother asked.

"Hilda. Hilda van Stromst." The woman squared her shoulders and straightened her back. "And yours?"

To me, this charade of civility after that first slap gave me a new insight into the nature of how women sometimes fight.

"Elsbeth Prins," my mother replied. "Are you prepared to fight me right now to try to take this room from me? Because if you do, I will scratch your eyes out. And if somehow you manage to outfight me tonight, tomorrow night, when you are asleep, I will sneak into the room and slit your throat and let your blood flow onto your children."

"You are making an enemy," Hilda hissed.

"You made one when you tried to steal this room from my children. What you don't know is that until a year ago, I was kept in a mental institute for outbreaks of violence." My mother paused, probably letting the other woman con-sider what she'd said—a nice touch to give credence to my mother's lie. "I would advise you to not only keep your distance from me but also

99

not to provoke me again in any way. So let me ask again, am I clear?"

I was as astounded at my mother's smooth lie about the mental institute as I had been to see the pencil sketches on her bedroom wall. She sounded so certain and true that Hilda's resolve collapsed. Hilda stepped backward, keeping her eye on my mother as if fearing an attack.

When the woman was in the doorway, my mother spoke again. "Stop."

Hilda stopped.

"Take your family to another house," my mother said. "I'm not sure I'll be able to control my mental illness if I have to live in the same house as you. If I kill you, your children will be without a mother, and so will mine when the Japanese take me away."

"You are crazy," Hilda said, a tremble in her voice.

"That's the point, now, isn't it?" my mother asked. "It can't be helped."

Much, much later, I would more fully understand the significance of that answer, but in that moment, as Hilda slipped out of our sight, I wanted to walk over and hug my mother.

But we didn't do things like that in our family.

Eleven

When the crying of a young child from another bedroom woke me the next morning, I discovered I was glowing with an unfamiliar emotion, the same one that had cradled me into sleep the night before. It was an ironic emotion, given that I had spent my entire life among the privileged Dutch in a large house attended by servants and now was sleeping in a storage room in a camp patrolled by Japanese soldiers.

For the first time ever, I felt secure.

Even though I was only ten years old, I could have articulated the reason for it if anyone had asked. Elsbeth had finally become a protective mother. Seeing another woman reach for her child with an intent to harm had been the catalyst for it. And if that weren't enough, Elsbeth put it into words the next morning.

The other three were still asleep beneath the blanket—each holding the other, back to front, back to front, with Coacoa at Pietje's feet on top of the blanket. I rubbed my eyes to see Elsbeth kneeling in front of her open suitcase on the floor.

She noticed I was awake and sighed.

"Look at this," she said, pointing to the contents. "The last months have been like a bad dream, and I'm waking to this."

I followed her instructions and knelt beside her to see what she had packed for life in camp. There were jars of cold cream, jars of hair coloring, eight bottles of Bols sloe gin, laced underwear that made me blush, packs of cigarettes, a silver hairbrush and matching comb and mirror, several straw hats, sunglasses, paperback romance novels, and rolls of nylon stockings.

I winced, thinking how much money this could have brought to our family. It would have taken two years of laundering ten hours a day to earn what this must have cost her, as the scarcities of luxury goods had soared in the first months of the Japanese occupation. How much of this had she purchased after that by scavenging our house and clearing it of furniture?

"Jeremiah," she said, "some days I do feel a little crazy. I can't help myself and I don't know what it is."

My father's words came back to me.

The way she is, is not her fault. You must do everything possible to help her in everything. nd when she is cruel or seems uncaring, don't blame her for it. Her illness is no more her fault than catching a fever."

"It will feel like weeks on end," she said, "that I'm in a bad storm that makes me blind and deaf to everything else."

She picked up a jar of cold cream and set it back into the suitcase. "And when the storm goes

102

away and the sun comes out, it seems like the world owes me happiness, and I should be more beautiful than a movie star, deserving of all the good things that a woman can have."

I said nothing. Tears started rolling down her cheeks, but unlike any other morning I'd ever seen her, there was no makeup to smear.

"Yesterday," she said, "when I heard shooting in the house, I thought you were dead. I'd never worried about you before because you are such a sturdy little man, and it's never seemed possible that you could get hurt. I'd never worried about Pietje and Nikki and Aniek either because they could depend on you more than on me."

She paused to wipe her cheeks. "I heard the shooting and pictured in my mind your crumpled little body with blood pouring out, and it tore my heart. But then you walked out like nothing had happened and made a joke like you were on a stage, and it all seemed normal again. But all day in the truck I thought of how it would have been if the soldiers had killed you. And I looked at Pietje and Nikki and Aniek who were so thirsty and saw that every other mother had taken along water. And I was so miserable at how I had failed all of you for so, so long."

She looked at me through her wet eyes and gave a slight smile.

"But last night," she said, "that was something different, wasn't it?"

"Yes. It was."

"And from today on," she promised. "I will be different. We don't know how long the Japanese will keep us in camps, but I will be as much a mother to my family as any mother here."

She closed the lid to her suitcase.

"What did you bring, Jeremiah?" Her bright smile dimmed. "I'm sure it's very practical and full of things I should have taken."

"Father packed it," I said. "I haven't opened it yet."

At my words, her face looked as stricken as if I had stabbed a knife through her heart. I remembered that expression with full clarity for decades, and only as an adult could I guess how she must have felt at the reminder of her husband's love and faithfulness to her. The baby in her belly made it obvious to anyone who did the math that someone else besides my father had been responsible, but the same conclusion was one that my ten-year-old mind did not comprehend.

Mother swallowed and took a deep breath. "Let's open it."

On top was a note in carefully printed pencil.

Jeremiah,
I am sorry for missing any things that you might need, but a suitcase is only so large. I can only guess at what is ahead for

you and how long I will be away from you.

You and your brother and sisters will grow, so the needles and thread and extra sheets will help you make the clothing fit. Don't throw away the clothes as you outgrow them but take them apart and sew on the extra material. Ask the women in camp to teach you and your sisters how to sew.

Cod-liver oil will give all of you the vitamins you will need, and make sure your mother takes her dosages too. DO NOT trade the cod-liver oil for anything else. It is the same with the mosquito netting. You must keep it and use it.

Use the soap sparingly, but try to stay as clean as possible. When it looks like you are halfway through the supply of soap, use it to wash only your hands and face.

Use the paper and pencils to teach your sisters and brother to read and write; every day, you must have an hour of school and you must be the teacher to them.

Read to them from the Bible every night and pray the way that Jesus taught His disciples to pray. It is okay if you skip the boring parts. I know you hate the begots and begets as much as I did when I was a boy.

Do not open the sealed envelope at the bottom. That is for your mother and she is to read it without telling you what is inside.

I love you and Nikki and Aniek and Pietje more than life.

Your father

The suitcase was filled as the note had promised. Mosquito netting and steel wire and hooks to hang it above us. Needles and thread and scissors and bedsheets for clothing. Half of the suitcase was devoted to jars of cod-liver oil. There were bars of soap, some dishes and cutlery, and a first-aid kit. The family Bible, inscribed to my father and mother on their wedding day. And a large, thick envelope addressed to Elsbeth Prins.

She took it silently and held it in her hands.

"The letter in the suitcase was addressed to you," she said. "Because he knew that you would take care of your brother and sisters, not me."

"Where we are now is where we need you," I said.

She took a deep breath and gave me a wide smile that made me feel as chivalrous as the bravest knight in all of history.

"See," she said. "There you are, helping me again. I promise I will be the best mother, and I hope you never stop helping me."

I felt a degree of hypocrisy because I had just made a decision to steal those eight bottles of gin from her suitcase to remove any temptation that might make her stray from her promise.

She held out her arms. That time, we did hug

and her soft perfume was the most beautiful smell I had ever experienced. I couldn't remember a hug like this ever happening. And so began, in the midst of accumulating hardships and struggles, the happiest months of my life.

Twelve

Later, at the first opportunity, I did steal and bury the eight bottles of gin. Elsbeth was furious at the theft but could complain to no one, because she knew she would get no sympathy. She kept her promise and began each day with a family prayer for my father and half brothers. We had heard no word from them, but neither had any of the other women in camp. Then she read a story from the children's Bible with the colorful illustrations that fascinated Pietje: the animals in the ark on tossing waves, Moses parting the Red Sea, Elijah calling down fire from heaven. This all seemed a miracle of sorts, that Elsbeth would gather the four of us at her feet and take time to read to us, like she was casting a wide blanket of love no differently than the disciples had cast their nets as fishermen and fishers of men. After a week or more of mornings like this, Pietje asked a question.

"Moeder," Pietje said, "how come they didn't fall through the roof?"

"Pietje?" She had just read to us the story about four friends who wanted to take a fifth friend to Jesus for healing, but the house was so crowded that they had to climb onto the roof and let the friend down through it and into the center of the crowd down below.

"In the story, there were five people. Four friends and the lame one. How come they didn't fall off the roof when they got up there?" He was stroking Coacoa's neck, who rested happily in his arms, occasional thump of his tail.

Coacoa wasn't the only pet in camp. Other families, like us, fed their pets by taking a little from each person's daily portions, and like other families, we felt it well worth the sacrifice for the joy those animals gave us with their unquestioning love and devotion in the grim circumstances.

"Especially the man who was lame. He would roll off the side of the roof if they let go, but if they held him, how could they keep their balance?"

Pietje, it seemed, had no difficulty with the healing itself when Jesus told the man to walk.

Elsbeth gave Pietje's question serious thought. This, too, was something new, that she would devote time and attention to us. "Pietje, where Jesus lived, the roofs were not pitched like ours. They were flat."

"Flat? But in a monsoon—"

"Ah," she said, smiling. "Where Jesus lived,

there was very little rain. They did not need roofs built to allow water to roll off."

Pietje chewed his lower lip. "A flat roof. When they broke a hole in it, did pieces of the roof fall on the people down below?"

"The Bible doesn't tell us that."

More lip chewing. "How come they didn't fall through?"

"Well, Pietje, it must have been a strong enough roof to hold their weight."

"But if it was strong enough to hold them, how could they make a hole in it big enough to lower their friend?"

"Because . . ." Elsbeth paused. We were outside, in the shade of a banyan, grateful to be out of the sun, even though it was barely past breakfast. Late in her pregnancy, heat gave her rashes, but she didn't complain.

"Yes?" He was expectant.

For a moment, her patience cracked. "It's just the way it is," she snapped.

Aniek was slow to pick up on her mood change.

"I don't think the mustard seed is the smallest seed in the world," Aniek said. Her blond hair shone because Elsbeth had brushed and washed it again that morning. "Jesus said it was. But I've seen mustard seeds, and I can find smaller seeds than mustard seeds here in camp. So was Jesus lying, Moeder? Because God is supposed to know everything. And Jesus is God, so Jesus must have lied if He knows everything. But lying is a sin, isn't it? I thought Jesus never sinned and that's why He was an innocent sheep and could die on the cross for us."

I could see the furrows deepening in Elsbeth's eyebrows, and I wanted to change the subject. I feared she might stop reading us Bible stories and stop asking us to pray for my father. Someday, she might go back to drinking gin and smoking cigarettes and to hours each day of vacancy in her eyes.

"Moeder, I think I can trade some cigarettes for canned milk," I said. "I have been watching the soldiers. I know when and where I can go to the fence and not get caught."

"Yes?" Elsbeth studied my face. She trusted me and often treated me like I was an adult equal to her. It was strange but enjoyable, wanting her protection and love, but also wanting to protect her.

Already canned milk was such a luxury that we all knew it was worth the risk involved in it for her. While it was a punishable offense for any-one caught trading with the natives on the other side of the fence, we had discovered that for the most part, the Japanese soldiers were reluctant to punish children. The mothers received their beatings instead.

"I promise," I said. "I would never do anything to hurt you."

It would take months and months for that comment to become a lie, and I didn't know then that those months and months would be the only remaining innocent days of my life.

"Go ahead. Canned milk will be good for all of us. Even for Coacoa." Coacoa thumped his tail again at the mention of his name.

With a tired smile, she closed the Bible and left Aniek's question untouched. Food was the primary focus of our lives. We were all fed from a central kitchen at specific times of the day and strictly rationed to a ball of rice, a vegetable usually impossible to identify, and a fragment of meat.

As well, all healthy adults were expected to contribute help in the camp. Mother's shift in the kitchen began in only a few minutes.

When we returned to our room, Elsbeth opened her suitcase that was filled with better currency than money. As she handed me four cigarettes, I took note of the fact that her previous self-absorption in choosing the contents of her suitcase was proving to be better for our family than the choices anyone else had made, except, perhaps, for my father's cod-liver oil.

Outside of the fence that surrounded our sixteen square blocks of residential imprisonment, life had not changed for the native Indonesians, whose impoverished lives had always fueled resentment against the untouchable wealth of the

Dutch. Now, however, the Indonesians had something we wanted. Freedom.

For the first weeks of internment, a barbed wire fence, eight feet tall with horizontal strands only inches apart, had served the purpose of confining the Dutch women and children. Japanese soldiers patrolled its perimeter to discourage outside contact, but nothing prevented us from standing near the wire and wistfully observing the natives in their daily lives. When this constant staring eventually irked the natives, they would hurl sticks at the fence that occasionally would make it through the barbed strands. Sometimes they threw larger objects, including garbage, over the eight-foot-high barrier. This led to the addition of vertical bamboo strips woven into the strands of wire, effectively forming a curtain that isolated us from the world.

The new barrier made the Japanese soldiers relax their vigilance on perimeter patrols, which, we soon discovered, made it possible to trade more frequently.

It was a simple system.

One of us, usually a child, would find a trading spot along the fence, push aside the vertical bamboo slats, and hold out our empty hand and wiggle our fingers. Like birds pouncing on a worm, it took only minutes, sometimes seconds, to hear the voice of a native on the other side. Then the negotiating would begin, and once an agreement was made, the transaction would occur. The system was rarely abused because the incentive was too great for both sides. The natives were so poor that many wore only loincloths, so our fabric was of high value to them. Their food, ranging from canned milk to bananas that we could see in trees on the other side of the wire, was of high value to us.

I had lied to my mother about understanding the patrol patterns of the Japanese soldiers. Instead, I positioned Aniek along the fence in one direction, and Nikki an equal distance the other direction, and their job was to call out if a soldier approached. It was near foolproof, and over the next weeks, we supplemented our rationed food with whatever I could barter with the natives.

One day, as I pushed aside the bamboo matting and stuck my hand out in the open air of freedom on the other side, Nikki called to me.

"Look, a chicken!"

I pulled my hand back with the four cigarettes I held and dashed toward her. A chicken! Sure enough, almost hidden in a bush and pecking at insects we could not see on the ground beneath it, was a fine copper-colored hen.

"Hey!" called a voice of disappointed outrage behind us. I glanced back. A brown hand was sticking through the fence from the other side, holding out a banana. That was an offer I would have scorned. For four cigarettes? Hah.

"How did it get here?" Nikki asked.

"Don't know. Don't care. A chicken!" This would be a feast for our family. We'd build a tiny fire and cook it slowly in small pieces, hoping no one would discover the rare smell of roasting meat.

"Who does it belong to?" she asked.

"To the person who catches it." I glanced up and down the fence again. "Stay here. Remember to whistle if you see a soldier."

I knelt. The chicken cocked its head and stared at me and blinked. I was the child who'd snatched a snake by the neck as a four-year-old. I made a confident quick thrust of my hand and missed.

The chicken clucked with disapproval and backed away, to the other side of the bush and into the open. I scurried forward in a half crouch, but the chicken easily outdistanced me to another bush, just inside the fence line.

When I reached that bush, I was stunned to see that the chicken had disappeared. I knelt for a closer look and felt my knees slope away from me. I pushed aside the lower part of the shrubbery and discovered how the chicken had disappeared.

It was a concrete pipe. A wide concrete pipe, its entrance completely covered by the bush. I heard clucks of disapproval fade as the chicken receded deeper and deeper into it. I pushed my head inside and saw light at the other end. This meant that the pipe could take me beneath the fence and into the Indonesian world.

This was such a magnificent discovery that I decided not even to mention it to Nikki. Someday, I realized, I might have need of something like this. But it would only stay in existence if the Japanese didn't know about it. Which meant if I wanted to keep it secret, I had to keep it to myself.

I went back to my spot on the fence and managed to trade those four cigarettes for two cans of condensed milk plus the original banana. We were so hungry that on our return to our room, we scraped the inside of the banana peel until it was translucent. Later, I returned to the pipe with blocks of wood and stuffed them into the opening so that no more chickens could appear and betray its existence.

With the contents of that suitcase keeping us relatively well fed, and with a mother who took joy in her children, our lives were generally happy. It lasted until the morning our black puppy with the lop ear did not wake with the rest of us.

Coacoa had died while we slept.

Thirteen

At my request, Elsbeth first lifted and carried away Nikki as she slept, then returned for Aniek. I had been the one responsible for bringing Coacoa into Pietje's world, and I would not shirk the burden that came with taking Coacoa out of Pietje's life. I had no choice but to remain beneath the mosquito netting and watch my little brother's innocent face as he slept, dreading what would happen when he opened his eyes.

I wasn't going to try to explain why the puppy was dead. Elsbeth had suggested that Coacoa might have eaten something that poisoned him or that because Coacoa didn't get enough food, it was just his time to die. I had begged her not to tell this to Pietje, for then he would blame himself for not taking good enough care of the puppy.

Pietje woke, and when he saw me, he gave me his quiet smile. Then, as he did each morning, he reached for Coacoa to shake him awake. I found the courage to tell Pietje the horrible news.

"I am so sorry, Pietje," I said. "Coacoa died."

I'd been expecting sobbing and disbelief. Instead, Pietje pronounced calmly, "He's not dead. He's asleep."

He lifted the puppy's underfed body and kissed Coacoa's nose, singing, "Wake up. Wake up. The sun is up."

"Pietje," I said, my throat thick with the tears I so badly needed to cry. "Coacoa won't wake up."

"I know my own puppy," Pietje said. "He's asleep. That's all. Please hold him. I need to get dressed."

Pietje passed me the puppy's body. For a moment, because of Pietje's certainty, I almost believed it. In the tropical heat, Coacoa was still warm.

I spoke as Pietje finished dressing. "We can have a funeral. Moeder said she would read a Bible story and then we will pray over Coacoa and bury him. She also said she would pay for some chocolate and that you could eat it all by yourself without sharing."

"Moeder is silly sometimes, isn't she?" Pietje said. He reached for Coacoa. "We always share our food. And Coacoa is just asleep."

Pietje crossed the threshold of our door frame, cradling Coacoa. He glanced back at me. I was rooted as I tried to absorb his reaction.

"What are you waiting for?" Pietje asked. "We can't let Coacoa sleep all day."

I stood and followed.

It was a day with no clouds and a breeze that carried the stench of the sewage away from our house. Within a week of arriving at the Jappen-kamp, the flushing mechanism on the toilet in our house had snapped, and we'd been forced to rig it so the lever was in a permanently open position. A bucket of water poured into the bowl sent the contents into the septic system, but after a few weeks, the septic had overflowed. Now we squatted over buckets that had to be carried and emptied into a large hole dug near the center of the former neighborhood, and the odor hung over the entire camp in a stench that seemed like oil clinging to our skins. Today, though, the breeze brought in the perfume of flowers from the gardens outside the bamboo curtain that separated us from the world.

As we walked, I did not see my mother or Aniek or Nikki. Boys and girls played games with marbles and sticks while the women labored according to their assigned duties. Pietje kept kissing Coacoa's nose as we passed several blocks of houses. We neared the houses where the camp commander and his soldiers stayed, and when we rounded the corner of one block, I saw the commander on the street, walking toward us.

"Pietje," I hissed. I pulled at his shoulder to bring him to a halt. "Commander Shizuka."

I stood ramrod straight and shouted a single word. "*Kiotske!*"

I would have been obligated to yell the Japanese word for attention even if it had been the lowest-ranking soldier.

All the children playing nearby immediately jumped to attention. We had all seen what happened when a woman or child forgot to pay sufficient respect or attention to any soldier or officer. If a child failed, the woman received a beating. If the woman failed, she was punished in the same way.

"Pietje," I whispered, arms straight at my side. "Put Coacoa at your feet. Do you want Moeder to get a beating?"

Pietje set the puppy's body on the road.

As Commander Shizuka came closer, I continued to follow protocol, as I had been the one to first give warning to everyone in earshot.

"*Kere!*" I shouted.

This was the signal to bow from the waist down, at a minimum ninety degree angle, arms straight back. It was unthinkable to make eye contact. Only equals could do that, and it had taken many beatings for the strong and independent Dutch women to conform. Already decades had passed since Dutch women could stand for election and vote, but as Dutch men often ruefully chuckled, they had been in control for centuries before that.

Pietje and I held our bow. Shizuka's black leather boots came into my view, and my stomach clutched with horror and dread when those boots stopped.

I dared not look at the commander. He had full authority over life and death in this camp, and there was no one over him to amend his decisions. As a result, we were intensely aware of his presence when he wandered among us. I could not hold my breath, as bowing took too much effort, but it still felt like I was not breathing.

Shizuka had the habit of men in power throughout history who were small in stature; he did not walk but strutted. He also smelled of cologne, a distinct lavender that I suspected was instead perfume, and grew his hair longer than his soldiers and held it in place with scentless grease. Mrs. Vriend had reported the source of a horizontal scar across his left cheek as a sword duel. The rumors said he had twenty sets of uniforms in his closets and changed three to five times per day, which I believed because of their crisp appearance.

The boots moved closer, now almost beneath our heads. I knew Pietje would say nothing. He was justly terrified of the man and had seen Shizuka slap an elderly woman for not bowing correctly, then slap a mother because her little girl had failed to hold a bow long enough.

One of the boots nudged Coacoa's still body.

Another nudge, closer to a kick.

Pietje fell to his knees and put his hands out to protect Coacoa. I envisioned soldiers dragging Elsbeth into the street and holding her as Shizuka beat her across the face. But I dared not speak because it would make her punishment worse.

I heard a snort of laughter, then a few Japanese words. Such was the concentration of my fear that I memorized the sounds of the words. Later that day, I searched for Mrs. Vriend, who translated them but would not believe that I'd heard correctly, not if Pietje had dared cover the puppy to protect it and Shizuka had let that action go unpunished.

Soon it will be gone.

I watched the boots withdraw, and once I was certain that Shizuka was far enough away, I yelled out the third command. *"Naore!"*

This was the signal that we could all resume our activities. *Kiotske. Kere. Naore.* Every child old enough to walk had practiced again and again how to respond to those words. Then I heard a shout from around the nearest corner as someone else saw the commander and gave the obligatory alert. *"Kiotske!"*

"You could have had mother killed," I said to Pietje.

"No. Today Coacoa is protecting us."

How could I respond? I asked a different question.

"Where are we going?" I asked Pietje. He had never led me anywhere before. "The doctor?"

"Coacoa is not sick," he said. "He is sleeping."

Pietje took us to the house where Mrs. Schoonenburg lived. She was older than most of the women and wasn't part of the labor duties in the camp because of her age. She walked slowly and heavily with a cane, and her gray hair was always in a bundle atop her head. She contributed to camp life, however, as the de facto pastor because her husband had been the pastor of one of the largest Dutch Reformed Churches in Semarang. Sunday mornings, Mrs. Schoonenburg led the church services and preached a sermon, drawing on her memory of forty years of listening to her husband's preaching.

Mrs. Schoonenburg sat in a chair on the shady side of the house, napping, with her hands in her lap, her glasses on her deeply wrinkled forehead.

"*Goedendag, mevrouw,*" Pietje said. *Good day, madam.*

I was impressed by Pietje's behavior. Not once had I seen him speak to an adult without being addressed first.

With a startled snort, Mrs. Schoonenburg awoke from her nap. "Eh?"

"Coacoa is sleeping," Pietje said. "Can you talk to Jesus and ask Him to wake my puppy?"

She blinked a few times as she focused on him and the puppy in his arms. Her eyes were pale blue and grew larger when she pulled her glasses onto her nose.

"Sleeping?" she said.

"Yes." Pietje set Coacoa on the ground at Mrs. Schoonenburg's bare feet. I was amazed at how blue her skin was, how crooked her toes and how yellow her toenails. "Coacoa sleeps with me every night and keeps me safe from the soldiers that took my father. Jemmy told me Coacoa is dead. But that's what people told Jesus about the little girl. Jesus said she was asleep and everybody laughed at Jesus, but He took her hand and asked her to stand and she did. Remember?"

Mrs. Schoonenburg's confused blinking resumed again, yet Pietje was so earnest that she did what any decent human would do. She reached down and stroked the puppy. "Sleeping?"

"You know Jesus," Pietje said. "I listen to you each Sunday morning when you tell us about Him. Ask Jesus to wake up my puppy."

"He wants a miracle," I explained. So did I. I promised God right then that I would never doubt Him if He would just wake up Coacoa. Maybe Pietje was right and something had made the puppy unconscious. If that were the case, it wouldn't even have to be a real miracle, just a good healing.

Mrs. Schoonenburg took Pietje's hands into her own aged ones where veins popped out of parchment skin. "My poor, poor little boy. I can't call up Jesus and expect Him to change the world for us."

He took her hands and placed them together, palms inward. "Pray," he said. "Talk to Jesus."

She gave him a slight smile, but her eyes looked sad. "I cannot do that," she said. She pulled her hands free. "For if your puppy doesn't stand, you will think that Jesus can't do miracles."

"You don't believe?" he asked. "I do. Every day, our mother reads us stories about Jesus. Wake up my puppy, and tomorrow maybe you can tell me how come five men can stand on a roof and not fall through but then can dig through it and put a man through the hole."

Mrs. Schoonenburg looked at me. I knelt beside

my brother. "Pietje. You must stop fooling yourself. Coacoa is not asleep."

He turned again to Mrs. Schoonenburg, who said, "Coacoa will be waiting for you in heaven. That's the best miracle of all, that Jesus made sure we can all go to heaven."

If she had intended this to comfort Pietje, it had the opposite effect. It forced him to realize that all hope was gone for Coacoa, and he collapsed into my arms and sobbed.

No matter how close one human is to another, we are still separated by flesh. I could think of no words to help him with his grief. All I could do was keep him from falling and hold him as he wept into my chest.

Mrs. Schoonenburg reached for him too, and he slapped her hand away. She had the sense to leave us, and it took a half hour for Pietje to become too worn out to continue crying.

I held his puppy as we walked back to our house in the corner of the camp. Elsbeth had already dug a hole and made a cross of two sticks of wood tied together. I could not help but note the proximity to a small tree, the spot where I had buried her eight bottles of gin.

How much better would it have been if I had not stopped that August afternoon and risked my marbles to save the puppy? I could not shake our mother's words that day: *If you really cared about Pietje and cared about the dog, you would have walked away and let that dog die a merciful death."* I alternated between grief and anger at myself.

Elsbeth, Nikki, Aniek, and I sang hymns for Coacoa, but Pietje only stared at the fresh dirt. Watching him while I sang, I said horrible things to God for taking away Pietje's friend and guardian and for breaking all of our hearts. I doubted God even cared to listen to me.

The next morning, I prepared for Pietje's grief by thinking of ways to distract him. I was explaining to Nikki and Aniek a new game I'd invented for Pietje when Mrs. Vriend came to the house.

All forty of our house's inhabitants gathered to hear what she had been telling the rest of the camp. Commander Shizuka had ordered that all families with dogs must bring the dogs to the gate, for dogs were no longer allowed in camp. It was—we were told—to prevent rabies.

I stood and absorbed the news for a few moments. We did not have to leave the house. Coacoa was already safe from the Japanese commander.

"He's in heaven," Pietje said as Mrs. Vriend left the house, showing the first bit of a smile. "The soldiers can't take him away from me! God has Coacoa already!"

Later, I heard what it was like. All the dog owners had lined up at the gate, and one by one, they were forced to hand over their pet to an Indonesian waiting outside. An old woman, whose dog had been with her for more than a decade, had pleaded to be allowed to give her dog to the lone Chinese man among the Indonesians, as she cried out, "*Andjing baik . . . bagus.*"

This dog is good . . . magnificent.

She wanted her dog to go to the Chinese man because she knew, as did all the others, that the native Indonesians would eat the dogs or, if they were Muslim, would kill them like vermin. It would have been unthinkable for Pietje to give up Coacoa and watch someone else walk away with his puppy, and even more terrible for him if he discovered what would happen to his lop-eared protector in the hands of an Indonesian.

When I knelt at Coacoa's grave later that day, thinking of Pietje's joy that death had rescued Coacoa from the Japanese, I was still angry at God, but not so much as the day before.

Fourteen

Each week, food rations had shrunk a little bit more. While we had not reached starvation levels, too many of the children in camp were beginning to show bellies as swollen as my mother's. I could not know it then, but the lack of protein was beginning to crumble their bodies, giving them stick arms and legs and flaky skin.

By now, those who developed diarrhea or worse, dysentery, could not recover because their bodies were too weak. Elsbeth, my sisters, brother, and I had been spared thus far, primarily because of my father's foresight. We each swallowed a half teaspoon of cod-liver oil, rich in vitamins A, D, and K, protein, and omega-3 fatty acids. Naturally, we hated the taste, but because of the lack of meat in our diet, it didn't take long for our bodies to crave the daily dose.

A few days after Shizuka had culled the camp of dogs, I heard groaning in the early morning. Elsbeth was sitting with her back against our bedroom wall, her arms limp and forearms exposed. I could see the tremble in her body from chills, and with her eyes closed, she was breathing so rapidly that she seemed to pant.

Her skirt reached only to below her knees, so I had full view of her shins. I knew enough about death to feel my heart lurch when I saw red streaks extending from two lines of scratches on her left leg.

"Moeder!"

She opened her eyes and tried to smile. I rolled off the mattress.

"Moeder." I lowered my voice so that the others would not waken. Sleep was a mercy.

"It's all right," she said. "It's just that the baby

inside me makes me tired. Give me a few minutes."

It was not all right. The red streaks going up her leg were ominous signs of blood poisoning. Children much younger than me understood that kind of danger.

"We are going to the doctor," I said. I leaned over and woke Nikki. "Take care of Aniek and Pietje until Moeder and I get back."

Nikki was so sleepy that I was glad I didn't need to give more explanation. I would worry enough for all of us.

I dressed in my shorts and shirt, then reached for my mother to help her stand.

"Not Dr. Kloet," she said, hardly able to speak.

Except for the Japanese soldiers, he was the only adult male in the camp, spared from the work camps because of the shortage of physicians, but nothing about his bedside manners suggested he was grateful for it. He was tall and heavy and young for a doctor. He liked to stroke his thick reddish beard in idle moments, and it had been noted early and commented upon that his bows to Shizuka were the deepest and longest.

"Dr. Eikenboom," I promised. We had seen her treat the younger women like she was a hen gathering them under her wings, and she dispensed advice with the same compassion that she dispensed the limited medical supplies.

The two of us struggled down the hallway. Every few steps took us past another open door frame and the family crowded into that room. I'm sure our progress was noted, but no women came to help. I already knew that my mother had no friends in the house. Or elsewhere. But I did not know why. Whenever I saw her in the kitchen, she was working alone, while other mothers shared duties and laughter.

Somehow we managed to hobble several blocks to the open-walled tent set up outside a former schoolhouse. The school building was our makeshift hospital. I'd been told the inside rooms were crowded with cots for patients, and two closets had each been converted into a residence for the physicians. The outside tent was set up to deal with those not sick enough to require a stay, and already, there was a line beneath the tent.

"You are too sick to wait," I said.

"No," she answered. "We ask for no favors."

At least we could wait in the shade of the tent. I made frequent trips to bring Elsbeth water and purposefully walked past Dr. Eikenboom's line of sight each time. She stood behind one table, waving new patients forward when she was ready, and farther down, Dr. Kloet sat behind another. I made sure I put very little water in each cup that I carried so that it doubled the frequency of my trips. Finally, Dr. Eikenboom stopped me.

"Bring your mother to the front," she said. "If she is that thirsty, the others can wait."

I rushed to get Moeder and ignored the snide

comments as I helped her to the front of the line. I glanced up and saw that those remarks had not left her unscathed, for she blinked away tears.

"Her leg," I said to Dr. Eikenboom.

Dr. Eikenboom was barely taller than I was, and I was not tall for my age. She had wavy brown hair, cut short. She wore a white jacket, much grimier than the immaculate attire of Dr. Kloet. Normally I would have respected the one with presentable attire over the one without, but here it was evidence that one was willing to get hands dirty and the other not.

"Please," Dr. Eikenboom said to my mother. "Sit."

Elsbeth lowered her body into a cane-backed chair, something made more painful by her pregnancy, and Dr. Eikenboom sat in the chair next to it and took my mother's hand.

"How long have you had the fever?" she asked, examining my mother's left shin.

"Since yesterday," Elsbeth said. "I thought it might be the pregnancy."

With a gentle touch, Dr. Eikenboom traced two long scratches from my mother's ankle to her knee. "Infection. How did you get these?"

"I scraped it in the kitchen," Elsbeth said. "There are always things in the way."

"This is an easy diagnosis," Dr. Eikenboom said. "Blood poisoning. And, with luck, we will stop this early enough."

She called to the other table. "Dr. Kloet, this woman needs sulfa."

She consulted her colleague, I would later find out, because of the protocol the two had developed. Sulfa was in short supply, but at that time, it was the only way to stop bacterial infections. The two doctors would confer on any prescriptions of the miracle drug because the limited supply meant that at times they were choosing between life or death for their patient. Here, Dr. Eikenboom saw that without sulfa, my mother would be dead within days.

Dr. Kloet stood over my mother and spoke sharply to Dr. Eikenboom.

"No sulfa for this case. Liquids and bed rest. She is young enough to pull through without any other help."

"Two lives are at stake," Dr. Eikenboom said.

"Yes, I've noticed she is the only pregnant woman in all of camp," Dr. Kloet said, not bothering to lower his voice to match Dr. Eikenboom's near whisper. "I'm assuming her husband was taken to work camp with all the others after the surrender. Count the months. Do you think the child will be born with white skin and blue eyes?"

I was trying to understand what he meant. Judging by the murmuring behind me, obviously it had significance. One word reached us, and I realized it had forced my mother to lower her head in renewed shame even as she panted to find her breath.

Harlot.

Even though I didn't know what the word meant, I knew what it had done. I turned and faced the women in line behind us. I was cold with my anger.

"Who said that?" I asked. My fists were clenched. "Who?"

"Why don't you return to our children all the marbles you have robbed," answered a woman halfway back in the line. "And let your mother tell you what it means."

I heard a small sob from my mother, like it had been wrenched from her despite a struggle to hold it in.

I marched toward the woman who had answered my challenge with a reply. She had long, stringy hair and wore a filthy dress. My first impressions of people often were based on whether they took care of their appearance. Shallow perhaps, but that was how I was. So even without her insulting words, I would have disliked her. She also held the hand of a boy my age, a boy I had played in marbles and whom I knew had a tendency to cheat. Another strike against the woman. Still, among children it was too deeply ingrained to treat adults with respect, so I shifted to an easier target.

"You, Albert, are a snot-nosed brat, and I'm not

surprised your momma is holding your hand. If you've lied to her about how you lost your marbles to me, you probably cried about it too."

"You impertinent boy," his mother said. "I'll turn you over my knee and spank you, since your mother obviously knows nothing about what is acceptable behavior."

Giggles from other mothers, combined with the direct insult aimed at my mother, drove me past the point of social convention, and for the first time in my life, I spoke disrespectfully to an adult.

"If you had done that often enough to Albert," I said, "perhaps he wouldn't be such a girl."

Albert ducked his head. I hated myself in that moment, but I wanted to lash out on my mother's behalf.

"Stop!" a voice from behind me said. "Isn't it enough we have to fight the Japanese?"

I felt Dr. Eikenboom's hand on my shoulder as she addressed the women. "Has it occurred to any of you that after our men were taken, that perhaps some of the Indonesian men forced themselves upon our women? And has it occurred to any of you that this is something of such shame that most of us, too, would make a decision never to speak of it? We are all children of God, and it is not how we treat each other in good times that allows us to demonstrate His love, but in times like this."

Her admonishment was greeted with the silence of respect.

Dr. Eikenboom guided me away from the line and back to my mother at the table at the front of the tent. She glared at Dr. Kloet. "You and I will have the remainder of this conversation in private."

"No," I said. "I will be part of it. It's my mother and if there is going to be a fight to help her, it's my fight."

Dr. Eikenboom said to me, "I like you, young man."

Dr. Kloet lowered his voice and asked, "You're the marble boy?"

"Yes," I said.

"I have my own collection of marbles," he said. "When I was a boy, I rarely lost a game, you know."

He stroked his beard and smiled. He had a prominent eyetooth on the right side, as yellowed as the rest of his teeth. "I've heard rumors about a china marble that the boys tried to win."

There had been an opportunity to win some chocolate, and it had been worth the risk. I nodded.

"It's been years since I've seen one," he said.

He spoke with an undertone of interest that I knew was in my favor. From my waistband, I pulled out the pouch that held my green statue marble and the china marble. I kept the green marble hidden and plucked out the china marble, then rolled the exquisite, tiny globe in my palm. Even though we were in the shade of the tent, the rich colors of the dragon gleamed.

"Here it is," I said. "I take on all challengers. Anytime."

His eyes bulged at the sight of the marble. If he would have asked for it in exchange for sulfa pills for my mother, I would have given it to him. But he understood my unspoken promise and must have realized that taking the marble in front of all the women would have looked like accepting a bribe.

"Give her the sulfa she needs," Dr. Kloet told Dr. Eikenboom.

As he walked away, two women broke from the line and walked to the chair where my mother was seated. These were young mothers, one dark haired and the other blond. The dark-haired woman had eyes filled with tears.

Both knelt beside her. The woman with tears spoke so softly I could barely hear.

"When you are ready," she said, putting an arm on my mother's shoulder, "both of us would like to help you back to your house. And while you are sick, we will help you with your children."

Fifteen

It seemed wise to recruit Dr. Kloet as an ally. But it couldn't appear that I was too anxious. I waited a couple of weeks before I made sure Pietje and I were sitting on the road down from the outdoor clinic late one afternoon. People would have stood in line all through the night if the Japanese had allowed it. But the ending time of each day's clinic was enforced to the exact minute.

When Dr. Kloet was finished, I was surprised that he didn't make his way directly to us, for I knew he'd seen us. Instead, he went into the house behind the open-walled tent. I made a silent bet with myself.

"Pietje," I said, "have you noticed that bigger pigeons are more easily plucked?"

Pietje squinted at me. "A pigeon sounds like a wonderful meal."

Easily half of our conversations revolved around food. Snails, lizards, mice. Anything that moved, we were willing to eat.

Pietje meant it literally. I did not. I won the bet with myself when Dr. Kloet reappeared within minutes. Where else would he have kept his marble collection except inside his residence, the closet inside the converted school?

I pretended not to see him or notice that he

was wiping his beard of crumbs as he strode in our direction. I had only arrived to lose some marbles to him, but the sight of those crumbs was an inspiration.

I took Pietje's hand and began to walk back toward our own house.

"Hey!" Dr. Kloet called.

Wasn't that the secret of life? When something hurts, don't let the world know. When you want something badly, don't let the world know.

"Don't look back, Pietje," I said. "Whatever he offers, you must not seem too excited."

I ambled with my little brother, just slow enough for Dr. Kloet to reach us. I heard the sound of marbles clunking against marbles in a sack that he carried. I thought it was one of the prettiest sounds in human existence.

"Marble boy," he said, panting slightly, "I was wondering when I would see you again. I've got something to show you."

"Hello, Dr. Kloet. With all respect, perhaps another time. I hope you don't mind that we don't stop. Pietje said he was hungry, and we need to be on our way."

"Nonsense. Let me see the china marble again."

"He's very hungry," I said. "Our family always worries about him."

Dr. Kloet grumbled, "I happen to have some bread remaining from my lunch today. Will that keep him happy?"

I shrugged, although I felt a moistening of saliva in my mouth. "We need to get home. Our mother has some cheese that she has been saving as a special treat."

"No, no," Dr. Kloet said. "Follow me back to the house. I have some cheese there too."

I was proud of Pietje and his careless shrug. Neither of us had eaten cheese in weeks.

Dr. Kloet made us sit beneath the roof of the open-walled tent as he hurried back into his house.

"Pietje," I whispered, "we don't eat anything here. We share it with the others. Moeder especially needs the cheese."

He nodded.

Dr. Kloet returned with cheese and bread wrapped in paper. By then, I was rolling the china marble across my open palm. He shoved the package at Pietje in his rush to have another look.

"How did you get it?" he breathed in awed respect. I almost liked him for that. I felt the same about this marble.

"My great-great-grandfather was a personal bodyguard at the Royal Palace," I said. "I'm told it belonged to William the Third when he was a boy, and that when my great-great-grandfather rescued him from drowning, William himself gave it to my great-great-grandfather. I don't believe it myself, but I like it as a story."

There. The perfect way to lie truthfully. I'd told

the story aloud to myself one day so that I could truthfully say it had been told to me. The truth was that I wished there had been a story like that. My mother's father had left a huge bag of marbles in his estate, and she'd forgotten about it being in a trunk. She found it a few years ago and had given it to me because she knew I liked marbles. The china marble was one of the few that I loved for the sake of the marble itself. I'd found it among all the chipped old marbles in that bag, and had often wondered about its history and how it came to be ignored among all the dross.

"William the Third!" Dr. Kloet said. "Let me hold it!"

"I cannot," I said.

He understood. He smiled what he must have supposed was a sly smile. "I used to be a fair player," he said. "But I've lost my skills, I'm sure."

He opened his marble bag and laid some of the round glass on the table. His shooters, of course, were larger. He had tiger's-eyes and swirlies and aggies and corkscrews. It was a decent collection, but I doubted he'd shown me his best.

"I'm fond of ringer taw," he said. "It would be an honor to play someone as good as I've heard you to be."

He added hastily, "Not for the china marble, of course. I wouldn't dream of that."

How a man this clumsy managed to become a

doctor must have been through family connections.

"Ringer taw," I said. "That's what I'm best at. And I happen to have some other marbles with me if that's how you'd like to start. My china marble is only for the day when I've lost everything else and don't have any more marbles to play."

I withdrew my own pouch from a pocket in my shorts. It wasn't my good collection of warrior marbles but middle-of-the-pack junk I'd won over the last weeks.

"Shall we start with five?" he asked.

"Pietje?" I said.

I didn't need to explain anything else. To play ringer taw, you drew a circle about seven feet across, and in the center, another circle about a foot across. Pietje was an expert at drawing these circles for me.

The day's heat was drawing down, but it was pleasant in the shade of the tent. The stench of the open sewage several hundred yards away wafted toward us, but I barely noticed it anymore. A gecko moved across the dirt just beyond our circle.

"Pietje," I warned.

I didn't need to explain that either. He was in tune with my thoughts. Now was not the time to be distracted by a hunt, especially with little chance to trap the gecko against a wall. Besides, we had cheese. Cheese!

I gave Pietje five marbles, and he spaced them out inside the inner circle. Dr. Kloet did the same, grunting with effort of a heavy man without flexibility. He wasn't thin, when most of us were, which said much about him.

This was a similar game to the X game where I'd lost to the Indonesian boy so badly. Players took turns shooting from anywhere outside the larger circle for the first turn. After that, a player would shoot from wherever his shooter came to rest. If the player knocked a marble out of the inner circle, he got to keep it. If he missed hitting any marbles, his turn was over. The game ended when no marbles were left in either circle.

It was tricky appearing to make the game seem close when Dr. Kloet was such a poor player. On one hand, he expected me to be great, because he'd heard the rumors about me. On the other hand, if I played up to his expectations, I would be cutting the pigeon's throat, not plucking it. I wanted him to return. Finally, I managed to lose my marbles to him.

"I can't believe this," I said. "You won't tell anyone, will you?"

He stroked his beard, smug with self-satisfaction.

"Tomorrow," I said. "Give me another chance."

"Of course," he said generously. "As many chances as you want. But be warned: the camp might face some disruptions soon. I've heard that we may get a new commander and that we also may be getting more families."

That surprised me.

"Yes?" I asked.

"I heard it from the guards," he said. He laughed. "They may have heard it from the kitchen women. Those females always know things before anyone else."

He patted me on the shoulder. "You put up a good fight. I'll look forward to another game."

He gave me that sly smile. "And don't forget to keep that china marble handy, right?"

"Yes sir," I said with proper earnestness. "And sir?"

"Yes, my little friend?"

"Thanks so much for helping my mother. It means a lot to me."

He gave me another patronizing pat. "Think nothing of it. Don't hesitate to bring her back anytime. She is pregnant, you know, and that means we need to take extra care with her."

Sixteen

Each night, the lights would go out in the Jappenkamp at a prescribed time, and each night, the bedbugs would begin to stir. We would stay awake as long as possible to hunt and kill them as they crawled to us from cracks and nail holes in the walls or fell on our bodies from the folds of our mosquito netting. It took a degree of skill, for the bugs were the size of pinheads, and in the dark you would have to accurately make a hard grinding squeeze to crush them between the pad of your thumb and forefinger. The reward would be a popping sensation and the foul smell of the oils from their bodies, an odor like rotting raw hamburger, or if it had been engorged with blood, a sickly sweet raspberry perfume.

The infestation had grown as hygiene had decreased from so many families living in such cramped quarters. Our family had already dis-carded our mattress for straw mats that Elsbeth had secured by trading the last jar of her cold cream. Other families had begun to do the same. If in every dark cloud there is a silver lining, then for Pietje and me, it was the fact that the cloth of a mattress cover was of great value to the Indonesians. We would prowl the yards first thing each morning, looking for the mattresses before they were taken away to be burned.

Not that this treasure came easily. Clouds of bedbugs would rise, then fall on us as we ripped the fabric, and there was no hurrying the process. Haphazard ripping resulted in smaller strips of fabric, so we'd have to slowly tear away the cover from the mattress in the widest strips possible, trying not to breathe in bedbugs. We would roll the fabric loose and then brush each other clean of bedbugs and then bundle the fabric before heading to the fence.

Braving the bedbugs of those mattresses seemed a worthwhile sacrifice, as we were able to trade for any type of food, including coconuts and mangoes and large grub worms to toast over our secret twig fires. The food was necessary to protect our mother. Even though the women in the kitchen had made a collective decision to let me work in Elsbeth's place, which still allowed her the extra rations that came with kitchen work, she desperately needed extra calories in the late stages of her pregnancy.

Pietje and I also had discovered *agaatslakken*— agate snails—living in the shaded outside walls of some houses. Each new find became vital protein. Before the war, Pietje and I would find them among the shrubs around our house and salt them with careless cruelty, imagining we could hear their screams as they withered. But in the Jappenkamp, as soon as we woke, Pietje and I would rush around to gather as many of the scarce mollusks as possible. Then we came home and gathered twigs for a small fire. Even though families weren't allowed to cook privately, we put the snails and a little bit of water in the bottom of a can, then heated it until the snails could be easily pulled from their shells. We cut them into small pieces and hid the pieces in our pockets until lunch. It was Pietje's job to distract our mother so that I could sprinkle the pieces into her watery soup. If she had known that the mystery meat was snail, she would have refused to eat it.

Pietje and I continued our marble games with Dr. Kloet too. He would win almost enough of my marbles to force me to pull out the china marble and then, from his perspective, hit an inexplicable losing streak that brought me back from the edge of bankruptcy. Pietje was a silent spectator with bread and cheese in his pocket to constantly take home.

As Dr. Kloet had foretold, these routines changed with the arrival of our new commander. On the first morning of his reign, we were roused from sleep by guttural screaming from a bull-horn on the street outside our house.

"*Tenko! Tenko!*"

This was a Japanese word I didn't yet know.

Then came the wail of a siren, rising and falling with the urgency that reminded us of the many times we had dived into makeshift bomb shelters before the capitulation.

Then it came in Dutch. Our translator had sent women out to run from house to house to give the instructions.

"*Allemaal naar buiten! We gaan julie tellen!*"
All outside! Head count!

Head count? Who would try to escape? Except for their willingness to trade, many, if not most, of the natives were openly hostile. All our radios had long been confiscated, but the truck drivers who brought daily supplies were happy to gossip, and the outside situation was clear. The natives called us *blandas*—whites—and now that every *blanda* on the islands was imprisoned, rebels had begun to form bands with the intent to make sure that centuries of resented Dutch governance remained overthrown after the Japanese were gone. It was doubtful any *blanda* would receive help outside a camp, and even so, there was nowhere to go. The Dutch East Indies was an archipelago; the nearest refuge, across shark-infested seas, was Australia. Anyone trying to escape would be killed by the Japanese if captured, and likely killed by Indonesians if not captured by the Japanese.

"*Allemaal naar buiten*! *We gaan julie tellen*!"

Families disgorged themselves from houses up and down the street. We milled in confusion and stood in tired family groups until Japanese soldiers moved up and down the streets barking out another word.

"Lekas! Lekas!"

This we knew. *Hurry! Hurry!*

Kicking and pushing the groups into lines along the streets, it still took the soldiers twenty minutes to complete the organization of making sure that every woman and child faced the street, forming a solid parade line on each side of the street as far down as I could see.

Then the soldiers pushed and shoved long enough for us to understand we were to remain in assigned groups of ten. That took another twenty minutes in the heat.

Then we were forced to count out in Japanese. *Ichi. Ni. San. Shi. Go. Roku. Sit. Hat. Ku. Juu.* Each group of ten would be ticked off against the total until the count was complete.

In places, some of the children urinated where they were standing. They had been rushed from the houses with no chance to stop at the toilet first. I began to feel dizzy from the heat, and I saw my mother swaying on her feet. Yet I did not hear a single child crying in front of the Japanese. The Dutch had too much pride, and the mothers would not permit it.

When all the counting was finished, we were given a real surprise. Dozens and dozens of more women and children walked through the gates of the camp. We did not know that the trucks with new arrivals had arrived just before dawn and that the new arrivals had been forced to stand in lines until sent to join us.

We could not gawk, however. As the first of the newcomers entered our street, soldiers bullied them into groups of ten and made them do a count as well. The single lines on each side of the streets became compacted, and any accidental jostling was immediately noticed and silenced by beatings and screams from the soldiers.

When the new count was finished, the soldier with the bullhorn yelled a single word.

"*Kiotske!*" *Attention!* The newcomers straightened instantly, as did we. So they, too, had been taught the same at whatever Jappenkamp had been their previous home.

Within seconds came the expected order to bow. "*Kere!*"

With my upper body forward at the proper angle, arms straight back, and eyes at the ground, I heard the approach of a Jeep. I tilted my head slightly, hoping that a soldier wouldn't notice, and I caught my first glimpse of Commander Isamu Nakahara.

He was standing on the passenger side of the open Jeep, holding the top of the windshield to steady himself. Sitting on the passenger seat, head at the height of Nakahara's hip and nose almost into the windshield, was a German shepherd, nearly black. Nakahara's shiny black visor and the sword strapped to the side of his uniform were clearly visible, even with the short glimpse.

The Jeep came to a stop, and, pointing his sword at a woman, Nakahara screamed a string of words at the nearest soldier, who in turn slapped a woman across the head for an infraction that I could only guess was an improper bow. I decided it would be prudent to keep my chin straight down and smother my curiosity. When the Jeep rumbled forward again, I relaxed slightly. That's when Elsbeth fainted, falling into the street just before the Jeep passed us.

I acted without thinking. I broke from my bow and hurried to her. Dimly, I was aware of screaming from Nakahara, but I was focused on trying to get my mother upright again. I heard the Jeep door click open, then saw a flash of black. I found myself pushed backward, and I lifted my arm instinctively against the monster that had bowled me over.

It was the dog, all the more terrifying for its silence. Its claws scratched my legs as it braced to a halt on top of my body, and before I realized it, it closed its jaws over my protective arm, inches away from my throat. I froze, lying on my back, with the dog's legs caging me in a perimeter around my body.

More screaming came in Japanese from Nakahara followed by the Dutch from our translator. *This dog will kill you at my command. Don't move.*

It was an order easy to obey. Frightened as I was, a part of my brain marveled at how gentle the dog's grip was on my arm. If it had been trained this effectively to hold without biting, I had no doubt it would do anything else that was commanded.

More Japanese words came from Nakahara, and the dog let go of my arm and backed away.

"*Kere!*" Nakahara said in a voice so eerily controlled that my fear intensified. *What will he do to Moeder?* I found my feet and forced my trembling body into a bowing position, leaving my mother motionless on the ground beside me.

God, God, I prayed in my thoughts, *please protect Moeder.*

"*Kere!*" Nakahara said again. For a moment I was confused. I was bowing in the perfect position, just as we'd been trained by the previous commander. Then, to my horror, I realized he was speaking to my mother. Her arm had fallen awkwardly behind her back. Her dress was skewed partially sideways, showing her lower thighs. Her belly pushed tight against the dress.

"*Kere!*" Nakahara said to her. I could see it too clearly, even with my head down. When she didn't respond, he kicked her in the side of her buttocks with such force that his sword slapped against his thigh. With the dog inches away from me, I was helpless to protect her.

"*Kere!*" This time, Nakahara screamed. My mother did not respond. He raised his foot to kick her again, and in the silence of hundreds of people frozen by this horror, one clear word came out in Dutch.

"*Niet meer!*"

From the corners of my eyes, I saw Nakahara

swivel to search for the woman who had spoken.

"*Niet meer!*" the woman said again. "*Ik zal haar straf.*"

Stop! I shall take her punishment.

I could not help but lift my head, and I saw that up and down the lines, others had too. No one received a kick or punch for this, because the soldiers, too, were transfixed by the sight of a woman stepping out of the line and marching toward Nakahara and his dog.

He smiled in anticipation as she neared, and I saw him moisten his lips with the tip of his tongue.

I had not seen her before in camp. She was one of the new arrivals.

Yet I had seen her before. I knew it.

It seemed like all sound in the world paused as the woman walked a straight line toward me and my mother.

The dog growled, but Nakahara silenced it with a gesture. When she was only a step away, she stopped, arms at her side, and bowed her head. I had a flash of memory that almost made me gasp.

The months had changed her, and hunger had etched out the bones in her still-beautiful face. The fabric of her clothing was faded and thinned from too many launderings, but this was the same woman who had stepped into the goat pasture and broken up the fight between me and Georgie.

Laura Jansen's grandmother. Sophie.

Just as I realized this, Nakahara crossed the single step between them and punched her full in the side of the head. He continued in a silent frenzy of kicks and punches that only stopped with Sophie on the ground, flies already swarming the blood that oozed from places where his blows had broken her skin.

Seventeen

I did not sleep that night, such was the anguish of responsibility that pressed upon my soul for the beating I had witnessed. It was wretched in the dark. An overnight storm had blown in, but it could not mask my mother's groans as she shifted on the floor, likely trying to escape the muscle pain from the vicious kick she'd received in the side of her buttock, much too close to her stomach. How much worse was it for Laura's grandmother?

When the rain stopped, I tiptoed past all the other families and found my own escape outside. I leaned against the damp house and let the darkness bury my shame for failing to protect my mother. I wanted to cry, but I was arid. I had not cried since my father had been taken.

Years later, my memories of the sleeplessness of that night remained so vivid that as an adult, when I questioned how it could be possible that

I had seen dawn arrive twice at the end of that night, I found it a relief to learn that it was not self-delusion. Sunlight had scattered off space dust in a diffuse white glow ahead of the path of the sun. Scientists called it zodiacal light, so faint that moonlight or light pollution renders it invisible.

False dawn. A dawn that dissipates when the light of the real dawn overpowers it.

False dawn. Just like the all-too-short time of peace that had found my mother in the days since women had begun helping her instead of ostracizing her. As the sky grew brighter with the second dawn, I dreaded what was ahead of us. My failure had caused another woman to be beaten near to death in place of the punishment that most surely would have been inflicted on Elsbeth. Surely our family would be forced to bear that same ostracism again. Surely that ostracism would swing my mother back into her darkness.

How can we ever get through all of this? I asked myself again and again throughout the night. *How can we keep going?*

Yet immediately after real dawn came, so came those same women who had earlier helped mother in front of all the others with Dr. Eikenboom—Mrs. Altink and Mrs. Meeuwsen, hardly in better health than Mother had been before her collapse.

At the usual morning time, Nakahara made all of camp go to the streets for roll call, and Mrs.

Altink and Mrs. Meeuwsen stood with her on the wet street to help her remain upright. Immediately after, when the Japanese soldiers dismissed us for our duties, Mrs. Meeuwsen stayed with Nikki and Aniek and Pietje, while Mrs. Altink stayed with me to support Elsbeth as she hobbled to the medical line. It took us such a long time to walk that already two dozen people were in front of us when we arrived. Mrs. Altink and I found a spot for her to sit.

"It's okay," I said to Mrs. Altink. "I can stay with her now."

I owe that nondescript, tired woman so much for her response. But I would not have a chance to thank her. Within a week of that morning, she would die of a fever, and her body would be buried as anonymously as if I had never known her. It wouldn't be until years later that I realized how much different the next months in camp would have been for my mother—and me—without Mrs. Altink there that morning to admonish me.

"Lift your head and look at me," Mrs. Altink said. She pulled me away from my mother to ensure our conversation was private.

I was reluctant to do as commanded, so she forced my chin up with pressure from her hand. I looked into a face that was splotched with rash.

"We will not let them win," Mrs. Altink said. "Do you hear me?"

Her cheekbones were pushing hard against skin that was drawn tight from lack of food. Her hair was limp with grease. But she had the eyes of a warrior.

"They can take our homes and our husbands," she said. "They can take our health. But we are Dutch. We will not let them take our spirit. Don't for a moment believe that you were at fault for what happened yesterday. When you assume you deserve the evil that someone else inflicts upon you, then you are choosing to be a victim. Do not give someone else that power over you."

Her intensity took so much willpower that after I nodded, she blinked back tears and whispered, more to herself than to me, "Do not cry."

This was something the children heard again and again from all the mothers. *Do not cry.*

The Dutch would not let the Japanese soldiers see our children cry. We were too proud.

"Do not cry," she repeated. "We will not let them win."

I took my place in line for Moeder, while Mrs. Altink returned to her and put an arm around her shoulders to keep a blanket in place for the half hour or so it took me to near the front of the line.

There, Dr. Kloet noticed my presence. He waved me forward.

I believe that had Mrs. Altink not been so fierce with me, I would have succumbed to the temptation to cut in front of the others still standing in front of my spot in the line. My earlier sense of defeat would have meant total surrender. When there is no point in even trying, what would it matter to push others aside and take only for yourself?

Instead, as he waved repeatedly, I pretended not to notice and tried not to feel scorn for Dr. Kloet's lack of political sense. I had been in school. I had seen the teacher's pets and disliked them for the fawning and the acceptance of favors from the teachers who did not understand how it was for the boys. Yes, there was a certain duplicity to this. I had no hesitation bilking the man for whatever food I could take from him in marble games at the end of the day. But it was different to take something here, for that would be like taking from the women and children who had paid their time to stand in line.

To step forward now would cost my mother the acceptance and grace that had so recently been extended to her. It would have given Nakahara victory.

When, finally, I was in front of Dr. Eikenboom, Mrs. Altink led Elsbeth forward.

I stepped away, my duty finished.

But Dr. Eikenboom would have nothing of it.

"Look at your leg," she said to me.

I glanced down. I was wearing shorts, and my legs were streaked with dirt. Two scratches, courtesy of the claws of Nakahara's killer dog, traveled from my knee to my ankles. In places, the scratches were wide enough and deep enough to have torn through the skin.

I shrugged.

"No," she said. "Remember what happened to your mother?"

Dr. Eikenboom called over to Dr. Kloet, just as a few weeks earlier she'd done for my mother; vital medicine would not be dispensed without a joint agreement. "We need sulfa for Jeremiah. If we give him a little now, we won't need a lot later."

Dr. Kloet was just grumpy enough at how I'd ignored his waves to walk over and make a show of deciding whether to agree with Dr. Eikenboom. He looked at the red scratches on my leg.

"Same thing as your mother, I suppose."

"No," I said. "She scraped her leg in the kitchen. This came from a dog."

A strange expression crossed his face, an expression that would not make sense to me until much, much later, when it was far too late to make a difference for what I should have also realized in that moment. Dr. Kloet was a blunderer in social situations, but not stupid, as I would also learn much, much later, when it was far too late to make a difference.

"A dog?" he asked.

"Yesterday. At roll call."

He blinked several times, putting together the stories he must have already heard about the previous afternoon. Most certainly, he would have helped Dr. Eikenboom treat Sophie after the beating.

"Fine then," he said and walked back to his desk.

"Dr. Eikenboom," I said, "will she be all right? The woman from yesterday."

Dr. Eikenboom knelt and made sure we were at eye level. "That is in God's hands. But whatever happens, she made the choice."

The tears that had failed me during the night now threatened to roll down my face. I blinked back the tears.

"Yes," I said. "We will not let them win."

Do not cry.

Eighteen

Naturally, I had questions about why Laura's grandmother Sophie was in camp. Hadn't she—and Laura—escaped by ship just before the Japanese invasion? This meant that I also had questions, naturally, about Laura. But these were questions I felt I had no choice but to keep to myself, especially because of the gravity of the beating I had witnessed.

I doubted I could comprehend how badly Nakahara had hurt Laura's grandmother, given that Nakahara's single kick to Elsbeth had penetrated the muscles so deeply she could barely walk that morning, let alone take her turn at kitchen duties.

Do not cry. We will not let them win.

I was determined that the Prins family, represented by me, would not let them win. Thus, I made my way to the kitchen to present myself for duties in Elsbeth's place.

The overnight storm had blown rain under the tin-covered roof, drenching the firewood and turning the dirt floors into mud. Someone had begun the fire in the stove, and because of the wet firewood, smoke hung shoulder high beneath the tin roof.

The women who had already gathered were sitting at a table, drinking tea before starting their duties. These were the women who heard rumors first because of their contact with the drivers who brought in supplies, the ones who had known ahead of the rest of camp, for example, that the dogs would be taken to prevent rabies. My mother would have been near or among them if she'd been able to help with duties. I was content to listen to their conversation as I waited for one of them to address me; one simply did not interrupt elders. It would have been nice, however, to have a cup of tea in my hand.

Mrs. Aafjes held court, and her voice was distinctive above the rest. She was a large,

159

intimidating woman who wore men's clothes—a loose, faded black shirt and ragged pants—and she was the mother to four children. Her face was ruddy from sun exposure, and she had a fascinating mole on the side of her nose.

"If someday these animals ever try to take us away from our children, I say that's when we make our last stand," she said. "Every one of us. Then the world will remember how we refused to surrender. Like Masada. That's a far kinder fate for our children than leaving them with these fiends."

"Take us away from our children?" someone asked.

Mrs. Aafjes leaned forward like she was going to speak confidentially, but the large-boned woman could have been heard in a cattle stampede. "The man who brings the bread. He said he's heard that the Japanese need more workers in Borneo. He says they might start taking women from camp and leaving the children behind."

"No," another woman wailed.

It seemed like Mrs. Aafjes savored the drama and the news she was delivering. "It's just a rumor, mind you. Still, if it happened, I say we gather ourselves in a group to choose our own deaths, just as the Jews did on the mountaintop. They knew if the Romans caught them alive that—"

The woman beside her tugged on her elbow

160

and pointed at me. "Not in front of the boy."

Mrs. Aafjes turned her nose and her mole toward me and glared. "Yes?"

I tried not to stare at the mole as I spoke. "My mother is Elsbeth Prins, and she cannot help keep the fires burning. So I am here instead."

Without rice, we starved. To cook rice, we needed boiling water. Vats and vats of it. This required constant fire in the stoves that were inefficiently leaky in the best of conditions.

"That will not be possible," she said. "Children are no longer permitted in the kitchen. Those are the rules."

"Yes," I said. "I must. I am not a child."

"Last month," she said, scolding me, "you didn't have to endure the tragedy that still gives me nightmares. A little girl, only three, tripped one of the women holding a vat of cooked rice, just before we drained the water."

The women had to lift these large vats of boiling water with bamboo poles. In the first months, it had been a task that required two women for two bamboo poles. Since then, as everyone in camp grew weaker, it had become a complicated task that required four women.

"That boiling water," Mrs. Aafjes pronounced, "spilled on the child and her mother."

She continued her glare. "It burned both of them, and both were dead two days later. So no more children in the kitchen. We don't want to have to see something like that again. A horrible, horrible thing for me. I can still hear the screams."

"I know how to split wood," I said. "I know how to wash dishes. I know how to stay away from boiling water. If my mother cannot be here, I will work in her place."

The woman beside her—the one who had interrupted the story about the Romans and the Jews—tugged again on Mrs. Aafjes's sleeve and whispered in her ear.

Mrs. Aafjes looked at me with new recognition. "You're the one the dog attacked at roll call."

I knew what that meant. I was the one whose mother fainted and drew a beating for Laura's grandmother.

"I am here to work in my mother's place," I said.

"I now understand why," she said. Her mole twitched as the moralistic tendencies of the Dutch triumphed within her. My work, I knew she believed, would serve as a payment for Sophie's sacrifice. "Very well then. If you chop off a foot, don't come running to me."

I searched for the driest logs in the pile. As I labored to split off small enough pieces to fit into the stove, I was so absorbed in the task that I did not know Laura had entered my life again until I heard her speak in a dull voice.

"I was told I could find you in the kitchen."

I turned and looked into the face of Laura. I had dreamed when one day I saw her again, I would be in fine clothes, driving a fine car, somewhere in Amsterdam. She would see me in the car and regret until her dying day how she had spurned me by sending an empty envelope in response to my beautiful sonnet.

"I've been asked to deliver a message to you," she said.

I was spattered in mud, smelling of smoke. I became more aware of how distasteful I looked in that moment than I had in months. That was the impact Laura's appearance had on me. It was the same horse's kick in the belly reaction that I'd had the first time I'd seen her. This time, however, I let it make me feel angry and churlish. With her in front of me, so beautiful despite the near rags that served as a dress, and the knots in her long hair, and with her facial expression and dull voice so obviously indicative of her disinterest in me, I honed in on the vivid disappointment I felt after that empty envelope had arrived.

"They were right, then, weren't they? This is where I am." I turned my attention back to the firewood. My goal was to say it in such a way that it hurt her as much as I felt hurt.

I succeeded. When I glanced back to see if she had remained, I found her staring at me with near hatred.

"Go away," I said.

"Believe me, I will. I didn't want to look for you, but my oma sent me because she wants to talk to you. So I had no choice."

I should have asked how Sophie was doing. I should have apologized that it was my fault that I hadn't done enough to stop Nakahara. Instead, I nodded without looking at her. I had every right to be angry, didn't I? I'd poured my heart into a sonnet that Ivanhoe himself would have been proud to have given to Rowena. Yet Laura had made a deliberate point of insulting me with her reply of an empty envelope. And her current attitude that made it clear she thought I was dung to be scraped off her shoe.

"I have wanted to be able to speak to your oma," I said. I did not know if I would be able to thank Sophie in a way that made sense. How do you express happiness to someone for paying such a large price to save someone you love? "But not with you there. So I will go to the hospital as soon as I can."

"She's not in the hospital," Laura said. "The doctors said that they didn't want her to catch an infection. She's at the house where they put us."

I didn't know which house Sophie had been forced to choose for their living quarters. The influx of newcomers had nearly doubled our population. Where families had once been able to keep a room all to themselves, now they had to share with another family of strangers. In our house, my decision to take such a small room, where five bodies asleep filled all the space on the floor, had paid off, and we'd been able to keep our privacy.

"Send someone else to get me then," I said, keeping my back to her. This was her chance to ask why I was so mad, and then when I explained, she could apologize and beg forgiveness for her betrayal.

When I didn't get a response, I turned my head to see why she was silent. But she was gone.

A few hours later, after all the rice had been dispensed—family by family, according to a check sheet so that nobody cheated and got second rations—someone did show up to lead me to the house where Laura's grandmother was recovering.

Georgie.

Nineteen

"I'm here to get you because I've been taking care of Laura and her oma," Georgie said. His age made him one of the oldest boys in the camp, and his size showed it. His shirt stretched at his shoulders, and he'd grown wider, though not heavier, in the last months. My clothes were still comfortable and slid around my body, to the point where I wondered if I was ever going to

165

get taller. "Oma Jansen wants to see you and I am to take you to the house. Our family shares the same house. That's what Laura wanted."

He looked me up and down, letting me know he was doing it, then gave me a challenging smirk. "I can't imagine Oma Jansen will have anything nice to say to you after you caused the commander to nearly kill her."

We were just outside the roof of the kitchen. The drizzle had stopped. Women in the kitchen were relaxing and chatting. This was not the place for a fight, but I could not help remembering the iron bar coming down on my arm. It took all my effort not to dive forward and tackle him. I felt like if I even let a single word escape from my mouth, it would burst the dam of rage I was trying to hold back, so I merely met his eyes and remained silent.

I was no longer Ivanhoe, but King Arthur; Laura no longer Rowena, but Guinevere; and I was tasting ashes of bitterness as I faced Lancelot, the knight that Guinevere had chosen for her betrayal of me.

I swallowed those ashes in silence, and I forced myself to walk away.

"Afraid?" he asked. "Chicken?"

I kept walking. He had to trot to catch up to me. This, at least, put me back in control.

"You have to visit Oma Jansen," he said. "She's asking for you."

I could see that my refusal to speak was infuriating him. As was my refusal to follow him.

"Hey," he said. "Aren't you listening? You have to go with me to Oma Jansen."

The streets were cobblestone, but the yards around the houses were grass. Or at least they had been, before the Jappenkamp. In many places, because each house held about fifty or more people, the grass had been worn to dirt, which had become puddles and mud after the rain. I walked directly into a huge patch of greasy dirt, and I made a splash. It didn't matter to me; I was filthy from tending the fires in the kitchen.

"Hey!" he said from the edge of the mud.

This was good. If he wanted to follow me and drive himself crazy listening to me not answer, he would have to endure my splashing.

"Hey!" He had not moved.

I reached the edge of one yard but stayed on a path that would take me past the edge of the next house, using a shortcut to the street a block over.

"I'm telling her that you're afraid," he yelled.

I disappeared around the edge of the house. Out of his sight, I ran to our own house. The cistern in the back had filled with rainwater, beautifully clean and lukewarm. I poured bucket after bucket over myself, standing in my ragged underwear. Modesty was a general commodity that had vanished weeks earlier.

After I dried, I noticed Pietje nearby, doing what he usually did—shadow my every move and observe everything.

"Pietje," I said as I walked toward him, "you need to stay with your sisters for a while. I am going to another house, and I will be back as soon as I can."

He giggled.

"*After* I get dressed," I said with pretended irritation.

My best shirt and shorts still looked good because I rarely wore them, and I made sure my hair was combed. Then I went back to the street, this time avoiding all mud and puddles.

It didn't take long to find out where Laura and her oma were staying. As I had anticipated, all I had to do was ask. The clouds had broken, and as sunshine lifted the gloom, women and children were spilling out of their houses. In such cramped conditions, there was no joy in listening to rain when another entire family shared your bedroom.

"*Mevrouw*," I said to the first woman I saw a street over. "I'm looking for Mrs. Jansen. She's the one that the commander attacked yesterday. Did you hear about it?"

This woman wore a wide straw hat and had curtains of skin hanging from her face and her arms. For some, who had been robust before the Jappenkamp, losing weight was happening faster than the body could adjust by tightening skin.

"I heard about it," she said. She wouldn't have seen it, of course, because where she was lined up during roll call was on her street, not ours. "It was a tragic thing. That poor woman couldn't help but faint. And the boy, I hear he was almost killed by that dog. Such a brave thing that Mrs. Jansen did."

"Yes," I said. "And Mrs. Jansen. Is she all right?"

"The doctor is with her." She pointed. "Four houses down. On that side of the street. I heard she was on a ship to Australia when it was captured by the Japanese Navy and everyone was taken back here and put into camps. She's lucky it didn't just get bombed like most of the ships. I heard that—"

Then she gasped at what she noticed in my hand. "You have an orange! Would you like to trade for it?"

A few days earlier, at the bamboo curtain, I'd been able to trade a few strips of mattress cover for it. I'd hidden it, even from my family, intending to surprise them with it on the birthday of the twins in a couple of days.

"It's not mine," I said. Because my family had not known about it, they would not be disappointed it would not reach them. "I'm sorry."

I followed her directions, not surprised she knew Dr. Eikenboom was there. Gossip and rumor spread faster and more thoroughly than bedbugs. When I stepped inside the house, the

169

familiar smell of body odor pressed upon me, as it did upon entering the house where our family stayed.

With all the interior doors removed from the frames, all I needed to do was walk down the hallway. Some families, in defiance of camp orders, had hung sheets in the doorways for privacy. Others, afraid of surprise inspections, had not.

Down the hallway, I saw the familiar figure of Dr. Eikenboom. Standing near her, blocking my view of the focus of her attention, were Laura and Georgie and a woman I did not know.

I cleared my throat, and all heads turned toward me.

"That's him, Mom," Georgie said without hesitation. "The boy who attacked me at the market. Remember? Who bit my ear? Before we got on the ship. He's the boy who didn't listen when I told him to follow me here."

Georgie's mother pursed her lips in instant disapproval. As an American woman, Mrs. Smith would have been automatically granted an air of mystique. Her appearance amplified it—thick, curly hair and the exquisite bone features of her face. I'd seen movie posters for *Santa Fe Trail*, starring Olivia de Havilland. The woman in front of me resembled and had the aura of that actress, but without the bonnet and frilly dress in the poster.

"Jeremiah," Dr. Eikenboom said. "It's nice to see you. I told them that we should expect you anytime."

At least she showed no pursing of the lips.

Beside her, Laura stepped away from the cot. I saw her seeing me see her, and I felt crucified by my regret for my churlishness.

"Mrs. Jansen asked for me," I explained. "So I am here."

"Yes," came the voice from behind Dr. Eikenboom. "Thank you."

Dr. Eikenboom moved aside, giving me a clear view of Mrs. Jansen, propped by pillows on a cot that had undoubtedly been moved here from the hospital. Her face was mottled with bruises, stitched in several places. Her swollen lips were split, with dried blood in the creases. She had an arm in a sling, resting atop the sheet of light-weight fabric that covered the rest of her body.

I stepped forward. "Thank you, Mrs. Jansen, for protecting my mother. I am very sorry for what happened to you. I brought this for you."

I held out the precious orange.

Mrs. Smith said, "An orange! Did you steal that?"

Instead of answering her insult, I froze my stare directly upon her. I could see that she wanted to rebuke me for my insolence, but Mrs. Jansen spoke first.

"I would like to be alone with Jeremiah," she

said. "If possible, this will be a private conversation."

"Of course," Dr. Eikenboom said. "I have hospital duties. Please send for me if you feel the need. We are all grateful for the courage you showed yesterday, and already, I am hearing that we all must stand together against the Japanese."

Dr. Eikenboom said to me, "And Jeremiah, when you hoodwink Dr. Kloet into a marble game this afternoon, ask him to put disinfectant again on those scratches. We can't be too careful, you know."

"Yes, *mevrouw*," I said. "Thank you."

As Mrs. Smith, Georgie, and Laura pushed past me, I heard Mrs. Smith say, "Hoodwink?"

The only response I heard from Dr. Eikenboom was laughter. Then I was in the room alone with Mrs. Jansen.

She studied me through one eye since her left eye was nearly swollen shut.

"So," she said. "I like how you look now, much better than seeing you only in underwear in a goat field."

I held out my orange for her. "Thank you for saving my mother."

"I'd like you to keep that for your family," she said. "I don't need thanks for what I did yesterday. I am so tired of how we've been treated, I've decided that I will no longer be a coward, even if it kills me."

172

She gave me a wan smile, and a touch of blood seeped from a crack in her lips at the movement. "That was a very serious thing to say, and it wasn't why I asked to see you. So I apologize if speaking of this frightens you, but I truly want you to understand my actions. You must not feel that you or your mother are to blame in any way for what happened to me. It was my choice and it gave me a chance to feel good about myself. Physical pain is a small price to pay for that."

"Yes, *mevrouw*," I said.

"If we become friends," she said, "I would prefer it if you called me Sophie. And I would like to become friends, but I want to ask you some questions first."

This was not at all the direction of conversation I expected. Friends with an adult? "You are the boy who wrote a letter to Laura?" she asked.

I nodded.

"Would you like to tell me what you wrote in the letter?"

"No," I said. It had been bad enough that Laura had humiliated me by sending back an empty envelope. "I would not."

I could tell my answer disappointed her. She took her time, as if gathering her thoughts.

"I've been told that you are cruel to animals," she said. "That you hit a pig in the head with a hammer. Is that true?"

I stood still, trying to keep my defenses in

control. "There are two sides to every story."

"Then I would like to hear the other side."

I did not like this feeling that I was on trial, and it made me angry. "Whoever told you that I hit a pig in the head with a hammer knows both sides to the story. Ask him or her. Then ask why he or she only told one side of the story."

That was either Laura or Georgie, who'd heard about it beneath the banyan tree. I hoped it had been Georgie trying to make me look bad, but now I wasn't sure about Laura.

"Fair enough," Mrs. Jansen said, and a hint of a smile returned to her face, though that could have been my imagination because of how puffed and swollen the skin was around her cheekbones. She studied me again.

"I am trying to decide about you," she said finally. She closed her eyes. "I saw yesterday that you tried to help your mother when she fainted, even though you risked a beating yourself and the dog was at your throat." She paused, then opened her eyes. "Dr. Eikenboom tells me that you work in the kitchen in her place and you carry buckets of sewage for her when it's her turn for that duty."

I expected then that she'd offer me unnecessary praise that I neither wanted nor deserved, but instead she said, "I've even heard the younger children adore you because you don't let anyone bully them and that you give marbles to the little children in this camp whenever you find them crying on the street."

She looked at me as if waiting for a reply.

"Only if they are old enough to know not to swallow them," I said. "I learned with younger ones that it upsets them to lose the marble, and then we have to wait until it passes through so that we can find it again."

More reflective silence on her part, perhaps as she sympathized with the difficulty of keeping happy a younger child that swallows marbles. Then, "You won't tell me what was in the letter to Laura?"

"I sent it for her eyes. If she wants to tell you, I can't stop that."

Sophie's eyebrows wrinkled slightly.

"Your arm," she said. "Outside the market where I saw you in your underwear tied to a rope to a fence post. Before we went on the ship to Australia. I heard that it had been broken that day. I heard that you fell from a tree after I took Georgie away."

"I'm sure that's what you heard," I said.

"Did you? Fall from a tree?"

"That's what I told my mother."

"What you told your mother might be one thing. But did you fall from a tree and break it?"

"I would like to know why you are asking," I said.

"I would like to know why, if it happened differently, that you keep it a secret."

"May I go now?" I asked.

"Do you remember that day in the market when you saw some money fall at the baker's stall and gave it back to the woman? I was there, at a nearby stall, and I heard her thanking you."

I shrugged. "To keep it would have been stealing."

"I also saw what happened at the fight with that piece of iron as I was walking up, when none of the boys had noticed me yet," she said, nodding toward my arm. "Georgie hit you with it."

"I have nothing to say about that fight."

"Laura told me that Georgie was the one who wanted to fight. I found it remarkable that you made it seem like nothing had happened, and I found it remarkable that you didn't try to get him in trouble for it. What I *can't* decide is how the same boy who could have easily kept the money and easily put another boy in trouble for breaking his arm is the same boy who would write something in a letter that would make my granddaughter cry for several days."

I said as respectfully as I could, "I think that if someone wants to judge me to see if they will approve of me, it makes me not care what they think. May I go now?"

Sophie's good eye had widened for a moment, but she only said in a quiet voice, "Could you give me some water first? I have difficulty reaching it."

There was a pitcher on the floor, with a battered tin cup beside it. I poured water into the cup, then took a cloth beside the bed and folded it. I tipped the cup so she could drink, and I held the cloth beneath her chin so that any escaping water would not drip onto her. This is how I'd seen mothers in camp with little children.

"Thank you," she said. She closed her eyes. "If you want to leave, I understand."

I set the cup down.

At the doorway, I stopped and turned and spoke. "Memories drift like leaves, blown by winds gentle before a gale heaves. Tears grace my cheeks, burning of love unspoken and deeply yearning."

"I beg your pardon?" she said, opening her eyes and revealing the exhaustion that was plain to see on her face, despite the camouflage of bruises.

"That's how my letter to her started." I maintained as much dignity as possible. "It's not my fault I'm such a bad poet I made her cry. Or that it was the wrong thing to send."

"Don't go," Mrs. Jansen said. "Please. Step closer and repeat that to me. So that no one else can hear but me."

I was reluctant, but did as requested. *"Memories drift like leaves, blown by winds gentle before*

177

a gale heaves. Tears grace my cheeks, burning of love unspoken and deeply yearning."

"It's the beginning of a sonnet," she said, kindly refraining from commenting on the straining of metaphors and the forced rhyming. "Did you write it?"

I nodded. With reluctance.

She closed her eyes again, and I thought she'd fallen asleep, but when I tried to move away, she stopped me again.

"Jeremiah," she said, "hearing that from you explains many things to me. Take my advice. Someday, speak those same words to Laura. I think you'll be surprised at how glad she'll be to hear it from you."

Not likely, I thought. But I didn't want to argue. I already felt as if I'd exposed too much of my soul.

"Jeremiah, I would be honored if you called me Sophie," she said. "And if there is anything I can ever do to help you or your family, please let me know."

Twenty

I did not trust Dr. Kloet. In this camp, he was too well fed. A boy of nobler spirit would have avoided the man, but hypocrite that I was, I had no pangs of conscience as I maintained our unspoken agreement. At our marble game at the end of each day, I would allow him the dream of someday possessing my china marble in exchange for the food he brought for Pietje the spectator. Late the next afternoon, as farmers in the surrounding valley were clearing for new fields by burning, Pietje and I made our way to the doctor's residence. The smell of smoke was a welcome change from the stench of the sewage pit, and the flat, gray, hazy sky was a relief from the sun. After Dr. Kloet had treated the claw scratches on my leg with disinfectant, I pulled my warrior pouch from its safe place under the waistband of my shorts. Under Pietje's silent observation, I made a show of counting out the final seven marbles that were the obstacle between him and the china marble.

"I can only afford to start our game with five today," I said.

Having set the hook deep enough—after all this time I thought it a miracle I hadn't ripped out all sections of his lips—I put one marble back into the warrior pouch and kept the seventh as my shooter.

"How about Dropsies?" Dr. Kloet suggested. He stroked his beard a few times. There was a creepy hypnotic rhythm to the way his long fingers would manipulate the hair. "Perhaps you need a change of luck."

This, on the surface, would have appeared to

be true to him. The day before, I'd lost all of my warrior marbles except the seven that he'd just watched me count. With those gone, he knew, I'd finally have to risk the treasure that made him lust, my ceramic china with the dragon.

"Dropsies." Normally, we played shooting games, and the level ground in front of Dr. Kloet's residence was a good enough surface that few bad bounces came into play. That was good for me. Better players prefer to rely on skill instead of luck because, of course, it gives them more control over the outcome.

"We'll each put five in the square," he said. "Don't worry. I'm not too good at Dropsies."

This meant he believed he was world-class, which matched his self-perception and self-deception in all areas. Time and again, he'd told Pietje and me how he'd deserved to be accepted into surgeon school and that the dolts who had left him stranded in the Dutch East Indies were doddering old fools who probably still prescribed leeches.

To play Dropsies, each player scattered five marbles anywhere inside a square. A player's toes could touch a line on the square as he leaned in, but straddling any part of the square wasn't permitted. To win a marble, the shooter would have to hit and knock a marble outside of the square without the shooter escaping too. If successful, the player took another turn, but if a player knocked both his shooter and the target marble out of the square, he would keep both marbles and lose a turn.

"Dropsies," I repeated, thinking through my odds. If Dr. Kloet thought he had a chance of winning, I was probably safe. However, Dropsies took away my key strength, shooting. I wasn't worried that I would lose a winner-take-all game if it came down to my china marble, but I still would have preferred not to risk it.

"I hope he's not chicken," a voice came from over my shoulder. My archenemy. Georgie.

I'd been so focused on a potential game of Dropsies that I hadn't noticed Georgie's approach. I turned my head and saw his habitual smirk.

"Hello," Dr. Kloet said. "I haven't seen you before."

"I'm Georgie Smith." He stuck out his hand and gave Dr. Kloet a firm and proper adult handshake that I could see impressed the doctor. "My mother met you today and told me what a wonderful man you were. She also said you told her that I should come at the end of the day if I wanted to play marbles."

"Ah!" Dr. Kloet said. "You're the American boy. So nice to meet you."

Dr. Kloet said to me, "He and his mother are new arrivals. His mother is very nice. When I met her today, she'd said she heard I liked to play marbles and wondered if Georgie could join us."

I recalled without any effort the final exchange I'd heard between Dr. Eikenboom and Mrs. Smith.

"And Jeremiah, when you hoodwink Dr. Kloet into a marble game this afternoon," Dr. Eikenboom had said, *"ask him to put disinfectant on those scratches. We can't be too careful, you know."*

And Mrs. Smith had responded with a single word. *"Hoodwink?"*

That told me several things. First, that Dr. Eikenboom was far more observant than I'd estimated. Second, that she'd probably shared—in the presence of Georgie—the nice little scam I had going. Third, Georgie had recruited his mother to angle his way into the scam and take advantage of Dr. Kloet or simply find a way to spoil it for me.

Dr. Kloet continued in his oblivious way, for any other adult would have caught the nuance in Georgie's opening remark about whether I was chicken.

"Jeremiah, Mrs. Smith said if we allowed Georgie to play, it might be a nice way for him to make friends because he is so new to camp."

Georgie smiled and offered me a handshake too. "It's very nice to meet you."

Hypocrisy can only go so far. I ignored his hand. "We've met before. Don't try to fool anyone here."

Georgie maintained the smile. "You mean like you've been doing to a doctor who only cares about helping people in this camp?"

I had set my own trap and stepped in it too. Dr. Kloet stopped stroking his beard in self-pleasure and frowned. "Someone's been fooling me?"

"I probably shouldn't say anything more," Georgie said. "That just slipped out of my mouth."

"No," Dr. Kloet said. "Really. Go on."

I could see how it was going to unfold— Georgie about to take my spot at this buffet table, and me with nothing to do to stop it.

"It's not me saying this," Georgie said, "but Dr. Eikenboom."

A well-played move. He had put the blame on someone with impeccable credentials that Dr. Kloet disliked anyway.

"Dr. Eikenboom?"

"She was telling my mother that Jeremiah stops by every day because he gets a free meal to take home to his family. It's all around camp, I suppose, how he loses on purpose until he's almost out of marbles and then goes ahead and wins them all back at will."

The touch about having it all around camp was masterful, especially adding the *I suppose* as an unproven qualifier.

The skin on Dr. Kloet's face grew almost as red as his beard. I could see that he was thinking through all the patterns of our wins and losses. Would any kind of protest erase his suspicion? I doubted it.

"What do you have to say for yourself?" he asked me.

My rage met with bitter revenge and I spat out my words. "I say that I owe Georgie something for breaking my arm."

I remembered how Georgie had secretly spit on my face when Sophie broke up the fight in the goat pasture. I stepped over and punched Georgie square on the nose. He dropped to his knees and howled with his hands over his nose, and it felt great to see blood running through his fingers.

Dr. Kloet was too flabbergasted to say anything. He opened and closed his mouth several times. I didn't care.

"Come on, Pietje," I said. "Let's go."

Pietje kicked dirt on Georgie and then marched away with me.

Because I hadn't won back all my marbles on the upswing cycle with Dr. Kloet, I was leaving behind all my wealth except for my final seven warriors. Good thing there were a lot of new boys in camp to help me replenish my supply.

Twenty-One

Within days of Nakahara's arrival, we realized that our former commander, Shizuka, had been a benevolent dictator in comparison. Each morning, wailing sirens would rouse us for *tenko*—roll call —and families would stumble to the street to line up and bow as he surveyed us from his Jeep. On sunny mornings, he would stand in that pose from the passenger side, his dog beside him. When it rained, he would get out and walk, with one soldier holding an umbrella for him, and another soldier holding an umbrella for the German shepherd.

Ichi. Ni. San. Shi. Go. Roku. Sit. Hat. Ku. Juu.
Each afternoon would end the same way.
Ichi. Ni. San. Shi. Go. Roku. Sit. Hat. Ku. Juu.
Immediately, Nakahara tripled the patrol duties around the bamboo curtain perimeter, and a half-dozen women were caught trading. They received a public beating during *tenko*. When another half-dozen were caught, it became apparent that the attempts would not end, so by the fourth day, he assigned permanent shifts of guards at the corners of the fence and every hundred yards or so down each wall. When one woman died during a beating, Nakahara had

185

touched the blood coming from her face, then had tasted it on his finger and smiled.

Nakahara also began sending guards into houses for surprise inspections. The soldiers upturned suitcases, dug through clothing, and tore up children's toys in an effort to find food, jewelry, and money. Then they seized the items and placed them into supposed storage on behalf of the owners.

Rations at the central kitchen were reduced by a third, bringing us even closer to starvation levels. Cutting rations was an obvious move to ensure rice could go to Japanese soldiers, but it also meant fewer mouths to feed. When women and children died because of malnutrition and a growing inability to fight off infections and disease, the Japanese found it less costly to keep us in the internment camps. The Nazis, we would learn later, set up killing factories, but the Japanese, whether it was an official policy or not, favored death by attrition.

More than ever, our ears would strain to hear the boys who would be sent from the kitchen to call out that food was ready.

"*Broodjes halen van de plaats! Pisang halen van de plaats!*"

Get your bread at the place! Get your banana at the place!

The "place" was the long row of benches that had been set up outside the kitchen after the newcomers had arrived. Women in twos or fours carried vats of prepared food to the benches behind which women and children stood in parallel lines to be served precisely measured portions.

At the kitchen, I'd seen fistfights between women over an extra spoon of rice. That's why I began to watch Mrs. Aafjes closely at her vat. I noticed that she had found a way to give her friends special treatment, and she was doing it openly but in such a way that no one else suspected what was happening.

I kept watch to confirm my suspicions, even as the women carried on conversations in the lines in front of and behind me. All the lines generally advanced one step at a time in unison with the others.

"Corrie Houtkooper wants her hair done," Mrs. Tenhove told my mother, who was standing behind me. Since Dr. Eikenboom had defended my mother, women had begun talking to her again, as if they'd never shunned her. "It's so sad."

This told us that Corrie Houtkooper had given up. She was in the hospital, fighting a cancer in her lungs. While this, at least, was not a death that could be blamed on the Japanese, it was no less difficult to watch. It had taken awhile for me to notice the pattern. When a woman requested that someone help her put on makeup and style her hair, she usually died the next day. Once decided, rarely did any amount of encouragement or begging change that woman's resignation and lack of willpower to fight. She only wanted to look nice when she died.

"At least she doesn't have children," Elsbeth said. She paused and took a deep breath, which she'd been doing all morning. "How horrible to go, wondering who will take care of them."

I had my eyes on Mrs. Aafjes, the one with a ruddy face and a mole on the side of her nose. There. I saw it again. It looked like she had just used the serving spoon to tamp down the rice she'd put into a cup for another woman who shared her house.

"I heard that Nakahara has put out orders for the Dykstra house to be emptied for soldiers to use," said a woman in front of me. Houses were named for the designated leader of each house. Families in each house reported to a spokes-woman, who also listened to any complaints. These spokeswomen in turn reported to a block representative, and the block representatives reported to Commander Nakahara via translator. The Dykstra house was closest to Commander Nakahara's residence. "Nakahara wants to build a walled private garden between the two houses."

"Where will the families go?" the woman across from her asked. "It's already too crowded as it is."

"That's not the worst of it," the first woman said.

"I hear he wants to make the Dykstra residence into a teahouse."

"Teahouse!"

A part of my brain wondered why someone would be so horrified at a teahouse, and the other part was focused on Mrs. Aafjes. There! She'd done it again for the next person in line.

"Teahouse," the first woman confirmed. "And I've also heard that Nakahara does crazy things every full moon."

"Ha! You can't believe all rumors. It's probably not even true about the teahouse. What does he expect? Dutch women to line up to keep his soldiers happy?"

I didn't hear the answer because I'd watched Mrs. Aafjes put rice in a bowl and moved to the front of the line to confront her. I kept my plate behind my back so it would be clear I hadn't moved forward to get food out of turn.

"I see what you are doing," I said to Mrs. Aafjes. "I don't think it's right."

She looked down her nose at me. I hoped she could see me past her monstrous mole. It was a strange time for me to notice a fine hair growing from the center of it.

"You get back in line," she said. She set the bowl down on the table and placed her hands on her hips. "Everybody takes their turn."

"When I get back in line," I said, "I'm going to keep watching you. And after I get my rice, I'm going to stand here and keep watching you. Because I know what you are doing, and it's not fair."

"You are making no sense," she hissed. "Stop your rudeness or your family will get nothing. Go back to your mother."

Sophie, whose face was now showing only faint bruises and no longer needed a sling for her arm, came to the front of the line. "What is happening here?"

I pointed at the woman. "She uses her spoon to press down the rice for people she likes."

It seemed like such a minor accusation, but around me, it became quiet. Food was so precious that it was like accusing her of robbing a bank.

"Ridiculous," Mrs. Aafjes said.

"There is one way to find out." I grabbed the bowl and turned it upside down. The contents held and not a single grain dropped.

Sophie said, "Please take off that apron. I will serve at this position now."

"I will not," Mrs. Aafjes said. She lifted her spoon.

"Are you threatening to hit me?" Sophie asked. "Go ahead. Your actions will condemn you."

Two women moved up beside Sophie. "If you hit her, we will make sure that you go without food for the next week."

Mrs. Aafjes glared. As she untied her apron, cheers and applause came from behind us.

Then it was interrupted.

"Jeremiah!" There was such a piercing quality to my mother's voice that I spun around, half expecting to see soldiers at her side dragging her away.

Instead, she was standing out of the line. Alone. With the dirt between her ankles turning dark from water that coursed down her legs.

Twenty-Two

To no one's surprise, Jasmijn Grace Prins was born with a mop of dark hair and soft amber skin. After watching my mother endure twenty hours of labor, I was not allowed to be involved in the delivery itself, no matter how hard I pushed at the women to let me be near as I heard the screams.

Jasmijn's weight deficiency, Dr. Eikenboom said, could be helped by condensed milk, which would replace the milk that she could not get from my mother, who was recovering slowly from the delivery. Dr. Eikenboom further explained that while fruits and vegetables would help Elsbeth, a baby's digestive system was not capable of dealing with any of the extra rations that my brother and sisters and I would gladly set aside no matter how pinched we were by our own hunger.

Everyone commented on Jasmijn's happy nature. When I held her, her beautiful black eyes steadfastly gazed at me with such apparent wisdom that they seemed to contain all the mysteries of the universe. I felt protective as a magnificent love grew for my little sister. I decided that her health—and perhaps her life—depended on my getting the supplies described by Dr. Eikenboom, so I took one of Elsbeth's sketches from their hiding place and made a list on the back of it. Paper was scarce, but the fear of forgetting something important for Jasmijn drove me. Then I went out to the bush near the small cross that marked Coacoa's grave. I made sure that I was unobserved as I dug out one of the eight bottles of Bols sloe gin I had stolen from my mother. I planned to go through the drainage ditch that only I knew about, but I would go alone, not wanting Pietje as an extra risk.

It took a slow hour to clear the way to the drainage pipe, pulling out the chocks of firewood that I'd used to block a chicken from returning, and checking for soldiers each time to make sure it was clear to crawl beneath the bush that had grown over the entrance. When I crawled beneath the bush again, holding the bottle of gin, it was around three in the afternoon. The parrots and warblers filled the air with cheerful notes meant to disguise their desperate pursuits of food, territorial rights, and mates. I was equally desperate as I crawled into the pipe headfirst, far enough for my shoulders to squeeze inside. The light at the far end may have only been twenty or thirty feet away. I knew an Indonesian might decide to take me back to the Jappenkamp for a reward instead of trading my gin for the supplies I wanted, but I was gambling on greed for the other seven bottles to guarantee I could trade with impunity. I was also gambling that there would be no snakes in the drainage pipe, or that if they were in the pipe, my approach would cause them to flee.

What I had not calculated was the effect of the tube of concrete around my body. I had my arms out in front of me, one hand on the bottle, with plenty of room to wiggle forward. But I couldn't. I began to hyperventilate, rasping in a fear that possessed me like claws of a monster. Sweat ran like thick blood into my eyebrows and dripped onto my cheeks. I wanted to scream in terror but was too frightened to do it only because I thought the sound itself might cause the pipe to collapse on my body and bury me alive.

Somehow I managed to push myself backward, and when I scrambled out from under the bush, all I could do was push my knees to my chest and hold my knees tight with my arms, until all the trembling in my body subsided. The bottle of precious gin was still in the drainage pipe, but the thought of going back in to retrieve it sent my body into more spasms. I knew it was lost to me and to my family. I was a coward, so ashamed that in the evening, when Elsbeth asked me to hold Jasmijn, I refused because I was unworthy of it and asked for Nikki to take my turn.

I could see only one solution. The next morning, in a light rainstorm, I walked a street over and visited Sophie for the second time. Her bruises had completely faded, and the beating had done nothing to diminish her aura of dignity. When I arrived, she was sitting on the porch, beneath an awning. With Laura in a chair beside her. At my approach, Laura stood and walked into the house, a pointed way to ignore me.

"Hello, Mrs. Jansen," I said.

She pointed at the chair that Laura had vacated. "Please sit. But don't expect any conversation unless you call me Sophie. I told you, I am a friend."

The usual noises came from inside the house, sounds of conversation, some crying, occasional clanking of pans. Ten or twelve families lived inside and were sheltering themselves from the rain in the stink of body odors and the mingling of bedbugs and lice. Others also sat under the awning looking for fresh air and relief from the crowding.

"Well," Sophie said, "there have been interesting conversations in this house about you and Georgie. His mother wants to hunt you down for what you did to his nose. And Georgie keeps saying he did nothing to deserve it."

"If he wasn't a sissy," I said, "he'd find me during the day and we could talk about it. But I noticed he gives me plenty of distance."

"I wish I could tell people about your broken arm," Sophie said.

I shook my head otherwise. "I prefer to keep things between me and Georgie."

"But that's not why you are here, right?"

I pulled a folded piece of paper from under my shirt where I had kept it away from the rain. "I wrote down a list of things that Dr. Eikenboom says my baby sister needs."

I caught Sophie's glance at the pencil sketch on the paper as I had unfolded it. This was one of a train, smoke flattening behind it, looking as if it were going to rumble off the paper and onto her lap. She made no comment about the sketch but gave her attention to the supplies.

"Jeremiah," she said, "it looks like many of these things can't be found inside the camp."

I nodded, then said, "I would like to ask a question, but it is only a make-believe question because, of course, a boy like me would not have a bottle of Bols gin. But if somehow I could get such a bottle, would you help me with the trading for it for things we *can* find in the camp? Condensed milk. Soap. I don't think it would do me any good to be caught with the gin, and since you are new to camp, others might believe it actually got here with you."

This time, when she tried to hide her smile, I could see the slight curving of her lips, as most of the swelling of her face was gone.

"I suspect that you would be able to get Bols gin, and I suspect that some of the mothers here would break another woman's bones for that gin. So perhaps, yes, some of the items on the list might be found within the camp. But not all— keep that in mind."

"Thank you," I said. "If somehow I manage to find a bottle, I will be back in the afternoon. And it will always be our secret, right?"

"Of course."

I rose.

"Would you mind waiting for a moment as I go inside?" she asked.

I nodded and sat back down.

Sophie limped into the house, taking my list with her. I had assumed she was going to make some immediate inquiries, so I was surprised when Laura returned in Sophie's place, holding the sheet of paper with my list.

"I suppose," I said, before I could stop myself, "you were told I would be found on the porch."

"No," she answered. "I was told you wrote this list."

She gave it to me and I took it. Up and down the porch, women in their own chairs were sitting out the drizzle, involved in their own conversations or simply just staring at the gray.

Laura had another piece of paper. This one, too, was folded. She opened it and stared at whatever was written on it. Then she folded it backward in such a way that I could see only the top third, which was the beginning of a letter, dated in February of 1942. Just before the Dutch capitula-tion.

"Read this," she said. "Not out loud. I don't want anyone else to hear."

I shrugged, not sure, of course, for the reason for the request.

It began with these words. *Dear Laura, you are very beautiful. Someday when there are no parents around, I would like it if we could find a private spot. There is a game called doctor and nurse, and . . .*

I gasped at what followed. Then became outraged and barely coherent.

"This . . . this . . . is . . . horrible."

"It gets worse," she said. "That's why I kept it folded, so you wouldn't read the rest of it."

"Who . . . Who . . . ?"

She took the letter from me, then folded it so that I could only peek at the bottom. Where my name was clearly written: Jeremiah Prins.

"I didn't—"

"This letter made me feel filthy," she said. "I was so ashamed that I cried for days. I didn't dare show it to anyone because they might think that I said something to encourage you to write this. And I didn't throw it away because I wanted someday to show it to you and make you eat this piece of paper and beg for forgiveness."

"I didn't—"

"Oma doesn't know what was in the letter, and although she has asked many times, I've never told her. And I always kept it hidden from her." She doubled the folds of the paper so that it compressed into a small square that fit into the palm of her hand.

"All she knew was that after I opened the envelope you had mailed, I was miserable. A few days ago, she told me to ask you to tell me what you had written. I refused. Why would I want to hear this again?" she asked, briefly opening her palm where I could see a glimpse of the paper.

Laura continued. "Except just now when she found me inside, she asked me if the writing of this letter looked like your writing on the list. It doesn't. That means someone else wrote the mean and nasty letter."

She took a deep breath. "What was in the letter you sent me?"

My mind was reeling from the contents of the letter in her palm, especially my forged name at the end. I wanted to be acquitted. "I am embarrassed to tell you. It was easier to send than to think I might have to say it in front of you."

She lifted her hand again and opened her fingers so that the paper was clearly visible. "Would you rather I believed you mailed this, even if the writing looks different than yours?"

Without hesitation, I began. "Memories drift like leaves, blown by winds gentle before a gale heaves."

I was not going to repeat the next line of my sonnet. Not to her. *Tears grace my cheeks, burning of love unspoken and deeply yearning.*

I stopped, but the next lines were spoken. By her.

"Tears grace my cheeks," she whispered, "burning of love unspoken and deeply yearning."

I was beyond comprehending. "Did Sophie repeat that to you? She made me tell her what I'd written. Did she pass it on to you?"

Laura shook her head. Her face flushed.

"Someone else told me," she said, and I saw her fists ball into knots.

"But nobody in the world knew I wrote it," I protested. Then it dawned on me. "Someone took my sonnet out of the envelope and put in that nasty letter and sealed it so it looked like that's what I mailed you! Someone stole my sonnet and—"

I stopped. Even though I didn't fully believe it, all I could think of was that one of my half brothers had done it in another attempt to torture me.

"And that someone gave the sonnet to me as if it were his," she said. "Our families shared the same post office, you know. He often delivered our letters to our home if he and his mother went to the post office first. I am sure now that he thought that once we were on the ship and away from the island, he would never be found out for taking your letter out and putting in another."

Laura's barely contained rage was frightening. She stood.

I stood.

"No," she said. "You stay here."

A grown man would have been a fool to defy her. I stayed.

She marched into the house, her back ramrod straight, while I tried to comprehend. *Someone had put in a letter to make me look bad and had taken my sonnet and pretended it was his. And that someone had pulled out my return envelope and mailed it to me empty.* His name entered my thoughts at the same moment I heard the thud.

Georgie.

I heard a responding scream of outrage to the thud, followed by high-pitched wailing that preceded Laura's return to the porch by only a few moments.

Now she stood at my side, her arms crossed, ignoring the curious glances from those up and down the porch. The wailing inside the house continued.

"My oma was right about what it does to a boy if you kick him between the legs," she said. "And I don't care how many spankings I get. That was worth it."

Twenty-Three

I was glad that there was no gin for Elsbeth to worsen the monthly mood swings that Pietje, Aniek, Nikki, and I had faced before the Jappenkamp, swings as predictable as a pendulum. Still, the first full moon of Nakahara's command showed it possessed him to a far greater degree than it did her.

Howling drew families to their windows. Those in houses closest to his clearly saw Nakahara outlined against the rising moon, standing on a thick branch of a tree in the center of his garden and clawing at the moon as if trying to pull it down from the sky. Many of the women prayed that he would fall from the branch, but God did not answer those prayers in the way they asked.

The next morning, Nakahara—his normal foul mood worsened no doubt by a hangover—called the block representatives together and declared, through a translator, that Japanese camp commanders were the head of a single military unit and could deal with prisoners as they pleased. No higher authorities would oversee the commanders' actions. Then he explained that he wanted the block representatives to choose a dozen dark-haired Dutch girls between the ages of sixteen and twenty for the privilege of serving teahouse duties in the Dykstra residence.

It was a morning I didn't have kitchen duty, so I learned about the teahouse from Laura, who'd learned about it from Sophie.

"A bad thing happened this morning," Laura said. She explained Nakahara's demand involving young women selected for his teahouse.

"What is bad about serving tea?" I asked. "Especially if Nakahara is promising they will be fed well."

"Oma told me that the soldiers will expect the girls to be like wives to them."

When I didn't respond, she added, "Like in Georgie's letter."

I stilled. "That's . . . that's . . ." Again, I was at a loss for words, because in my naiveté, those things were not only utterly senseless but went well past a basic invasion of privacy and vastly overshadowed the humility of living in such close proximity at the Jappenkamp.

"Oma said all the women have to stand up for the sake of those girls. All the mothers, not just the mothers of the girls. Someone said that Nakahara might begin killing mothers who don't obey him, and Oma said then that Nakahara could begin with her."

I detected the fear in Laura's voice.

Pietje must have sensed it too, for he put his head against my side. He said, "I don't want him to kill Moeder."

"I won't let it happen," I told Pietje. "Nobody is going to kill her. I promise."

Those were words that would torture me later.

A single tear rolled over the dirt on the left side of Pietje's face, and he squeezed me as a thank-you.

"I don't want it to happen to my oma either," Laura said. "But she looks like she is ready to make it happen."

I couldn't think of any way to console her that wouldn't sound like a falsehood. The reality that we understood as children was that Nakahara was far worse than a vicious headmaster who could and would do as he pleased. So I chose a different subject to distract Laura from her fears.

Construction.

By then, Nakahara had begun building the walls that would connect his residence and the former Dykstra house. Inside the walls would be his private garden. It was a simple design, ensuring that access to the enclosed space between the houses came only from the rear doors of either house.

The walls were built of concrete blocks, mortared in place by his Japanese soldiers. The work had gone slowly because Nakahara refused to hire

Indonesians who knew the craft, and the soldiers were learning by trial and error how to mix cement and sand and water and stone so that it would set properly.

But, the world over, children usually gather to watch construction projects. Especially when there is nothing else to do.

"Look at the walls," I said to Laura, pointing at the soldiers who were at work. "I bet a person could climb them."

As sloppy workmen, the soldiers failed in many places to scrape the mortar away from the blocks. The curled slop provided footholds and handholds that would have made climbing a fun challenge for any boy.

"How would a person get over the top?" Laura asked.

Jagged broken glass jutted upright from mortar that had been set on the top blocks.

"Sneak at night and break them," I said. "Just in one place where it might not be noticed."

"Soldiers would hear you," she answered. "Anyone caught after curfew will be beaten."

"What is Nakahara going to do behind the walls?" Pietje asked.

"Nobody knows," Laura said. She shuddered.

"Hey," I said, as an idea occurred to me, one to take her mind off the teahouse girls, "we should make sure we can always know. Let's poke some holes."

I explained my idea. If the soldiers had been experienced in masonry, my idea would have been as ludicrous as it sounded. But they weren't.

During my architecture courses long after the Jappenkamp, I would learn that, after water, cement is the most used human product on earth, dating back to well before Roman times. Cement and water and sand and stone produce concrete. Aside from reinforcement with rods of steel, two important factors make the difference between a finished product that is one of the strongest structures engineered, or something that appears strong but will crumble under pressure.

The first factor is the correct ratio between cement—a binder that sets and hardens because of a chemical reaction with water—and the water and sand and stone. The second factor is how evenly these components are mixed. A rotating barrel will do a much better job than humans with shovels, especially if these humans are soldiers far from home and resentful of their job.

I did not know all of this when Laura and Pietje and I were watching so many years ago, but we did know that the concrete was watery because we watched it ooze from between the blocks. Cement is the expensive portion of the mix, and diluting it meant that less was used, something that I'm sure Nakahara encouraged. This also meant the concrete wouldn't set as quickly as it should have, something I also didn't know then but proved to be a lucky accident.

"Laura," I said, "do you think you can run to the kitchen and borrow one of the wooden spoons the women use to stir rice?"

I envisioned the long handles, just the perfect diameter for my plan.

"They won't just give it to me," she said.

"Then borrow it. What's the worst they will do?"

"Tell my oma."

"And then we will tell your oma why we wanted it. Do you think she'll like the reason?"

"She won't like that we are taking chances at getting caught."

"It will look like only a marble game. I promise."

Laura thought about this. She was, I was learning, not an easy girl to push around.

"Wait here," she said.

I had full confidence she would find a way to steal—borrow—a wooden spoon. She was back within minutes.

"We will wait until they stop work for lunch," I said. "Then you watch. Pietje and I will do the rest."

"Don't make me angry with you," she answered. "I'm not a servant girl. Treat me as you would any other boy."

Treating her as a boy would be a good rule until Holland, after the war, when for obvious reasons, I would hold her as a woman.

I remembered her straight back as she'd marched into the house to confront Georgie. I remembered that she had not told a single adult why she had kicked him without warning because that would have revealed the shame of the letter, and I remembered how she had accepted the necessary spanking from her oma without complaint. Together, Laura and Sophie served as the first and best lessons I had in realizing that not only are both sexes equal, but it verges on idiocy to make any other point about it except quickly dismissing any suggestion of inequality.

I grinned. "Like a boy? If you are going to play marbles, it will be for keepsies then."

"I don't have any marbles," she said.

"I will lend them to you. After you lose them, I will lend you more."

"After I *lose* them? We will see about that."

I grinned again, almost forgetting our purpose of sabotage against Commander Nakahara.

I had a sudden inspiration.

"Hey, everyone," I said. "Laura thinks she is going to beat me in marbles!"

That drew the attention of the surrounding children, about a dozen or so.

"What are you doing?" she hissed.

"The more children that watch, the safer we will be."

She kicked my shin. Hard enough to hurt.

"What?" I said. "It's a good idea."

"Next time," she said, "you discuss the idea with me first."

"Yes," I said. She saw enough humbleness in my eyes to relax, but I made a note of how quickly she could lose her temper.

Boys and girls drifted toward us. When they were gathered, I explained that Laura and I were going to play Off-the-Wall. It was a simple game. You mark off a line about five feet from a wall. The first player throws a marble at the wall to serve as a target. To win that marble, the second player needs to bounce the shooter marble off the wall before hitting the target marble. We decided that the first one to hit five marbles would be declared the winner.

As a plan, it was more successful than I had hoped. The soldiers went for a break, and all of us drifted over to the wall. I chose a spot down from the wheelbarrow, far enough away from where the next blocks would be mortared so that any discrepancies would be invisible.

As Laura and I took turns, with the children cheering us on and full attention on the game, Pietje wandered farther down the wall and in various places, with a quick look to ensure it was safe each time, pulled the spoon out from his shirt and used the handle to poke a hole between the blocks where the weakened mortar was still setting. In some places he set the holes lower, and in others, he reached above his head. He was sneaky and did it with a smile.

We intended to daub those holes with mud that we could remove and replace anytime in the future, but the second part of the plan failed partly because the marble game was so successful at drawing everyone's attention that no one noticed that Nakahara had turned the corner. With his dog.

"*Kiotske!*" one of the boys behind us finally shouted, but too late.

Such was our conditioning to the phrase that my first reaction was to stand straight, arms at my side, before registering that the approaching Japanese man was Nakahara himself, wearing black aviator glasses, with his dog at his side. As I was coming to attention, I gulped down a shriek. There were over a dozen of us, all literally frozen with that shared fear, rigid in the hot sun.

My fear was greater than the others', however. If Nakahara noticed anything wrong with his wall, he'd be sure to wonder why. And if that led him to the spoon hidden beneath Pietje's shirt, a spoon with bits of wet concrete clinging to the handle, the conclusion would be obvious.

I decided to draw attention to me.

"*Kirih!*" I shouted.

Half of the children began to bow, but the other half—those who understood the Indonesian language—looked at me in confusion. I had just shouted out the Indonesian word for dog, a word similar to the Japanese command to bow, *kere*. I'd nearly made the mistake many times before, only because *kirih* came to mind so often when I saw the soldiers that I'd been tempted to shout it out as an insult.

"*Kirih?*" Nakahara screamed in guttural rage. "*Kirih?*"

So he did understand. He put his hand on his sword.

I moaned and pointed at the German shepherd, saying "*kirih*" two more times, making it clear I was in terror at my mistake. That took little acting.

I bowed now. "*Kere, kere.*"

I straightened and pointed again at the dog. "*Kirih. Takut! Takut!*"

Takut. The Indonesian word for fear.

For a tipping point of about a second, my fate hung on whether Nakahara would first understand that I was trying to tell him that the fear of the dog had made me mix up my words, and second, if he did, on how he would react. But at least it was my fate in the balance, not Pietje's, for Nakahara's entire focus was on me—not Pietje or the wall behind us.

I wondered if he would motion for the dog to attack. The tipping fell in my favor. The time of the full moon had made him crazy, for Nakahara began to laugh like a maniac and even slapped my back in glee.

Some of the children began to laugh with him, but he cut them off by screaming, and when their eyes widened with fear, he lifted his hands and said, "Boo!" When they jumped back, he burst into more maniacal laughter.

He was still laughing as he walked away from us, and because he forgot to shoo us away from the wall, I made sure from that day on to play marbles there as frequently as possible. That would make it all the more natural, I knew, for the times we wanted to peek through the holes in the concrete.

Twenty-Four

Jasmijn worsened, despite the condensed milk and other supplies we had found for her, and after examining her at the hospital, Dr. Eikenboom gave her pronouncement to me and Elsbeth.

"All the symptoms lead me to believe that Jasmijn has developed diabetic ketoacidosis," Dr. Eikenboom said. "This happens when a baby has so little insulin that the calories from milk can't be used for energy, and the body starts to burn fat. It makes the blood acidic, and as she burns up her fat reserves, it leads to all the other difficulties."

I was holding Jasmijn, as Elsbeth seemed to be giving up the fight and the hope. My tiny sister had been vomiting constantly, and any touch on her abdomen led to sharp cries of pain. She didn't seem alert—her black eyes were a dull gray and failed to watch me with any intensity as I held her. When she breathed, it was a deep sighing respiration that was so unnatural, I had to fight tears as I listened to it.

"Then there is nothing we can do," Elsbeth said, settling deeper into her depression.

"Not without insulin," Dr. Eikenboom said. "And with the camp up in arms and ready to revolt against Nakahara because of the deadline he has given for us to choose the teahouse girls, I can't see any way he would let us go outside of camp and purchase some."

"There is insulin outside?" I asked. I kissed Jasmijn's hot forehead and she stirred slightly in my arms.

"If you find the right person," she answered. "And you have something worth trading."

Sophie had already done trading for me, but not for insulin. Beneath the bush at the drainage pipe were four remaining bottles of Bols sloe gin, and a fifth partway down the pipe were I brave enough to retrieve it.

"If we find the insulin, will it save her?"

Dr. Eikenboom nodded. "I don't want to give you false hope because there is no way to get insulin, but the answer, if this were a normal situation, is yes."

Right then, I told myself I would find the courage to crawl through the pipe.

But I was wrong. That afternoon, when I snuck toward the bush, I wasn't even given a chance. Guards had been doubled along the fence. Then, after curfew, when I returned in darkness, no matter how hard I tried to push myself into the pipe, I could not do it. I loathed myself. And worse, the next morning, I had no choice but to admit it to Sophie.

"I've heard from Dr. Eikenboom about Jasmijn," Sophie said when Pietje and I stopped by the house to see Laura. "We've been praying for you."

"Pray instead for insulin," I said. "And pray that I won't be such a coward."

She knelt and put an arm around my shoulder, and I couldn't help but break down and tell her of the drainage ditch and my fear. As I explained the situation, I didn't even notice that Laura was listening. But when our trio walked away from the house, she looked over her shoulder to make sure that we were out of earshot of Sophie and said two simple words.

"I'll go."

"No," I said. "You're a girl. It would be too dangerous."

"I can do anything a boy can do."

"That's not what I meant. The Indonesians on the other side. It would be dangerous for you

213

to wander the streets at night. If they see that you are a girl, it will be very bad."

Laura spun and ran back to the house, leaving me speechless. Pietje and I looked at each other in mutual puzzlement over how I could have possibly insulted her enough to make her that mad. The mystery was explained when she returned fifteen minutes later with short-cropped hair.

"Huh?" I said.

"It was getting to be a bother," she answered. "I didn't like my hair anyway. Now if there is mud on my face, people will think I'm a boy."

"You can't do it," I said. "Sophie won't let you."

"Does Elsbeth know when you sneak places? Did she know you were going to go through the pipe to outside?"

I didn't answer. It would incriminate me and prove Laura right. But, of course, so did my silence.

"We are not going to let Jasmijn die," she said. "I've already cut my hair. If you don't help me, I'll find a way to do it by myself."

She put her hands on her hips. "So. What's your decision?"

A Dutchman can be stubborn, but even he knows he will not prevail against a female of his nation.

Twenty-Five

It was a couple of days past full moon, but the natural light of the waning moon was sufficient illumination for escaping notice of the guards. I hid under the bush as Laura crawled into the concrete pipe toward the bottle of Bols sloe gin I had left behind, and the hope that somehow, on the other side, she could trade it for insulin that would save my sister.

She had bravely wriggled into the darkness, wearing pants into which she had tucked a rock to use for communication. I held a similar rock.

It took only a few minutes. From my side of the drainage pipe, I heard two quick raps of stone echo against concrete, the signal that she had made it to the other side. I, in turn, was to signal twice to let her know that I'd heard, but before I could do so, I heard a brief scream roil toward me through the pipe.

I froze, then whispered, "Laura?" We were past curfew. I could not be loud. "Laura?"

She did not answer. She was supposed to rap three times if she encountered trouble, but she'd rapped only twice upon making it through. I rapped my rock against the concrete three times.

"Laura!" I hissed.

I peered into the drainage pipe, hoping for some kind of miracle of vision.

"Laura!"

In daylight, I could see bushes silhouetted against the opening at the other end, but now in the darkness, I could see nothing. And I could not shake the terror I'd heard in that brief scream. I squirmed into the tunnel, carrying the rock in my hand. I was overwhelmed by panic and every cell in my body revolted. For a moment, I was so terrified that I was unable to move.

"Laura!" Now I was pleading. I moved a few body lengths into the pipe so that I had no choice but to move forward. I squirmed and slid, fighting a sensation of drowning. *Forward! Forward!* My knees scraped against the rough concrete but I didn't notice.

Finally, my hand felt the scratch of bushes. I flailed through the end of the pipe, landing on my stomach in soft dirt, then rolled over and sucked in a gulp of air. As I scrambled to my knees, I began to call out her name, but then my eyes locked on a nightmare before me. My throat closed. I couldn't even whisper.

Pythons don't hunt. They ambush. Some, like the reticulated python, ambush from trees near a water supply. The geometric patterns of their scales make them near impossible to see among the branches and leaves.

In the light of day, I would later learn that this

drainage pipe directed water that collected in a low spot of the Jappenkamp down a hillside to the other side of the fence. There, it was held in a pond that fed a banyan tree near the bank. Although I was aware that a venomous snake like a cobra could be a danger if it was resting in the cool shade of the pipe, it had not occurred to me to give any thought to the banyan on the other side of the fence, that I could see from inside the Jappenkamp.

Pythons of staggeringly large size lived in the Dutch East Indies, but they stayed invisible. The Burmese python used water to hide and was able to submerge a body up to twenty-five feet long, leaving only eyes and nostrils above the surface. While it was rare that a python would enter a hut in pursuit of a child, it had happened. Much less rare were ambushes from trees by reticulated pythons. We would discover later that in the town outside our Jappenkamp, two Indonesian children in the previous year had disappeared. While the Indonesians had been unable to find it, they sus-pected a massive python somewhere was respon-sible, for the snakes are capable of taking down small deer.

It had been three months since the last child outside our fence had vanished.

In the moonlight, I stared at a tableau of horror, the figures set in a Dante's Eden painted by a madman, the girl child and snake in a bizarre embrace of death.

All I could see of Laura was the pale of her upper face and the shine of the moon reflected in her terror-stricken eyes. A coil of the python draped her lower face. Had she not instinctively ducked her head and pinned her chin to her upper chest, that coil would have already crushed the bones of her throat. The snake had struck by grasping the top of her head in its backward-pointing teeth. It had rolled the upper third of its body into a ball around the rest of her, pinning her arms against her body. She was on her knees, legs braced apart to keep her from falling, and the lower coils of the snake were tightening and curling toward her in preparation of dragging her sideways, then down to the ground.

I had a rock in my hand. Almost as a reflex, I smacked the python's head, hoping to dislodge it or distract it, but that only created a dull thud and made no impact on the snake. How could I smash the python's skull without hurting Laura? What if one of my blows missed the snake?

I ran behind and grabbed the python's neck, just below its head. It was so massive, even at the thinnest point I couldn't fully get both hands around it and, even so, didn't have the strength to strangle it. The python wasn't crushing her, but with each breath that she exhaled, it squeezed tighter, making it impossible for her to get more air into her lungs.

When the cold rage began to build, I shoved

aside my panic. I jammed my fingers into its upper jaw line, searching for leverage. The pliable flap of skin that could stretch wide enough to allow it to swallow an adult goat easily gave way, but I could not fit my fingers between its jaw and the top of Laura's skull.

I felt my foot hit something hard, and registered that it was the bottle of gin that Laura had dropped when the python struck.

I grasped the neck of the bottle and raised it, ready to swing down like an ax. I saw the terrible risk of missing the python's skull and hitting Laura, or of the bottle sliding off the python's skull and directly into hers. But what choice did I have?

Then I remembered the burning taste of the gin on the day my father had given me a sip and I'd run to spit it into the sink.

I gave a shove against the coils, and as Laura fell, I tried to scrape the seal off the top of the bottle, tearing my thumbnail in the process. I ripped at it with my teeth and finally managed to pull away a strip so that I felt the top of the cork. But the cork was too tight to remove.

With each new constriction, the snake sucked her life's breath. My rage intensified, giving me clarity. A coil of the snake brushed against my ankle, and I stepped over it to find the rock that I'd dropped. It took two hard blows to snap the top portion of the glass neck. Then the sharp sting of alcohol hit my nostrils.

The python held its grip on Laura's head, and with her now on her side, the python's throat was in a position where I could pour the gin inside. I peeled away the skin that covered its jaw line, tipped the bottle of gin sideways, and poured the liquid against her skull so that the alcohol could find its way into the python's mouth.

Electricity could not have jolted the snake into a faster reaction. The head snapped backward and a rasp seemed to come from somewhere deep in the snake, a rasp of the same rage that I felt. Just as its jaws released Laura's skull, that massive head struck my left arm, and I felt searing blades bite into my flesh.

Had it struck my right arm, it might have jolted loose the bottle. But I was able to tip the bottle and jam the broken neck into the snake's mouth, ripping my own skin against the jagged glass. Gin poured freely into the snake, and as it lessened the grip on my left arm, I grabbed the snake below the neck. With my right hand, I shoved the bottle down as deep as it would go and tilted the remainder of gin down its throat. By then, the coils had slipped from Laura, and she had rolled clear of the snake.

The burning of the alcohol must have put the snake into a panic. With a deceptively fast rolling of those massive coils, it reached the banyan tree and began to climb up into the shadows.

I felt something touch my arm and I flinched.

It was Laura. She was trying to speak. She stared at me as she drew sob after sob into her lungs and shook so hard she was going to fall. I pulled her against me and we clung together, shaking, until finally, when she could make noise, she wept.

That's how we were found—a minute later or a half an hour later, I couldn't guess—by an Indonesian teenage boy, who spoke with difficulty.

The words he forced out were accompanied by a high-pitched nasal grunting.

"What is going on here?" he asked.

Laura let go and took a step sideways. I became aware that blood was running down my arm. Laura's hair was stained too, from my tears as I held her and from the blood that seeped from dozens of puncture marks where the snake had held her in its jaws. We both needed disinfectant badly.

"Two boys?" he said. "What is this? Holding each other?"

There was enough moonlight to make Laura and me distinguishable, but I hoped it was still dim enough to conceal the paleness of our skin and our Dutch features. My hopes were dashed immediately. Bright light hit our eyes from the flare of a match as he lit a candle.

"You are Dutch!" he said, holding the candle toward us and as far away from his face as possible. In the brief flicker of light, however, I'd seen a glimpse of his face and understood why he sounded the way he did. His face was deformed by an upper lip and palate that were completely cleft. It seemed to form a fissure between his upper lip that cruelly twisted all the way to his nostrils, revealing gums that formed a V and teeth that pointed horizontally.

"From the camp!" It came out as a near squeal in raised nasal tones. "How did you get here?"

Vegetation obscured this side of the drainage pipe, so I wasn't going to tell him. Not yet.

"Not so loud," I answered. Enough light reflected off his skin that I could see his upper body was bare, but this was not unusual when fabric was so scarce for the Indonesians. He was about six inches taller than I was, but his shoulders were hunched in what looked like a perpetual cower. It was cruel, but instinct told me that I could use that to my advantage.

"Please, blow out the light," I said. If I did it, we would be opponents. If he did it, that would be the first step toward becoming allies. "It will be worth it for you, I promise."

A second later, it was dark again. He whispered with suspicion, "How?"

"Python," I said.

"Python! How big?"

"Big enough to kill a human."

"The elders have been hunting that snake for months," he said. "Where is it?"

There was a heavy thump behind us. We all turned. The bottom half of the python had fallen from the tree. The gin, Dr. Eikenboom would decide later for me, had worked with spectacular swiftness. The snake had been hungry enough to feed, and on an empty stomach, the alcohol would have spread quickly through its body.

The boy groaned and stepped back, as if the snake would give chase.

The remainder of the python's body fell.

I walked to the banyan and grabbed the snake by the tail. I tried to drag it toward the Indonesian, but it was too heavy.

"What's your name?" I asked.

"Adi."

I would discover later he preferred to walk the streets of his town at dusk and evening, when anyone he passed had difficulty seeing his deformity. That he spent most daylight hours inside the family hut while his parents worked as laborers, an only child who preferred solitude to mockery and trusted only a handful of people with a full view of his face.

"Adi," I said, "imagine how much meat and skin will come from this snake. If you are smart, you could help us do some trading for it."

Twenty-Six

The next morning, my arm had already started to swell at the puncture marks where the python had clamped onto my arm. After the wailing siren for *tenko*, I took a place in line at the crowded hospital tent. Two boys, Pietje's age, were trying to console their mother, who was hunched over in agony and clutching her stomach, and an elderly woman kept trying to pull her blouse away from her body so that the fabric wouldn't touch her skin. We all understood why, as the rash of dengue was obvious on her shoulders and upper arms. Her expression was stoic, however, as she bore the muscle aches of what we called break-bone fever. When all of her pain passed in the next week or two, she at least would be immune to further attacks. This couldn't be said for the unlucky ones who shivered with malaria.

There was no question that I needed medical attention or that I needed to line up for Dr. Eikenboom. I waited an hour for my turn at her table. My arm was throbbing, and I rested it on the table so she could examine it. Blood seeped from the deepest gash of the broken bottle.

"Aside from these cuts, those marks are in a peculiar pattern," Dr. Eikenboom said as she examined the series of dots in a U shape on the top and bottom of my arm. It didn't take much imagination to see that it was an animal bite.

"I don't want it known," I said. "But Nakahara caught me at his wall again, and as punishment, he ordered his dog to bite me."

Dr. Eikenboom let out a deep sigh. "You are not the first patient to lie to a doctor, Jeremiah. But that doesn't make it acceptable either."

She called for Dr. Kloet. He saw that it was me at her table and gave a slow shake of his head.

"Frederick!" she said in a raised voice. "Do not ignore me."

Enough patients in line heard her that it made it embarrassing for Dr. Kloet to submit to her sharp tone. In my mind, he walked over as if he were wearing a skirt.

"Remember the girl you asked me to check earlier?" she asked him. "The dozens of marks on her skull that you treated with iodine?"

With Laura's hair cut short, I'd also had a chance to look while combing aside her hair with my fingers as if looking for lice. Many of the small punctures showed the first signs of infection, so there had been no choice except to send her to Dr. Kloet.

"Of course," he said. Irritated.

"That was a rhetorical question," she told him. "I wanted you to compare those marks to this."

She ran her fingers lightly over the bite marks,

ignoring the deeper gash where I had slashed my arm with the broken bottle neck.

"Similar," he said. "Satisfied?"

He did not look at me.

"Dr. Kloet," I said, "just so you know, Georgie lied to you. It was my secret. Nobody at camp was talking about our marble games."

That was the only part that bothered me. I deserved the shunning by Dr. Kloet, for I had played marbles for no other reason than food. He didn't deserve to believe that the camp had been laughing about it behind his back.

"Except for Dr. Eikenboom, apparently," he said. "Besides, can you expect me to believe anything you say? Georgie, I have learned, is not the type of boy to punch another boy without warning. He is just like I was as a boy. Sensitive and brilliant. And misunderstood."

Dr. Kloet stomped back to his table.

Dr. Eikenboom gave me a thoughtful gaze. "I've noticed he's been particularly unhelpful to me lately. Can you explain what that was about?"

"Georgie told him that you told his mother I was hoodwinking him at marbles. So I punched Georgie." Then I continued, almost to myself, "Less for that than for something else."

Dr. Eikenboom's gaze remained thoughtful. Then she said, "I'm sorry for that, Jeremiah. I thought my funny little story to her was harmless, but in this camp, I need to learn better that tongues will wag. Will you forgive me?"

I stared at her for a moment, unfamiliar with the wonderful feeling of an adult actually owning up to a wrongdoing, much less offering me an apology for it. I nodded.

Dr. Eikenboom unwrapped the dirty cloth around the tip of my finger. She inspected where I had torn the nail loose in my frantic attempt to take the seal off the bottle of gin.

"And this?" she asked.

I hesitated.

"Don't bother thinking of an excuse," she said.

She leaned forward. "Jeremiah, if I were a detective, I would suggest the puncture marks on your arm came from the bite of a large snake. I would also suggest that a blond girl with short hair had the same bite on her head. I would have expected that Laura would come to me for medical help, but instead she chose the other line. Almost as if the both of you didn't want the same doctor comparing the wounds."

She took out a curved needle and some black nylon thread. She coiled the thread in an open dish of disinfectant to let it soak. She paused, holding the needle above the dish.

"And if I were a detective," she said, "I would do some deducing, like Sherlock Holmes. I would first suggest that a snake big enough to leave bite marks of this size does not exist in the walls of this camp. Otherwise, I would have heard about it by now. We are far too crowded for a predator like that to move about unseen, and the soldiers would have taken great pleasure in shooting it and cooking it."

This was true. It was no secret that the soldiers were facing their own shortages. Snake meat would have been a tremendous luxury.

"There is something else strange," Dr. Eikenboom said. One of the drivers who delivers the rice said he heard about an Indonesian boy who found a python last evening, just on the other side of the fence. He said that somehow the boy had managed to kill it and made a good trade for the skin and meat. He said he heard it was twenty feet long and hundreds of pounds."

"An Indonesian boy," I echoed with relief. So Adi had lived up to our bargain. After claiming the snake and showing him the bite marks that proved Laura and I deserved our bounty, I'd promised him that tonight I could deliver excellent gin as a commodity for trade. But, I'd said, if word got around town that it came from a Dutch boy, the Japanese commander would turn the camp upside down to find out who that Dutch boy was and seize the gin.

"That boy must have been very brave," she said. "It's a good thing the python didn't kill him. Or at the least, give him trouble. Because if it did, you would expect to see the same kind of bite marks on him that you seem to have."

I maintained an innocent expression. I believed I was very good at that.

"An Indonesian boy," I said. "It couldn't have been anyone else but an Indonesian boy. Otherwise the commander would hear about it from the delivery drivers, wouldn't you say?"

"Aaah," she said. "That's true. Unless somehow some very smart Dutch children found a way to stain their hands and faces with a dye made from the juice of a betel nut."

It was my turn to give her a thoughtful gaze. That was an excellent idea, and I stored it, thinking that someday it might come in helpful. But why was she suggesting it to me?

She dipped the same needle in disinfectant.

"You know I have to stitch the deep cut beside the bite mark, right?"

"Yes, doctor," I said.

"Some children cry or pull away," she said. She handed me a small wooden dowel. She didn't have to explain why. "But that's not a worry with you."

She threaded the needle, and I put the dowel crossways in my mouth. Not much of a painkiller, but it was the best available. Morphine was saved for more severe pain than a minor thing like stitching a wound.

I bit the dowel hard between my teeth, and with sure and steady movements, she sewed the gash in my arm. I breathed so hard through my nose that my jaw muscles began to ache. I wanted to cry, but she had predicted that I wouldn't. I wanted to live up to her expectation.

When she was finished tying off the final knot, she dabbed iodine on the punctures and pulled out a container of sulfa tablets.

"Perhaps you should save that for others," I said.

"We are so short on supply that it almost doesn't matter," she said. "Any day now, what we have will be gone. Nakahara doesn't care. He wants more of us to die so there will be fewer to feed. And that is the bigger worry."

She patted my good arm. "If you hear of anyone who has somehow found a way to sneak out of the camp at night, will you let me know? If that person would be willing to help trade for medical supplies, it could save many lives. There is money in this camp, you know, money that Nakahara hasn't found. I think I could convince the block representatives to find some of that money to purchase more sulfa and other necessary things."

She looked away to count out the sulfa tablets, then back at me.

"Naturally," she said, "I would be very worried that the person might get caught, but if it was a smart boy, he probably knows how to stay safe. And, so far, the Japanese have not yet started executing children. Normally, I'd hate for that smart boy to take a risk like that, but I see no other choice. Of course, this arrangement would remain between me and that boy."

"Of course," I said.

"Well then." She stood. "Is that it?"

I stood too. I pointed at my knees where I had scraped them along the inside of the drainage pipe. "Do you have some disinfectant for this? Any boy smart enough to get out of camp to help a doctor better be smart enough not to get blood poisoning."

"Of course," she said. Her smile was all I needed.

"At the end of the day," I said, "perhaps Pietje and I could come back and talk about this with you?"

She nodded agreement.

"And perhaps," I said, "you might be able to bring along some cheese or sweets? Dr. Kloet always did when we met with him."

"I have none," she said.

I'd expected that answer, but it was still worth a try.

Twenty-Seven

With Dr. Eikenboom's help and using Adi as an intermediary, trading with the world outside the Jappenkamp held little risk. We managed to do it without breaking curfew, and that saved trying to consistently sneak out at night where dozens of families could observe us and ask questions.

Without Laura's involvement, the system would have failed. The irony was that we discovered our roles had been reversed. When I'd heard Laura's scream that night, I'd been able to make it through the drainage ditch, and having conquered it once, I no longer felt claustrophobic. For Laura, who woke from nightmares believing she was still in the snake's coils, the drainage pipe became an obstacle of fear. The only way she'd been able to force herself through to get back inside the camp after the python attack had been the over-whelming need for comfort in Sophie's arms.

Dr. Eikenboom agreed that if only four of us knew about the drainage ditch and how we were trading, the secret would survive. The fourth was Sophie, of course, for Laura had had to answer to her the mystery of the puncture wounds on her skull. I hadn't needed to involve Elsbeth. The months of happiness under the care of a bright, cheerful, and affectionate mother had swung back the other direction, and rare was the day that I did not think about the dark, brooding sketches I had seen on the bedroom wall of the house we had lost to the Indonesians. Elsbeth was largely unaware of her family's activities, and even her breast-feeding of Jasmijn seemed like an absent-minded task, for my sisters had to remind her again and again to tend to the baby.

The night after the python attack was the only night I had to break curfew again. I crawled underneath the fence to the outside and found Adi waiting. My currency for him was only a small jar of gin that he could trade for some coconuts and vegetables for our family. It had seemed wise to stretch out the remaining supply of Bols by dividing it this way. But to Adi's surprise and delight, I also had money for him to purchase medical supplies.

During this meeting, Adi and I agreed on the system that Dr. Eikenboom had suggested. The foundation to it was that as a middleman, he would be able to take a consistent profit. I showed him where to find the drainage pipe hidden on his side of the fence. In the mornings, with enough sunlight filtering through the bushes covering both ends of the pipe for me to see that it was clear of snakes, I would crawl through. On the other end, just inside the pipe, I would leave a list of items for Adi to obtain, along with the necessary goods or money for his exchanges.

He would make sure that no one observed him as he took the list and goods from the pipe, and then he would wander around town to barter with people who had been exposed to Adi's appearance long enough to look past it. In the evening, Adi put his spoils inside the end of the pipe, and I would retrieve them the next morning when I brought a new list and goods and money.

This meant that Laura and I would need to go to the drainage pipe only once a day and that neither of us needed to dye our skins with betel nut juice to go into town ourselves. Laura would play dolls on the ground near the bush that hid the drainage pipe. She watched for soldiers and let me know if it was safe to come out.

The system seemed like it depended on trust, but it didn't. Adi knew that if I returned the following morning and the goods weren't in place, there would be no list and no goods or money waiting for him until he delivered on the previous list. The first time he wasn't able to find what I needed, he had been waiting in the vegetation at the end of the pipe the next day so he could explain why. By the following morning, what I needed was there.

It was a good system. Adi, as it turned out, was an adept trader, and he procured the insulin that Jasmijn needed to survive. Within days, she became healthy again, and as I held her, her eyes would search my face and she would respond to my smiles. My sisters took turns trying to teach her the names of different parts of the body—elbow, hand, nose, ear, fingers—giggling and singing, although we all knew it would be a while before Jasmijn would be old enough to talk. Now, at least, we could look forward to that day.

Yet while it seemed Dr. Eikenboom had solved

one crisis facing the camp, Nakahara's determination was growing to find the girls he needed for his teahouse.

Sophie met that challenge in her straightforward way. She wanted Laura to be part of the conversation so that her granddaughter would be aware of this injustice and could stand bravely alongside her grandmother. By then, Sophie had become like my own grandmother, so I was with Laura, at the kitchen, when Sophie met with Mrs. Bakker and the other block representatives.

About twenty women were gathered around the tables and huge vats that later would be filled with more water and rice.

"Tomorrow," Sophie said to all of them, "Nakahara wants us to present him the young women for his teahouse."

"It's against the Geneva Convention rules," Mrs. Bakker said. About Sophie's age, she was a mother of four boys, all in the men's work camps, and had the habitual expression of a woman sucking on tart lemon candies. This had been Mrs. Bakker's standard response in private conversations with Sophie, which is why Sophie wanted a broader audience.

"And it's against the Geneva Convention rules for him to withhold our Red Cross supplies," Sophie said. "But we know he's doing it."

"We *think* he's doing it," Mrs. Bakker said. It was hot, even in the shade of the tin roof. The armpits of her dress were damp. "There's no proof. Surely he knows we need those supplies."

Mrs. Bakker, Sophie had explained to Laura and me, lived life with her head in sand, her big bloomers puffed out like the hind end of an ostrich.

"I have a woman who says she wants her daughter to go to the teahouse," one block representative said, utter exhaustion on her thin face. "So does the daughter. They say she will get fed well and won't have to work."

Sophie turned over a vat and stood on it so that she could see every woman and they her. She looked them in the eyes as necessary.

"Think about this," Sophie said. "Stop and really think about this. Are we going to agree to be pimps for our enemy? If we allow even one woman to send her daughter to the soldiers, that is what we have collectively become. When the war is over—and it *will* end sooner or later—do you want to leave this camp and have that on your conscience forever? Do we want even one of our daughters spending the rest of her life not only remembering how those animals treated her, but remembering that we allowed it to begin and allowed it to continue?"

"They might kill us if we resist," the woman said.

Sophie stepped down from the vat. She turned over another vat beside the first one, then motioned for Laura to stand on it beside her. She put her arms on Laura's shoulders and addressed the women again.

"And you think the shame of handing daughters over to be deflowered is better than living with that shame?" Her voice rose. Sophie was furious. Not at the woman who radiated exhaustion but at the situation.

"These are our children!" Sophie looked from woman to woman. "If one of your children was drowning, wouldn't you rush into the water even if you couldn't swim? If a lion attacked one of your children, you would face it with a broom or your bare hands, would you not? And would not that lion flee to discover how savage you would be in driving it away?"

I saw many of the women stand straighter as if saying, Yes, they would attack a lion. Yes, it would flee.

"Tomorrow morning, Nakahara expects one of us to bring him the girls at his deadline of nine o'clock." Sophie spoke clearly, her voice radiating strength. "I will be the one to go to his office and tell him that we refuse to grant his request."

No one spoke. I assumed they were thinking, as I was, that Sophie would receive a savage beating for her defiance against Nakahara.

"If I don't return," Sophie continued, "it is up to the rest of you to be leaders for all the women. We must hide all of the girls that meet his age requirements. We cannot give him those girls."

"And if the soldiers come to get those girls?" Mrs. Bakker asked. Serious as this situation was, I had difficulty getting the image out of my head of this old woman bent forward with her head in the sand and her bloomers exposed.

Sophie stepped down and reached for one of the stirring spoons. She stepped onto the vat again so that everyone could see as she tossed it to Mrs. Bakker. "If the soldiers come to get those girls, you will have this to defend yourself."

"A spoon against a rifle!"

"No, all of us with any kind of weapon. We have table knives and paring knives and scissors and forks. There are three thousand women and only a couple hundred soldiers. Nakahara might be willing to kill one woman, but would he kill us all? And are his soldiers willing to shoot us down for him?"

Sophie scanned the women's faces and met as many eyes as she could. "Every woman in this camp must choose this moment to stand up against Nakahara. If we don't stop him here, who knows what he will ask for next."

She put her hands back on Laura's shoulders. "And who knows if the next girls he wants will even be of age."

Again, silence. One of the women stepped forward and turned a vat over. She found her balance on it and, at Sophie's side, faced the women.

"I will stand with her," Mrs. Schoonenburg said. Normally, when she preached to us, she was strong and confident, a pastor's wife whom we depended on as if she were the pastor herself. But now, her voice was trembling. "I will go with her tomorrow to Nakahara, and I will face his rage with her."

She gulped for air and struggled to continue speaking. "When Paul and Peter were asked to deny the Christ, they suffered beatings and imprisonment. When the first Christians in Rome were told to deny their Lord, they went into the arenas and sang hymns as wild animals advanced on them to tear them apart. If we give Nakahara our girls, we will be denying our Lord as surely as if we put the nails in His hands. And if tomorrow I die, when I enter heaven, it will not be with shame, and I will be able to look my Lord in the eyes and tell Him that I followed Him even unto death."

"I will stand with her!" another shouted.

"And I!"

"And I!"

Then someone shouted, "We will stand with her!" It became an echo affirmed by all, repeated and repeated and repeated.

Sophie began to shudder as she, too, released her emotions. Then she began singing, so softly that it took me a few moments to realize it. "A wretch like me . . . was blind, but now I see . . ."

Mrs. Bakker, at the front, heard it too. She moved up and stood beside Sophie, then took Sophie's hand and joined in. " 'Twas grace that taught my heart to fear, and grace my fears relieved . . ."

The ostrich was out of the sand, and her voice carried to the others. Like a flame touched to dry grass, it took only seconds for all to lift their voices, reaching out, hand to hand, many weeping as they sang.

"When we've been there ten thousand years, bright shining as the sun, we've no less days to sing God's praise, than when we'd first begun . . ."

As these women began to sing the final chorus, I saw Nikki running toward me. Her face was pinched with grief.

"Amazing grace, how sweet the sound . . ."

Nikki darted among the women and reached me at Sophie's side. I, too, was singing.

"I once was lost, but now am found . . ."

Nikki pulled my hand and stood on her tiptoes so she could speak into my ear and so I could hear her above this wonderful hymn of hope, poured out to their Lord by women so sad and afraid and resolute.

"Was blind, but now I see . . ."

"Jeremiah, Jeremiah," she said. "Come home. Jasmijn won't wake up."

Twenty-Eight

Each day, dozens of bodies were prayed over by immediate family members or by Mrs. Schoonenburg before being removed from camp. There was no dignity in wrapping the bodies in blankets, and no remembrance stones were left to mark a loved one's passing.

Stone-faced mothers dressed their children's bodies in their finest clothing, then let someone else take the child away. At least it spared her the final image of her child being stacked beside other bodies in a death wagon.

When a mother died, the children often responded with incomprehension, their reactions ranging from hysterics to denial. Sometimes a little boy or girl would refuse to let go of the mother's hand in a futile attempt to prevent the body from being removed.

Elsbeth, Nikki, Aniek, and Pietje and I had placed our hope in my obtaining insulin for our little Jasmijn, but it hadn't saved her. While we weren't alone in our grief, we each faced the loss independently. I responded with a determination that Jasmijn would not be added to the bodies on the wagon, and I told Dr. Eikenboom of my decision as she filled out the death certificate.

Jasmijn's soul had been gone only an hour or so, and she truly looked asleep.

Dr. Eikenboom shook her head. "But soldiers would see the freshly dug soil of a grave plot. Or a neighbor would know and others would hear about it. It wouldn't be allowed because if you were able to bury your sister, others would want the same privilege."

The tip of a small feather from her pillow extended from the edge of Jasmijn's lips. Her mouth had not dried out, and the feather was still wet and bedraggled. I pulled it out.

"I will take her to Adi," I said.

"Adi? The boy who does our trading in town?"

"I will ask him to take our little sister and provide her a grave. After the war, we will be able to visit her."

"Jeremiah," Dr. Eikenboom said, "Mrs. Schoonenburg will join you and perform a funeral ceremony and you can say good-bye to Jasmijn that way. That is how it must be done."

I don't know what she thought she saw in my eyes, because her expression changed and a sad smile formed on her lips. "That is not how it must be done. I think your suggestion is a beautiful idea. I trust you not to get caught."

Pietje nodded. Aniek and Nikki came to a telepathic agreement and both nodded too. Their faces were blotched with grief and exhaustion. They had spent the last hour singing to Jasmijn, not songs to teach her what to call finger or nose, but hymns of comfort to her still body.

"Now," Dr. Eikenboom said, "we need to see to your mother." She knelt beside Elsbeth, who pushed her away. This, at least, told us that Elsbeth still heard and understood what was happening around her.

Dr. Eikenboom rose. "Please do your best to make sure that your mother eats what you give her. She needs rest."

"Yes," I said.

When Dr. Eikenboom left, we placed Jasmijn in the family bed and sang her lullabies, as if she were still with us. I glanced over at Elsbeth once, and she was managing a small smile as tears were rolling down her face. That gave me a burst of joy because it told me that perhaps our mother was breaking through her hard shell.

I knew what was ahead of me for the rest of the day. Mrs. Schoonenburg would lead us through a funeral, and I would promise to be responsible for taking Jasmijn out of the house. Mrs. Schoonenburg would assume I meant the wagon, then would leave us alone. I would spend the day with Jasmijn, and after curfew, I would hold my little sister to my chest and crawl through the drainage pipe. Then I would wait on the other side in the darkness for Adi to arrive with the items on the list that I'd left for him before Sophie had called together the block representatives. It wouldn't matter to me if my vigil took all night.

The funeral came and went. With the knowledge that she would join Sophie the next morning to face Nakahara, Mrs. Schoonenburg had a powerful presence to her that illuminated her prayers over Jasmijn, as if she were already in the fire—like Daniel's friends with the angel —and singing praise to God.

The only time I left the house and my vigil over Jasmijn was when Sophie came to see how our family was doing. I allowed Sophie to hug me, but Laura stared at me in a daze. The next morning, Sophie and Mrs. Schoonenburg would face Nakahara with their message of defiance, and Laura was trying to be brave about her own fears. We were both aware that today might be the last time for Sophie to hug either of us.

I waited about an hour after the siren sounded for curfew. Then I safely snuck to the bush that hid our pipeline to freedom, and I cried only a little as Jasmijn and I made our final journey together beneath the fence. On the other side, I found a spot in deep shadows to lean against the banyan that once held the python. With Jasmijn cradled against my chest, I let the night sounds settle around me. Frogs in high pitches and bullfrogs in low pitches. The occasional screech from trees outside of town. The tropical heat was a blanket, and I whispered lullabies to Jasmijn, grateful for each minute that Adi did not arrive.

I had no way to track time, but eventually, I fell asleep. It was only the rustling of brush that woke me, and I saw Adi kneeling as he prepared to crawl through the vegetation to the entrance to the drainage pipe.

"Adi," I whispered.

He groaned with fright.

"It's me—Jeremiah."

Adi backed away. He had a bag in his arms.

"Jeremiah?"

"Over here," I said.

Adi came forward. He set the day's supplies on the ground.

"What are you doing?" he asked.

"Light your candle," I said.

He did. The glow showed Jasmijn's tranquil face. It also showed the twisted turn of his upper lip that made him an outcast in his own world.

"My sister," I said. "Jasmijn."

"She's so beautiful." He saw that her hair was dark. "She's one of us."

"Yes."

In the candlelight, he reached over and lightly stroked her cheek. I could not help it. I shuddered with grief.

He drew his hand back as if he'd touched the flame of his candle. "I'm so sorry. Forgive me."

"There is nothing to forgive," I said. I took his

hand and brought it back to her face. He stroked her cheek again, as if lost in the perfection of her face.

"Don't let her wake," he said, a grunt escaping his mouth as he tried to form words. "Sometimes the little ones see my mouth and they don't understand I am not a monster . . ."

In that moment, I wanted to hug him as Sophie had hugged me earlier in my grief, but that was impossible. Adi would have misinterpreted my compassion as pity.

"Remember how you've found me insulin?" I said to Adi. "It was for her. But she doesn't need it anymore."

He looked at me. And understood.

"My brother," he said, "I am so sorry."

"Will you truly be my brother?" I asked. "Will you find a grave for her and a cross? Beneath her shirt, I've written a note with her name and her date of birth and today's date for the cross."

"I will," he said. "As God is my witness. You honor me with this."

"Tell me what it costs," I said. "I will leave you the money when I leave a list."

"This is not something that a brother does for money," he answered, and it was an answer that gave me certainty that I could trust Jasmijn to him.

I tried to thank him, but I could not control

246

my shuddering anymore and became incoherent.

Adi blew out the candle. He knelt and took Jasmijn from my arms and walked away into the darkness, leaving me with the night sounds beneath the banyan.

Twenty-Nine

I could not permit myself the luxury of solitude for my grief much past dawn, because I could not fail to be there for the usual roll call after the wailing of sirens took our family out to the street with all the other women and children of camp.

In line, waiting for the soldier to appear who would do the count for our block, I first heard the news: Sophie and Mrs. Schoonenburg had been taken away by guards the evening before, and no one knew where they were.

With the deadline less than an hour away, I heard the whispers up and down the line. *"Who will face Nakahara now? Who will go to him and tell him that we will not give up our girls for the teahouse?"*

With sisters too young to be affected by the teahouse, my fears were for Sophie and Laura. During roll call, it was impossible to go a street over to see Laura, but as soon as the soldier had satisfied himself that everyone on our block was accounted for—Jasmijn's death certificate had reduced it by one—I dashed between two houses on a familiar shortcut to find her.

Laura was sitting on the porch of the house, back to the wall, arms wrapped around her knees.

"I've heard," I said as I sat beside her.

"He said they will be released when the teahouse girls are brought to him," Laura answered. "What is there to do?"

I grappled with the answer that had already been decided. Sophie and Mrs. Schoonenburg had said that if necessary, they would sacrifice their lives in telling Nakahara of the camp's refusal to give him teahouse girls. How had anything changed? That was a logical answer for Laura.

Yet only the day before, too many adults had tried to comfort me with logic. *It's a mercy that Jasmijn is in heaven. This camp has too many hardships, and the poor child was in so much pain so much of the time.*

The heart is not engineered for logic, because the heart is not engineered.

I knew the answer to give Laura because Sophie had given me the best answer the day before. She had held me and whispered, *"I'm sorry for you, Jeremiah. I don't think anyone can understand how much it hurts. I wish I could carry your pain for you. I'm so sorry for you."*

"Laura," I said, "I don't know what there is to do. I wish I knew. And I'm so sorry for you."

We might have remained on the porch all day, each in our own private griefs, but in the next minutes, Mrs. Bakker, the block representative, stepped into the middle of the street and called in a voice that was surprisingly loud.

"Ieder een er uit! Ieder een er uit!"

Everybody out! Everybody out!

All the houses began to discharge the adult women as if the sirens had wailed again for roll call. When the women got to the streets, instead of forming lines, they began to march down the street toward Nakahara's residence.

We began to follow, and Mrs. Bakker noticed.

"Stay behind," she said. "No children."

"It's my grandmother," Laura said. "I will not stay behind."

"And I will fight anyone who tries to stop Laura," I said.

Any other time, this open rebellion would have earned spankings and forcible removal. Laura and I knew it, and Mrs. Bakker knew it. However, Mrs. Bakker only said, "I will deal with your disrespect later."

The women from the other blocks streamed in from all streets to converge on the stretch of cobblestone in front of the Nakahara residence. He was inside, no doubt, waiting for the deadline to come and go so that he could send his soldiers to gather some teahouse girls. Or perhaps he expected that with Sophie and Mrs.

Schoonenburg captive, the camp's resolve to defy him would collapse.

Hundreds upon hundreds of women gathering in front of his residence spoke otherwise. Soldiers scurried up and down the street, pointing their rifles, but the fear was obvious on their faces. With no orders, they were uncertain about what to do. Several bolted into the Nakahara residence.

The women formed orderly lines up and down the street. There were too many for the customary roll call formation of one line on each side of the street, so when all the movement had stopped, the women stood four lines deep on each side, with enough space between the lines for the women to bow.

Laura and I took spots at the front line where we had a clear view of what might happen.

Soldiers continued to walk up and down the center of the street, yet each woman remained motionless. And silent. It was an eerie tension-filled bubble of time.

Then, down the center of the street walked the woman who intended to replace Sophie and Mrs. Schoonenburg in defiance of Nakahara. Laura grabbed my wrist in an unspoken gesture of support.

It was Elsbeth. Head bowed. Plodding step by step. Wearing a faded dress with a dotted pattern and walking in bare feet.

Much, much later I would understand what had

driven her, an attempt at redemption for an act that I would never fully comprehend. But in this moment, I could only question whether my eyes were deceiving me. Out of all the women in this camp, it seemed impossible to me that my mother —who in her despondency over the last weeks had rarely left our cramped room and in so doing had become as invisible as the dead thrown onto the wagon—would have made a decision not only to face Nakahara's wrath but to put herself at the center of attention.

"Moeder!" I ran out to her, uncaring that it put me squarely on the same stage of attention.

"No, Jeremiah," she said in a dull voice. "It must be done."

"He will kill you," I said. "Please, don't."

"If he does, you will take care of the family as you have always done. Go."

I pulled on her hand. She reacted by slapping me across the face with her other hand.

"I am your mother," she said. There was sudden strength in her voice. "Do as I say."

I backed away, blinking with the same disbelief that had overwhelmed me upon seeing her walking alone down the center of the street. I stumbled back to Laura.

I felt a woman's hand on my shoulder. From the line behind me. I pushed it away. I looked straight ahead. I would not let my eyes follow my mother to the steps of the Nakahara residence. In the silence, however, the sound of the closing door betrayed me, and I knew she was inside.

Time remained suspended. Even the soldiers stopped the nervous patrolling of the center of the street. When screams came from inside the house, every woman stood like a statue. Except the woman behind me, who must have anticipated what I would do, for her arms grabbed me and prevented me from running to the house. No matter how much I squirmed, I could not move. As the unseen beating inside the residence continued, I was enveloped in the peculiar smell of that woman's unwashed body, her hand around my mouth to keep me from screaming. What little shaking of my head I was able to accomplish showed me that while some of the women were watching our struggle, all of them maintained the discipline of formation.

When the screams stopped, so did my struggle. But the woman behind me did not let go.

The door opened. Nakahara stepped outside.

"Kiotske!" Attention!

It was an unnecessary command. All the women had been standing at attention from the moment they had formed into lines.

"Kere!" Bow!

Only then did the woman behind me let go of my body.

In the moments that followed, there remained total silence. Total obedience. All these hundreds of women crisply bent forward at the waist and held position. Although I raged inside, I, too, bent forward.

Five minutes passed. Maybe ten minutes. The older women must have been in agony, because I felt horrible strain on my back. Some groaning began to break the silence. When the moment came that Nakahara was satisfied that he had proven he was in control, the final order came.

"Naore!" At ease!

Perhaps this was when he intended to speak to all the women through an interpreter, but when the women straightened, he discovered how mistaken he was in believing he had managed to quell the revolt by taking away its leaders and beating the woman who had replaced them.

When the women straightened, they pulled out weapons that had been hidden in their clothing and held them at chest level. Not a word was spoken. From my position at the front line, I saw the resolute determination on the face of the women who stood facing me across the street.

No translation was needed because no one spoke. Nakahara faced knitting needles and scissors and forks and paring knives and wooden spoons and the jagged necks of broken bottles. The soldiers formed tiny circles in the center of the streets, backs to each other, rifles pointed outward.

Had a single shot been fired, there is no doubt

that the entire group of steadfastly disciplined women would have become an unstoppable mob, releasing its fury on the dozens of soldiers, who would have been overwhelmed by hundreds and hundreds of women seething with hatred at the daily roll calls and the reduced rations and the misery inflicted upon their children.

Nakahara broke the silence and shouted in Japanese. It took several moments, then the translation came. "No teahouse deadline. Volunteers only."

We knew it was defeat for Nakahara, because there would be no volunteers. Mrs. Bakker took a step forward and spoke in a moderate tone that was still clearly heard up and down the street.

"We will not leave until Mrs. Jansen and Mrs. Schoonenburg and Mrs. Prins join us."

Nakahara shouted again, and the translation came again. "No teahouse deadline. Volunteers only."

He turned quickly and retreated to the house, leaving his soldiers in their tight circles to face the women. Within minutes, the door opened again. Sophie and Mrs. Schoonenburg framed my mother as they stepped outside, supporting her as they helped her walk to their freedom.

This time, when I tried to break from the line to race past the soldiers toward my mother, no one held me back.

Thirty

As Elsbeth recovered from the beating that Nakahara had given her, Sophie had taken it upon herself to nurse her, and they became like mother and daughter. During those weeks, one day to the next had the numbing effect of making everything seem unchanged. The siren wailed each morning, and families stumbled to the streets for roll call. Mothers tried to comfort children who cried from hunger, and women and girls over sixteen carried out the duties of camp routine. Rice and stale bread were served at every lunch and dinner. Sirens wailed for end-of-day roll call and then wailed again to impose curfew.

In their lives before camp, my sisters had lived like beautiful china dolls, pampered and exhibited accordingly by Elsbeth. Now their legs were streaked with dirt, their knees scabbed, and they wore tattered dresses far too small for their growing bodies. They knelt in dirt to search for snails and squealed in delight on the rare occasion they found a frog for our boiling pot. Even so, when Elsbeth could, she insisted on brushing their hair every morning and lectured them if they allowed their faces to be dirty.

Georgie was unable to find his own group of boys as friends and made sure that when I was in sight, he disappeared. It felt to me like a justification of my hatred for him, as in a large part he earned the dislike of those he tried to befriend. He wasn't alone, however, for he had Dr. Kloet, a man in the mirror image of Georgie. While it didn't appear that he suffered physically, Georgie no longer had the arrogant swagger of an American boy whose father was the big boss of an oil refinery. It's an easy assumption that he was fearful and lonely, yet he could have eased both afflictions if he had joined our collective defiance of the Japanese by sharing chores and food and hymns. Perhaps, had any of us reached out to him, he might have reciprocated. Instead, we enjoyed ignoring him and making it obvious we were ignoring him.

So, happily without him, we roamed and made the best of our prison. Part of my own routine was a fake marble game with Laura, Pietje, Aniek, and Nikki, played along one of the walls that formed protection around Nakahara's private garden. As often as possible, Laura and I would peek through the holes that we had once formed with the handle of a wooden spoon.

Our amusement consisted of watching Pietje mainly lose marble games to kids in their own little gangs on each street. I was Pietje's banker, supplying him with an ample number to distribute among the camp through his losses. I had managed to establish an unspoken agreement. A day or two after Pietje lost his marbles, I would be allowed the chance to win them back again, which invariably I did. It wasn't as much of a thrill as earning marbles that weren't mine in the first place, but it was a way to pass the time. Occasionally, something out of the ordinary would feed new rumors, eagerly passed along and discussed in minutia as a welcome change from conversations that often revolved around the first meal a woman would cook and eat once the war was over. In innocence, I contributed to a rumor that swept through the kitchen lines with delicious self-righteousness and indignant speculation.

Through the holes in the garden wall, we could see that Nakahara was growing his own vegetables and using some of the produce to feed a pig penned in the corner. But this was not news worthy of passing along. The squealing and grunting of the fat sow already had reached us, tormenting us with visions of bacon and cured ham. Also, the women responsible for cooking his meals daily entered the garden for vegetables and were able to report the bounty with expected degrees of frustration and hatred.

These same women confirmed that Nakahara was keeping American Red Cross parcels for himself, storing them in stacks in one of the unused rooms of his residence. These parcels contained bandages and ointments and disinfectants and painkillers that would have alleviated so much suffering in camp. The parcels also contained soap and chocolate bars and powdered milk and tins of food.

Nakahara's cooks reported that Nakahara made no effort to hide the opened parcels, eating chocolate as they took away the dishes after his meal. They saw him give soap and tins of food to soldiers as rewards. They also saw him load the medicines into larger boxes to sell outside of the camp. Because Nakahara was the ultimate authority at this camp, he had no reason to hide this from them and would even smile, they said, when he noticed them staring at the items that rightfully belonged to the families of camp.

From day to day, our view of the private area did not change. We could see the pig, and often, we saw Dutch women weeding and picking vegetables under the guard of Japanese soldiers who were there to keep them from eating from the garden. Occasionally, we saw Nakahara snoozing in a chaise lounge in the shade of the banyan near the center of his garden, his monster guard dog on the ground beside him, tongue out and panting, head on paws, one eye open. In the middle of one afternoon, however, when I peeked through a spy hole in the wall, what I saw shocked me: the back of a woman in a silk robe crossed my small circle of vision, then moved toward Nakahara in the chaise lounge. Her identity was obscured by a towel wrapped around her head and the robe covering all of her body. I did see Nakahara sit up and smile at her and that her skin was white on her shoulders as she began to pull the robe away.

I saw nothing else because Pietje tapped my shoulder.

Soldiers.

I straightened and shouted automatically. "*Kiotske!*"

Pietje shouted, "*Kere!*"

We had to wait in a bowing position until they passed by.

"*Naore!*" Laura said, and we all relaxed. Farther down the street, another boy yelled "*Kiotske!*" to warn all those around him, and then came "*Kere!*"

When I looked again through the peephole, the chaise lounge was empty.

What I'd witnessed was so astounding that I immediately had to tell someone, who was Pietje and Laura and Nikki and Aniek, and what I'd seen gave us such an air of self-importance that we first stopped at Dr. Eikenboom's table to tell her. Enough of our conversation reached Dr. Kloet that he broke in with questions that were overheard by some of the women in line. By supper, women I did not know were coming up to me in small groups and asking for an eyewitness account and then walking away to speculate on the identity of the woman in the robe. Not one of those women, however, would answer my own questions about why a woman in a robe would have been in the garden with Nakahara or why the woman had so much of her skin exposed or where they could have gone.

It wasn't until the next morning that I realized how much of a mistake my lack of discretion had been. When our little gang wandered over to the garden wall as part of our routine, our spy holes had been plugged with fresh concrete. Until then, it had never occurred to me that the mystery visitor would hear the rumor about herself and report it to Nakahara, thus securing her identity. I should have known, however. After all, someone had denounced Sophie and Mrs. Schoonenburg and their intent to defy Nakahara about the tea-house. Thus, I feared that Nakahara would know it had come from me, but after a day or two had passed without incident, I relaxed. That was my second mistake.

A few mornings after that, as I was crawling out of the drainage ditch with supplies left for me by Adi, I was met by Nakahara on the other side of the bush, waiting for me. Laura had been standing guard, and if soldiers happened nearby, she was to yell Pietje's name, as if calling him to come and play dolls with her. Once every few weeks, she'd been forced to use this ploy. The first time, we had both been terrified, but after our system had worked then and every time since, much of our fear of using the tunnel to the outside had disappeared.

I crawled from beneath the bush as I always did, headfirst, but then I saw boots. Army boots. I saw legs of soldiers. And beyond those legs, I saw Nakahara's dog with Laura's arm in its teeth. I saw Nakahara with a triumphant grin as he made eye contact with me. He and the soldiers had been waiting.

Nakahara shook his head as if he were addressing a naughty boy. He put his left forefinger to his lips and made a shushing sound, and with his other hand, he opened and closed his thumb and fingers as if they were the jaws of his guard dog.

I understood. I remembered when the dog had attacked me and clamped down on my arm. Nakahara had screamed and our translator had made it clear. *This dog will kill you at my command.*

Now, Nakahara's smile was more frightening than his screaming. He was a man in control and savoring revenge.

I crawled out, and he motioned for me to stand. As I did, he barked a command at his soldiers. One of them kicked aside the bushes and found the cloth bag that held the day's supplies of sulfa and ointments for Dr. Eikenboom. The soldier gave that bag to Nakahara, who looked inside and grunted acknowledgment.

Nakahara gazed upon me again like a lazy lizard in the sun. Then he gave a quick stream of Japanese that I didn't understand. A soldier on each side of me grasped each of my arms and lifted me.

My instinct was to kick and struggle, but Laura's eyes were wide with terror because of the dog clamped to her arm. Nakahara had made it clear if I made any noise, he would order the dog to tear into her arm. Or worse.

If Nakahara was trying to scare me as well, he was failing. I felt my rage build. My eyes locked on the sword in the scabbard on Nakahara's belt. I could feel myself pulling the sword loose and impaling Nakahara with a joy I knew I would never regret, even if it cost me my life.

His eyes narrowed, as if he understood the depth of my anger. But he smiled again, with an exquisiteness of someone who had planned to enjoy the first moments of torture. He calmly spoke more Japanese. While I was still in the air, another soldier grabbed at the waistband of my shorts. It took me several moments to comprehend. The soldier was looking for my marble pouches and found the first one almost immediately. Often enough, others had seen me reach for it, so it wasn't a camp secret.

But Nakahara barked at him, so the soldier kept searching until he pulled the other one loose from my shorts. Then he squeezed out the two marbles —my precious china marble with the dragon and the far more precious marble that my father had given me with the tiny statue inside.

The soldier walked across to Nakahara and gave him both marbles. Nakahara rolled both of them across his open palm so that he knew I saw them in his full possession.

He spoke to his dog, and it released Laura.

Then Nakahara said, "*Kere!*"

Laura and I bowed. He laughed as the soldiers walked away, and just before they turned around the corner of the nearest house, Nakahara called out in a mocking voice, "*Naore!*"

Now, I realized, I was a personal enemy of the commander, who knew me well enough to know the one punishment that would hurt and haunt me. But it wasn't enough, for he and the soldiers marched to the medical tent and, in front of all the women in both lines, Nakahara dumped the confiscated supplies onto Dr. Eikenboom's table. She was standing, so he punched her to the ground and kicked hard and repeatedly enough to break her ribs, an act that I knew was directly my fault.

Only one person could have confirmed to Nakahara my story about using the peephole to see a Dutch woman in a robe in his private garden. Someone who heard me tell Dr. Eikenboom about it himself. The same man who knew about my pouch with the china marble and where I kept it hidden at all times.

The same man, of course, who had lusted after that marble and felt he'd been made a fool over his desire to win it from me.

The round-faced, well-fed Dr. Kloet.

Thirty-One

Dr. Eikenboom struggled to push away a wet cloth in my mother's hands. "Elsbeth," she said, "you have used too much. I'm not the only one in this camp who needs this." She rested in a tattered armchair in the schoolhouse hallway, just outside the large closet that was her residence. The beating she'd received had been so bad it had taken her four days to be able to leave her bed. During that time, Sophie and Laura had tended to her in one shift, and my mother and I in another.

Elsbeth held the wet cloth above a pan where it had been soaking. The pan of lukewarm water also had pieces of torn leaves from the hibiscus plant. We'd harvested the leaves from the area of camp that Dr. Eikenboom had set aside just to grow the flowers. A vegetable garden would have been unthinkable, as the crops would not have served more than a handful of people. But it was understood that medicinal plants would be useful for everyone in the camp, and the patch had flourished under careful tending.

The largest percentage of the garden held

hibiscus plants because of all of its uses. Tea made from the leaves was not only a natural diuretic that relieved swellings of the limbs, but it also contained vitamin C and many minerals. More importantly, the slimy water that was produced by soaking leaves was a natural disinfectant, and Dr. Eikenboom prescribed it for those with skin diseases. Like everything in camp, however, it was a limited resource.

My mother dipped the cloth into the pan and admonished Dr. Eikenboom. "You need to look out for yourself first. Until you recover, we are down to one doctor. If something happens to you, it won't make a difference how much extra hibiscus is left for the others, because we need you far more than the camp needs the hibiscus."

Elsbeth squeezed drippings from the cloth onto Dr. Eikenboom's nearer arm and cleaned the skin.

"Dr. Kloet," I said with loud derision. I was holding my book, *Ivanhoe*, that Pietje had stored in his bag the day the soldiers had arrived at our house. I'd been reading it to Dr. Eikenboom, and we were at chapter fifteen. "We'd be better off without him."

"Hush," Dr. Eikenboom said. Her forehead was mottled with bruises, and every time she shifted in her chair, she winced. "He may complain at times, but the poor man has been doing the work of two for a week now."

"I've been saying nothing so far because I

wanted to wait until you were better," I said. "But he's the one who told Nakahara about the drainage pipe."

"What?" This came from my mother, and I felt satisfaction that both my mother and Dr. Eikenboom gasped.

"Moeder," I said, "did you know I've had two marbles hidden in a second pouch beneath my waistband since we came to camp?"

"No," she answered slowly, trying to figure out how this had anything to do with the discussion.

"No is correct," I said. "The other pouch has always been my secret. From everyone. Except Dr. Kloet. He knew about it because once he saw me take a marble out of the pouch and then return it."

"Yes?" Dr. Eikenboom said.

I described how, after orders from Nakahara, his soldiers had known exactly where to find those marbles.

"Dr. Kloet," I pronounced, "is the only person who would know that somehow the camp was not running out of medical supplies. He's the one who could spy on you and see that I was delivering those supplies. I'm sure he told Nakahara. He probably told Nakahara about Sophie and Mrs. Schoonenburg too."

"Just to get two marbles?" Dr. Eikenboom asked.

"He's been furious with me ever since he

found out that I could beat him at any time," I said. "I bet if I searched his room right now, I could find them both."

It was a tempting thought. Dr. Kloet was at the medical tent and his door was only down the hallway.

"So," Dr. Eikenboom said, "you think that doing something wrong like sneaking into his room is justified?"

This was such a silly question that I couldn't even find an answer. Dr. Kloet had stopped the entire camp from receiving the supplies Adi found for us, simply because he wanted to punish me and get the china marble. Of course I thought that stealing back the marbles was justified.

"As soon as you are better," I said, "we need to tell everybody what he did."

"Can you prove it?" Dr. Eikenboom asked.

"It's plain for anyone to see," I said.

"You think it's right to destroy a man's reputation without proof?"

"It's plain for anyone to see. I don't need proof. But if I go into his room and find those marbles, I'll show you the proof you need."

"So again, it's okay to do something wrong to fight what is wrong?" Dr. Eikenboom sighed. "Then you have become the same. Remember Mrs. Aafjes and how she was stealing food by tamping the rice for her friends? Would you steal rice for your family to get back at her?"

"That's different," I said.

"How?"

"It just is."

Another sigh from Dr. Eikenboom. "And if you proved Dr. Kloet is reporting to Nakahara, what then?"

"He gets a beating," I said. "From the block representatives. As bad as the beating you got. And I get my marbles back and everything is even."

"How does that help all the people who depend on him every day?"

I could see that I was making no progress in trying to convince Dr. Eikenboom of the error in her thinking. Some people can be too stubborn for their own good. Also, it struck me that I shouldn't make too big a fuss. I would just wait awhile, then sneak into his room during the day and find those marbles. Then we would see who was right about all of this.

As my mother dripped hibiscus water into Dr. Eikenboom's hair, I asked, "Would it be wrong to steal the Red Cross boxes that Nakahara keeps from us?"

My mother mopped water from Dr. Eikenboom's eyebrows.

With her eyes closed, Dr. Eikenboom said, "I need to give that some thought. You are right that, in a sense, it's no different than you stealing back your marbles." She paused and I waited impatiently. "But it would be impossible. And if Nakahara caught you, all of the camp would be punished."

My mother said, "You heard Dr. Eikenboom say it would be impossible to get those boxes. I forbid you to even think about it."

What they didn't know was that not only had I snuck out of the house to climb the privacy wall the night before, I'd done so with a straw mat to put on the jagged glass. With it protecting me from the glass, I had discovered it would be very possible to sneak into Nakahara's garden, then through the door that led into his house. There was only one problem. His dog. It knew I was there. It had not barked but only stared upward at the base of the wall directly below me and whined slightly, wanting me to descend into its jaws. Nakahara had the perfect sentry. Someone who would not fall asleep, and someone who would take care of intruders without waking Nakahara.

"Even so," I said, "I would like to know if Dr. Eikenboom thinks it would be okay to steal those boxes from Nakahara."

Not only did I want revenge on Dr. Kloet but Nakahara too. It was time someone taught him a lesson, and stealing those boxes would suffice.

"It would save lives," she said. "Your marbles would not. And I make no apology for the distinction. Someone with higher standards than

I would insist that if something is wrong, it is wrong in all situations. I, however, would lie if it meant pro-tecting someone from the Japanese, even though it is wrong to lie."

"It doesn't matter, though, does it?" Elsbeth asked with artificial brightness. "Because no one is going to risk going into Nakahara's head-quarters to steal those boxes."

She, of course, meant me.

"That would be crazy," I told my mother. So I waited until she departed to read another chapter of *Ivanhoe* to Dr. Eikenboom. Before beginning, though, I asked, "Dr. Eikenboom, what's the best way to poison a dog? Rosary pea?"

Poison would complete my revenge. Dr. Kloet. Nakahara. And the monster dog from hell that was in the private garden at night, stopping anyone from dropping down inside.

"I won't answer that for you," she said. "Unless the dog was poisoned slowly, Nakahara would know someone in camp had done it, and I don't want to think about the consequences. Always, Jeremiah, we must think about the consequences of our actions."

She was absolutely right.

I began to read chapter fifteen to her. "No spider ever took more pains to repair the shattered meshes of his web, than did Waldemar Fitzurse to reunite and combine the scattered members of Prince John's cabal . . ."

The next day I read aloud chapter sixteen, and I continued to read to her day by day until she was able to return to the table in the medical tent. That gave me many days to think about the consequences of sneaking into the house to find my marbles. Consequences for Dr. Kloet.

So I did it, and it was as simple as I had imagined. Dr. Kloet was busy at the medical tent just after the lunch break. He had just returned to the lineup of women and children, so I knew there was no chance of getting caught.

Except when I opened the door to his room, Georgie's mother was there. Mrs. Smith. On his bed.

"Back so soon?" she asked in a drowsy voice, rolling over on the bed to turn toward the door. That's when our eyes met.

And I fled.

Thirty-Two

In a place where no fathers lived to impose discipline, some of the older boys had become wild, refusing to fulfill camp duties, forming gangs, and often hassling or threatening older women. The risk to his men also apparent, Nakahara decided to send all boys over the age of thirteen to a men's camp. This sent a seismic wave of grief through camp with mothers clinging to their boys and boys trying not to weep in return as soldiers loaded them onto trucks.

Before then, Georgie had existed among the fringe of boys that exist everywhere. Some live a solitary existence without enough courage to form their own group or the courage to stand up to older boys. Others are invisible to the ringleaders and, like geckos, scurry away from the moving shadows of danger. I always tried to earn enough respect from older boys to be left alone. Then finally, there are the Georgies. They need attention, and probably because a mother or aunt excessively doted on them, they expect to be treated like royalty their entire lives. They have a stench of obnoxiousness and bluster that serves well to push around younger or smaller boys, but it also draws the predators above them in the food chain. Georgie's only refuge had been Dr. Kloet, and he often spent hours at the medical tent with him, sometimes running errands Dr. Kloet requested.

In the space of hours after the last of the trucks transported the older boys out of the gates, Georgie's role shifted from that of one bullied by his elders to one of an elder happy to bully those beneath him. After the culling of the older boys, he could dare to form his own group and was delighted to leave Dr. Kloet's protection. He led this uncivil group of five or six boys as they took marbles and dolls from younger kids, taunted them to the point of tears, and punched and hit at whim. He'd seen me in line at lunchtime and promised to make my life miserable as soon as he could catch me away from adults. I think he thought that would make me afraid. Instead, I looked forward to it and wondered where and when would be the best time for it.

In the meantime, and ever since Dr. Eikenboom had returned to her table under the medical tent, I had begun collecting seeds from the rosary pea plant. Like a weed, it would twine around shrubs and trees as it flourished in the tropical conditions of the Dutch East Indies. Because none of the plant was edible, though, no one in camp bothered it for anything except the seeds, which were like hard beans the size of ladybugs and used for jewelry. The seeds were colored like ladybugs too, with most of them a shiny red with the top tip black.

Small children in camp would occasionally swallow the attractive seeds, but mothers would not be worried. The shell of the seed was too hard to be digested, and the seeds would pass through in normal fashion. I did know, however, that some-times a mother would get sick after making jewelry with the beans. Using a needle to bore holes through the seeds, she would string them together to make bright ankle or wrist bracelets. But if a woman pricked a hole in her skin while boring the seed, the toxin inside could enter her bloodstream. All it took was a minute amount of abrin—the poison inside the seed—on the tip of the needle to bring on the fever and cough and nausea, but that small amount wouldn't lead to death. I needed to gather enough seeds to crush and mix into meat to poison Nakahara's dog. It would take days to die, which meant that long after the animal had eaten it, the evidence would be gone.

I was deterred from that plan, however, because as in all of life, good fortune and timing were what truly mattered. One morning, our little group had gathered beside Laura's house. Pietje, Nikki, and Aniek sat in a small circle with us because Laura was trying to teach them to read.

Laura noticed them first, climbing down a tree trunk. "That's a long caterpillar! Really long!"

She walked to the tree for a closer look, and I followed. The front of the caterpillar looked like it had almost reached the ground.

"It's a bunch of them," she said.

Indeed, an unbroken vertical line of caterpillars stretched down one of the few pine trees in camp. Each was only an inch or so long, with orange-brown backs and bands of blue-gray, and covered with soft-looking blue-gray fuzz. They had formed a parade, with the nose of one caterpillar touching the tail end of the one in front of it.

I moved beside her. "Those are called

processionary caterpillars. You can see why. We need a marching band for them. This happens only once a year."

High up in the tree would have been the remnant of a nest built of white silk to protect them as they ate pine needles and patiently went through the stages of molting and growing. When ready to leave the nest, they paraded down the tree to look for a place to dig underground and pupate, emerging at the end of summer as moths with cream-colored forewings and white hind wings.

"They look cuddly," she said, reaching out to stroke the blue-gray fuzz.

I snatched her wrist and pulled her hand away. "Not a good idea."

She giggled. "They bite?"

I shook my head. "There's a reason they are not afraid of birds or animals. You'll see lines of them crossing open ground and nothing touches them. All that fuzz is poisonous. When I was eight, a boy from the Netherlands visited my dad's school . . ."

My pause wasn't for effect or because I was searching for words. It was just that I had been struck by an image of myself at the school at the end of a day, sitting by my father's side for what seemed like hours as I sketched out buildings of all shapes and sizes and he graded papers. I fought off the sadness. "This boy didn't know about the caterpillars. Just like you. He began to play with them. Then his face swelled up and his hands got blistered and . . ."

My voice faded as another, much less sad, vision struck me. Of Georgie reaching into a bag of marbles stolen from a little kid only to discover the processionary caterpillars and their thousands of follicles like poison darts.

"Hey," I said to Laura. "I want you to watch something. Pietje, where's a stick?"

Dutifully, he went running. By the time he returned, the line of caterpillars had flowed from the tree onto the ground. Sometimes the procession would be over a hundred feet long.

"Thanks, Pietje," I said. His obedience and worship of me was something I gave little thought to. With Laura and my sisters watching, I used the stick to flick aside some caterpillars about six feet from the front of the line and form a gap. Now there were two processions—the short one at the front, and a second one that continued unbroken all the way back to the trunk of the tree and up into the branches where it had started.

I nudged the lead caterpillar of the short line to change its direction. The caterpillars behind it remained in the nose-to-tail formation. With a series of these nudges, the lead caterpillar was taking all of its followers in the beginning of a circle, and soon enough, it had reached the tail end of the final caterpillar and the circle was complete.

This was a parlor trick I'd learned from my half brothers. Before the capitulation, I'd watched them do it one afternoon in our own yard. The next morning the caterpillars were still moving in that circle in the same place. They did that for two days before succumbing to starvation.

"You try," I said to Laura.

She used the stick to get another circle started of the same size. I allowed Pietje to form a third circle. Nikki and Aniek made a fourth and fifth circle. Even so, the line from the tree continued to move forward, and when the final caterpillar descended, the straight line that departed from us was still twenty feet long.

As their comrades marched away, we were looking at five circles of caterpillars, their backs undulating as they crawled nose to tail, nose to tail.

"They are not going anywhere," I said. "Now we need some bags to hold them."

I stood guard as my henchmen ran to various places to find any remaining bags that the women once used to carry goods from the markets—before the Jappenkamp had become the only way we were allowed to live.

When they returned, we put marbles in each bag, enough for the clunking sounds to be heard. After that, it was simple to guide the caterpillars into the bags. We finished with three bags full. It was deliciously satisfying to hold the top of the bag open and see the curled masses of caterpillars writhing inside.

I explained my plan. We would go through camp and give the marbles to some of the younger boys, sternly warning them not to reach into the bags themselves. Sooner or later, Georgie would try to take away the marbles, and when he reached into the bags, he would pay the price. He was an American. He wouldn't know the danger.

"Please don't," Laura said. "Maybe Georgie will get really sick."

I understood the implication. If he got really sick, he likely wouldn't be able to get the medical help he needed. Medical supplies were getting scarcer and scarcer, and mothers were terrified that something as minor as a scraped knee could lead to something far worse. That fear was also matched by anger; despite the continuous incoming of Red Cross supplies, none had reached us.

"All the better," I said. I would not mind if Georgie became so ill that he lost his swagger. Neither would all the younger boys he constantly bullied. "*We're* not making him reach into the bag. And we won't be hurting him. The caterpillars will do the work for us."

"If he gets blisters, they might get infected,"

she said, sticking to her argument. "He could die."

That was more difficult to argue against, for I had to consider how much trouble Georgie's death might make for me and maybe my family.

I'd been so proud of coming up with a way to turn the caterpillars into weapons, but now I had three bags of caterpillars that would live for at least two days without food, and nothing to do with them except turn them loose.

Then came my next flash of insight. Nakahara's dog.

Thirty-Three

In terms of excitement and adventure for me, the rest of the day rivaled any day in all the pages of *Ivanhoe*.

We heard the bell from the kitchen area, signaling that it was time to prepare the lunch rations of rice and mystery meat. Even though Elsbeth was in good enough health to do her chores at the kitchen, Laura and I had made it part of our daily routine to help her and Sophie.

"I will see you there," I told Laura. I needed to run to our room at our house a block over so I could tie the bags shut and hang the bags on a hook. There, they would be safe until evening.

I left Pietje with Aniek and Nikki and began

carrying the bags weighted with marbles that clanked with each long step. I rounded the corner of a house and saw a blur of movement, but too late to react.

Georgie and his gang had been waiting for me. One of his friends blindsided me with a tackle. I fell sideways, landed with an *oomph,* and let go of the three bags.

In a flurry of action, two more jumped on me, pinning my arms and legs to the ground so that I was on my back, helpless.

Georgie, bare chested in sandals and shorts like all the other boys, stood over me.

"I told you this day would come," he said. He kicked me in the ribs with the side of his foot. Then he kicked me three more times, each blow a heavy bounce that lifted me off the ground, despite the boys holding me down.

Another boy handed him the three bags that had fallen. It was a diversion that gave me a momentary reprieve.

"What have we here?" Georgie asked.

Now I was torn between several outcomes. If I let him reach inside and touch the poisonous caterpillars, I would have the satisfaction of seeing his pain, and I was so angry I didn't care about any other possible consequences.

But if that happened, I had no assurance as to the fate of the caterpillars. If Georgie and his friends took the bags away or dumped out all the caterpillars and stomped on them, I would not be able to use the poison against Nakahara' dog. There were so few pine trees in our Jappenkamp, I didn't know if I would be able to get any more caterpillars.

Yet if I warned Georgie about the caterpillars, he might still destroy them, and I wouldn't have the satisfaction of at least seeing Georgie suffer.

I waited too long. The decision was taken out of my hands.

Georgie looked inside the bag. "Caterpillars?"

He showed it to one of the boys standing beside him.

"Don't touch," the boy said. "Those ones have a sting to them."

"These?" Georgie asked. "Really?"

Another of the boys looked in and confirmed it for them. "Poisonous. Very poisonous."

"What would he be doing with them?" Georgie asked. "With those marbles?"

Georgie kicked me again. "What are you doing with them?"

I hardly felt the kick, although I was sure my ribs would ache later when my cold rage dissipated.

He kicked once again, harder. "What are you doing with them?"

I could come up with no answer that seemed like it would stop him from doing what he chose to do with the bags and the contents. It seemed like my silence infuriated him, and since I was helpless to strike out in any other way, I kept that silence as he kicked my thigh.

"What are you doing with them?"

"Maybe that's enough," one of the boys said, the one pinning my left arm to the ground. Georgie's savageness must have been frightening to him.

Georgie sneered. "Poison caterpillars. We'll see about that."

He turned one of the bags sideways, and marbles rained on my chest first.

"Hey," one of the standing boys said. "You don't mess with those kinds of caterpillars."

"I do," Georgie said. "How bad can a caterpillar be? That's what I'd like to see."

Georgie tilted the bag more and a few caterpillars plopped onto my neck and lower face. Although I felt an immediate sting, like a light dusting of hot embers on my skin, I wasn't going to give him satisfaction.

"You guys are wrong," he said with a continued sneer. "They're not poisonous."

He plopped a few more, then shook the entire bag free of caterpillars. His mistake was that some of the caterpillars landed on the bare shoulders of the two boys pinning my arms. As native Dutch boys to the Indies, they knew exactly how much those caterpillars should be avoided. They yelped in outrage. And frantic, they released my arms to dust themselves of the caterpillars.

My legs were still pinned, but that gave me a chance to half turn at the waist and grab Georgie's legs with my free arms. There is no sense trying to describe the depth of my fury. My hands were no weapons because my fists against his legs would have done no damage, but I had teeth.

Georgie struggled to slide loose. He twisted to keep from falling backward on his head and landed stomach first. The back of his calves were exposed, and I bit into the meat of the calf muscle on his left leg and held on as he screamed.

Blows landed on my head and my shoulders from the other boys, but I was locked on. I tasted his blood flowing from his leg out of the sides of my mouth. Because my arms were wrapped around both his legs, Georgie couldn't try to kick me loose. I had become his lamprey.

"Get him off me!" Georgie screamed.

I endured more blows and kicks but it took two hands around my throat to pry me loose; one of the boys finally realized the only thing that was going to stop me was cutting off my airflow.

I fell to the side, gasping for breath. When I found my feet, the boys stepped back, staring at me with awed horror.

Georgie was still on his stomach. The gash in his calf showed tangled bits of muscle fibers. I thought that was why they were staring. I wiped my face with the back of my wrist, and blood streaked my skin. Georgie's blood.

So that explained the horror. I must have looked like a monster. Georgie's blood was probably staining my teeth.

"I've marked each of you," I said. I spit blood and wiped my face again and saw more of Georgie's blood across the back of my wrist. "If I hear of any more children crying at your hands, I'm going to hunt you down, one by one. What he got, you'll get ten times worse."

I meant it and they knew it.

Georgie rolled over and hopped onto his good leg. He lifted the back of his other leg and looked down at the wound and groaned. "Look . . . look . . ."

He didn't get a chance to finish.

"No, you look at this," one of the boys said through teeth gritted with pain. He held out his arm where narrow and inch-long angry red welts already were pushing up from where caterpillars had landed. "We told you the caterpillars were trouble but you were too stupid to listen."

"You dumped them on us." The other boy who shared the rain of caterpillars swung hard and punched Georgie in the belly. "Here's what you get for that."

Georgie clutched himself, his wind gone.

The boy who punched him said, "Not a word about this to any of the mothers, understand? Or it will be much, much worse when we find you."

They walked away.

So did I, in a shamble that betrayed how much my body hurt. I had two consolations. The aches distracted me from the severe stinging of the caterpillars. And I was able to pick up the remaining two bags.

Maybe there was a third consolation.

My wounds, I believed in *Ivanhoe* fashion, were the wounds of a man who had survived an injustice. Not so much for Georgie.

Thirty-Four

Before going to sleep that night, I drank as much water as my stomach could hold. I did this so that my bladder would wake me in the early hours of the morning. It turned out to be an unnecessary precaution, however, because I was unable to fall asleep.

I had used a narrow stick to move marbles out of the bags without touching the caterpillars. My weapon was ready.

In the dark I listened to the sounds of my family and squeezed the occasional bedbug. I needed to take shallow breaths because if I inhaled too deeply, I'd feel a stab by my ribs where Georgie had kicked me. Dr. Eikenboom had washed my caterpillar stings with hibiscus water, which reduced the swelling. But the aches of the blows to other parts of my body would not let me relax.

Dr. Kloet had tended to Georgie's wound. Rumor had gone through camp that Nakahara's dog had bitten Georgie. That told me he had chosen to believe the threats made against him if he told any adults.

I had no way of counting time in the darkness, and I tried to keep my mind on the task ahead. I did not want to think about the letters that had reached the camp earlier in the day. For weeks there had been no correspondence, and today, a bag full, as if Nakahara had been hoarding letters to release all at once. Family after family had rejoiced to hear from fathers and older sons who were working on the construction of a railway between Bangkok in Thailand and Rangoon in Burma. No letters had come for Elsbeth, though. She told us that she was sure it was because of how much my father hated writing. I had my doubts. A headmaster who hated writing?

I knew the truth but didn't want to admit it. If he could have written a letter, he would have. Even Pietje saw through my mother's lie, and I reassured him by pointing out that some letters contained news of the deaths of fathers and sons. So really, no news was good news, I told him, something I couldn't quite fool myself into accepting.

To avoid wondering about my father, I focused on what I planned to do with the two bags of

caterpillars that still hung in our room. I visualized the route I would take and the likely places where Japanese soldiers might patrol. Finally, when my bladder ached to the point of bursting, I decided it was late enough to sneak out. I rolled my straw mat into a tube and took it, along with the caterpillars, outside where I first knelt to empty my bladder.

Clouds blocked the moonlight, and I was grateful for that. When I reached the wall of Nakahara's garden enclosure, I crept over to where it connected to the old Dykstra house. I hung the bags from my neck, letting them rest on my back so that I wouldn't squish the caterpillars between me and the wall. I slipped the straw mat tube down the front of my shirt as I'd done the first time I'd climbed the wall.

The curlings of dried concrete made the climb simple. Just before reaching the top of the wall, I grabbed a goodly piece of concrete with my right hand and reached for the tube with my left hand, balancing on my footholds. This was not a complicated balancing act, but my sore ribs protested.

I put the mat across the top of the wall, covering the shards of glass that had been embedded in more concrete. Then I shinnied up and found my balance, straddling the row of glass by placing my feet in the narrow space on each side. I shifted the bags from my back to my chest, then pressed my back against the Dykstra house. I hoped it melted my silhouette into the structure.

It gave me a view of the open space where we played marbles during the day. Beyond it, I saw a small flare of light. A match to a cigarette.

A soldier.

Below me, I heard a small warning woof. The dog had stopped directly below me, panting. But it wasn't the threat a soldier was. My entire focus zeroed in on the small glow of that cigarette. At each inhalation, it brightened, and it was getting closer. I was trapped. Moving to climb down on the outside of the wall would put me easily in his vision. Dropping down on the inside of the wall would deliver me to Nakahara's dog.

I remained as motionless as possible. If the dog barked . . .

The soldier stopped so close to the wall that I could smell the cigarette smoke. He turned to the wall, then urinated and sighed. After a yawn and a stretch, he resumed his patrol, leaving me with only one enemy. Who stood below me, just as motionless as I was.

I cannot pretend that I did not know my actions would be cruel to an innocent animal. The terror it inflicted was terror it had been trained to inflict. I cannot pretend that I underestimated how painful it would be. I'd spent hours earlier enduring the sting of the poison. But this was a camp where a dozen people died each week, often in horrible pain. Cruelty was the reality of this life.

However, I did not know how much suffering my actions would cause.

I fumbled with untying the bags even though they weighed very little without the marbles inside. I squatted, and then just as Georgie had done earlier to me, I shook the bags loose of their contents.

I could only imagine the flight of the caterpillars as they drifted downward to settle on the dog. I had to imagine the first contact on its fur, where the poison of the protective fuzz would have had little effect. I pictured caterpillars landing on its eyes and in its mouth because it had been panting and staring upward.

I've since learned from veterinarians what I didn't understand then. Often a dog will swat at the processionary caterpillar with its paw, where the sensitive skin burns immediately. The dog's impulse is to lick the paw to ease the pain, which then spreads the poison to its mouth. Because dogs have such powerful salivation glands, the poison soon reaches the dog's bloodstream, where it often delivers a severe allergic reaction and lowered blood pressure. But I had inadvertently delivered caterpillars directly into the mouth of Nakahara's dog. The agony must have been incredible on its tongue and the inside of its cheeks, not to mention its eyes if one had landed there.

All that I could dimly see was that the dog had

rolled over. It pawed frantically at its mouth and nose, uttering a piteous, choked whine that haunts me whenever I remember it.

Miserable as I was at my success, I climbed back down and snuck back to the house, where I could join my family in sleeping on our straw mats.

I left behind a dog that was going into convulsions and would die in the arms of Nakahara before morning.

Thirty-Five

It was fortunate for all of us that two other pine trees in camp began to disgorge lines of caterpillars. In the first light of day, Nakahara had seen the corpses of the caterpillars matted in the dog's hair where it had rolled over them, so his fury was directed at the dog for not knowing enough to leave the caterpillars alone. We knew this because he'd demanded an explanation from our translator, who had explained to him about the poison the caterpillars contained and then left the house to joyfully pass along the news about the dead dog to anyone who would listen.

It had been my plan to wait to sneak into his house as many days as necessary until hearing Nakahara was drunk, when he went on his rampages. Whenever he did this, all of camp knew. He would stagger down the streets, yelling at his soldiers and threatening them with his waving sword. When he ran out of violent energy, he would disappear into his house, and all of camp would feel an ease of tension.

I found it fortunate that in his grief later that day, Nakahara started to drink himself into the type of oblivion that he usually reserved for a full moon. I had little knowledge of how long a person would be unconscious from alcohol, so in the evening, I didn't wait long. Instead, I snuck out of the house as soon as I heard the comforting snores of my family.

I was on a righteous mission, a boy like Ivanhoe, fighting to help the poor and downtrodden, and I knew that God would ensure my safety. Where I should have felt fear, exhilaration drove me forward. I would be the knight presenting Red Cross supplies to Dr. Eikenboom, and Laura would adore me even more for my braveness and cunning.

This time when I climbed the wall with my rolled-up straw mat, the bag hanging from my neck was not filled with poisonous caterpillars but with peelings from the kitchen. I stood on the top of the wall with my back pressed to the Dykstra house and surveyed the garden as best I could in the darkness to make sure it was clear below.

Soldiers lived in the Dykstra house. Not once—

when the peepholes had been open—had I observed them moving freely in Nakahara's garden, and I assumed they were as forbidden to enter his private reserve as any of the Dutch women and children. I was not expecting any of them to step into the garden, but I did wonder if Nakahara had posted a sentry to replace his dog. I could see no movement, but I wasn't in a hurry to make a mistake.

A light breeze during the day had brought relief from the heat and from the stench of the open sewer, and it had picked up in strength with nightfall. The leaves of the solitary banyan in the center of the garden made for rustling that masked any sounds that could have given me cues to whether anyone was hidden in the shadows. But it would also mask any sounds I made.

As I studied the open area below, I took a deep breath and noticed the sweet perfume of the small white flowers of the melati. The rough plaster of the wall of the house at my back was still warm from the day's heat, adding to the moistness of the skin of my neck. The shrieks of distant monkeys seemed to tunnel directly into my brain. It was the type of moment, I would learn later, that soldiers share when the body is at full alert for fight and the senses are hyper. It's the knife-edge moment when life on one side of the blade is most vivid because death on the other side of a razor-thin margin is so near.

I blinked a few times. I delivered a silent prayer. Then, using the handholds and toeholds of the outcroppings of mortar, I descended into the private garden. I took a few steps, then froze. The straw mat!

I had left it on top of the wall. What if a soldier saw it there?

I climbed up again, retrieved the mat, and climbed down again. I tucked it into the back of my shorts and stayed along the wall as I moved toward the rear door of Nakahara's house. I had to trust that it was unlocked; otherwise, all of what I had planned would fail.

The pig caught my scent and grunted. Geese, I knew, often served as sentries. I'd wondered if pigs were the same, so I'd brought the bag of peelings just in case. I tossed the bag into the enclosure, trusting if it could smell me, it would also smell the scraps.

The grunting ceased.

I moved to the door. I had an extra surge of adrenaline at the thought of Nakahara walking toward it from the other side, awakened from a drunken stupor and wanting fresh night air. I could see his hand reaching for the doorknob as I reached for it from my side, and for a long period of time this fear paralyzed me.

I told myself that I was too far to turn back. I gently turned the doorknob slightly, and it slid easily. But was it bolted on the inside? I pulled, then pulled harder. It remained in place, not even the squeak of a bolt holding it in place. I felt the sag of defeat and let out a deep breath. It wasn't until I let go of the door handle that I felt it shift and realized how stupid I had been.

I turned the doorknob again, and this time pushed the door instead of pulled. It opened. Here was my Rubicon. I was still not committed to the theft. I could still pull the door shut and sneak back out of the garden and return to the tiny safe haven that was my family lost in their dreams for the night.

I almost succumbed to the temptation to leave. But I remembered Nakahara's satisfied sneer as he rolled my two marbles in his hand. I remembered how he had kicked and beaten Sophie and Dr. Eikenboom and my mother, and that renewal of cold rage was enough impetus for me to continue.

I had done intelligence work ahead of time, asking the Dutch ladies who cleaned the house and cooked for him to describe the interior for me, so I knew it was designed much like most of the other houses of the camp. The rear of the house contained rooms on each side of the hallway, and the front of the house had a sitting room and the kitchen and dining room. I'd been told that the Red Cross boxes were in a room ahead on the right-hand side, two doors down the hallway, and opposite the room where Nakahara slept.

Yet as I took the first step into the house and

into a soft light, my chest felt like it would explode at the surge of my heart rate. A lamp was on in the sitting room, around the corner from the end of the hallway, so it gave enough glow to show the hallway was clear. But was someone in the sitting room? My mouth open, I listened as intently as I could for any signs that my entry had been detected.

The house remained still. I tiptoed past the doors on each side of the hall. When I reached the final door, I heard irregular snorts, the sound of a man too drunk to sleep soundly. Still, was there a soldier in his sitting room? I dropped to my knees to peek around the corner. The furniture was arranged with the delicacy of balance that I'd seen in the homes of our Dutch friends before the war; it had a woman's touch. Nice prints on the walls. Doilies on the backs of chairs. A fine rug on hardwood.

It was also empty of anyone to enjoy it, so I crawled across the room to the front door with the intent to unlock it, making it an escape route should I need it. I had been told by the Dutch women that there was a bell on the front door, and I had no intention of triggering it. But if Nakahara caught me, the noise of the bell would be the last of my worries.

With my hand on the lock, I felt, rather than heard, the creak of the floor of the sitting room. I turned my head.

I'd made a huge mistake. The sitting room had not been empty. Rather, from the hallway, I could not see the person in the armchair because that person's head had not been high enough to be visible.

It was Georgie's mother. Mrs. Smith. Rising from the armchair. Wearing a silk robe, tied around her waist. A nearly empty glass of red wine was on the small table beside her, a wine glass that the chair had also screened from my view when I had first looked into the sitting room.

Her expression was unmistakable fury. Muted fury. She had a forefinger to her lips to indicate silence, and she pointed with her other hand to the bedroom door. I understood the message completely. Not a sound.

I complied, trying to grasp the situation. She was the mystery woman I'd seen through the peephole? But she and Dr. Kloet . . .

Although her robe clung to her in a way that I'd never seen with the big towel robes my mother had worn before the capitulation, I was incapable of giving any realistic imagination to what happened between her and Nakahara or between her and Dr. Kloet. Still I had absorbed enough hints from other sources to know it was not good. Even the story about King David in the Bible said that after he knew Bathsheba, they had a baby, and whatever they'd done that consisted of a man knowing a woman, it was not good.

She motioned for me to rise. I did. Then she walked over to me and leaned in so close that I could smell wine on her breath when she whispered. "Garden."

She kept a hand on my shoulder as she guided me down the hallway, past the room where Nakahara was snoring, out the door, and back into the night air. She shut the door and pushed me to a spot beneath the banyan tree.

"You stupid, stupid child," she hissed. Her nails dug into my shoulders. She was holding me there with both hands, looking into my face. "What has possessed you to go into the house?"

I could have asked her the same question, but she had strength I would have never guessed.

"Red Cross boxes," I said. "They belong to the camp."

"You thought you could steal them?"

"He is drunk," I said.

"And he wouldn't notice in the morning?"

"I would take the boxes from the back."

"And every woman and child in this camp would suffer." Her fury was rising, not abating. "Is that what you want?"

"I would take the boxes from the back."

She slapped my face. "You stupid, stupid child."

I dared not slap back. At least not with my hands. I said the worst thing I could think of from the Bible. I knew it was a woman who did bad things.

I spat back at her, "Whore of Babylon."

She slapped me again.

I was glad to see that she didn't like what I'd said. Since Babylon had been a city in the Bible, it must have been the other word.

I refused to rub my face and give any satisfaction.

"You have no idea what I go through!" she said, leaning in so close I could smell the alcohol again. "No idea I've already saved your life once! Nakahara was going to have you shot for the peepholes in the wall, and I convinced him to take your marbles instead."

As I tried to absorb this new information, an indistinct shout came from Nakahara's house.

She hissed at me. "If you tell anyone about me, I will make sure that you and your family are destroyed by him. Understand? And from tomorrow on, you will protect my son. Someone hurt him bad and he can hardly walk. But he's too scared to tell me what happened. You will protect him. Do you understand? Or next time you will lose more than those precious marbles and your mother her precious drawings."

What was this? My mother had been punished too and had said nothing? I was given no time to grapple with it.

The shouting from inside became louder.

"Do you understand?" As she hissed again, she squeezed my shoulders so hard that it forced a yelp from me. "You tell no one! You protect my son!"

The door opened, spilling soft light into the garden area.

She pushed me away. "Hurry. Up the tree. Or he will kill you."

I scrambled to the first low branch and was pulling myself upward as Nakahara lurched into view below, wearing only a towel around his waist.

I climbed higher, terrified that I would be caught.

It was an unnecessary worry. He had other things on his mind, and below me, in the darkness, soon came sounds that I'd never heard before.

Thirty-Six

Much later, when it became apparent that Mrs. Smith was pregnant, the whisperers passed around with certainty that Dr. Kloet was the father. Because Mrs. Smith was a widow and Dr. Kloet a single man, opinions were divided. Some passed no judgment and said that in these circumstances, each was entitled to find comfort. Others took the middle ground and said if the two performed a marriage ceremony before the birth of the baby, none should see this as scandalous.

At the far end were those who clucked their tongues and wore the self-righteous satisfaction of all those who are first to cast stones.

I heard the conversations in the lines at the kitchen or on the porches, but despite my hatred for her and her son, I found no difficulty in keeping secret what I knew about Mrs. Smith and Nakahara and who the real father might be. Had I passed along the story of how she spent evenings with the Japanese commander, she may well have been lynched as a focal point for how much Nakahara was detested. But she would have known the one source of the information, and she had the power to send Nakahara and his soldiers directly to our family's room and punish us beyond my worst imaginings.

I also knew that when her baby was born, if it had Japanese features—not reddish hair—then everyone would know what I'd known all along. My silence was delayed gratification. It would be all the more satisfying for the camp to be astounded in that manner rather than by a story from me that would hurt my family. When that vindication came, I would no longer have to go from block to block, threatening anyone against mistreating Georgie.

As the weeks passed, though, the camp became more decrepit and the people more destitute. Hundreds of families were packed into an area that should have only held dozens, and hundreds of families lived off rations that could only sustain dozens. Nakahara managed to make the filling of the death wagon an ordinary part of life. Those who wanted to survive learned vigilance, for as the saying went, *een ongeluk ligt in een klein hoekje*, or accidents were waiting in the smallest corners. One of Laura's friends received news that her father had died on the railroad project in Borneo, but she told Laura she didn't know if she was crying because of that or because she was worried about her toothache.

Even something as simple as not promptly closing the front gate behind the daily bread truck held dire consequences. I was farther up the street as it entered the Jappenkamp. In each hand I carried a bucket of raw sewage to be dumped into the collecting pond. Pietje and Nikki had been racing toward the bread truck, along with many other children, because occasionally a loaf of bread spilled off as it turned and backed up to the kitchen area.

From behind me, I heard screaming at the gate. *"Andjing gila! Andjing gila! Andjing gila!"* *Mad dog! Mad dog! Mad dog!*

I could not see beyond the bread truck until it finished backing into position, but when the view came clear, there was a dog nearly as big as the one that had been Nakahara's running in a staggering gait that betrayed the later stages of rabies. It drooled and growled so loudly that I could hear it fifty yards away. And the nearest children to it were Pietje and Nikki.

When the first camp commander had cleared the camp of dogs, cruel as it was, it had been an act of prudence. Rabies was common in the Dutch East Indies, and even prewar, the vaccine for it rare.

Nikki reacted first. She shrieked and fled, trying to catch up with the other children. The three guards at the gate reacted nearly as swiftly. Not since the revolt of the women against teahouse girls had any soldier in camp been forced to unsling a weapon from his shoulders, but they were able to train their sights on the lurching dog within seconds. Behind it, though, were children and the too-real danger of hitting one of them.

Pietje had not moved. He was as transfixed with fear as a rabbit facing a cobra. The soldiers began to run to find a better position to shoot the dog, but the animal's movements were unpredictable. As it neared Pietje, they couldn't risk a shot. At that moment, Nikki turned her head to make sure Pietje was still with her. When she saw Pietje still behind her, she stopped and screamed for him to bolt.

As did I.

I began running toward Pietje.

As did she.

The Japanese soldiers were screaming at her, but she ignored them.

As did I.

I had closed the gap to under ten paces when she reached Pietje and shoved him away from the dog. That broke his paralysis, and he stumbled into a full run. When she tried to follow, the dog had gained on her. Seconds later, the soldiers' gunfire bowled the dog over, and I welcomed Pietje into my arms. Nikki was close behind, and her impact into us almost knocked the three of us onto the road.

"Pietje," I said. "Pietje."

I had one arm around his frail and shaking body, and I reached for Nikki with my other arm.

"Nikki. Nikki."

As I said her name, she began to sob. Both of them clung to me, and I drew in a deep breath of relief that we were all safe. It took a few more seconds to register the other noises around us, and a few more seconds to notice the soldiers pointing at the back of Nikki's leg.

I peeked over her shoulder and saw the gash in her ankle where the dog had managed to nip the skin. And my world seemed to shrink to silence again.

The next hour passed in a disjoined series of events. As Dr. Eikenboom closed the small wound with a couple of sutures and bandaged it, first Elsbeth wept over Nikki, then Sophie, then Dr. Eikenboom. Aniek, Pietje, and I were told to hug Nikki and say good-bye. She would be put in a small room away from others in the camp, and when it appeared that there was no danger to anyone, she would be let out again to play with us.

We were too young to understand that rabies generally has an incubation period of two to twelve weeks. It was probably just as well. If we had known that this was the last time we would hold her while she was alive, those moments would have been far too painful to bear. It was just as well, too, that Nikki had no idea of the fate that was awaiting her.

Our reprieve of false hope lasted several weeks, and we were allowed to come to the door and open it and talk to her from the hallway. Then, she became ill with what seemed like the flu. My mother's artificial optimism on our behalf crumpled, and that was the last we heard my sister's voice.

Not until I became a father could I fully comprehend the horror that those final days were for Nikki and for my mother. Fully incubated, the virus is untreatable and the progression of symptoms as predictable as the fatal outcome. From the first shaking of her body—well after the sutures had been removed and the skin of her heel completely healed—Elsbeth and Sophie knew they would have to watch Nikki's fever worsen to the acute pain of headaches, violent spasms, and mania, to hallucinations and delirium, then paralysis and coma. Each day, the two of them would enter the room and face this with Nikki, watching her endure the agony of one stage and knowing the next would be worse, until they were forced to keep her bound to the bed so that she could not attack them. Elsbeth could not walk out at the end of the day without Sophie's support, her arm on Sophie's shoulder, grief sagging her body almost to collapse.

It took ten days of suffering for Nikki to die.

Thirty-Seven

In her final month of pregnancy, Mrs. Smith, along with Georgie, vanished from the Jappenkamp. Left behind were most of their belongings, except for photographs and any personal mementos.

This should have fueled massive and delicious speculation. After all, if she and Georgie had escaped, where would they go? A white person would not be able to travel unnoticed, and collaborators in any village would have immediately turned them in to Japanese authorities for a reward. She and her son could not have escaped either. The perimeters of the Jappenkamp were secure, and the gates guarded. At the very least, gossip should have focused on the significance of taking photographs and mementos but leaving behind straw mats and clothing.

I was bursting to tell someone, anyone, about Mrs. Smith and Nakahara, but that would have involved confessing to my invasion of Nakahara's residence and bearing witness to what I had seen. I remained afraid of reprisals against our family, especially after Nikki's death had made Elsbeth so fragile.

This time, however, my mother's withdrawal into darkness did not have a detachment that made us invisible to her. Instead, she would not permit us to be out of her sight. Her fear was that she would be taken away while we were gone and that Aniek and Pietje and I would be left behind in a camp full of children guarded by Japanese soldiers, or worse, the fence around the camp would be taken down and all of the children would have to fend for themselves among the natives. Her efforts to keep us in her sight at all times should have been seen by Sophie and Dr. Eikenboom as a warning that the agony of the darkness in her soul had grown too large, but unfortunately, her fears were not irrational.

Rumors had again reached camp that the Japanese were going to send women to work the mines of Borneo and there would be such a shortage of food that children would not be allowed to stay with their mothers. We should have seen this as a sign that the Japanese were losing the war. Otherwise, their resources would have been ample. We didn't have a radio, and in the camp it felt as if the world had forgotten about us. We didn't even know that the Americans had joined the battle against Germany, or that it was pouring men and planes and ships into war at such a great rate that no matter how well Japan fought, an eventual bankruptcy of resources would doom them.

Then came the letter from Borneo that made for our mother's final undoing. Aniek and Pietje and I learned about it when Elsbeth gathered us in our room and pulled out the large envelope she had kept in her suitcase since the day we moved into the Jappenkamp. "This," Elsbeth said in an eerily calm voice, "was something that I hoped would remain sealed until we were reunited with your father." With the tip of a kitchen knife, she cut the top of the envelope. She poured loose smaller letters from the inside onto the straw mat at our feet.

The one on top had a name printed in my father's strong and clear handwriting: Nikki.

Elsbeth lost her eerie calmness and swallowed down a sob. She held the letter to her cheek for a few moments, then with tenderness, she placed it back into the larger envelope.

There were three other letters on the straw mat. Jeremiah. Aniek. Pietje.

"Pietje," she said, "you are too young to be able to read. So you and I will find a private spot and I will read to you the letter from your father."

She handed Aniek and me the letters that were addressed to us. "Your father asked me to give these to you if he never had a chance to speak to you again."

"Moeder?" Aniek said, not understanding. She was coughing because of a stomach virus that gave her skin a fevered pitch, and beads of sweat ringed her forehead.

I did understand, and I had that same horrible silence in my brain that had come when I'd noticed the bite of a rabid dog on Nikki's heel. The shift of a world tilting and with nothing to hold on to as I slid into the abyss.

"Moeder?" Aniek said again.

"Your father has died," Elsbeth said. Then her face contorted. "Haven't you children faced enough? He is dead and I don't know how much longer I can continue."

Sobs wracked her. She shook off the arms of comfort that Aniek and Pietje tried to place on her shoulders, so violently that Pietje began to cry.

I could only stand there, holding the letter unopened in my hand.

Our father was dead. He and my half brothers had joined the thousands and thousands worked to death, or beaten to death, or starved to death on the construction of the Borneo railway. What hurt me the most was that I had not thanked him for the marble he had given me, that I had not been able to catch up to the truck for a final shout of good-bye.

I left Aniek and Pietje with Mother and walked out of the house with the letter. I sagged back against the wall and sat there with no focus on the other houses or the bamboo fence behind them that kept us away from the world.

As I read my father's simple letter of love to me, I tried to cry when I realized I could not picture his face anymore. But I could not find tears.

Looking back, it is plain that Elsbeth lost her will to live because of the accumulation of tragedies: Nikki's horrible death, followed by the strain of Elsbeth's terror of the Borneo plan, the news that our father and half brothers were dead. To add to it, that night, Aniek succumbed to her infection as we slept. I woke to see Elsbeth holding Aniek's lifeless body, weeping tears that rolled across Aniek's face.

There was nothing left of my mother, and she died too, the next night.

All of this devastated Pietje, and instead of those events drawing us closer as the two survivors in our family, it was as if I became a reminder to him of all that he had lost, and he fled from me as if I were the dog with rabies that had begun this recent chain of events leading to my mother's passing.

For refuge, he clung to Sophie. Literally. There

would be hours when he would not let go of her hand, almost catatonic in his grief. He moved in with Sophie and Laura, and after curfew, I was alone on the straw mat in our tiny room.

I would lie in the dark and count time by the seconds. Each heartbeat brought a literal squeeze of emotional pain, and I would find myself on my back on the straw mat, my spine rigid and arms pressed to my side, hands in fists and eyes closed as tight as possible while I waited in vain for tears to run down my face.

Do not cry.

I hoped that I would die too as I slept, but each morning my traitorous body would begin to stir and sunlight would bring me back to the reality that I had no family.

Thirty-Eight

Within weeks of the passing of Elsbeth and Aniek, I, too, joined the dead.

It began with the usual commotion around the arrival of the bread truck, the same truck that had driven through gates that had once opened to allow a rabid dog into the Jappenkamp.

I was among the women who were unloading rectangular bamboo baskets filled with the round loaves of rough-grained bread. The driver never stepped out of the truck; he was lazy and knew that dozens of volunteers were waiting for the precious cargo. To feed a camp with hundreds upon hundreds, it took much of the back of the flatbed truck to hold the baskets. One tumbled, and several loaves rolled onto the dust beneath the truck.

When portions were cut in exact amounts and doled out to women and children who would take minutes to chew each bite, it was unthinkable to throw away the bread. I got on my belly and rolled beneath the truck to gather the bread.

Had I crawled instead of rolled, I doubt I would have noticed. But I didn't want to hit my head on the underside of the truck. As I rolled, for a moment I was on my back, staring upward at the drive shaft that ran lengthways down the underside, connecting the engine up front to the rear axle. The wood planks of the flatbed above the drive shaft were ninety degrees to the drive shaft and were supported by beams parallel to the drive shaft. There were gaps in the wood planks, and it struck me that the gaps were enough that I could have reached up and grasped the top of the planks with my fingers. And that if I held on and waited, as the truck pulled away, my heels would drag on the ground and I could escape camp hidden beneath the underside of the truck. Or, better yet, if I could fasten a strap and tuck my heels into the strap, I would be unseen with nothing to drag. That wouldn't be too difficult.

The driver just sat in the cab, oblivious and uncaring of what happened behind him. The greatest danger posed by the driver was getting splattered by the juices from the leaves of the betel nut that he spat out of the open window.

A few days after that, I was sitting with Dr. Eikenboom, Laura, Sophie, and Pietje on the porch of Dr. Eikenboom's residence. It was the time of day, a little before curfew, when the heat had faded just enough to make the approaching dusk comfortable.

"I don't know what we can do now," Dr. Eikenboom said to Sophie. "We have nothing left for sulfa and disinfectants. Nothing. I used the last of what we had this afternoon."

The image I'd formed of me clinging to the underside of the bread truck remained in my brain like a burr.

"We trust in God," Sophie told Dr. Eikenboom. "We take comfort knowing that our life on earth is only an eye blink."

I snorted. It was an accident, but it drew her attention.

"Jeremiah?"

"Nothing," I said.

"Jeremiah."

I'd been hiding anger. There was no doubt of that. I woke up angry and I fell asleep angry. It was a blessing of sorts, because I was so angry I didn't even want to eat.

"I don't need those lies," I said.

All eyes turned on me.

"Jesus loves us? God loves us?" I snorted again.

Had Sophie admonished me for my doubts, she would have turned me forever away from any hope of returning to faith. Instead, she nodded.

"I understand," she said. "It is sometimes difficult, with evil around, to believe in what is good."

"It's not that," I said, although, of course, it was. "The Bible is filled with lies."

Again, had she admonished me for this declaration, I would have entrenched my position and fought for it. I was Dutch, after all.

"I suppose," she said, "there are parts that seem difficult to believe. Sometimes, it takes effort to understand what is not plainly spoken."

"It's plain to me," I said, "that Jesus was a liar. The mustard seed is not the smallest in the world."

"In His world, it was," she said. "And those He spoke to in that world understood what He meant."

"Well, I know that men cannot stand on a roof that will easily break apart when they want to lower a friend."

"What's this?" She was genuinely curious, and because of it, I did not feel threatened, and because I did not feel threatened, we were able to explore my question.

I explained to her that I did not believe the

313

story where men lowered their paralyzed friend into a crowded house for Jesus to heal.

"Ah," Sophie said. "Isn't that strange."

"Not strange. Simply a lie."

"No," she said, smiling. "Strange that I had often asked myself the same question, among others. So I was relieved when I finally found the answer to this one. You see, Jeremiah, in the time that Jesus lived, the roof was made flat and sturdy so that families could spend time on it as extra living space. It was supported by frames to make it sturdy, with materials laid across the frames that held the weight of the people above it. Yet all one needed to do was lift off those materials, and there would be space between the crossbeams to lower a friend."

I blinked. The explanation was simple. And years later, as an architect, I easily verified it.

"Yet," Sophie said, "that does not mean I am telling you that you should live without doubts. Jesus Himself doubted the Father, on the night before He accepted death on the cross."

I think she knew me well enough to know I would give this serious thought.

"It still does not bring back my family," I said. It was one thing to answer the question about the roof, and another to rid me of my anger.

Her response was to try to hold me to comfort me. I pushed her away.

Probably to break the awkward silence, Dr.

314

Eikenboom spoke again. "All the new Red Cross boxes—a soldier confirmed that Nakahara's been selling them on the black market."

At the time, her statement seemed of no significance, and I gave it the lack of consideration it apparently deserved, because I was seeing a different solution.

"Can we still find money and other items to trade?" I asked. "Like before, when Adi found what we needed?"

"Sure," Dr. Eikenboom said, "but none of that stuff has been able to leave camp since Nakahara closed the drainage pipe."

"I found another way," I said. I told them about the delivery truck.

Dr. Eikenboom's smile was the kind reserved for a boy with silly dreams.

"Tell me why it wouldn't work," I said. I knew that if I could convince her it was sustainable, she would consider it.

It should have also occurred to me how strange it was that she had taken this long after the drainage pipe had been sealed to remark on the desperation of supplies.

"Where would you stay at night?" she asked. "You would be forced to live outside the camp."

"Sleeping in the streets is no worse than where I sleep now."

"You could only come and go with the delivery truck each morning," Sophie offered. "While you are gone in the evening, it will be discovered during roll call."

"You are the one who makes up death certificates," Laura said to Dr. Eikenboom. "That would take him off the list and he wouldn't be counted anymore. Then, if he only leaves with the truck every second day, he could stay in camp and hide in the house during roll call at least some of the time."

"Look at his skin," Dr. Eikenboom said. "No one would mistake him for a native."

I thought again of the driver of the bread truck, spitting out his window as he chewed on slices of betel nut wrapped in betel leaves.

Pinang. The combination of betel nut and betel leaf, sometimes sprinkled with cardamom or clove or other spices. For the driver of the truck had without intention reminded me of what Dr. Eikenboom had said when she'd slyly encouraged me to go out of camp following the python attack . . . *"unless somehow some very smart Dutch children found a way to stain their hands and faces with a dye made from the juice of a betel nut."*

The betel nut is a seed of the areca palm. Fresh, the husk is green, and all it takes is a soft knife to cut it. When the fruit has dried, it takes a special cutter to slice it like almonds. When chewed with leaves, the combination of nut and leaf gives a mild stimulant, like a strong cup of coffee. This had been a tradition in South Asia and the Pacific for thousands of years. Swallowing a few teaspoons of powdered betel nut removes tapeworms and other internal parasites. It was also used to freshen breath.

More than that, it deadens hunger and gives energy, and it's a social glue, with households owning beautiful and ornate pots of silver or gold to hold the juices. It was a common sight to see a person with what looked like blood gushing from his or her teeth dribbling the juices into a shared container.

The nut was also used to make a brown dye.

"Remember?" I asked Dr. Eikenboom. "You once suggested the juice of a betel nut. If I rubbed it on my skin and in my hair, I would look like a half breed. There would be no danger."

She gave that serious thought. "But then you couldn't return to the camp. The dye doesn't wash off easily, and here, the soldiers would see you sooner or later and ask why you are dyed brown."

"Then," I said, "I would just live outside the camp. I would sneak beneath the bread truck and ride into camp under it. Laura could crawl under the truck and take the supplies that I'm delivering. And while she takes the supplies, she could give me a new list, along with money and what I can use to trade. I would leave with the truck again. Each day I would make new deliveries."

"No," Dr. Eikenboom said. "That is entirely too risky."

"Where are the risks?" I asked.

"It is unfair to ask you to live on the streets outside our camp."

"Sophie and Laura already take care of Pietje," I said. "Think of the extra food and medicine I could bring you every day."

"And if you are caught?" she asked.

"How would I get caught?" I answered.

"No," she said again.

But a week later, when a dozen children had died from lack of a simple sulfa pill to stop the spread of infection, she changed her mind. And by then, I had already rigged the truck with straps beneath the flatbed. I'd done it partially in case she changed her mind, and partially to prove to myself how easy it was to remain unseen beneath the truck as the bread was unloaded.

Because it was parked there for at least a quarter of an hour each day, there had been no difficulty not only preparing three straps that sagged like hammocks but also finding ways to securely attach them to the support beams of the flatbed. I was even able to prove how simple it was to get into the straps. On my knees beneath the truck, I would lift my feet and slide my lower legs into the rear strap, almost to my thighs. Once my feet were in, I pulled myself into the middle strap and wriggled forward so that the weight of my upper body was supported by my chest, with the straps running upward around my armpits, and the rear straps supported my knees. Then I would reach for the forward strap and hold it with my hands stretched in front of me. It converted me into an arrow, hanging below the truck, facedown and looking at the road. I knew that I could hang the bags from my arms and travel like this for miles.

Dr. Eikenboom spoke to me about it again at the end of a day. Sophie and Laura and Pietje had joined us on her porch.

"There is a problem with writing a death certificate for you," she said. "I hadn't given it much thought until now, because things have been so desperate. The soldiers count the bodies at the end of the day to make sure the number matches the amount of death certificates that are turned into the commander."

She put a hand on my shoulder. "It would mean that you would have to be placed among the bodies on the death cart and you would have to stay there until the count is complete."

I nodded. "After soldiers count the dead bodies, I will sneak out of the death cart, hide in camp, and not report for roll call. And the next morning, I'll leave with the bread truck."

This was possible—I wouldn't be noticed among the children who always ran when the bread truck arrived. If my skin was dark, I would be part of the town, not the camp.

It was her turn to nod. Her face was solemn.

"I will do it," I said.

Yet nothing in my imagination could have prepared me for the sensations and smells that came the next afternoon as Dr. Eikenboom and Sophie lifted me into the death cart. They placed me near the top, knowing three more bodies remained to cover me. This way, even a sharp-eyed soldier wouldn't notice the movement of my ribs as I breathed. The slightest of mercies was that they waited as long as possible to add me to the dead, so that I had only a half hour among the corpses.

There are times I still wake from nightmares with the stench in my nostrils. Of bodies riddled with gangrene and pus, of bodies not cleaned of the vomit or diarrhea. The flesh was not cold or clammy but instead warm from the sun, and gasses inside the bodies shifted, giving a sensation of life. I had to hold myself still for that eternity, until I felt the touch of a soldier's stick on my heels, for the bodies were all stacked in one direction, exposing our feet for the count.

When it was over, and Sophie and Dr. Eikenboom returned to pull the bodies off of me, I was shaking in tight spasms.

They rushed me away from the death cart and into Dr. Eikenboom's residence, where they had prepared buckets of hibiscus water to cleanse me of the filth.

My spasms would not ease.

"Jeremiah, Jeremiah," Sophie said, stroking my forehead. "This is such a brave and noble thing you've done. You are now a lifeline for the women and children of this camp. I have no doubt that God will be with you as you save so many lives."

Thirty-Nine

The next day when the truck arrived, I scooted beneath it again, and in an awkward position in the shade below the flatbed as women unloaded the bins of bread, I rubbed betel nut dye on my arms and legs and face and neck and into my hair, transforming myself into a half breed. I was also equipped with a bag of currency that Dr. Eikenboom had gathered from block representatives and a list of items to return to the camp.

As I discovered when the truck lurched forward with a grinding of gears that rattled with disturbing closeness, it was less than a ten-minute drive from the Jappenkamp to the bakery. It was not difficult to remain hidden beneath the moving truck for that journey. The swaying of the straps mitigated the jolting of the vehicle over potholes, and the movement of air swept away the exhaust. It was disconcerting to know the drive shaft was only inches from my head, whirling in a blur. Had my hair been long enough for a sideways gust of wind to blow the ends into the drive shaft, the instant wrapping of hair would have pulled my face into it and I would have died a horrible death as it continued to rotate my head. But my hair was cut to a buzz to prevent lice, and I was relatively comfortable and safe in the makeshift hammock beneath the flatbed.

Instead, the difficulty on the first day was finding the right moment to leave the straps and crawl out from beneath the truck, something I had not given much thought to during my planning.

At the bakery, the truck driver remained in the vehicle when it came to a stop and he shut off the engine. I saw the bare feet of boys and the sandaled feet of men who unloaded the empty bins from the back of the truck and replaced them with full bins. It was certain I would be discovered here.

It appeared I had no choice but to go along for the ride as the truck made its next deliveries. I tried to anticipate what might happen at the next stop. What if someone there saw me on the ground as the truck drove away? When the driver heard about that, he might get curious enough to look beneath the vehicle and see the straps.

What about on the road? I asked myself. Traffic

jams were frequent, and while it was stopped, I could roll out from beneath. That too had risks. I would need to depend on luck and disinterest from those on scooters and motorcycles, and indeed on no Japanese soldiers spotting me and asking questions.

So I remained in the straps and fought the gradual ache that came at the pressure points on my thighs and chest. I decided that when the truck was parked back at the bakery overnight, I would sneak back and add padding to those straps.

It was fortunate then that at the next delivery, the driver needed to pull as far off the road as possible for traffic to get around the vehicle. Drivers sat on the right side of the vehicle, as the Dutch East Indies had established a pattern of left-side driving. It meant the left side of the truck was very close to the wall of the building. It was a very simple matter to work out of the straps, roll toward the wall, and sneak backward and out of sight.

I was free. Homeless, but free. For the next hour, I fought an impulse to flinch as any of the natives glanced at me, but the dye must have been effective enough, for I drew no attention. My appearance was no different than any other poor Javanese half breed, roaming the streets out of boredom and in vain hopes of spotting anything of value.

I roamed. Naturally, since all that the Japanese

had done was confiscate homes and surround them with a fence, the nearby residential streets were identical to those of the Jappenkamp, except that the yards were much less worn because outside of the camp, one house held at most three families. None were Dutch—these were homes taken from the colonizers after the capitulation and left open to be scavenged and for squatter's rights.

When I reached the first market area of this unfamiliar town that I had lived in for months and months and months, I was astounded at the variety and availability of fruits and breads and butchered chickens and sheep. Did no one realize that hundreds and hundreds of women and children were in a desperate fight against starvation on the other side of the bamboo fence?

The answer perhaps was that few cared.

Anti-Dutch graffiti was everywhere, and I was to learn that in return for cooperation, the Japanese had promised self-governance. The war might end, but life on the colony would never be the same.

I spent the remainder of the afternoon among the crowds in the market. If this town was anything like Sukorejo, where I had been raised, gangs of boys from homes of the poor would roam in their established territories. I had been given permission by Dr. Eikenboom to use some of the money to feed myself, and the glorious taste of fresh cantaloupe nearly brought me to tears that leaving Pietje behind had not done. I didn't know if it was the taste or the wish that somehow I could get some of the slices to the brother who was now lost to me.

When the shop owners began to empty their stalls, I hung around the periphery, waiting until darkness provided a blanket of safety. And when the night insects began to call from the trees, I made my way toward the Jappenkamp, sealed by that bamboo fence in the center of the town.

I came to the drainage ditch and the familiar tree that had hidden the python that attacked Laura. I sat against the trunk of the tree and waited.

Was Adi even still alive?

I could not know. I could only take the chance that his life was still one of solitude because of the cleft lip and palate that disfigured him. I could only hope that his habits had not changed. I needed him. The women and children of the Jappenkamp needed him.

The breeze shifted and brought the stench of open sewage from within the Jappenkamp. With that came memories that I wanted buried, the funerals of Nikki and Aniek and Elsbeth, the last night that Elsbeth was alive, how morning had shown Pietje the lifeless body of his mother and his reaction of horror to me.

Our bodies are the carriers of our souls. Too often we get lost in the physical world when our souls should focus elsewhere. Just as often, we get lost in the darkness of our souls when our bodies can so easily provide escape and distraction.

Sitting against the banyan tree, I banished my melancholy by listening to every night sound, trying to sort and categorize each one, plucking them out of the cacophony. Shrieks of monkeys, the hoot of an owl, the slamming of a distant door, the roar of a motorcycle. I examined each new scent, from the perfume of the flowers to the vague sulfur smell of the bog that was formed by the water from the drainage ditch. I let my skin tingle for the sensation of ants that crossed my bare shins, allowed grass to itch at my thighs where my shorts touched the ground.

I managed to make time pass by getting lost in each moment of the present, and when my mind was tempted to stray into the future or the past, I pictured Laura on the first day I met her, radiant in a dress, her long blond hair clean and bouncy. I pictured her on the porch of Dr. Eikenboom's house, solemnly listening to the plans for me to become a way of getting medical supplies back into camp. I imagined photos of Amsterdam and placed the two of us there as a young couple, beneath streetlights along a canal.

This was how I banished my demons until Adi arrived.

I didn't want him startled into fleeing, so I called out to him.

"Adi, it's Jeremiah. From the camp!"

He ran toward the banyan tree, and I heard joy in his voice that brought a lump to my throat.

"Jeremiah!"

Thus began my final months of the war, as a half-native trader and Dutch boy smuggler.

Forty

A few weeks passed without mishap or any real danger. Adi and I would do our trading with those he carefully selected, none of whom gave me a second glance, as Adi did most of the speaking and negotiating. Every day or every second day I would enter camp hidden beneath the bread truck with goods for Dr. Eikenboom and leave with what she had collected for me to use to barter. At night I stayed with Adi's family, pretending I was happy not to be alone.

Then came the morning at the market when I heard my given name and surname called out from behind me. Had I been more alert, I would have pretended not to hear. Jeremiah Prins, after all, was supposed to be dead and certainly not supposed to be wandering the village with his face darkened by the brown dye from nut juice.

I couldn't help myself. For I knew the voice. I turned to see the smug and triumphant face of Georgie. He held a canvas bag filled with fruits and breads, obviously the results of his own market shopping.

"I knew it!" he said in clear Dutch. His voice rose above the din of the crowded market. Adi grabbed my hand and tried to pull me away. He, too, understood the danger if I was recognized.

It was enough of a warning that I didn't reply in Dutch to Georgie, for my articulation in that language would have drawn attention to me from the Javanese.

Georgie pushed in close. "I knew it. I knew it. You've run from camp, haven't you?"

I could see by the expressions across his face that he was calculating how best to hurt me.

Adi stepped in.

"You," he said to Georgie. "You're the one whose mother was given a house and servants by the Japanese. The one whose mother had a Japanese girl. Everyone knows who the father is."

Adi spat. "And the commander still visits every few days, that's what I hear. If you say a word about my friend to anyone, you won't spend a safe moment outside the house. There are gangs, you know, that will kill you for whatever reward I offer."

Georgie backed away slightly, enough of an indication that I knew the leverage was back on our side, and the hatred spilled out. "After the war," I said, "everyone will know what I know about her and the commander."

It hit him like a punch. But I didn't expect the counterstrike.

"And I will be happy myself to spread the word about your own mother," he said.

"She is dead," I answered, closing my heart to any emotion that came with memories of her.

"That won't matter," he said. "Will you want everyone knowing what she did to Jasmijn? I know about the feather in her mouth. From a *pillow.*"

If I didn't stagger physically, whatever showed on my face was enough to goad him.

I didn't answer.

"See?" he asked. "See? The commander told my mother if she doesn't do what he wants, he will kill me. At least my mother does what she does to keep me alive. Your mother—"

I punched him square in the mouth, and he dropped to his knees.

Adi scrambled forward and pulled him back up again. Adi hissed at me. "No fighting! We cannot draw attention to ourselves!"

Adi put his arm around Georgie's shoulder like they were friends. "Both of you. Stop. You must each pretend the other does not exist. Then you will stay alive. Understand?"

"I understand." Georgie wiped blood from his split lip. "I understand that if Jeremiah ever speaks a word about my mother, the world will learn about his."

Georgie smiled at me, the smile of a victor. "Am I right, Jeremiah?"

"The same in return," I said. It was the best I could manage. "If you ever speak of my mother, the world learns about yours. And remember, I was the one who got in the last punch."

That didn't diminish his smile as I had hoped.

"And you remember," he said, "that I'm the one who has the green statue marble that I stole from Dr. Kloet's collection. The one with a tiny horse statue inside. Didn't it once belong to your father? I think I'll go home now and throw it in the sewage."

Before I could take another swing at Georgie, Adi pushed me away and propelled me forward, through the throngs of shoppers at the market.

From behind me, I heard Georgie's vindictive laughter, much more painful than any punch he could have thrown.

Forty-One

I was fortunate that Adi's family was Protestant, as it prevented some of the awkwardness that came as they sheltered me in their home. I had had little exposure to Muslim or Hindu traditions. What I did know about the native Indonesians I had gleaned from my time at the laundry, watching closely as someone invisible to them.

Understanding the social customs helped considerably when Adi first brought me to the small thatched structure that was his home, at the far edge of the town, with rice paddies behind, stretching to the distant volcanoes that ringed the valley. It was hardly larger than a hut, with a single room, a dirt floor, and a smoke-leaking stove.

When he introduced me to his father, Sukurno, I was prepared to show respect by performing *salim*, touching the top of his hand with my forehead as we shook hands.

Sukurno was sitting on a bamboo chair outside their home when Adi led me there, and he surprised me by remaining seated and opening both hands, palms up, in his lap.

I looked into his wrinkled face. I would find out later that he was only in his midforties, but labor and constant cigarettes had added a decade to his appearance. I think he understood my hesitation, for he nodded.

I bowed and put my nose deep into his hands, almost placing my head on his lap. He was greeting me as if I were his son.

What I didn't know was that Adi had spent long hours describing me to them, and describing the previous nights where I'd passed the hours lying on a thick branch of the tree outside the drainage ditch that had once held an ambushing python. I also didn't know that his mother, Utami, who ruled the household, had forced Sukurno to accept my inclusion on the mats that served as their beds.

She was a short, squat woman, with thick calluses from the basket handles used to carry rice. Yet I would learn that her touch was velvet. Adi was her only child, the one who had been born last. All the others before him had died before reaching school age, and she adored him, often kissing him lightly on his nose and lips, as if to tell him that she found his deformity to be beautiful to her.

Sukurno had argued against my presence among them because of the risk and the need to hide my true identity. There was no reason to not fear punishment for treason against the Japanese war efforts. Rumors of my existence would surely spread once even a single person outside the family knew, but long before such news reached Nakahara, the family would have been attacked by the older teenage sons of their neighborhood friends, the radical and independence-minded *pemuda*, the youth groups, who wanted neither Japanese nor Dutch rule on the island and, like the Hitler youth groups in Europe, were barely more than thugs who roamed unchallenged by their elders.

Why had Utami fought on my behalf?

The trading that Adi and I accomplished did have economic benefits to the family, but I doubt that is why I was accepted into their home. I had co-opted Adi into my cause of helping the women and children of the camp survive with our daily delivery of food and medicine, and most of our profits went to those rations. And even if we had been driven by the greatest gain for ourselves, our increased earnings would not have been worth the risk his parents took in pretending that I was a cousin from Semarang, staying after I'd become orphaned.

Instead, I believe she was driven by love for Adi. I was his first and his only friend, someone who accepted him as they did.

I could never forget the moment, on the evening that I trusted him to bury her, when Adi stroked the perfection of Jasmijn's face, when he believed that she'd been asleep. Nor could I forget his words and the sorrow in his words. *"Don't let her wake. Sometimes the little ones see my mouth and they don't understand I am not a monster."*

He was not a monster. I would never have known that, had not circumstances put us together long enough for me to no longer notice his horribly distorted face and the peculiar noises he made and the high nasal tones of his speech.

As I would learn in adulthood, with no separation between his nasal cavity and mouth, it was physically impossible for Adi to accomplish what the rest of us take for granted, indeed what takes no thought during the process of forming our words as we speak. To make our sounds, it requires air pressure in the mouth; correct speech requires the soft palate at the back of the mouth to lift and move toward the throat so that air and sound can be directed outward. We also require the area of hard tissue at the roof of our mouth for our tongue to tap and touch as we articulate different sounds. Adi's soft palate was incapable of closing off the nasal cavity through his mouth, and the cleft of his palate had robbed him of most of the surface area for his tongue to deliver consonants with any precision. Worse, as a little boy still unaware of his handicap, for years he'd strained without success to mimic those around him and had learned grunts and growls that had become an unconscious habit he could not escape.

It is not difficult to imagine Utami's anguish in the months after he was born, her attempts to suckle him as he vainly tried to create a vacuum with his mouth against her breasts. Later, his isolation as a child, bewildered at his different-ness, would have torn her heart, and when he learned to understand the words he struggled to speak, the taunts of unkind strangers would have been barbs piercing her just as deeply as they did Adi. To watch him step out of the hut in the evenings, when darkness would protect him, would have been gut-wrenching, to know that he would be unlikely to share a first kiss or hold hands with a young woman, to understand he would not be able to whisper poetry in the ear of a woman to take as his bride. All of that because of a genetic aberration seemingly placed upon him with arbitrary indifference.

To someone, however, who believes that good comes from bad, who believes in divine purpose, Adi was paying the price for the dozens of lives that were saved by the food and medicine we brought into camp. Had he not been disfigured, he would have not been at the drainage ditch on the night that Laura was attacked by the python; had he not been disfigured, he would not have been willing to join another outcast, me, in those efforts.

If this is true, it would mean that I, too, had paid a price to be in the same position. If my sisters and mother were still alive, I would not be strapping myself beneath a bread truck on a daily basis and roaming the village like a native to procure those supplies.

While I had volunteered—without doubt because it didn't matter to me whether I lived or died—it wasn't a willing sacrifice. I was angry and depressed, which would be expected, given what had been taken away from me. But I was too young to realize that it should be expected. I had no appetite. I could not sleep and spent most of each night on the mat in their home listening to Utami's soft snoring on the mat she shared with Sukurno. And I seethed with a rage I dared not admit, even to myself. Yet I also dared not look up from that task because it would have allowed for a sorrow that I could not bear. All that anchored me was the sole purpose of self-imposed heroics, a purpose that outweighed my rage, as I was to discover on an afternoon when three boys, barely older than Adi, managed to trap us in an alley.

It began with a barked order to halt.

Our first mistake was to look back.

We saw them at the entrance to the alley; each carried a rifle hand-carved from wood; each was marching toward us with the butt of the rifle resting on an upraised palm, the top of the rifle leaning on the left shoulder. It showed the officiousness and self-importance of a petty bureaucrat. Worse, as we immediately discovered, it was combined with a degree of fanaticism.

Our second mistake was to ignore the order and continue walking toward the end of the alley, where it spilled out to the town square.

"Halt!"

Apparently, as soldiers in training for future battles in the independence movement, they fully believed they had authority and were irked that the authority was ignored.

We heard rushed footsteps and turned to face

what was obviously a gleeful test of their military endeavors.

Naturally, Adi and I stopped.

"At attention," the middle one stated, the commander of the small army. He was slightly taller than his companions. All three, in ragged shirts and shorts, wore shoes. This was significant. Not many natives were able to find shoes.

I saluted. It was mockery, but he took himself so seriously he didn't understand that and gave me a salute in return.

"What's in the box?" Commander asked Adi.

Adi and I stood side by side. I was by far the smallest of the five of us. Adi carried a small box. It held a few bottles of sulfa pills, a real score for us.

Adi didn't like to speak. Around anyone but me or family, he kept his jaws clamped, as if somehow that could mitigate the gap of exposed upper gums and teeth. He had small balls of muscle at the joint of each side of his jaw from that continuous pressure.

As always since beginning the trading business with Adi, I focused on matching the local accent. I was close enough to be believable as a cousin from the city. "Whatever it is," I said, "it's his business."

Commander narrowed his eyes at me. "Silence!"

"Come on," I said to Adi. "This is a waste of time. Let's go."

Instantly, all three of them pointed their rifles at us, belly height.

"Please," I said. "Be merciful. Don't shoot."

I was the only one who thought I was funny. Adi nudged me to be silent. He knew them. I didn't.

"Guard them," Commander snarled to his friends. "If they move, shoot to kill."

Commander moved closer to Adi. "Show me what's in the box."

I stepped between them, and Commander swung his rifle and cracked me across the ribs.

"No!" Adi said. "Leave him alone."

Under normal conditions, the words he forced out reached the world as a high-pitched nasal grunting. Now, under stress, it was even more distorted.

Commander imitated Adi, and his friends laughed. I saw the hurt in Adi's eyes, and I fought a cold surge of rage and the immediate impulse to kick him in the groin. That would have diverted any further teasing of Adi and satisfied my emotions.

But I was highly aware of my status as an imposter, and I realized how any escalation of this might draw closer attention to my identity. Truly, I didn't fear for my own safety, but I was acutely aware that no one else but me could deliver the sulfa pills and all the other supplies that Dr. Eikenboom needed so badly.

"Sing us a song," the one on the left said, using the same nasal grunting sound and poking Adi in the belly with the end of his rifle. "We need a good laugh."

This would have been the moment to protest on Adi's behalf. Even if it would have been useless in preventing more mockery, it would have shown him that I was clearly on his side. That I was his friend.

"And you," Commander told me.

"What?"

"You sing a song like he would. You know, like this." And Commander sang a lullaby as if he too had a cleft palate.

I shook my head in protest. This was going too far.

"No?" he asked, drunk on his own power. "No?"

He cracked me across the ribs again, then grabbed my hair and pulled me down to my knees.

"And you," he said to Adi, in the mocking nasal voice. "On your knees. This is how we treat anyone who defies our orders!"

We knelt.

The entire time, I memorized their faces.

If there came a time that the Japanese were gone, I would find them and make them pay for how they had humiliated Adi.

Forty-Two

Months and months before, on a warm, dark night, Adi had taken Jasmijn's tiny and still body from my hands and promised to bury her as if she had been his own sister.

It had been no easy task. Taking her body to a priest for a church burial would have led to questions he could not answer. But a hidden and unmarked grave somewhere not easily found or disturbed—where untamed vegetation would have been a desecration in itself—would have been too disrespectful.

He'd chosen to sneak at night into the pauper's cemetery where his own brothers and sisters had been buried. Near the small headstone of his own sister's grave where no one would tread— she had died of influenza at age two—he'd carefully removed sod, dug deep into the moist soil, wrapped Jasmijn in a blanket, covered her with dirt, prayed over her, patted the sod in place, and carried away the excess soil in a cloth bag that had once held twenty pounds of dried rice.

Daily, I sat near the headstone and mourned her as if only the day before death had taken her from me. Daily, I would search my memory to wonder if there was anything else I could have done to keep her alive, and that would invariably lead me to grief over losing Aniek, Nikki, and my mother, thoughts that renewed my rage, not dissipated it.

Adi knew better than to interrupt those thoughts, so on the afternoon his shadow fell over me, that told me something of importance had occurred, and it was not difficult to guess.

"The trains have arrived," I said.

"Yes."

We both knew what that meant. British and Australian soldiers would begin the task of guarding the women and children as they marched from the camp to the train stations.

Officially, the war had ended a few weeks before. But real freedom had not come to the camp as a result. The women and children had simply woken to an unfamiliar sound. Silence. No screaming from Japanese soldiers, no roll call, no counting to ten in a foreign language.

They found the front gate open and the soldiers gone. But it had taken less than a day to realize they were not safe outside the gates, for the villagers, goaded by the young men who had carried wooden rifles and marched in forma-tions, refused to trade with the women and were openly hostile, to the point where they soon realized they were in more danger outside the gates than inside.

The Indonesians had learned to live without colonialism, and Dutch were not welcome on the island. For them, now that the weed had been eradicated by the Japanese, they did not want roots to take hold again.

British soldiers had arrived to protect us in our prison, bringing with them food and medicine. But I was too restless to stay among them. So I had stayed with Adi and his family, acutely aware of the danger of the independence movement from all the rumors and gossip around me.

"You cannot stay," he said.

I stood. "You of all people know I will make my own choice."

Yet I was only delaying the inevitable. I really didn't have a choice. While I had family through Adi, unless I was going to spend my entire life applying the dye from betel nut juice to my skin, eventually I would have to become Dutch again. And the Dutch were not welcome in this land.

"One of the boys is near death," he told me. "It is rumored that he will live, but I have heard at the market that the police are looking for someone like you."

It was the talk of the village, that at three separate times, just before sunset, each of three teenage boys had been ambushed and attacked by an unknown assailant armed with a cricket bat, and each had been left battered and bleeding. It was speculated that gang members of an opposing independence squad were responsible, but apparently the police thought differently at this point.

I looked at my arms and hands, and Adi understood.

"Come home," he said. "My mother has prepared the bath for you."

We ran and found that the hut was filled with smoke. Utami had filled pots with water and had warmed the water on the stove. On the floor were the rinds of the lemons that she had squeezed into the water.

She handed me a small stack of rags cut into squares. My modesty to them was amusing, but they had always respected it, and both of them left me alone with the water.

I soaked the first of the cloths in the water and squeezed the mixture of water and lemon juice on my other arm and wiped with vigor. The rag absorbed a hue of brown, leaving my skin mottled.

What was more important was my hair, and the lemon juice cleaned it almost completely of the betel nut stain. I was Dutch again. Utami had foreseen the danger in that too.

The neatly folded clothes did not consist of shorts and a shirt, but a dress. And somewhere, somehow, she had found me a wig.

Perhaps we could have had the luxury of waiting until nightfall before sneaking me bac to the camp, but it wasn't a certainty. Nothing had been certain for a long time. Rumors had swirled as the war neared an end, rumors about the arrival of British and Australian soldiers, about whether the Dutch would fight back against the Indonesian rebels. It had been no different with speculation about when the women and children would be escorted from the camp to ships on the coast, or indeed what would happen once we were on the ships.

It could easily happen that the train would be loaded in a matter of hours, and that by night-fall, the camp would be empty.

Utami knelt in front of me and inspected my appearance.

"Very attractive," she said. "Don't get in a fight on the way."

"Yes," Adi said. "There are dangerous attackers armed with cricket bats."

He knew.

"I will be back," I said. I was sad. Very sad. I should have been fighting tears. But most emotion had already been squeezed out of me. "Someday I will be back. I promise."

"Of course," she said. She straightened. It was obvious that she could not speak without bursting into tears.

"Come on," Adi said. "But first, this."

He drew me in and hugged me. I wanted to push away, but sensed that would be far too hurtful for him.

"Only here could I do that," he said. "Not at the camp gate. If anyone saw me close to a girl, they would wonder who you really were."

It would have been patronizing to deny that. No girl would allow Adi near. My sorrow for his future overwhelmed me.

"If that is the case," I said, "then I shall do this here too."

I hugged him in return. Less from my own need than what I knew he needed.

That's the closest I came to breaking down since the death of Jasmijn. Holding him, smelling the garlic of his skin and the adolescent tang of hormones, understanding that when I let go and when he walked away from me at the gate, he would be alone again.

But then, so would I.

And it's a feeling that never left, through seven more decades, and a feeling that still shrouded me in the holding cell in DC where, at age eighty-one, I faced my daughter, the lawyer.

Forty-Three

Journal 35—Washington, DC

"One. Question." This came from my daughter, Rachel Prins. Divorced and back to her maiden name. I'd expected more anger. But instead, she sounded sad. She was across from me in the holding cell. It had come full circle, just over an even three score and ten years after the marble game beneath the banyan tree that had led me here.

She was in her late thirties, and thus you can conclude I was past forty when she was born, late for first fatherhood. I looked at her, wondering if there really had been a time when she fit in the crook of my arm and I'd wept with joy at holding her. Time heals all wounds, but it also wears away at some of the best memories a man can have.

"Just one question?" I asked. I kept my hands on my knees. Best way to hide a tremor that came and went with unsettling unpredictability. "It must be said. You do have a habit of poking around."

I tried to breathe through my mouth to avoid the odor of vomit and urine in the holding cell.

"I do have a list of questions," she answered. Her hair in no-nonsense corporate business style matched the blandness of her expensive pants and jacket. A strand of hair had fallen across her forehead and was stuck in place by the humidity. It, like the rest of her hair, was ash blond, the way it had been since her childhood, and I didn't think she needed to assist it yet with coloring. My own hair had resisted gray until my late fifties.

She gave me a resigned smile. "You have a habit of avoiding most of them. So for now, I'll stick to the most important and salient question for this situation."

She was unaware of how deeply I grieved my inability to open up to her. I studied her and marveled that she was my child, grown or not. I'd never lost that sense of wonder, just as I'd never been able to express it.

"One, you fly out of town and fail to tell me," she said, holding up her index finger. Then doubled it with the second finger. "Two—"

"I suppose," I interrupted, adding disdain to my voice to conceal my anxiety, "next you're going to tell me this police station is in the Capitol Hill precinct?"

I wasn't near the point where I couldn't recognize people or where I would mistake someone for another person and, for example, blissfully chatter to Rachel, thinking that she was my long-gone sister Nikki. When I arrived at that stage, I would be so far gone that I wouldn't realize I was at that stage. Would that be a blessing? Or a snake eating its own tail?

No, my problem was that the episodes were more frequent. It would feel as if I had snapped out of a daze, with no recollection of the immediate time span before it, or even how long I'd been in the daze. With Rachel across from me, my last meaningful short-term memory was sitting for tea in a hotel with Laura, but the agony was in trying to recall what city. Washington, DC, I hoped.

The room I was in didn't have any windows. A police officer had just escorted my daughter in. Good evidence of the kind of room that held me, just not the geographical location of the room. If this was Washington, DC, nothing good could have come out of it. At least in my daughter's eyes.

I waited, trying not to show that I waited.

"As if you don't know where we are," she said. "I'm not going to fall for your distraction techniques."

I took that as a yes. Capitol Hill. If I was here, something had happened, then. The police had confiscated my moleskin notebook, so I couldn't be sure. Hopefully what had happened would have been worth recording in my daily diary, and more hopefully, I would have logged it in, or at least logged in my intentions.

"Two," she continued, "the phone call that I get isn't from you, but a woman I've never heard of before. Who expected me to jump on an airplane and fly across the continent merely because she asked."

"Her name is Laura Jansen," I answered. Good. Laura had not abandoned me. Yet. "I had hoped, eventually, to introduce her to you."

The hope was probably overly optimistic, given my situation. There wouldn't have been any point in an introduction if Laura decided to go back to the Netherlands.

"Yes, I know her name is Laura," she said. "She told me over the phone when she asked if I would fly all the way here to DC to help. If she hadn't described the interior of your condo and her large suitcase that was sitting in the hallway, I wouldn't have believed her story."

In the spider webs of my memory, I was able to pull forth the recollection of my own flight to DC from Los Angeles the day before, with Laura and I each taking only a carry-on for what was supposed to be a short stay in the capital. The large suitcase is what she'd taken from Amsterdam and left behind. That had given me satisfaction, knowing the suitcase had anchored her enough that she would at least return to Los Angeles.

"You went to my condo?" I asked.

"On the way from my office to the airport," she said. "For all I knew, someone had stolen your identity and it was some kind of scam. If you ever bothered to answer your home phone, or if you had a cell phone, it might help."

"I don't think they allow cell phones in here."

"They allow one call," she answered. With me too ashamed to admit to the police in Laura's presence that I couldn't remember my daughter's phone number.

Rachel continued, exasperation obvious on her face. "And who the woman is should be at the top of my list of questions."

She challenged me with another stare and it

took effort for me to maintain eye contact. Any reaction from me except studied indifference would be like a poker tell that Rachel would immediately spot. I was an expert at studied indifference.

"I met her at the hotel before taking a cab here," she said. "After all these years of your self-imposed monkhood, she's the one? I've seen them much younger show some real interest in you."

"She is the most beautiful woman I know," I said. "And I resent your obvious ageism."

I wasn't going to share how my heart had thumped like an adolescent boy, earlier in the week, when I'd opened the door for the totally unexpected sight of the return of Laura into my life after more than a sixty-year absence.

"If that's the case, why separate hotel rooms? At the least, it would save money."

"That would not be proper," I said. "Nor would I ask her to be improper on my behalf. What time is it? As much as I resent your ageism, I resent it more that I have to admit I'm tired because of my age."

"Time for you to tell me why you are here," she said. She did something out of character for her. She reached across and placed a hand on mine. I did something out of character. I allowed the touch.

I tried to piece it together. I was in DC. That

had been established. I'd made it to Capitol Hill. With that to jog my memory, I could picture the Rotunda. There was a long underground hallway that led from the Rotunda to the offices of the senators.

I didn't remember much after showing my visitors pass to the female guard.

Rachel removed her hand from mine and took a breath. "Please. Tell me. Why?"

"Do you ever listen to yourself?" I asked. I needed more deflection that might bring out more clues. "Why is the scariest question in existence. Why does the earth exist? Why is there evil on this earth? Why—"

"You are truly a horse's ass. Why would you tackle a senator and try to pull his pants down?"

Aaah. There it was. The detail I needed to open the floodgates. Much of the day's earlier events swooshed back to the front of my memory. I had tackled the senator; but a man had to defend himself against injustice.

"I did not try to pull his pants down," I said with dignity. That had not been my plan. "I'm sure that's been misinterpreted. I was trying to pull his pants cuffs upward. To expose his calf. That is only possible when you are sitting on a man's back, looking downward at his shoes. You grab a foot and bend it toward yourself and hold with one hand while using the other hand to pull the pants leg and expose the calf.

351

Doesn't that sound much more like the truth?"

I held my breath and waited for her answer. Not everything had swooshed back into my short-term memory. I wondered if my plan had succeeded and hated the need for a third-party confirmation.

"I suppose it could have happened," she said. "Although witnesses have conflicting reports. That still begs the question. An eighty-two-year-old senator and you attack him in a hallway outside his office. Why?"

"For the record, I did not try to pull his pants *down*. Please clarify that wherever and whenever possible."

"He walks with a cane," she said. "His partial flew twenty feet down the hallway when you tackled him."

My own teeth are all in place, I would like to mention. No bridges. No partials.

"I asked him politely to show me his calf," I said, more of the memory emerging from my cobwebs. "I even warned him of the consequences if he didn't. *And* he had the audacity to swing at me with said cane. Again, I was not the bully in this situation. I was firmly taught as a child that I was not allowed to fight until someone took the first swing at me."

This was something my father had been adamant about, and, with the exception of attacking Georgie, I'd not once broken that rule since my first fight at age seven. Yet, in reflection of my own ageism, it had not occurred to me that someone as old as the senator could swing so fast. My ribs ached where he'd made contact with his cane, and I'm sure the bruise was already black.

"Why?" Rachel asked. "Why did you fly from Los Angeles to DC to try to pull down the pants of a senator from Wyoming?"

"Up," I corrected. "I tried to pull his pants up. Did the cops mention if there was anything on his leg?"

"The senator from Wyoming?"

"Like I pulled someone else's pants up? Who else would I mean?" I had set aside my recent fear of travel and flown a long way to find out. Hadn't risked much, though, in attacking the senator. What were they going to do, give me a life sentence? If you get to the point where you can't remember why you are in jail, how remedial is that?

"Let me make sure to put that at the top of my legal inquiries," she said. "Check the senator's leg for birthmark."

She was fishing.

"Tattoo?" she asked.

I didn't reply. That would require explaining that I had been looking for the scar of teeth marks. My teeth marks from nearly seven decades earlier.

"Let me get right on this birthmark-tattoo

question," she said, defeated but not prepared to admit it. "First thing, say, next decade?"

So no marks reported on the senator's left calf. I sure hoped I'd remembered to pull up the pants on his left calf. Be stupid to come all the way here and grab the wrong leg. That left three alter-natives. I'd grabbed the wrong leg, or there was nothing on his left calf and I was wrong about his identity, or no one had cared to watch closely during the commotion.

I hid my disappointment at the new realization that I'd not yet discovered what I had come to Washington to confirm and accomplish. I've had a lifetime of practice at hiding disappointment. And, I can say with confidence, at my age, that means much more practice than just about anyone.

"I'm here to make an offer," she said. "I will do what it takes to rescue you from this. In return, what I want is not reimbursement for my flight or my lost billable hours."

"What do you want?"

"I want your story."

"Story?"

"Over the phone, Laura Jansen said she'd known you since you were children. Old flame?"

Her eyes widened as she repeated herself. "Old flame. Flying here, that's all I could decide. There never was anything tender between you and Louise. I'm long past caring that I was born six months after the wedding. Is that it? Laura is your true love?"

Louise. The woman who had been my wife for thirty years, then left me to find a new life before she died. And died of cancer six months after that. I had a couple of photo albums somewhere to remind me of that life, if I ever wanted to find them.

Rachel leaned in and spoke in a teasing tone. "Mawidge. Twue wuv and mawidge."

"I don't understand," I said.

"That's because you always refused to watch *The Princess Bride* with me. Was this why you always refused? Your own heartbreak about your one true love?"

I grunted. Noncommittal. I hoped.

"See," she said. "I want to know. Was there ever a time you had feelings? This Laura, was she your one true—"

"Stop," I said. "You are mocking me."

I didn't want to be reminded of my biggest regret. Laura had agreed to meet me at the base of a statue in a square in Amsterdam, me almost twenty by then. How differently the rest of my life would have turned out had I had the courage to show up as we planned.

That feeling of regret never failed to stab me. Older memories are so vivid, it takes no effort to find them. There are times, I've discovered, that it seems like I am a boy, and the Jeremiah Prins at age eighty-one is a convincing dream, and that as soon as I wake, I will be that boy again, on a straw mat, pinching bedbugs, a belly aching from hunger.

Rachel leaned back. "She said that the two of you spent part of your childhoods at a camp. In the Dutch East Indies. Where you were held prisoner by the Japanese for most of the Second World War."

I made another noncommittal grunt.

"How old am I?" Rachel asked.

"That's rhetorical, right?" This was habit. I'd learned over the last months that this was a wonderful evasion and often resulted in helpful answers to questions I should have easily been able to handle but couldn't.

"I'm a fully grown woman," she said. "I am a partner in a law practice, and yet only now do I learn you were born in Indonesia."

"Dutch East Indies," I corrected. The Dutch had not relinquished it as a colony until 1949. That's how it is. The older memories are right there in front of you, yet daily events recede and return like an unpredictable tide.

"And," she continued, "you spent time in a concentration camp? This, I had no idea of either."

I closed my eyes, trying to push away the one memory that was my greatest shame. Losing all my other memories would be worth it if that one disappeared as well.

"Yes, I spent time in a Jappenkamp."

"That's what I want then. Your story. Write it or dictate it. I don't care. I want it. That's my price."

"Why?" I asked.

"I want to understand you," she said. This time, her voice was soft. I could see in her face the little girl she once had been. "When you are gone, I want to weep over what I lost, not what I never had."

"Maybe," I said, trying to push away that one memory, "there wasn't much for you to lose."

Tightness returned to her face, even as a single tear rolled toward her chin. "Then *I* want to be the one to decide if there was much to lose. Not you."

I knew what she needed from me. What she had always needed from me. A father who hadn't spent a lifetime resisting any kind of emotional closeness. A father who sat with his little girl to watch *The Princess Bride*.

With the memory of why I had come to Washington to face the senator successfully triggered by Rachel's presence, I realized that if I had decided to reconcile with a boyhood enemy while I still could, what justification did I have to deny my daughter, the one I loved more than my own life?

"I will do it," I told her, with the sensation that I was swaying at the edge of a precipice.

Still, it would be on my terms.

357

Forty-Four

In my hotel room, my morning's second cup of tea was cold long before the sun had risen. Tired old men wake early, even when they are exhausted. Words from Ecclesiastes about old age taunted me. *Those who keep watch over the house begin to tremble . . . one is awakened by the sound of a bird, and all their songs grow faint . . . because man goes to his eternal home . . . the silver cord is removed . . . the golden bowl is broken . . . the pitcher is shattered.*

I looked out the window, at a parking lot. I had a notebook in my lap. Not a notebook computer. But a notebook. A journal. Number 35. It had a moleskin cover and a snug band to hold my fountain pen. I took an architect's pride in neat handwriting and always wrote with deliberation, so on the occasions when I had to scratch out a word or a sentence, my single horizontal stroke still left a sense of tidiness that I was vain about.

When this one was filled, I would store it in the office of my condo, with the previous thirty-four journals on a shelf, surrounded by walls that were covered with the different-colored sticky notes that I also used to help organize my daily tasks. The system worked and would continue to work until my neurons could no longer piece together the reason for the stickies.

When this journal was finished, I would begin filling another. And another, until I could no longer make sense of why I was determined to store my recollections of each new day on paper as a way to ward off the growing inability to store them in my mind.

I knew why I spent so much time on journals to record the daily events of my life that would hold little interest for anyone else. To be human is to tell story, and to tell story is what makes us human. Our lives are unfolding stories, and when we lose our stories, we lose ourselves. At this early stage of Alzheimer's, I could not shake the terror of losing who I was. On this morning, only hours after agreeing to Rachel's terms, I could admit to myself that I was also motivated to grant her request because of the fear that once those memories were lost, so was I, like a sailor clinging to the debris of a shipwreck finally slipping beneath gray waves.

I sipped on cold tea and studied in my note-book what I had written about my time in the holding cell with Rachel the previous night, pages 17 to 26 of Journal 35. Here, it was easier to make sense of it, because I could flip back to earlier pages and day by day retrace how the journey to Washington began, with the appearance of Laura, to our flight, to my walk in the corridor beneath the Rotunda.

There was a second notebook beside me. Every page blank. I purchased them by the dozen because I wanted them with lined pages and a page number at the bottom. Without the numbering, I would be lost.

I picked up the second notebook. On the inside cover, I gave it a label: Journal 1—Dutch East Indies.

At the top of the first page, I scratched away the emptiness and I wrote these words: *See 35, 17–26.* When the inevitable happened, and I wanted to know why I was reliving my child-hood in the Dutch East Indies on paper, all I would need to do is open Journal 35 and reread pages 17 to 26, and learn that I was paying a debt and hoping to give my daughter a reason to mourn what she had lost when I was gone. And months from now, in following my own written instruc-tions, I would be obeying someone from my past who was no longer me.

I stared out the window, not seeing the parking lot and the cars. Would it be important for Rachel to know that, immediately after the war was over, at the port of Semarang, in a holding camp as we waited for a ship, that one night we had been woken by grenades tossed over the wall by Indonesian rebels? That Pietje still refused to sleep with me and stayed instead with

Laura and Sophie? Or what it felt like in the port of Suez, lining up for secondhand clothing donated by people in the Netherlands, trying to comprehend that I would need the ill-fitting thick woolen jacket when I felt the first real cold of my life—the gale winds that swept the ship as it neared the North Sea?

Or my numbness when Sophie succumbed to influenza after days of fighting it, and how the ship's captain ordered her body wrapped in a blanket and slipped into the water after a brief funeral, no differently than had been done for dozens of others during the weeks of travel from the southeast Pacific and the turquoise waters to the angry swells of the Atlantic? As her body disappeared into the water, I had no sense then that my last protector was gone. On our arrival to the Netherlands, Laura was whisked away by her wealthy family, her father and mother ignoring her pleas to take me and Pietje to their home. Instead, Pietje and I were put in a foster home, where the militant father was appalled at our wildness and ill manners when we snatched food and gobbled it the way our instincts had been trained to do by three years of near starvation. His solution had been to allow us one small piece of bread at a time, and not until we chewed slowly and finished it would he allow us another. I hated him for how he would watch and smile in satisfaction at the triumph of his willpower over us. I hated myself because I was so hungry I capitulated to his pettiness.

Or how my buried rage and helplessness at Pietje's determined rejection of me led to a horrible moment on a bridge over a canal where, at age nineteen, I had struck a man so hard that I had to flee Holland as a murderer?

After long thought, however, I realized there was only one place to begin my story for Rachel. Where the circle began that was ending here in Washington, with the day that I met Laura. So on the first page of Journal 1—Dutch East Indies, I began the transfer of memories that were preserved in protein and DNA and tiny bursts of electricity that jump from nerve ending to nerve ending, putting those memories into lines of blue ink.

A banyan tree begins when its seeds germinate in the crevices of a host tree. It sends to the ground tendrils that become prop roots with enough room for children to crawl beneath, prop roots that grow into thick, woody trunks and make it look like the tree is standing above the ground. The roots, given time, look no different than the tree it has begun to strangle. Eventually, when the original support tree dies and rots, the banyan develops a hollow central core.

In a kampong—village—on the island of

Java, in the then-called Dutch East Indies, stood such a banyan tree almost two hundred years old. On foggy evenings, even adults avoided passing by its ghostly silhouette, but on the morning of my tenth birthday, sunlight filtered through a sticky haze after a monsoon, giving everything a glow of tranquil beauty. There, a marble game beneath the branches was an event as seemingly inconsequential as a banyan seed taking root in the bark of an unsuspecting tree, but the tendrils of the consequences became a journey that has taken me some three score and ten years to complete.

That took most of the first page of Journal 1—Dutch East Indies. I began the second page, but only after writing across the top of the left-hand side: *See 35, 17–26.* It might take a year to complete the DEI journals; if I failed to do this on every left-hand page of every journal that recounted my time at the Jappenkamp, the clumping nodules of my brain might have well pushed the neurons to the point where I'd forget where to look for the key to why I was writing.

I looked out the window again. How clearly it came back to me. On the second page, I continued.

It was market day, and as a special privilege to me, Mother had left my younger brother and twin sisters in the care of our servants . . .

I felt some comfort in the clarity of that recollection and satisfied that I'd chosen the right moment and place for the beginning of the first DEI journal. I set that notebook aside, and opening the latest page to Journal 35, I recounted my time in the holding cell and underlined the portion where Rachel insisted on this story as a condition for helping me. It was more important to stay in the present, so that at the end of each day, when the terrors of losing myself grew too dark to withstand, could reassure myself by hearing from the pages the continuing unfolding of my life, proof that I was still a person, not a body that merely functioned as a machine.

Over the next few days, while the events were fresh in my memory, I would continue to journal this trip to Washington as the events occurred, no matter how it ended. Later, back in the safety of my condo in Los Angeles and trusting that my oldest memories would be the last to fade, I would take as much time as I needed to give Rachel my boyhood story, beginning with Journal 1 of DEI. Then, although I would have written this ending first, and would finish the beginning last, I would arrange all the journals chronologically, starting with the marble game beneath the banyan. The bundle of journals would be hers as I had promised, a drawn-out plea for understanding and forgiveness for failing her as a father. But she would not get it until I was gone.

Rachel arrived at my hotel room at 9 a.m.

Her look of concern frightened me.

"What's wrong?" I asked.

"Nothing," she said from the doorway.

"Okay," I said. I shrugged.

I saw her battle with thoughts. Then she said, "Okay, it's not okay. It's not nothing."

I shrugged.

"See," she said. "That's how you and I have lived our lives. Nothing. Nothing. Nothing. All the time. Speak of nothing that's inside."

She stepped inside and shut the door. I backed away.

"A daughter should hug a father," she said. "A father should hug a daughter."

As she moved closer, I fought the impulse to keep the space between us.

She reached up and put her arms around my shoulders. She put her chin on my chest and spoke into the bathrobe that I was wearing.

"Do you know how much courage it took me last night to ask for what happened to you as a boy? How vulnerable that made me feel? That's not how it should be."

She trembled in my arms. Or was it my arms trembling, my own tired flesh and skeleton betraying me?

Hesitantly, I patted her on the back.

"More!" she demanded. "Hold me. Squeeze me. Like you love me."

I did. I felt like a tin soldier, but I waited until she broke the embrace and stepped back.

"Why is that so difficult for us?" she asked.

"Does this dress make me look fat?" I countered.

"No." She became angry. "No deflections."

She grabbed my hand. That was twice. Once the night before. And now. She led me to the mirror at the hotel closet.

"Look at yourself," she said.

"I'd rather not," I said.

My gray hair was limp and messy. There were patches of stubble that I'd missed when shaving. A stain of egg yolk on the robe. My neck was wattled, and my face sagging.

"I don't want to see you like that," she said. "You are the rock. Invincible to erosion. That's the way I want you. I don't want to see you and know that too soon—"

My own face must have shown horror. Why was she sharing this?

"Don't run from my feelings," she said. "At the same time, I don't want you to be the rock and invincible. I want—"

She closed her eyes and I saw a familiar set of her jaws as she squeezed the muscle at the joints and took control of herself. See, she *was* my daughter. She opened her eyes. "What I want is room service."

She marched to the phone and made an order.

I took a set of ironed clothes from the closet, went into the bathroom, and shut the door. I shaved again and wet my hair and combed it and dressed and stepped outside in a suit and tie. I was a new man.

"Better?" I asked.

"Just forget my outburst," she answered. "Hormones."

"Okay," I said. But was wise enough not to shrug.

She said, "I have good news. I wanted to deliver it in person."

"Another future ex-husband lined up?" Perhaps now was the time for artful deflection to be welcomed.

She answered, "I've heard from the senator's office. There will be no criminal charges."

I sat on the chair beside the small couch at the end of the small room. I pointed at the couch. She sat.

"Have I ever lied to you?" I asked.

"My entire life, you have withheld information, continuously deflected my questions, ignored me, and in many senses, abandoned me. To the point that I just made a fool of myself."

"Who I am to you is something I grieve every day," I said. "Next time, perhaps, I will be the one to step forward and hug you."

"You don't need to force yourself. I'm over whatever flash of hormones it was that hit me."

I was surprised to feel a nudge of disappointment. We both let a few moments pass in silence.

"Have I ever lied to you?" I began again.

"No," she answered.

"Even if someone wiped my memory clear of what happened, when I tell you the senator assaulted me, that is the truth. Not once in my life have I instigated a fight. *He* assaulted *me*. Ensure that charges are filed. If not, then ensure that the press hears about an attempt to cover up charges against a United States lawmaker. I *will* have my day in court."

Was the surprise in her face at the sudden strength in my voice, or my unexpected demand?

"The press won't care about two octogenarians engaged in a pillow fight," she said after some thought. "Neither do the police. No one assumes you are a threat to homeland security."

"If you won't do it, you are obligated to put together a file that another lawyer can take over. I expect you to do so by the end of morning. Send me a bill."

"Just so I understand. I drop all my appointments to fly to Washington because the police arrested you, and now that you are clear of any trouble, you want to—"

"How much clearer can I make this? I was assaulted by a US senator. I will not let this injustice go unpunished unless you arrange for me to privately meet the senator."

"Is this somehow related to your time in the Dutch East Indies?" she asked. "And the legal investigation into war crimes that you spent the better part of the 1970s trying to establish? What was the name of the Japanese commander you tried to track . . . Nakahara?"

Even to me, my voice sounded like a croak. "You . . ."

"Learned enough to track it down with LexisNexis. It only took a few hours. Your name is everywhere. If you had done this a few decades later, Google would have flagged it for me."

"Laura told you," I said. I was so intent on this, I didn't think of how it would look as I fished for Journal 35, flipped through pages, and found what I needed between pages 17 and 26. I spoke without looking up from my notes. *"Laura vertelde jou dat ze jou ontmoed had in haar hotel kamer voor dat ze naar het politie station ging."*

When she didn't confirm, I glanced up.

Rachel was weeping in silence, eyes wide open as she stared at me.

"Hormones?" I offered, knowing it was weak. Why couldn't I move myself closer and hold her? Her divorce had broken her; not once during the months it had taken for her to piece together her life had I consoled her by holding her.

"You were just speaking in Dutch," she said.

"No," I said, a reflexive denial. But I realized she was correct.

I cleared my throat and said it in English. "Last night you said you met Laura in her hotel room before going to the police station."

"And you had to confirm that by looking at notes." Tears glistened. "This is what happens. Lapsing into your mother tongue. The journal. Stickies . . ."

"Stickies." My voice was flat. If she suspected what was happening to me, it explained the demand in the holding cell for me to share my story before I was gone.

She took a deep breath.

"When I was in your condo yesterday, I looked through your office."

The tears flowed, and she was barely in control of her voice. "I thought maybe I could find something there that would give me a hint as to why you would be in jail for attacking a United States senator."

"My office. That's private."

"Under the circumstance," she said, "I'd say that I was justified to disregard your privacy."

She reached into her purse and pulled out a black-and-white photo and handed it to me. "While I was in there, I took this from a photo album that I'd never seen before. Who is it?"

I glanced at the face in the photo and had to

look away. This was not the time or place to become weak with emotion.

"Not only this," she continued, "the album had dozens of black-and-white photos. Family, I'm guessing. Don't you think I have a right to know? Was it you, the little blond-haired boy on a horse with palm trees and a volcano mountain in the background? He looked so happy, with the man beside him. Was that my grandfather?"

After the war, a cousin in the Netherlands had given me a package with those photos, sent to his father from my father during happy years in the Dutch East Indies. Aside from memories, it was all that remained of my family.

"I made my promise to you last night," I said. "I have already begun to journal my childhood for you. My promise should be enough for you until you get those journals."

I remembered that day with my father when I was on a horse. Just as I remembered standing beside a white wooden cross long after the war had ended.

I'd flown back to the islands to search for Adi and had also sought out my father's grave site in Burma, one of thousands who had died as the Japanese pushed them to build the railway and the bridge over the River Kwai.

To emphasize my point, I continued. "You will get my story. It's not something I can write in one day."

"That man," she said, pointing at the photo I still held. "I only brought that photo along because somehow, I know I know him. Didn't he visit us once when I was a little girl? Tell me that's true. Tell me I'm not imagining it."

"He did," I admitted. "His name is Adi."

"And he is . . ."

"Was," I said. "Two years ago, I went to his funeral."

"In the United States? He looks Indonesian to me."

"He was buried in Batavia," I said.

"Batavia?"

I corrected myself and spoke formally. "My apologies. It is now called Jakarta."

"Indonesia, then. I didn't know you'd gone there. Why do you make me drag information out of you?"

I shrugged.

She said, "Don't you think I saw the other photo of him in that album?"

"Some things I want to keep to myself."

"Some? How about all! Tell me about the surgery."

I shook my head. It was already difficult for me, being in Washington for the purpose that I was. Too many memories to fight. Too many memories I was afraid of losing.

She grilled me as if I were an opposing lawyer in court. "Adi, you said. The first photo, that poor man. Where did you meet him? How did you know him? And this photo . . ."

She reached for the photo and took it from my unprotesting fingers, then examined it again and, as if she could not help herself, smiled. "Look how happy he is. Total reconstruction of the mouth and nose. Why would you have kept the photo of him before the surgery if you had not been involved in some way?"

"He was a friend," I said. "Can that not be enough?"

"How can you pretend to be untouched by this? On your office wall, a framed photograph, this same man, much older, white hair against his dark skin, surrounded by people who are probably his children and grandchildren. I know it means something to you."

"It does," I said. "Please let that answer be enough of a satisfaction to you."

"You arranged for the surgery?"

"Do you share all parts of your life with me?" I asked. "No, you don't."

"I would like to," she said. "You are my father. I am your daughter."

What answer could I give to that? I kept my silence.

"I don't want it like this," she said. "Here we are. You know I've been in your office, yet still you say nothing about the elephant in this room. The same elephant in your office.

You want both of us to pretend it doesn't exist?"

"Do not cry," I could hear my mother and the other mothers say. *"Don't let the soldiers see you cry. We are Dutch. We are strong. We will not give them the satisfaction. Do not cry."*

"Then I will talk about the elephant," she said. "The stickies on the walls. Different colors. Like you were keeping track of your life?"

"Private."

"A stack of journals."

"Private."

My obstinacy served to drive her to irritation, which gave her strength, and the tears stopped. "When I saw all that, I realized what I'd known for a while but didn't want to admit to myself. So why not tell me yourself?"

"Private."

"Let me ask," she said. "Just now, why did you have to go to that journal to learn what I had said last night?"

"I like accuracy," I said. If I remembered correctly—irony, I thought—there had also been a stack of nonfiction books on how to deal with Alzheimer's. She hadn't needed the stickies and journals to point her to that, but I had taught her well to come at things obliquely.

"Who is the president of the United States?" she asked.

So typical. And unoriginal. I could remember the physician asking me the same question. But when I tried to answer, I found myself stuck. The contemptuous tone I'd started in my thoughts vanished. My mind said Reginald Reagan, but I sensed it was the wrong answer.

"Your poor clients," I said. "How much do you charge them per hour when you need help with a question like that?"

She took a breath. A quivering breath. "How long have you known?"

"Private."

"There it is," she said. "You and me. In a nutshell. You'd think a daughter would have a right to hear it from her father. Just as she should have known what happened to him during the war."

She began to weep again. I was angry that she had invaded my office, but now the timing of her request to learn my boyhood made sense. She knew too soon I wouldn't be able to tell her anything about my past. To tell our story makes us human, and to be human is to tell our story. If she didn't know my story, when my memory was gone, her father would be gone. My golden bowl would be long empty before it broke, my pitcher long dry before it shattered; she had just dis-covered how I was destined to spend my last years. There wasn't much time left to find out who I was, and whether I was worth mourning.

I moved to the couch. Beside her, I reached with one arm and drew her close and held her tight as she shook with the fierceness of her grief. I wanted to weep too, not for myself, but for all that I'd failed to give her and what I had lost for myself because of it.

Forty-Five

Laura and I had agreed to meet for a late breakfast, and that gave me time to leave the hotel around 9 a.m. by taxi. The driver had agreed to wait while I went into a jewelry store, and it hadn't taken long to find what I needed.

At the hotel again, I pushed open the rear door and eased out of the cab. I didn't feel the usual twinge in my right knee; I felt eighteen again.

"Fifty-five bucks," he yelled to my back as he leaned across the front seat to speak through the open passenger window. "Don't think you can outrun me, Gramps."

Gramps—spoken like that—is a word that can spoil your mood in a hurry. I understand why it's insensitive to mock or criticize obesity; it's now been classified as a disease and gets treated accordingly. But why are wrinkles open game for anyone who wants to be a comedian?

I wasn't going to let it spoil my mood. I had a diamond ring in my front pocket.

"Fifty-five bucks," he repeated. "You deaf?"

Again, deaf is not something you have much choice about, so to pose the question as an insult is just another example of blatant ageism. But personal hygiene? That *is* a choice. Taxi Driver was unshaven—in a patchy, greasy way, not in the Hollywood style, where shavers are set at the correct length to give a suitable virile look. He smelled too. I'm not cranky about this—okay, I am, but I won't apologize, as the formative years of my boyhood were spent in a concentration camp where dozens shared one house and overflowed one toilet, so I think I have a right to be sensitive about the issue.

I walked back to the cab.

"I've got your money," I said. "And I apologize. My mind was on other things."

I wasn't going to propose to Laura immediately. But I wanted the ring with me, if there came the moment I could do so with honor.

I was carrying my leather satchel, the one I'd had since architect school, battered and comforting. I set it on the hood of the taxi.

I unzipped an outer pocket for my wallet. It wasn't there. I unzipped the larger pocket inside. Not there either.

"Hurry up, old man!" Taxi Driver shouted.

I pulled out the contents, carefully setting articles one by one on the hood of the cab. Two moleskin notebooks. A camera. Some paper novels. Folded city maps. I didn't feel a sense of panic; I had put a system in place that I knew I could rely on. These days, I was all about backup systems.

I carefully placed each article back into the satchel and zipped it closed.

Ah, yes. The outer zipper pocket. That's where my wallet was. No, it wasn't.

All right. The larger zipped inner pocket. Not there either.

Maybe it was inside the satchel. I carefully pulled out each article. By then, Taxi Driver was standing on the other side, strumming his fingers on the hood, beaming hostility in my direction.

I vaguely remembered why I didn't feel a sense of panic. Travel and unfamiliar surroundings made me anxious these days, so I had begun the habit of wearing a money belt instead of a wallet that could be easily misplaced. The money belt held cash, a credit card, my government-issued identi-fication, and the key to get me into my condo. I reached for the small of my back and was com-forted to feel the slim pouch in the center of the money belt when I patted my shirt.

I began to lift my shirt to turn it around where I could reach the pouch, but somehow time slipped past my awareness and when I returned from the reverie, I was looking at my satchel, thinking that the wallet was in the outer zipped pocket. But I also noticed that someone had pulled out the notebooks and city maps and paperback novels, so I carefully placed each piece inside the satchel.

"If you weren't so old," Taxi Driver said, "I'd pop you in the face."

"That wouldn't help you get your money," I said. "How much do I owe you?"

"Sixty-five bucks," he said. "A drive to L street, a half-hour wait with meter running, a drive back here. And just now I turned on the meter again so I could enjoy this little charade of yours."

What was my task? Right. Wallet. Outer zipped pocket of the satchel was where I kept it. But it wasn't there. I felt no panic for some reason. I checked the main front pocket inside but then remembered I wore a money belt.

My shirt was already untucked. I frowned. Normally, I wasn't that sloppy. Stop caring about little things, and soon enough, the big things are totally undisciplined.

There it was. Beneath my shirt. My money belt. I found the pouch, withdrew cash, counted out fifty-five dollars, and handed the cash across the hood.

"Seventy-two dollars," he said, holding out a grimy palm for more.

"For some reason, fifty-five sticks in my mind," I said. "That's all you get. If you want a tip, I'm happy to offer one. Don't call someone 'Gramps' if you want a tip."

"Didn't expect one after that little senile routine

you just pulled. My tip? If you're young enough to actually have a day job, keep it. Your acting is horrible."

He slammed the door and tried to squeal tires as he floored it.

The spring in my step was gone. I was tempted to drop the diamond ring into a sewer grate. Laura didn't deserve what I was becoming.

Laura Jansen had grown into an exquisitely beautiful woman. It was not the fragile beauty that some women managed to magnify, becoming porcelain and brittle like fine china held together with invisible glue.

At breakfast, she wore a long blue dress of expensive material. It radiated the warmth of her eyes. She wore her hair short. Not gray. Not platinum. Not blond. But an ageless blend, and it wouldn't have surprised me if that was the color that was natural for her.

Grace Kelly. It's a reference that you need to be as old as I am to understand, but who today in Hollywood has effortless elegance without haughty superiority? Laura didn't deserve what I was becoming, and I certainly didn't deserve her. But my heart still soared at her presence.

At the restaurant table, she looked over a cup of tea at me. She spoke with the curve of a smile on lips that I longed for with the heat of an adolescent. We'd been together only a few days since her arrival in America. Long enough to share our histories, the events that had happened over sixty years. But we'd yet to approach what really mattered. It would have been unseemly to rush it, and I hoped she was enjoying the slow journey as much as I was. Eventually, however, she or I would get to the question neither of us had asked; sixty years ago, I had not shown up on the evening we agreed to elope to America.

"Your daughter is a lovely woman, Jeremiah."

"Yes," I said.

"She and I had a lovely conversation this morning."

"She and I had a conversation this morning as well."

"I hope you don't mind. I called your room to see if that would be all right to introduce myself to her properly, but there was no answer."

"Had I answered," I said, "I would have merely warned you that she likes to ask questions."

"She did," Laura said, setting her cup down on the saucer, without a hint of china clinking against china. "She started by telling me that she was born six months after a civil service marriage in front of a judge."

"Ah."

"I understood what she was trying to tell me. That it was a loveless marriage. Was it?"

"I made the best of it," I said.

Laura let out a long sigh. "That's what I told her

about mine. She asked me if I had pined for you."

"Mawidge," I said. "Twue wuv."

Laura giggled. "My favorite movie. English, with Dutch subtitles. But I had learned English by then."

I'd already made a note in my journal to watch the movie so I could understand what was meant by those words. Mawidge?

"And did you?" I asked. "Pine?"

"I told her that Holland is a small country," Laura answered. "I explained to her that my family was among the pampered elite. Early on, because those were different times, I knew it was unthinkable to marry outside of my class. I told her that I had been ready to leave all of it and begin with nothing in America. With you. Then she pointed out I had married someone else. Someone at the outer edges of Dutch royalty. It wasn't what I wanted, but I made the best of my life."

"So," I said, "she asked the natural question after that."

"I told her on the night we were going to elope, you did not appear where we had agreed to meet. And that you had disappeared from Amsterdam, so eventually, I married the man that it had been determined I should marry. Then, when my hus-band passed away, I flew to America. To find out why you had abandoned me when you had promised otherwise."

Here it was. The question we had avoided.

"I was in a jail cell," I said.

She raised an eyebrow. "Is this a pattern?"

"An attorney hired by your parents gave me a choice. Stay and face murder charges. Or take his offer to bail me from the jail and accept his help in fleeing the country."

The memory was never far from me. Like all the old memories, it remained clear. I could find myself in my armchair in my condo, staring at a cup of near-cold coffee, returning to the present from the dank, still waters of a canal in the gloaming of an evening in the fall of 1949. I would still have the smell in my nostrils—a whiff of cat urine from the alley where I'd finally found Pietje near the canal. I would still see the pale gleam of the man's face as it had rolled once, then twice, in the water below the bridge, as if a carp had been at the surface and bellied itself to the air in throes of death.

The scene itself on the bridge had been brief, anger rushing through me with the force of a nova. Beneath the single light at the entrance to a cheap hotel, a street girl had smiled with blackened teeth at the description of Pietje and given me directions.

Pietje, by then, was beyond caring about anything except how to find just one more pipe. The opium had wasted him horribly, his own teeth black, his eyes jaundiced, and his hair as stringy and dirty as his clothes. He was a wild and feral teenager, living the life of an ancient addict.

I had reached the bridge in time to see Pietje standing in the center, by the iron rails, accepting a pipe from an older teenager.

"Ah, the brother's keeper," Pietje said, his voice dreamily high-pitched and mocking. "Yet again you find me. Doesn't this crusade tire you? I can promise, it certainly tires me."

"Pietje . . ." I could not find any words.

"Where are my manners?" Pietje said. "Johannes, this is my only remaining family member, Jeremiah. I refuse to call him brother. I've done my best to lose him, but you have heard about bad pennies. Jeremiah, this is Johannes. He truly is like the brother I never had. Never judges me, always keeps me happy. With him around, never am I short of the bliss of poppy."

"Pietje . . ." Again, trying to find something to say. Close to a bridge farther down, at another cross street, well in the shadows, was a light splash in the water of the canal. A fish, maybe. Or someone dumping something out of one of the houseboats.

I had begged. Cajoled. Threatened. Promised money. Anything to get Pietje away from the underbelly of Amsterdam.

I turned my anger on the man beside Pietje. "Go away!"

I advanced, motioning with my hands like I was shooing at pigeons, and raising my voice. "Go! If you dare give my brother—"

Johannes laughed. "You really are the judge and God that he claims you to be. How long is it going to take for you to understand that you are no longer his brother?"

Both of them began to cackle.

"He needs help!" I said to Johannes.

"From you?" Pietje said. "Like you helped Mother?"

Pietje swayed as he cackled again. "You thought I didn't know? Every night I try to forget. And now I have help from my friend to help me forget."

Pietje put his arm around Johannes, at the waist.

"No!" I shouted. "You don't understand!"

From a houseboat below came a circle of light, catching the two of them squarely in a tableau.

"Shut the noise," came a bellow. "I'll call for police."

I ignored the shout. I reached for Pietje, to pull him away from Johannes, but Johannes reacted by swinging at me.

It was truly a nova of anger. A bright explosion of cold rage, and I returned his blow with all the frustration that had been bottled inside me. It was a punch that hit Johannes along the side of the jaw, snapping his head back, and his body followed the momentum. Johannes hit the railing waist height and plummeted.

There was a thud of impact against the hull of the houseboat, then the splash.

The man on the houseboat put the beam on the water, finding Johannes in time to see the rolling. Once, twice. The face of Johannes like a belly of a carp each time before disappearing into the water.

Frozen, I watched from the bridge as the man used a fishhook to search in the water. The canal water was shallow. Johannes could have stood in it. If he was alive. It didn't take long for the man on the houseboat to snag clothing and pull Johannes to the edge of the boat.

Then he turned the beam squarely on me again, painful against my eyes, and I realized that Pietje was clawing at my face, ripping my skin with jagged fingernails.

In the light of that beam, I grabbed each of Pietje's frail wrists, needing little strength to hold off my brother's rage. We could see each other clearly because of the light from the houseboat.

"This is how you solve problems," Pietje said, his voice flat. "Am I next?"

"No," I croaked.

"Run," Pietje said. "Run. I will not protect you from the police. They will hear from me how you killed."

I found myself in the restaurant again, Laura's eyes gentle as she tilted her head listening to my story.

"I fled jail," I said. Pietje died an addict's death within months of my abandonment. "I thought the solution was to go to America first, then have you join me as soon as possible. I sent letters. And letters."

She nodded. "At first, I did not receive them," she said. "My family, and the man I married, I see now, made sure of that."

"Here, in America," I said, "I had the freedom to turn my back on the mechanics trade that had been decided for me in Holland. I worked and worked, saving money to go to architect school. That was a dream I did fulfill. But I still waited. So long I waited for an answer, believing that I would always wait. One weekend, in an act of carelessness and weakness, I shamed myself with a secretary from the office that I knew adored me. I married her, because that's what a man should do. Then waiting was something I could no longer do."

"I waited too," Laura said. "You know that. We had promised to meet, and I waited. Each night at the time you had promised and the place you had promised, I waited. Until I could no longer wait. One letter, finally, reached me. A servant was careless, I suppose. I was ready to break my engagement. Then my fiancé told me he had a friend in the police, and that he'd learned something about you but had never wanted to tell me in case it destroyed the image I had of you. He said you'd killed a man and let your brother die of a drug overdose that was likely a suicide. He said that because I was engaged to be married to him, he had wanted to protect me by protecting you."

Laura gave me a tight smile of sadness. "There were papers I found after my husband's death. The attorney who arranged for your bail was not from my family, but his. The man you believed had died, did not."

That hit me with the impact of a hammer. I groaned.

Laura reached for my hand. "When I learned from my husband that he knew you had fled the country for killing a man, I felt a joy that I didn't dare reveal. You *hadn't* abandoned me. I love you. What happened on the bridge is nothing that you could have prevented. If you had stayed, any jury would have found you innocent. How I wish it could have been different. But at least we know the truth now. And it's not too late. For us."

I trembled. I should have been relieved that I was innocent of murdering a man in a moment of rage. I should have rejoiced that this amazing and wonderful woman had just declared love for me, that we had a chance to begin again. This was the moment to pull the ring from my pocket.

With cruel clarity, and bitter irony, I remembered that I couldn't remember how to find money to pay the taxi driver. The ring remained in my pocket. I would not propose. For Laura, marriage to me would be like putting her in a prison.

"Rachel is trying to arrange for she and I to meet with Georgie early this afternoon," I said.

Her brief pause before answering told both of us that the moment had been offered and that I had declined.

"I'm glad to hear that," Laura said with polite neutrality. "And, of course, I will be hoping for the best for you."

Forty-Six

As we settled in for the discussion with Wyoming Senator Michael Knight and the attorney who represented him, I doubt Rachel was impressed by the physical setting of the Capitol Hill office where she had insisted on the meeting. Not compared to where she worked.

I'd been in her Century City office, knew exactly what kind of impression it gave to clients, measured in terms of the fee she billed them per hour. The view of the Malibu mountains through the floor-to-ceiling windows from the corner suite on the top floor of the tower; the original artwork on the walls; the photos of her shaking hands with politicians who were high powered enough to be recognizable years—maybe decades

—after the posed shots that were the privilege of those who made generous enough campaign donations; the gleaming deep brown of furniture that most assuredly did not come from Ikea.

As a former architect, I could also guess at what it had cost her to give that kind of impression; the infighting and maneuvering with partners, the endless evening hours devoted to her computer, and the lack of family photos anywhere in the office. Her partners could display the warm and fuzzy arms on shoulders of children and spouses, photos that fooled nobody into believing a Beaver Cleaver existence. Rachel was three years, at most, from the expiry of any kind of biological ability to have a child, and she had chosen a career.

I suspected that when a new client was led into her office, with the secretary offering coffee in a china cup, the client would pause and evaluate— whether consciously or not—exactly what this visit was going to cost. The smart ones knew that whatever they paid, it would be a worthwhile investment. Nobody came to Rachel with simple and easy-to-solve problems. They needed a shark, and most often were sharks themselves.

I was glad she was going to be my shark for this meeting. We had both agreed I wouldn't speak. It wasn't the time or place to say what I wanted to say to the senator; nor did I want to reveal any weakness that would be exposed if I was unable to answer a question because of short-term memory loss.

Rachel had told me before the meeting that she hadn't cared where it would take place.

Instead, she'd wanted to establish control. If they had wanted to meet on Capitol Hill, she would have insisted on the conference room of Knight's attorney, Justin Davey. Since they'd requested the conference room of Knight's attorney, her demand had been Capitol Hill.

The senator's inner suite, like the outer offices where a prune-faced woman had registered our signatures, had a fifties dinginess to it; desks with yellow varnish, dull beige walls long due for fresh paint. It felt Cold War era, complete with photographs of Eisenhower and Nixon. No Democrat presidents, I noted. Wyoming was not a liberal stronghold. For proof, all I needed to see was the portrait-sized photo of Charlton Heston with a hand on the shoulder of a much younger Michael Knight.

Now, the paunch and wrinkles were more developed, the roundness of Knight's face blurred, and his goatee gray and wispy. Same paisley bow tie, bland suit jacket, and matching pants, as if long ago he'd taken to heart someone's marketing advice on how to brand a politician.

Knight ignored me. It was like showing contempt to an ant. Boots don't notice where they step.

He was staring at Rachel with an intensity of

one of the hawks that swept the skies of his home state. I hoped she would not be fooled by the Colonel Sanders charm that Knight obviously put forth as public image.

Knight was probably waiting for her to speak. They had already exchanged the necessary pleasantries that fooled no one. I guessed that Rachel had no intention of breaking the silence. Although she was outnumbered, she wasn't intimidated; she'd had a lifetime of facing me down.

The silence lengthened.

As to which person in the room would first break this silence, my bet was on Justin Davey, who looked like he was working too hard at rolling back a decade, going with a facial grooming for the French élan that had been in fashion for the Three Musketeers movies back in the eighties, and which I'd seen on a poster for a movie, *Metal Man*, *Iron Man*, or some name like that. Expensive suit, bad tailoring.

While Knight's focus was on Rachel's eyes, I'd caught more than a few glances from Davey at Rachel's calves and the part of her thigh exposed by how her skirt slid up her legs when she sat. That angered me, but Rachel had told me ahead of time that there was no sense in having a biological weapon unless it was used with art.

Knight coughed, and that broke the staring match.

"Rachel," Davey said, "the senator is a busy man. Perhaps you could get right to the point of the vague threats you used to set up this meeting?"

He was choosing to ignore me too. Since Rachel had let both of them know ahead of time that I would be with her, he was probably heeding Senator Knight's instructions.

"Ms. Prins is how I expect to be addressed," Rachel told Davey, with the scornful coldness reserved for a man who had made an indecent proposal.

I hid my smile. This was going to be a street fight, only Davey didn't know it.

I'd been in office politics. A response to an aggressive opening gambit like this was typically one of three things: Apology. Or embarrassment. Or aggression in return. It was a gambit that gave her an early chance to rattle her opponent, and a way to get a read on the situation.

Davey surprised me. I'd expected retreat in the form of apology.

Instead, he went with the third option and stood and extended his hand. "I am sorry this meeting won't continue, Ms. Prins. Neither the senator nor I will be interested in a conversation where you want to play games."

"Wonderful," Rachel said, not bothering to stand or accept the offered parting handshake. "Then let's get right to the charges of attempted murder that I intend to take to the prosecutor later this afternoon."

I thought that would rattle Davey, but it didn't.

"As I said," he told her, "this meeting is over. It is clear by all reports that Senator Knight was defending himself and graciously asked that no charges be pressed against an elderly man who was obviously confused."

"The attempted murder by Michael Knight took place on January 22 in 1942 and involved a piece of rebar against an unarmed boy. I have a list of surviving witnesses and I am prepared to discuss the situation at a press conference. One of the witnesses, Laura Jansen, is connected by marriage to Dutch royalty, so I expect her credibility won't be an issue."

"Nineteen forty-two? That was . . ." It took Davey long enough to calculate that it exposed a certain lack of quickness. "That was over seventy years ago. You expect any sane prosecutor to—"

"Are you implying I underestimate how the media becomes judge and jury?" Rachel asked. "Think about it. Seventy some years ago, Senator Knight tried to kill the same man he assaulted in the halls of Capitol Hill. I, for one, like that as a sound bite. The Dutch royalty is a nice touch too."

Rachel opened the top of her file folder. It was her meeting now. "You look silly standing there," Rachel said to him. "If the meeting were over, you would have left it at that. Sit down so that it will be less awkward for you when you finally admit you have no leverage here."

Davey looked to Senator Knight for support.

Rachel put up a finger to halt anything Knight would say. In control and showing it. "In case it isn't clear, Senator, I am here to talk about a boy named George Michael Smith, and the Wyoming rancher named Bruce Knight that George's mother married shortly after World War II, and the subsequent adoption of George Smith and the name change that followed. I have details in a comprehensive report put together by a high-profile Hollywood private investigator, if you, or the national press, need them for the record."

The Hollywood investigator part was nothing but bluff. Still, I was impressed that the senator didn't glance my way. He must have anticipated something like this; his hawklike observation of her did not change.

"As I understand it," she continued, much like a comedian who gives an almost imperceptible pause after a punch line and discovers no laughs, "your son is slated to run for your senate seat when you retire in a few months. Is he aware of the place you spent 1942 to 1944, the name of the Japanese commander involved, and what your mother was doing during those years so that both of you would survive? The country is in a patriotic mood, Senator. You and I both know what that means."

"This meeting is over," Senator Knight said from his chair, fingers steepled in a thoughtful pose. His voice was deep and calm. Unafraid.

As Davey beamed, Rachel nodded and closed her folder. The aggressive tactic and laying out her aces early was how she'd decided to play it, and I was proud that she wasn't going to second-guess herself now that it had failed. Or beg for more time with the senator. She'd meant what she said about the press conference, and that was the next step. She'd promised that to me.

Rachel began to stand.

"I am sorry you misunderstood," Senator Knight told Rachel. "What I meant was that any official representation by my attorney is over. I would be grateful if you remained after his departure so that you and I can have a private conversation."

"Senator . . . ," Davey said, his face blanching beneath his handsome tan.

"It irritates me when I have to repeat myself to an employee," Senator Knight told him. "She thumped your butt, and I am not going to forget how easy she made it look. At this point, because the remainder of my conversation is going to be a private matter between Ms. Prins and me and her father, I will assume that if I hear any whispers about World War II that involve my family, you and your firm will pay the consequences, as I will also assume that you have

396

broken the confidentiality of the first part of this meeting. The meeting that is now over for you."

Davey pulled in a deep breath and held it. That was the only dignity he could find as he walked from the room. The door clicked behind him.

Still pretending I wasn't in the room, Senator Knight spoke with a sigh of regret. "If an offer to retain you as my attorney wouldn't be seen as an attempt at bribery or conflict of interest, I would attempt to do so right now, Ms. Prins. You obviously have the same steel that your father does, and I have always envied that in him."

He sat taller and shifted in his seat so that I was now partially in his field of vision, but he didn't address me. "You weren't there when I hit your father with the rebar. It broke his arm and he didn't flinch. Seventy plus years later, it's as vivid in my memory as if I were standing in front of him right now, both of us tied to a fence. I doubt that charges of attempted murder would stand at this point, but as you pointed out, it would not matter to the media. And the thing is, I really did want to kill him, nor would I deny that in front of a jury. I felt the same way swinging my cane at him the other day. I should have known better, but Jeremiah is a man that can raise the worst types of feelings."

Still not a glance at me from the senator.

"I understand the feeling," Rachel said, not looking at me either.

"Laura Jansen," Senator Knight said. Another sigh. "How could two boys know instantly that she would be worth whatever fight it took to win her heart? Boys, no less."

"I understand that too," Rachel said. "I've met her. And Jeremiah promises to tell me all of the story."

Senator Knight's attention on her flickered, as he tried to calculate the implication that she didn't yet have the entire story.

He recovered well. "Please, no need for threats. We are past that. You know the power my past has over my son's future."

Rachel nodded. Aces on the table.

"Do you think people can change?" he asked. "I am not that boy anymore. I am less concerned about my son's political career than you might believe. Instead, I wouldn't want him to know me as that boy. My stepfather taught me a lot on the ranch. I was proud to take his name."

I hoped his charm was not working on Rachel.

"People change," she said.

Senator Knight smiled as if she had bestowed upon him a blessing.

"Well then," he said. "What does Jeremiah want after all these years?"

"He wants two things. The first is a green marble with a horse statue inside. And the second thing he wants is time alone with you."

"So he can try to pull my pants down again?"

I had to clench my jaw to keep myself from speaking.

"Up," Rachel said. "He was attempting to pull your pants leg up. That's an important distinction."

This was my girl. I loved her so much.

"Then why does he need to be alone with me?" he asked.

Rachel said, "I believe all it involves is an apology. That's why he is here in Washington. I've written up a contract for you to sign to promise delivery of the marble. Once you've signed it, I'll leave the room and the two of you can be alone for the apology."

"I have no idea what marble you mean."

"Yes, Senator," she said. "You do."

Rachel was taking my word for this, so her certainty was a convincing piece of acting.

Finally, Senator Knight turned his gaze on me.

I held his gaze and said nothing.

"I am not a fool," he said, turning back to her. "I'm aware of how today's technology makes it easy to hide recording devices. The last thing I want is to give Jeremiah Prins the power of a recorded conversation that can embarrass me politically."

So, he still assumed the worst of others. He would have expected me to bring a piece of rebar to a fight because that's an option he would want for himself. I wondered where in this office he had that kind of voice recording technology, and how he had leveraged it on other occasions.

The senator put up a hand to forestall whatever protest of innocence my daughter would issue.

"We will meet tonight at 6:30," he said. "Give me a number where I can reach you. Stay near the Capitol building. At 6:15, I'll give you the location of the restaurant. At the front door, you'll meet someone who will take you into the coatroom and discreetly but thoroughly do a wand sweep to ensure you are clean. Those are my conditions."

"And my conditions now are that you give him the green marble before you speak to him."

"I have it," he said. "But it's at my primary residence in Wyoming."

"Then make a phone call and arrange for it to be flown here. There's time for that if the jet leaves within an hour."

He stared at her. I admired her toughness.

"That would make it an expensive marble."

"Yes," she said. Cool. Determined. Frightening. "Not as expensive, however, as the alternative."

"Conditions met," he said.

He paused. Even though he spoke to her, there was no doubt he meant his words for me. "After all, when it comes to protecting a child, a parent will do nearly anything."

Forty-Seven

Laura and I had agreed that I would find her on the steps of the Lincoln Memorial after the meeting with the senator who had once been named Georgie Smith. Sixty some years earlier, we had had another agreement to meet that I had failed to keep.

The afternoon air was soft and warm, and I waited at the edge of the Reflecting Pool, the water as flat and perfect as the mirror it had become for the Washington Monument on the other end. The length of the image of the monument in the water stretched almost the length of the Reflecting Pool. Poetic. There was a rare daytime moon behind it, the edge behind the monument, three quarters of the way up. It was a tourist moment, with the iconic images meshing with the elegance and majesty that the designers had intended. Architecture should always be beautiful like this.

But the beauty that truly mattered to me was not here to share the image with me.

Because of what I was determined to tell her, I already feared this might be my last day with her. That she would abandon me like she would abandon her luggage in my condo, and take a flight directly from DC to Schiphol in Amsterdam.

To distract myself, I pulled my moleskin notebook from my suit jacket—Journal 35—and reviewed the main points I'd made about my breakfast with her. Yes, I saw with a twist of my heart, she had opened the door for me to suggest the rest of our lives together, and I had firmly closed the door. I pushed my sadness aside and reviewed the meeting with the senator. Later in the day, alone, I would use those points to bring the impressions back, and I would use them to flesh out the details that I hoped would bring life some future day to a rereading of the events when I would not be able to pull them from my mind. My body was too healthy, and I would not quit by committing suicide. So, unless an accident occurred, there would come a time when the gaps between lucidity grew longer and longer; when I returned from those gaps, I wanted to be able to know who I was.

Time passed at the front of the reflection of the monument in the water. I wondered if I had misremembered the time and location.

Another look at Journal 35. No, there on page 33, I had underlined this time and location. Two neat, thin lines, so close to horizontal that it would have taken the edge of a ruler to determine exactness. Old habits and such.

I needed to fight my anxiety.

I eyed the reflection of the Washington Monument. I took out my moleskin. I walked and measured some deliberate paces. I wrote down the numbers, for future reference, careful to add bullet points to explain why I was writing the numbers. Then I began to use those numbers for calculations. The task immersed me. As I finished, I glanced back at the monument in satisfaction and saw Laura walking toward me, a paper cup in each hand.

True love. I heard the echo in my mind of Rachel mocking me in the holding cell. *Mawidge and twue wuv.* I told myself that when Washington was over, I would invite Rachel over to watch *The Princess Bride* and make bowls of popcorn for us to eat as we watched.

True love.

What a gift given to me, that at my age, I still felt that little catch in my heart at an unexpected glimpse of her. I remembered how it had felt so long ago, at the marble game, seeing her for the first time, that sensation of emotion coursing through me as thoroughly as if it were the very blood of my veins, a feeling I thought would never be repeated until later, in Amsterdam, when I'd seen her walking on a sidewalk outside the brick walls of the private school that she attended.

It was an accident. I had not been looking for her, but wandering up and down the streets of the canals, in the shade of the tall bricked buildings and the stately trees, looking for Pietje, who was living on the streets, drifting from friend to friend, staying in the wrecks of ancient houseboats that should have been condemned.

I'd been drafted into the army because even though it was postwar peacetime, all male Dutch citizens were obligated for a stint. Architect school was not a possibility for someone of my economic and social status, not in postwar Holland, in a cramped country where rules and obeying rules mattered most. In the army, I'd been given the mechanic trade. If war broke out, I would fix vehicles. If I followed those rules, once out of the army, I could make a satisfactory living and pay my taxes and let the state take care of my needs.

Our eyes had met, and she'd run, unheeding of startled glances from schoolmates, toward me and had flung her arms around me.

"Jeremiah, is it truly you?"

Thus, our brief time together in Amsterdam had begun, evenings at cafés, long walks hand in hand, a desperate melding of bodies in alley shadow-embraces, tormented by our restraint and the purity of love that would not allow us to indulge in anything bawdy or tawdry, with the only blight in my life the knowledge that Pietje lived on the streets, an addict who had no heed for following rules or desire for a life plan laid out neatly for him.

My mind returned to the present, and I saw her

along the side of the Reflecting Pool, pigeons scattered into the air in front of her.

She was unaware, for a moment, that I was watching her approach, feeling the same feeling all these years later.

She carried a leather-handled bag over her left shoulder. She wore an emerald-green dress, long enough to reach down below midcalf, and a gray cashmere sweater. Just enough heel in her shoes to show curves in the portions of her calf that were exposed through sheer white stockings.

There was an aliveness to her, a luminescence that was breathtaking, and she drew admiring glances from those gathered at the pool's edge. When we made eye contact, it was like the touch of static electricity from brushing a fingertip.

"Jeremiah!" She lifted the cups. "It took forever for the street vendor to make these. Espresso."

When I had opened the condo door a few days earlier, I'd had to grasp the edge of the door frame to keep my balance against the shock of surprise and joy. We had squandered a lifetime apart. I could not bear the thought of losing her again, but I had steeled myself for the possibility. Yet it would be stupid to allow myself to throw away the time I might have with her now.

I held out my elbow, and she took it. Each sipping on espresso, we began to stroll, and I was aware that the two of us drew smiles from younger couples. Yes, if *GQ* had a special edition for geriatrics, I told myself, we could be on the cover, a benevolent image of romance that refused to fade.

"Let's make this last forever," I said. It was a courtly thing to say, and while I meant the sentiment, I knew that if she stayed, it was at best only a matter of years until she became a stranger to me.

"Or," she said, with light elegance, "return again and again."

We spent five minutes in comfortable silence. She knew where I had been, with Georgie, and that when I was ready, I would tell her. I hoped I would not need to refer to Journal 35 as I recounted it for her.

It could wait. It had to wait.

I pointed at a bench, inviting her to sit beside me, a bench beneath a streetlamp. It vaguely felt like a scene from a black-and-white movie, and that added melancholy to the moment for me.

She sensed it. "Jeremiah, you are troubled. I understand. The meeting with Georgie could not have been easy for you."

I shook my head and explained that it would be delayed until the evening.

"So," she said. "You and I have the afternoon to be tourists here."

"Yes."

"You don't sound as delighted as I feel."

"There is something that must be said." I

pulled out the moleskin notebook and peered at it.

She reached into her purse and dug out reading glasses. "Don't be vain."

I slipped the dainty frame onto my nose.

"While I was waiting for you," I said, "I was admiring the architecture of the Washington Monument. Thinking about the foundation it would take to support the weight. I wanted an idea of how much all the stones would weigh."

I glanced back at the monument. The pale outline of the daytime moon had risen so that it was just above the tip, as if the point were trying to burst a balloon.

"Looks smaller, doesn't it?" I observed as she glanced that way. "The moon. But it isn't. The moon only looks bigger when it's near some-thing to give it perspective. Try it some night when the moon is at the horizon. Hold out your hand and put the tip of your thumb beneath the moon and close one eye and you will see it is about the size of your thumbnail. Then later, do the same when it's in the middle of the sky. Same size."

"The things you know," she said. It didn't appear to bother her that I was drawing things out. Impatience was for the young. Ironic. They are the ones with so much time.

"To calculate the weight, first I needed to know how tall the monument was," I said. "I couldn't remember, although I should have known, because we studied this in architecture school. The tip of the reflection of the monument almost reached the end of the pool. I went to the side of the pool and I paced off the distance from the tip to the end. It was twelve feet. That meant if I stood at the edge of the pool, from my feet to the tip of the reflection, it would be twelve feet if I wanted to walk into the water and touch it. But, of course, I didn't. The elderly are too often viewed with suspicion."

She leaned against me as if nothing fascinated her more than my rambling.

"My eyes are just under six feet above the ground," I said. "It meant that I knew the two sides of a triangle. Twelve feet from my feet to the tip of the reflection was the horizontal length, and six feet the vertical length to the ground from my eyes. Knowing those two sides was an easy task to calculate the length of the third side, the distance from my eyes to the tip of the reflection. That gave me the proportions I needed, so with a final measurement, the length of the reflection from the base of the monument to the tip, I would be able to deduce its height based on the proportions. After pacing that, I can tell you it is somewhere between five hundred twenty-five feet to five hundred seventy-five feet tall. And that would have been a close enough estimate to begin calculating the weight of the stone blocks."

I drew a deep breath and paced out my words.

Later, with this journal to help me remember, I wanted to be able to convince myself that I had made the correct choice, the correct risk. But that wasn't why I was telling her this. I loved her. She needed to know; otherwise my selfishness would be proof that it wasn't love, but a need for ownership.

"When I opened the door and saw you that evening last week," I said, "I was ten years old all over again, determined to write a sonnet and win your hand. I knew with certainty beyond certainty that I still loved you as no other man has loved a woman. Here, this morning, I went to a jewelry store and found a ring. This morning, there was a moment I could have presented it to you on my knees."

"Yet," she said, "you didn't."

"My love for you is such a love that I cannot bear to chain you to me for the remainder of my life. You deserve more than that."

Laura tried to shush me.

"Don't," I said, feeling a bitter curl of my lips. "What I want to do is convince you to marry me so that you are chained to me. After you cannot leave, then I will tell you who you married. In Holland, you didn't leave your husband until his death, didn't even reply to my letters. If I can chain you to me now, you'll stay with me, no matter what."

"You think there is something about you so

horrible that if I knew, it would keep me from choosing you?"

No doubt, she was thinking of the Jappenkamp.

"Yes," I answered. "There is."

She stroked my face, and I was aware of how her knuckles protruded from her fingers, aware of the age spots on her hands. One of the minor indignities of aging. "We are old. Think of what it was like for us as children. We have survived the worst that life could have given us. Tell me and we will face the monster together."

I let out a long, ragged breath. "I'm so weak, I want to hold you to that promise. But I can't. Hear me out, and if you go back to Holland, I will accept it without a fight."

She studied my face until I could no longer meet her gaze, and I again examined my notebook.

"I began to calculate the height of the monument," I said as I looked at my neatly drawn numbers, "but even now, I need to read my notes to know why. In the time it had taken to pace the length of the reflection in the pool, I'd forgotten why I had started."

She didn't interrupt.

"You see, I know that the structure is classic architecture. I learned it as a draftsman. The monument is a narrow, four-sided structure capped by a small pyramid. I can calculate the height, and I can decide the foundation it needs, but I can't remember why I'm doing it, or the name of the structure."

I took one of Laura's hands. Kissed the knobbed knuckles and the age spots. "In two years, three years, seven years, I won't be here, Laura. My body will be as strong as ever, but only a shell. I have a disease that is slowly ravaging my mind. You shouldn't have to endure that. Yet I am so selfish that I'm terrified there will be times when memory returns, when I know who I am and that you are gone."

"You only know how to do one thing, Jeremiah," Laura replied. "And that is not quit. You refuse to feel sorry for yourself and all you are going to do is keep fighting the forces of the universe, although in the end you won't win. In the end, time steals our glories and our loves."

She paused, struggled for words. "Unless there is more to life on earth than this life on earth. Like my grandmother, I believe there is, that we have a soul and another destination. That's what gave her courage in the Jappenkamp. Now I need to find that same courage."

She stood. "Let's walk. This is too difficult for me. I can't look at you as I talk."

I followed her example. This time, she didn't take my elbow. It filled me with dread.

"With you beside me, I want to weep," she said. "But I can't find the strength. What I want to do is beg you to propose, what I want to do is accept your proposal and run with you and find a justice of the peace, and while you are strong and vigorous and the man that I love, I want to chain myself to you so that when the darkness comes, I will have no choice but to care for you like the woman you need me to be. But I don't know if I have that courage."

Each step felt like my feet were stuck in buckets of concrete.

"I understand," I said. There was nothing else to say. She had come to America to accomplish something, and after I met Georgie Smith in the evening, it would be accomplished. This was life. If she returned to Los Angeles with me to get her suitcase, I would try to enjoy each moment with her, and I would refuse to beg as she left again for Amsterdam.

"Do you?" she answered. "Because I am telling you that all I want is time to absorb what the future holds if we are bound together. If I beg you to marry me, I want to be certain that I will have the courage for what lies ahead."

"Obelisk," I said.

"Obelisk?"

"It just came to me. That's the name for the Washington Monument. It's an obelisk."

I pulled out my moleskin notebook again and wrote a single word in it, repeating it aloud. "Obelisk."

Forty-Eight

That evening, Rachel and I endured a wand sweeping by a man in a black suit who seemed bored at his task. Then we were escorted out of the cloakroom. A waiter led us to Senator Knight.

I knew nothing about Washington power circles, but I recognized the obvious aura of exclusivity, an established restaurant that showed no signs of trendiness with its dark-paneled walls, dark carpet, and low lighting. It was an atmosphere soaked in discretion, dispensing generous drink portions and steaks of even greater proportions. Rachel had expected this and had dressed for it. Dark skirt with a hem below her knees, suit jacket over a dark silk blouse. She clutched her purse at her side. I, too, wore a suit, with my moleskin journal in my jacket pocket. Rachel had promised I wouldn't need it. She had promised that if it appeared I was searching for a piece of a jigsaw puzzle, she would handle the conversation until I rejoined.

This was a new sensation for me, the feeling of being able to trust the help of someone. I was proud of my daughter and, more importantly, was able to tell her that by leaning in and whispering. My reward was a radiant smile from her.

Knight was waiting for us in a booth near the

back, away from the kitchen. A large candle centered on the table gave the only real light, and he was facing away from the traffic area, holding a glass with lime on ice and beaded with con-densation.

He stood as she sat on the opposite side of the booth, then sat and sipped his drink when she and I were settled.

I was happy to follow Rachel's lead. He was drinking a soda, so she ordered two sodas, one for her, one for me.

He frowned. "I try, but I don't like soda. What's the point of health if you don't enjoy it? Not that I'm healthy. Is extending life a few extra months worth drinking this stuff?"

A waiter stopped with another drink on a tray.

"Johnny, make a note that I lasted nearly five minutes with the soda water before succumbing," Knight told him. He smiled at Rachel. "Gin and tonic."

"Yes sir." The waiter glanced at Rachel. "And for the lady and her companion?"

"Still sodas." This, I thought, was subtle gamesmanship on her part. Had she changed her mind, it would have appeared her initial order of soda was a flattering move to mirror him.

Knight raised his eyes to mine. "You are going to speak at this meeting?"

"The marble," I said. I'm sure my tone was terse. "It's mine. I want it back."

I needed possession of it before the apology. After, I doubted he would part with it.

Knight pulled a small box out from his suit jacket. It looked like a box that held a ring. He pushed it across the table.

I opened it. A surge of sorrow threatened to bring me to tears. It brought me to the moment when my father had handed it to me. It brought me to the memory of chasing the truck that held all the Dutch men and boys that the Japanese were taking away from me.

I could only whisper when I spoke to Knight. "Thank you."

Rachel and I had earlier rehearsed how I would then tell Knight that I had something to give him in return. But choked by memories, I found it difficult to speak.

She interpreted that as a lapse into blankness and spoke for me.

"My father has something to give to you as well," Rachel told Knight. "After you read it, then you will have the conversation that we agreed would occur between the two of you."

"I'm not interested in games. I'll make my apology, all right?"

"You're going to need to know what my father and I have learned from Laura," Rachel said. "Think of me as a mediator that you can trust."

Knight made a grunting noise that Rachel took as assent.

"I'm going to start with the catalyst," Rachel said. "There is no coincidence about the timing of all of this. Jeremiah didn't wake up one morning after seven decades and decide to find some resolution to those years in the internment camp."

Rachel paused, because the waiter had returned with her drink. His experience at a restaurant like this was apparent, because he read their body language correctly and didn't linger.

"I'm not interested in being treated like a puppy, with my nose rubbed in my mistakes," Knight said. "I'm prepared to apologize. Let's leave it at that."

"Laura Jansen, as you might know, married into the outer circles of Dutch royalty," Rachel said. "That is relevant here, because her husband had a bureaucratic position at a high level. You understand that kind of power, don't you?"

Knight took a long gulp of his gin and tonic. I took the green marble out of the box and held it inside a clenched fist.

"In the late forties," Rachel continued, "Queen Juliana began to give royal recognition t citizens who had been heroes during the war. Those who hid Jews, those who led underground resistant movements. It was a program where citizens nominated candidates, and careful background research was done before royal recognition was given. It was a great honor to receive such a letter."

Knight was more interested in his gin and tonic than her preamble.

"The short of it—" she began.

"For this meeting, my favorite phrase," Knight said. "Let's get this over with."

"—is that Laura's husband was the one to dispense those letters, usually with some kind of ceremony, depending on who had received royal recognition. One of the letters went to this woman."

Rachel opened her purse and pulled out the photograph. She placed it on the table.

"Too dark here," Knight said.

On her smartphone, Rachel turned on the flashlight app, and the bright light on the photograph showed a blocky woman standing beside one much more elegant.

"Queen Juliana," Rachel said.

Knight straightened in surprise. "And Dr. Eikenboom."

"Survivors from your camp put her name forward as a candidate. She received a royal commendation."

"Wonderful. You mentioned something about the short of it."

"Dr. Eikenboom used this recognition to pursue a commendation for Laura's grandmother, Sophie, who was granted a letter from Queen Juliana within the year."

Rachel paused and gathered her thoughts.

"Dr. Eikenboom also successfully pushed for two others from the camp to receive commendations from the queen. The research was done—which Laura's husband oversaw in his official position for Queen Juliana—and the letters written, but when it was convenient, he found a way for the letters to be filed in such a manner that they never reached those other two from the camp. He worried the two of you might someday be reconnected."

"Look," Knight said, "I'm not a fan of ancient history."

It didn't ruffle Rachel. She spoke as if she had not been interrupted. "Laura found those letters in his papers after his death. That's why she flew to America. To share those letters with Jeremiah. She found him through my Facebook page."

Again, Rachel reached into her purse. This time to pull out a letter on heavy parchment, with a royal seal.

Rachel said quietly, "Senator Knight, this letter is written in Dutch. I'm glad Washington hosts so many nationalities, because it was a simple matter to find a translator on short notice. I had it done in case it's been too long since you've used your Dutch. It's a letter that never reached your mother."

He had his glass halfway to his mouth, but those words stopped him and he set the glass down.

"My mother."

"Did she ever talk to you about her camp years?" she asked.

Knight gave Rachel a challenging look, someone too proud to acknowledge an act of shame. "My mother gave birth to a half sister who was half Japanese. My mother raised the child in a village outside the camp, because she would have been ostracized by the Dutch for becoming impregnated by the commander's rape of her."

"Dr. Eikenboom's account of the situation is different from that, Senator Knight. Dr. Eikenboom's testimony is that it wasn't rape, but consensual. Over a period of weeks."

She'd spoken gently, but he slammed his glass down, shattering it across the table. He ignored the shards. As did she.

"If you are now threatening me with—"

Rachel reached across and put her hand on the senator's wrist. The waiter had come to the table. With her free hand, and without looking up, Rachel waved him away.

"Senator," she said, "Jeremiah hasn't shared much with me about his time in the Dutch East Indies. I only know enough to have wept on your behalf when I learned the truth. I could only imagine how you would have fought to understand what your mother did, and how a part of you must have been aware of her nightly visits to the commander."

"Enough!" He began to slide out of the booth.

She did not let go of his hand. "I am begging you, read the letter."

"We are finished here." He was now standing, his voice almost choking.

I could not pretend that I liked him now any more than when we first met. Even so, I ached with his pain.

"Your mother," Rachel said, "saved hundreds and hundreds of lives. God Himself only knows the price she had to pay for it. Read the letter, Senator, and find the peace that you deserve after all these years."

She pulled on his wrist, and he sat, grudgingly. He did not reach for the letter, but struggled to keep control of his emotions.

"Then let me read the letter to you," Rachel said. "The translation."

He didn't protest, so she unfolded another piece of paper. I could not imagine how I would have found the strength to do this, and I felt gratitude wash over me for my daughter's strength on my behalf.

She read to Knight, lifting her eyes occasionally. "In recognition of the sacrifice and risks that Georgina Ruth Smith took to ensure that Red Cross supplies reached those in desperate need of medicine and food, I declare, as the Queen of the Netherlands, that royal recognition should be bestowed upon her for—"

"Red Cross supplies," Knight said, with vague bewilderment.

She gave him the original, and the translation.

That's when I spoke. "Georgie—"

"I am Senator Knight."

"Senator Knight," I said, swallowing a prideful reaction of anger at his admonishment, "I have been wrong for seven decades. I am ashamed of that, but I will not be ashamed of what I must say."

Knight's hands, on the table, were trembling. He did not pull them away from the spreading puddle of gin and tonic among the shards.

"Senator Knight," I said, "there was a night that I snuck into the commander's house. I was determined to steal the Red Cross supplies that he had been withholding from the camp. Your mother caught me and prevented me from doing so. I thought she was collaborating with the Japanese. I was wrong. She was using her time in the house to pull medicine out of full boxes in such a way that Nakahara wouldn't realize she was stealing medicine for the doctors in camp."

Rachel continued for me, "Each dose of sulfa that saved a life was a dose of sulfa that your mother had to risk a beating or possible death to steal. Doctors Eikenboom and Kloet knew this but had to pretend that, indeed, she spent evenings with the commander for her own benefit. No one knew that much of what Nakahara gave her for food and luxuries to be his mistress was what she in turn gave to the doctors to distribute."

This was the truth that I had been incapable of seeing as a boy. Georgie's mother was a heroine, not a whore of Babylon.

"Make no mistake," I said to him. "I do not see some kind of maudlin reconciliation between us. It would be a pretense by both of us. But I am the one who owes you an apology for the words I said to you about your mother when we last faced each other in that village in the Dutch East Indies. I am sorry. Very sorry. You did not deserve that, and I feel shame for the years you lost when you should have been able to love and honor your mother as she should have been loved and honored by you as her son."

In the candlelight, tears ran down Knight's face, sliding in and out of deep wrinkles in his skin. I didn't like him, but in that moment, I could feel love for him. It would be wonderful if we could always see that what we have in common as humans outweighs our differences.

"Don't you tell me how and when I should love and honor my mother." He spoke as if fingers were squeezing his throat. He was angry. "Don't assume I didn't love and honor her no matter what she appeared to be. Can you say the same about your mother?"

"For that too," I said, knowing that with Rachel in front of us, my answer would be and had to be ambiguous, "I am sorry."

Senator Knight made the waving motion of someone indicating it didn't matter. "If your apology is finished, then go. I will make no pretenses about reconciliation either."

Rachel said, "Not yet. Laura gave me another letter. Both of you need to know about it too. She told me, Senator, that she wanted you to be with Jeremiah when he learned of it."

She pulled it out of her purse. "In recognition of the sacrifice and risks that Jeremiah Prins took to ensure that food and medicine reached those in desperate need of medicine and food, I declare, as the Queen of the Netherlands, that royal recognition should be bestowed upon him for—"

"Enough," I told Rachel. This letter was a surprise to me. "That changes nothing for me."

"Or me," the senator said to Rachel. "Your father as a boy wanted all of camp to know that my mother was a whore. And you know what stopped him from telling?"

He turned to me. "I knew the truth about your mother. And so did you. And you knew I knew the truth from Dr. Kloet. Your mother did what she felt she had to do to help her children. That makes her no different than mine. With one difference. I am alive. My mother could live with what she did. Yours could not. Does Ms. Prins know what happened at camp?"

I had been prepared for this. I didn't want it.

But I had owed him an apology and had no choice but to risk this when my leverage over him was gone. The consolation was that he did not know how accurate it was to say that my mother could not live with the choices she had made.

It was a horrible secret that I had kept. Conscious that Rachel was at the table, I tried to convince him there was no need to continue our war. "I wish you peace, Senator. It's something that will always escape me. Can't we stand and shake hands and agree those were terrible times?"

The senator sneered. "You've always sickened me with your self-righteousness. You didn't come here to apologize, but to trade. You knew if you didn't deliver the letter, Laura would. Think I haven't thrived in this kind of politics here for decades? Your bet was that a pretended act of nobility, in front of your daughter, would serve to keep me quiet after I learned this about my mother."

I had guessed correctly, then, about the marble. Had it been in his possession now, it would have remained there.

Still sneering, the senator turned to Rachel. "When it's convenient for you, ask Jeremiah about how his baby sister really died. About a feather in her mouth that Dr. Kloet observed, an observation he later shared with my mother. Jeremiah knows the truth. But I doubt he'll tell you."

Knight waved for a waiter's attention and pointed at the mess.

As the waiter walked away, Knight said to Rachel, "Thanks for the letter. In these patriotic times, it will make a wonderful campaign prop for my son. And if your father tries to go public with the details of how the letter was earned, then the world can find out that Jeremiah's mother murdered her own children."

He gave me a cold smile. "You and I, we are finished here, are we not? I hope I never see you again."

I held the marble in my hand and let Rachel lead me out of the restaurant.

Forty-Nine

I paced the sitting area of the hotel room. The curtains were open, and it was a sunny morning. I did not feel sunny. I had slept less than usual. It had been painful adding to my journal the conversation in the restaurant the evening before. But if I had not included it, I would have been lying to myself. It's one thing to hide a secret. It's another to deny it.

"Will you sit?" Rachel asked me. She was in an armchair, opposite where Laura sat on a sofa. They'd ordered coffee from room service, and the empty cups were on a table, the pot untouched. I was very conscious that Laura had not given me any indication of whether she had the courage to live with me as my identity left me. I didn't blame her. It was one thing to prop myself up by believing I could read my journals in an effort to hold on to who I was. She would need more than memories as I grew older; why choose for future companionship a body that would eventually carry an empty mind?

I looked at her, and she must have sensed I needed strength. Laura stood and walked to me and held my forearm and stroked my hand.

I could not allow myself to learn to lean on her. I disengaged myself, moved to the window, and stared at the parking lot that was becoming as familiar as a friend. "I can't sit down because when I say what needs to be said, I want to be able to look away from both of you. If I am trapped between you, that won't be possible."

Some of the lines painted on the pavement were crooked. I would have rather made that my focus. I said, "His mother spent nights with the camp commander. But my mother . . ."

I shivered as if fighting malaria. Not once had I spoken of this. The growing suspicion after Jasmijn had died in her sleep. Then, at camp, tracing the memories of those months. Still not believing it, pushing away the thoughts.

Yet . . .

After rumors had reached the kitchen that all

the dogs would be removed from camp, eaten by the Indonesians, Pietje had woken up with his black puppy Coacoa dead, a blessing, we all believed, because Pietje had buried his friend, not watched it be taken away.

What had my mother said? *"If you really cared about Pietje and cared about the dog, you would have walked away and let that dog die a merciful death."*

And in the days that followed, my mother had nearly died from blood poisoning from long scratches down her leg. The scratches of a dog's claws as it fought suffocation, not scratches from the kitchen as she'd said.

Then Jasmijn. Sweet, sweet Jasmijn. Almost dead and certain to die soon. A mercy. Then I had brought her to life again by finding the insulin, which was only prolonging the inevitable. So cruel. And then the blessing returned. She was lifeless the very next morning, a feather in her mouth. The feather from a pillow.

Later, the rumors of the Borneo plan grew stronger, that the mothers would be taken with none left to care for the children. With Aniek growing weaker and weaker from hunger until a fever attacked her. So weak that death would be a mercy. A mercy that my mother bestowed.

Georgie knew too. His words from the previous evening were already transcribed on the pages of Journal 35. *"Your mother did what she felt she had to do to help her children. That makes her no different than mine. With one difference. I am alive."*

"Elsbeth," I said, willing myself to breathe out the words, "my mother, Elsbeth, killed Jasmijn and killed Aniek."

I've often wondered if Mrs. Aafjes's rants about Masada and Jews committing mass suicide on a mountaintop had planted the idea in the mind of a woman with an existing mental illness, or if it had been a natural progression of mercy killings from a dog that was going to die anyway, to her suffering baby who would not be able to receive adequate treatment, and then Aniek.

It was quiet behind me. I stared down at the crooked white painted lines of the parking lot and the dusty black roof of a compact car. I spoke, needing to get it out. "My mother tried to kill Pietje. That's what broke him. Broke us. She wanted to protect Pietje by killing him."

I turned to both of the women I loved. "Tell me. My mother murdered two of her daughters and nearly killed Pietje. How could anyone expect me to fix that?"

Hidden in a drawer in my office is a sketch I take out occasionally to remind myself of a time in my mother's life when demons were not clawing at her soul.

It's the only sketch that survived the

Jappenkamp, the sketch she had drawn that showed me as a boy, the two of us holding hands, her dress swirling as if the wind were flirting with her, the smile on her face showing the joy of a purity of love.

I am glad it survived to remind me of a happier time in her life, because something remains to be told. As I admitted in the hotel room, Jasmijn had not died peacefully in her sleep and Aniek had not succumbed to infection. As promised, I did write the journals for her, over the course of a year, upon my return from Washington. They have been stacked in chronological order, and these pages will be my last for her.

In these final pages, I confess it was a deception earlier in the journals to suggest that Elsbeth lost her will to live because of the accumulation of tragedies: Nikki's horrible death to rabies, followed by the strain of Elsbeth's terror of the Borneo plan, the news that our father and half brothers were dead, and Aniek succumbing to her infection that night as we slept.

Pietje knew better. That is not why Elsbeth died.

It was a lie in the Washington hotel room to tell Rachel and Laura that Pietje's knowledge of Elsbeth was of a mother who believed it would be a mercy to suffocate her children. It was the opposite. Pietje did *not* know that she had killed them, and when I tried to tell him, he wouldn't believe it.

Pietje never saw what I saw in the dark hours before he woke that morning to find Aniek dead in Elsbeth's arms. I had lain awake in the dark for hours, trying to comprehend what I had witnessed—Elsbeth's choice to end Aniek's suffering.

A slight mewing sound had woken me. Half-asleep, in dim light from the moon through the small window high in the wall, I had seen Elsbeth straddling Aniek. I had seen Aniek reach up with both arms, as if imploring. I had seen Elsbeth lean down and Aniek's arms wrap around her mother's neck.

I had heard my mother half sob as the strange embrace continued, until Aniek dropped her arms from my mother. I had seen my mother stand and leave our small room. I had heard my mother vomit as she fled down the hallway.

I had crawled over to Aniek, to ask if she knew why our mother had fled. I had pulled the pillow off her face, still not realizing what had happened. Aniek hadn't answered, no matter how hard I tried to shake her awake.

I'd crawled back to my sleeping pallet and pretended not to notice when my mother returned. She had lifted Aniek's lifeless body and taken it into the corner of the room to huddle against a wall, cradling the body and continuing to weep.

In the dark, that's when I'd begun to understand. How Pietje had been spared the pain of giving up Coacoa with all the other dogs taken from the camp. How the scratches had appeared on my mother's leg. How Jasmijn had died in her sleep and why the feather had been found in her mouth.

I still agonize over the choices I faced. What was I to do? Tell Sophie or Dr. Eikenboom that Pietje and I could not live with our mother because she might kill us? That would mean telling them what only Dr. Kloet suspected. That would mean betraying my mother by declaring to the world that she was far, far worse than a whore of Babylon.

I couldn't flee with Pietje. There was no place to go.

I couldn't ask to live with another family.

I couldn't tell my mother what I'd witnessed her do.

I could only do what I'd vowed to do since the soldiers had taken away my father and my older brothers. Carry on and protect my family.

The next night, I'd tied a string from Pietje's wrist to mine because I was afraid I would not be able to stay awake to protect him. The string had woken me. There she was again, in that same embrace with my brother, his arms up around her shoulders as she straddled him and he fought to breathe against the pillow against his face.

In the warm tropical darkness on that night in

the camp, I could not see the future. I could not anticipate that no matter how I tried to explain, Pietje's memory of that night would drive him away from me and to the amnesia that came with opium. I could not anticipate how my own insulation against the memory would turn my heart into a hard and tiny kernel, what it would do when I became a father myself, how guarded it would make me in showing love to my own daughter. I could not know the night of my mother's death at the internment camp would send me into the dark for decades after, isolated on the other side of the fence from the campfires of humanity.

Yet had I known, it wouldn't have mattered. What choice did I have? Pietje needed my protection.

I am grateful, beyond anything that can be expressed by words, that the undiminished love between a boy and a girl, which began seventy years earlier at a marble game beneath the banyan tree, eventually became an open gate to bring me back through the fence, to those camp-fires.

For in my twilight years, Laura decided to stay with me.

I am also appreciative that circumstances thwarted our marriage for sixty years, for her time in the Jappenkamp had done something to her body, and she was never able to bear children.

If I hadn't fled to America and married another, I would never have received the greatest gift in my life, my daughter, Rachel.

It is with the same breathtaking gratitude that I realize I have been rescued from my past and present and future by my daughter, who did so by granting me our reconciliation.

Thus, in solitude one night all these decades later, while still cognizant of the words I spoke, I found the strength and courage to fold my hands together and bow my head and finally ask His mercy.

I etch these last words not from a need after my death to share and dissipate the shame of what I did on the night my mother died at the internment camp, but from a desire to comfort Laura and Rachel, who led me, for the first time since that horrible night, to find the courage in that solitude and pour out my soul in prayer and finally weep with all the anguish I had denied myself for far too long.

In telling what remains to be told, I want my daughter and my one true love to know that they helped me find a way to defeat what I thought could never be defeated: the boyhood memory of the resolute action of protecting Pietje from our mother by pushing a pillow down on my mother's face and holding it there while she clawed at my arms and thumped her feet on the floor until her body stopped quivering, with me unaware that Pietje had returned to the room and was trans-fixed as he watched every cold moment, fleeing in silence, and even through opiates unable to escape that memory until his own death years later.

For as I near my end, I understand.

Against any horror that we may face in this world, and in the face of knowledge that for each of us time is a thief of glory, what matters most and what gives meaning to our lives and deaths is love and hope, if we are willing to share and accept.

When time comes to take me, I will go in peace.

Author's Note

Growing up, what I mainly knew about my grand-father, Simon, a headmaster in the Dutch East Indies before the capitulation to the Japanese, was that as the first born, I would have been named after him. But my mother, new to Canada and the English language, had found out that "Simple Simon" was a nursery rhyme, and she didn't want me teased for that name.

Because Willem, my father, spoke so little about his boyhood time in a Jappenkamp, I only knew that Simon had died during the war. Simon Brouwer had joined the army and was taken prisoner of war when Japanese forces were victorious. His fate can only be gleaned from a single letter, written to my grandmother, Grietje, from someone who did survive.

The letter is haunting to me in its sparseness of detail: "In November of 1942 we were transported to Soerabaia. There we had a bad time . . . later that camp was named Camp Makassar. Not a very good camp."

(The Pacific War Online Encyclopedia gives this description of Makassar: "The camp commander, Yoshida, was a sadist who engaged in frequent beatings and other abuse of the prisoners. Prisoners were forced to climb trees full of fire ants and were beaten unconscious for the least infraction.")

From Makassar, my grandfather was sent to Singapore, where he first contracted dysentery. And from Singapore, as told by the letter, "In the middle of April we were sent to Siam. In Ban Pons we started a march through Siam. But after two days of marching, your husband had to stay behind in Non Pladuk."

No details, either, of the march.

But even a cursory reading of any material about the Burma Railway paints a horrible picture, for my grandfather had become one of tens of thousands of prisoners of war forced into slave labor on what became known as the Death Railway. The building of it took the lives of 356 Americans; 6,318 British; 2,815 Australians; and 2,490 Dutch. Simon Brouwer was among those Dutch soldiers who perished.

Simon carved his own chess pieces and was a chess champion, as the letter informed my grandmother, and he was a man of strong faith and excellent spirits, leading fellow inmates to the same faith. This, in essence, is all that I know about his character.

My father was fortunate. Unlike so many children, he survived the war with his mother and all of his sisters and brothers. They returned to Holland, where my grandmother tried to rebuild a family life without her husband. My father dated my mother while he was in the army and she was a nurse, and he would have to bicycle for miles for the chance to spend time with her.

Much of what I learned about what my father endured in the Jappenkamps came from accounts of children who were older when they were sent to the camps, and I've listed those books at www.thiefofglory.com, along with the few photos that exist in our family archives, the letter about my grandfather, and my grandmother's description of the best birthday present she received, during her years in camp.

I was brought to tears by a video that you will find at the *Thief of Glory* website via a YouTube link to the footage of the most infamous of these camps—Tjideng Internment Camp. While the footage shows the considerably better conditions of post liberation, it was the closest I could come to understanding those three years of my father's boyhood.

I was also touched deeply when my research about cleft palates led me to the "before" and "after" photos of children whose lives are transformed by Operation Smile, where we can help bring new smiles and joy and hope to children like Adi, a character who really came to life for me during the writing of the story. (www.operationsmile.org/Sigmund)

My grandmother, Grietje, with her children, posing
for a photo in Holland in 1946 after arriving by
ship. My father, Willem, is on the far right.

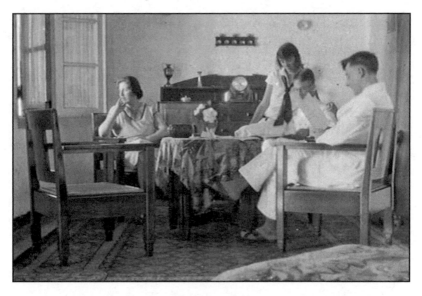

My grandparents, Simon and Grietje, having a
quiet family moment in the house in Magalang.

My grandfather, Simon, before the war.

Soldier 3602: My grandfather's grave site in what was then Burma, showing the KNIL for Koninklijk Nederlands Indisch Leger, the Royal Netherlands Indies Army.

My father, Willem, at age four on the steps of his house in Magalang on the island of Java.

Gerda and Willem Brouwer, my parents.

Readers Guide

1. What is thematic significance of the book's title *Thief of Glory*? The phrase is mentioned only once, at the end of the novel when Jeremiah says, "Against any horror that we may face in this world, and in the face of knowledge that for each of us time is a thief of glory, what matters most and what gives meaning to our lives and deaths is love and hope." What, then, is the meaning of this phrase to Jeremiah? What is the meaning of it to you? In what ways was time stolen from various characters in this novel? What "glory" is out of reach for the characters?

2. Discuss the living conditions in the *Jappenkamp*. Which element was most horrifying to you? Which scene, if any, held the most hope?

3. At the beginning of the novel, Jeremiah remarks about Georgie, "Georgie had no idea how easily I had taken control of the situation. But then, I had no idea of the extent of his cruelty and preference for inflicting pain. Yet." To what extent is this an adequate characterization of Georgie? How would

you expand upon Jeremiah's observation? When meeting Georgie again in the present-day part of the story, has your perception of him changed? Why or why not?

4. Jeremiah's mother, Elsbeth, suffers from an unidentified mental illness that Jeremiah's father says is "no more her fault than catching a fever." Her illness often caused her to retreat to her bedroom for long periods of time. On the day the Japanese arrive to take the rest of the family to a Jappenkamp, Jeremiah discovers that Elsbeth had drawn intricate sketches during those reclusive times. What images did he see in these drawings? What meaning do they hold for Jeremiah?

5. Identity is a key concept in *Thief of Glory* since a number of characters and groups are displaced and trying to assimilate into one or more cultures. Prior to the opening of this story, Indonesia had been a Dutch colony for nearly 350 years. Where in the story do you see this struggle for identity? How do the Dutch and the Indonesians view one another in this novel? What stereotypes are present? What elitist attitudes among the Dutch are described?

6. Only a very young boy when the story begins, Pietje is the last of the Prins children.

Describe his character at the beginning of the novel. Why does he respond so well to Jeremiah? Discuss how he and Jeremiah react to their experiences in the Jappenkamp. What reaction did you have to Pietje's adult lifestyle in the "underbelly" of Amsterdam, smoking opium?

7. Consider the native Indonesian characters in *Thief of Glory*: the *djongos* in the Prins house-hold; the launderer who hires Pietje and Jeremiah; Adi and his parents, Sukorno and Utami; the extremists who raid house-holds for furniture; the radical *pemuda*— young soldiers in the independence move-ment; and others. What do these characters and voices add to the novel?

8. Freedom is an underlying desire of many characters and groups in the novel. Identify those who desire freedom and why. Also discuss the avenues to freedom that exist in the novel, such as Jeremiah's "pipeline to freedom."

9. Much of *Thief of Glory* is about power. Political unrest is a driving force in the novel, and in the midst of war, many characters crave, gain, and/or lose power. Why is power so important to the female characters in the

Jappenkamp? Compare how and why certain forms of power are desirable to certain female characters and not to others. How much are they willing to sacrifice for it? And, when they finally have it, what do they do with it? Consider these characters when answering: Dr. Eikenboom, Laura Jansen, Sophie Jansen, Elsbeth Prins, Mrs. Georgina Ruth Smith, Mrs. Baker, Mrs. Schoonenburg.

10. Were you shocked when it was revealed how Jeremiah's mother died? How did it change your opinion of Jeremiah's character? How did this act affect Pietje? How do you think it does, or will, affect Laura? What does Jeremiah mean when he says he was "rescued from my past and present and future" by Rachel?

11. Adi's cleft palate ostracizes him from people of every nationality. He knows that his speech and appearance scare children who think he is a "monster" and that many adults prefer to avoid him. However, Adi becomes a lifeline for the women and children in the Jappen-kamp. What symbolic role does his character serve in *Thief of Glory*? What contradictions does he bring to light?

12. Identify where Christianity is evident in *Thief of Glory*. How do certain characters

interpret or apply their Christian faith while in the Jappenkamp? Discuss the underlying ideas about good versus evil in this novel and at this point in history. Have these ideas changed at all? If so, how?

13. When Sophie Jansen volunteers to take Elsbeth's punishment and receives a terrible beating from Commander Nakahara, her sacrifice could be seen as a parallel to the crucifixion of Jesus. Would you agree? What is the significance of the next day's "zodiacal light" or false dawn?

14. What role does Jeremiah's father serve in the story? How is the father/son relationship portrayed and what impact does it have on Jeremiah? On Jeremiah's half brothers? On Pietje? Take into consideration Jeremiah's description of his father as a "strict disciplinarian" who "detested whining or excuses in any form" and displayed "unemotional severity."

15. Why do you think the author chose to include marbles in the story, particularly Jeremiah's fascination with them? Describe Jeremiah's prized marble and explain its significance. Based on the type of marble player Jeremiah is, what do you think he believes about

calculating risks and taking chances? Do you think the games serve as a vehicle for making sense of his environment and circumstances? If so, how?

For an extended Readers Guide, visit
www.thiefofglory.com